The

Manila Galleon

Jason Schoonover

Author photo credit: Su Hattori

Website: jasonschoonover.com

Rolling Thunder Publishing
720 University Drive
Saskatoon, Saskatchewan
S7N OJ4
Canada

Jason Schoonover's books are also published and available from asiabooks.com and pilgrimsbooks.com.

What Critics Say about *Thai Gold* and its sequel *Opium Dream*

"A tour de force . . . accurate to a fault." Bangkok *Post*

"*Opium Dream* was such a riveting read that having taken the book on a visit to Bangkok I had to ask for a late check-out from the Amari Watergate Hotel, because I could not possibly wait to read the last two chapters later at home!" Lang Reid, Pattaya *Mail*.

"[An] exciting, high powered novel . . . Schoonover pulls it off." Toronto *Sun*

"One wonders why this book has not been made into a screen play. In many ways it is a Bond style movie still in the written form." Pattaya *Mail*

"Indeed, if there is criticism to be made here, it's that there is too much action—they will never get it all into the movie." Winnipeg *Free Press*

"A fast-paced Robert Ludlum-meets-Stephen Spielberg romp." Edmonton *Journal*

"One wonders whether this work was penned with the intention of its being snapped up by Steven Spielberg as another vehicle for Harrison Ford in the ongoing celluloid series." Bangkok *Post*

"In my review of his previous book, *Thai Gold*, I said that it should be made into a movie. The movie moguls should also snap up *Opium Dream* for the sequel. This is one helluva good yarn. Get it! You will enjoy it!" Dr. Iain Cornell, Pattaya *Mail*

To my many Ifugao friends in Banaue, and on Palawan,
Philippines. I shall return.

Books by the Author

Fiction

The Bangkok Collection
Thai Gold
Nepal Gold
Opium Dream

Non-fiction

Westward from New Amsterdam: The Schoonover Epic. Thirteen Generations, One Branch, One Tree, One Forest

Watch for

Adventurous Dreams, Adventurous Lives: Today's Explorers Recall the Youthful Dream Launching their Remarkable Lives

Pre-Expedition Notes

Outside of obvious license, I have stayed true to archaeological, anthropological, historic and geographic fact. This is true also of Dr. Robert Fox, author of *The Tabon Caves* and discoverer of Tabon Man, who was one of the most important archaeologists to do field work on the beautiful Filipino archipelago. Virtually everything written about the island of Palawan and its hundreds of caves, filled with centuries old, still undiscovered burial jars is true. Palawan's south-west side is one of the few untouched regions still ripe for discovery and adventure on this small planet.

I say, virtually. While the Batak are indeed protected, the area around the underground river is only off limits for the purposes of this story. It's entirely possible to explore. The background to Abu Sayyef, the Islamic terrorist group, is true. They did a dramatic kidnapping on Palawan which garnered worldwide headlines, and tried to blow up several US bound jumbo jets.

Disappointingly, the dungeon as described at Fort Santiago was destroyed in the 1990s by government approved treasure hunters seeking Yamashita's gold.

Finally, Chantico, the headhunting Ifugao's Goddess of Love, is a figment of my imagination, but the God of Locks is, indeed, very real.

Acknowledgements

Thank you to the late Mel Fisher for vetting early drafts of the treasure dive chapters.

I would also like thank the following for answering questions and pointing me in research directions: William Trousdale and Dr. Robert M. Laughlin, curators with the Smithsonian Institution's Department of Natural History; Dr. Michael Ames, Director Emeritus of Vancouver's UBC Museum of Anthropology; Dr. David Simmons of the Auckland Museum; Dr. Gabriel Casal, Director of the National Museum of the Philippines, and; the late Dr. William Scott of Segada, the leading authority on the ex-headhunting Igorots.

A special thanks to Ting de los Reyes of the Philippine Deparatment of Tourism. Three times over twenty years he lent me carta blanc support to travel anywhere I wished in the Philippines, twice for six weeks and once for a month. Thus I was able to discover the fascinating nooks and crannies of this beautiful country, as well as its hospitable people.

Finally, thanks to Hal and Janet Baldwin, Gene and Judie Hattori, the late Jay Headly, past Media Relations Chairman of The Explorers Club, Garth and Kumiko Ramsay, Verl Sabourin, Steve Voth and my readers Su Hattori, Doug Birkmaier and Silvia Martini.

There is something about a treasure that fastens itself upon a man's mind. He will pray and blaspheme and still persevere, and will curse the day he heard of it, and will let his last hours come upon him unawares, still believing that he missed it by only a foot.

Joseph Conrad

Some things have the power to seize hold of one's imagination but perhaps nothing like treasure or gold. The word fever implies weakness but nothing could be further from the truth. It gives courage and strength. The allure of wealth and everything it promises—you might say the worst human emotion, greed, pure and simple greed, but there is more to it than that. It is "The Quest," that primeval search that harks back to the beginnings of man.

Kawthoolei Dreams, Malaria Nights, Martin MacDonald

The Philippines

Luzon

Banaue

Baguio

Manila

Corregidor

Pasa de Acapulco

South China Sea

underground
river

Ulugon
Bay

Puerto Princesa

Palawan

Mindanao

Solo Sea

Prologue
Acapulco
April 1704

The sweating peons, like a trail of black ants, wrestled the last of the wooden chests through the fort gate of San Diego to the docked galleon.

At 2,000 tons, 175 feet and carrying 1,000 souls, the *Santa Maria de la Immaculate Concepcion* was the most enormous ship ever constructed. Eighty cannons on three levels, plus 300 soldiers consigned to relieve the remote colonial outpost of Manila, also rendered her a veritable floating fortress.

On the beach were clustered some twenty sunbaked, mud huts. In their scant shade huddled many of the vessel's 200 outward bound passengers. They stared with anxiety, admiration and anticipation at the vast barge which would be their home for the next two to three months.

They also stared in awe at the endless, well guarded procession before them. It was no secret what the three foot iron strapped wooden strongboxes contained—pieces-of-eight—most in payment for the exotic goods the annual treasure ship carried from Manila.

A sigh of relief breezed though the assembly when it appeared that the last chest rumbled by on its crude dolly. A regal, young couple—she aglow in the early stages of pregnancy, burgundy and lace, he stiff and proper in a purple tunic and white tights—stood in preparation for boarding when an order to stand clear was barked from the fortress gate.

There was one strongbox yet to board.

As it creaked by, the passengers noted that it was different—constructed entirely of iron and six inches shorter, though broader and deeper. Such was its greater weight that it required an extra effort on the part of the stevedores. Murmurs rippled through the crowd that the chest must surely contain gold. A special escort of soldiers, arquebuses at the ready, caused the whispers to quicken. Why such vigilance for such a relatively small amount?

Speculation was cut short when a tall, thin apparition appeared behind the troops and slashed his cold, blue eyes like scythes through the assembly. The man had long, blond hair and a beard cascading in a golden waterfall to the waist of his black robe. From his neck hung a six inch golden crucifix. Emeralds surrounded the tortured Son of God in a sparkling halo. A Jesuit. Such was the coldness that radiated from his lean figure that some shivered despite the searing heat.

He supervised the carrying of the chest into the ornate stern-castle. After stationing a double guard, the man of the cross climbed the companionway where he towered like a praying mantis over the captain-general at the poop's hurricane rail.

"Is this flying pig ready then?" the Jesuit snapped, using the Spaniards' own derisive term for the galleon style.

"As soon as we take on the livestock and rabble, Father Atagar," the captain-general replied, his normally booming voice failing to disguise a quiver. "Then we'll be ready for Mass."

Father Ignatio del Atagar did not deign to reply at first. His ceramic orbs, eyes filled with unbridled pride and ambition, had fixed on his glorious, secret mission ahead—one he had personally been entrusted with by King Philip V and sanctioned by Pope Clement XI themselves. The priest was a man who reveled in the sure conviction that Providence had fated him for Greatness.

"Good," he finally said, as the young couple were escorted to one of the few private cabins, and the remaining passengers began scrambling up the gangway. Each huddle claimed a cramped corner of the spardeck, which they would share with farm stock during the crossing. Mass was sung by a bishop from the fortress' low ramparts. Friars chanted while the Effigy of the Virgin—patroness of the galleon—was piped aboard. Finally, to ear-numbing booms from San Diego's cannons bounding around the barren bowl of the bay, rowers in longboats towed the wooden leviathan toward the narrows and the awaiting tide.

The Manila Galleon was ready to sail.

1 New York
The Present

"My gawd!" Liana Eastlake exclaimed, sweeping ahead into the open beamed hall. "So *this* is the famous Trophy Room of The Explorers Club!"

"It's quite a sight alright," Chase Ballantyne replied as he followed her in, his eyes firmly fixed on her equally firm backside. Not bad. Not bad at all. And legs right up to her earlobes under that tan jumpsuit.

Her eyes swept from beasts from the Serengeti staring from the rafters, to a huge portrait of a peg-legged explorer glaring down from above an enormous fireplace. She glided across the Oriental carpet appraising the casual clutter of curiosities filling the room.

Chase forced himself to make more appropriate appraisals himself. As he patted a dog-eared book against his palm, he took stock of how her camera bag swung with ease from her shoulder. He noted her lack of self-consciousness, mixed with a certain sensitivity, necessary in a good photographer. He liked both in a woman, particularly a pretty one—and with full features surrounded by a bonfire of red hair, and emerald eyes sparkling with enthusiasm, it was easy to describe her as that and more. She was a fit, beautiful thirty-four-year-old—at least that's how old the senior editor at *National Geographic* had told him she was.

Chase was a senior writer there and had been looking forward to working with her ever since she had been suggested for the assignment, her first for the magazine. He was familiar with her work, having admired it in numerous high profile publications and coffee table books. He also liked the photographs of her on their sleeves, and wondered how much they had influenced his decision to give her the nod as his photographer. But it had been a safe one because she had a reputation for getting great shots, no matter how tough the situation.

While she inspected a wooden statue on a table, Chase glanced around the room. The aroma of pipe tobacco telegraphed that they weren't alone. In a far corner a shrunken, old man sat crunched in his usual leather-bound armchair. They exchanged nods though Chase was relieved when the man, recognizing he had a guest, returned to his book. Chase enjoyed many of the old gent's fascinating, if endless stories about his treasure diving days—but he also knew Barnacle Ben Gordon would wear out your eardrums if given a chance.

"Poor fellow," Liana joked, "looks like he could use a suppository."

Chase grinned when he realized she wasn't referring to Ben, but rather the statue. It was two feet tall, of a naked man with slightly bent knees, the surface black and mottled. Its expression was constipated, to say the least. He strolled over and tapped a brass plaque on its base.

"Careful what you say." He caught a whiff of fresh, green-grass fragrance. "This used to belong to a headhunter. It's a *bo-lul*—an Ifugao-Igorot rice god from the Philippines." He thought of telling her that the out-of-print book he held—*The Igorots of Luzon: A Culture Which Won't Die*—was about them, and that the anthropologist they were linking up with in the Philippines had written it, but decided that could wait.

She raised her Scotch glass in mock gratitude. Her emerald greens held his hazel browns before she lowered her glass and moved on. She was aware that he had been evaluating her, but she was comfortable with it and was doing the same with him. Wasn't that the purpose of his invitation? So they could break the ice in a little Lagavulin before the expedition?

She looked forward to working with him for other than professional reasons too. In his early forties, with tanned, taut features and careless mahogany hair, he was an attractive man. She judged he was only six inches taller than her five-foot-five, and though she actually preferred her men taller, he was lean and had the supple movements of a javelin thrower. And he had other assets as well. Following him up the stairs she'd had ample opportunity to check out the buns in his tight safaris. Not bad. Not bad at all.

Liana studied an exhibit of Sri Lankan Devil Dance masks, then drifted on to a large display case. She started, spilling a lick of Scotch.

"My gawd! Tell me about *this*!"

Chase drew to her side. The exhibit was a new one. The case contained rows of human heads.

A tag identified one with swirling facial tattoos as a Maori trophy head; another as wearing an Etruscan death mask; a third Chase recognized from Borneo, the owner's features recreated in mud; beside it was a skull encased in gold with large emeralds for eyes, clearly Mesoamerican; below that was an Auca shrunken head; a sixth, from the Denmark's peat bogs, wore an oily cap; a seventh, of a man wearing a powdered wig, was crudely pickled in an old jar. Chase glanced at the label. It read Marquis something or other—a royalist whose head had tumbled from a French revolutionary guillotine into the brine. The expression was one of shocked indignation.

"Hmmm. Mustache could use waxing," Chase offered.

"*Look* at these two!" Liana pointed at two heads given prominence. "Aren't they incredible?"

Chase leaned forward with her for a closer examination. They *were* amazing.

In identical handblown jars, the bubbles and green in the glass testament to their age, floated two extraordinary heads.

The one on the left was of a gorgeous young woman—a girl really no more than seventeen. The sensuous lips, high cheekbones and flawless, caramel skin clearly were those of Filipino ancestry. Her ebony hair drifted free as if in a tropical breeze. Her expression was serene, as if she were asleep, dreaming of butterflies or birds or babbling brooks. If the eyes were to drift open, one *knew* they would be warm, promising love.

Chase's eyes flickered to the other jar. In it rested the head of a young man, equally well preserved. The writer was taken aback when he saw that they weren't the features of a native. Rather, the tousle of blond hair—though cut in a native style as if a bowl

3

had been used—and sprinkle of freckles across the nose belonged to that of a northern European. His handsome face bore nascent fuzz—he had been no more than eighteen. If his eyes were to open, one *knew* they would gleam a bright blue. His features, too, were enigmatically tranquil.

"I wonder what they're preserved in?" Chase said, recalling the macabre pickled snakes and pig fetuses in his old high school biology lab. "Formaldehyde wrinkles—and they're as fresh as the day they, uh, died." The word seemed like a blaspheme they looked so alive.

"Extraordinary . . . they're so . . . *beeeautiful*," Liana whispered.

They were aware that their shoulders brushed.

"What's it say on the card on your side?"

"Uh . . . 'Acquired from a Hong Kong Curio Dealer circa 1932. Found by missionaries in Banaue, Philippines. Heads believed to be eighteenth Century'. *Eighteenth Century!* My gawd! There's got to be a great story behind this!" Her look contained an invitation for another collaboration. She didn't wait for a reply but instead set her drink on a table, and reached for a Nikon.

Chase mulled the offer. He was pressed for time. He had just flown in from his last assignment in Peru three days before, hardly time to do more than water his cacti—forget about catching up with friends—and to polish his Inca article before flying off again. Indeed, that expedition had been so deluged by rains that he had warned the senior editor that he might need a delay on this one and he, in turn, had notified the Philippine-based leader, Dr.. Garnet Quinn, and cautioned him that a postponement until the next dry season might be necessary. But Dr. Quinn had replied that he didn't want to risk wasting the precious Writ of Permission granted to enter the restricted area—another might not be forthcoming—and he planned to continue alone.

Then the rains in the Andes had stopped, allowing Chase and his photographer to finish their climb to recently discovered burial sites. If the almost postponed expedition was cause for concern for Liana, she said nothing. Another indication of her single-minded rep for charging into the future.

"We'd need more background," he said, then remembered they weren't alone. He had hoped he could diplomatically avoid the old man, but he was the only other person in the room. "Hey, Ben, what's the story on Hansel and Gretel and their buddies?"

The old man eagerly fumbled his yellowing demi-tasses off

and looked up with watery, gray eyes. Above them hung eyebrows threatening to tumble down the weather-worn crag of a face betraying his eighty-three years. A semi-halo of windblown hair the same tarnished platinum of old sails circled a liver-spotted dome. In his worn canvas pants, workman's shirt with nerd pack, and sockless deck shoes he looked like a cross between a retired diesel mechanic and a sailor, probably because he was both and more.

"Remember old Barney Barnett who kicked the bucket a month ago?" Well smoked barnacles on his vocal chords gave his voice a husky rasp. "He willed the collection to the club." He pulled himself from the armchair. "It must have been quite a love story for these here two kids to lose their heads over. What do you make of the scrimshaw on the lad's forehead?"

Liana and Chase had noted it—crude tattooing disfiguring the flawless face. Red dots formed a line wavering across his brow like the homeward course of a drunk sailor.

"The lettering is *reversed*—he did it *himself* using a mirror!" Liana puzzled. "'6 Z-e-e-m-i-j-l-e-n.' Zeemijlen. What does that means?"

"It's the Dutch word fer 'sea miles,'" Ben explained while fingering tobacco into a battered pipe. "In the old sailin' days, the Dutch didn't have a 'league' as such, which was usually about three miles. Six zeemijlen would be 6.89 miles."

"It looks like a . . . map," Chase said. Like a treasure map, he almost added but caught himself. That was ridiculous.

"Thet's the consensus," Ben replied.

Liana nodded. So Hansel was Dutch. The romance of buried treasure filled her head. "Well, Chase? Newspapers love human interest items like this. My agent can handle distribution."

Liana's determination was swaying him. It would amount to little more than a cutline. He grinned. "I'll write something up."

Her eyes warmed before she turned them to the task at hand. "How do we get this thing open?" Liana jiggled the display case's handle. The two heads hulaed in their jars.

"The concierge has a key," Ben offered. The old treasure diver bent an ancient Zippo to his pipe, and stoked up a fogbank while drifting closer like a crocodile.

Chase knew this was preliminary to him stoking up a monologue that would go on until your ears fell off. "Right!" Chase agreed. "Uh, Liana. . . ." He had let the old reptile out of his cage. There would be no coaxing him back until he had a few bites. She pulled herself away from the case and took the introduction. Chase patted her camera bag and grinned. "Liana's our bag lady on a river expedition to Palawan in the Philippines." He named the archipelago's most remote island, considered the Last Frontier by Filipinos.

"'Bag lady,'" Liana laughed.

"Ooooh, is thet soooo?" the older man said in his foggy rasp, taking an immediate interest along with her hand. "Liana is an appropriate name for someone goin' on a jungle expedition."

"Yes, I suppose it is," she laughed again. "What's your background Ben? You obviously know a great deal about nautical matters."

"Oh, I used to rattle around the Caribbean, doin' a little divin'."

Liana tilted her head, knowing she wasn't getting the entire story. Chase was more puzzled. It wasn't like Ben not to seize an easy prey.

"What Barnacle Ben's neglecting to tell you is that he worked on just about every major treasure dive since World War II. You want to know *anything* about diving for doubloons, this is the man."

6

Liana looked impressed.

"Or was," Ben said. "Those days are over, I'm afraid. Most old boogers like me in New York retire to Florida but I got it back asswards, pardon my French. But Myrtle had enough of Key West and me being at sea and insisted we move to Manhattan when I retired. I've never felt comfortable here"—he looked more lost than usual—"especially since she passed on."

"Why don't you return to Florida then?" Liana asked.

Ben shook his head. "Not without a job. I refuse to become one of them old geezers sittin' around Sloppy Joe's borin' the crap outta everyone about the good old days. I just realized a few days ago thet's exactly what I do around *here*!" His gray eyes betrayed embarrassment as they flickered to Chase. "I've put the word out among the boys on the Keys thet I'm available, but they all think I'm too long in the tooth." His eyes lit up. "But if you run across anything in the Philippines—especially a Manila Galleon—be bloody sure to gimme a call! I've still got my equipment, mostly rented out."

"Manila Galleon? What's that?" Liana asked.

"What's thet! The Manila Galleons were the largest, richest treasure ships ever!" The light in his eyes spread to his face. "They sailed between Acapulco and Manila for 250 years between 1565 and 1815. All us salty old geezers would give our false teeth to find one. They were loaded to the gunwales with silver!"

"The richest?" Liana asked. "How rich?"

Chase glanced at his dive watch. Like most resolutions, Ben's was fading along with the New Year's Day hangover.

"A pope's ransom! It would be several hundred million dollars in today's money!" he replied, then caught himself. "But as I say, I flap my gums too bloody much. Now, please, tell me about this here trip of your—"

He broke into a coughing fit that bleached his face. Chase steadied the old man but he waved him away and leaned against the table.

"Never mind," he wheezed. "It's just . . . some smoke that went down . . . the wrong . . . the wrong bloody pipe. Go on—*your* trip!"

Liana looked at Chase. His pipe had gone out.

"It's a short one, not a major feature," Chase said, feeling sympathy for the ancient mariner. "Are you familiar with Palawan, Ben? No? If you can imagine the Philippines to be some kind of enormous, dislocated Martian insect, it's the long arm that reaches out to the bedbug that is Borneo, or Kalimantan as it's called now. Palawan is about 250 miles long, but only twenty wide. A range of old mountains runs the length. There's hardly anyone on it, mostly on the south-eastern side. The north-west side is pretty well uninhabited. Back in 1962, Dr. Robert Fox discovered some 200 caves there, most of which contained burial jars. In one of them, he dug up a skull he named Tabon Man which was the basis for his book *The Tabon Cave*. He found that it had been inhabited for 40,000 years."

"Nice to have been collecting rent all that time!" Liana laughed.

Chase found himself grinning again. More than anything, he liked women with a sense of humor. "Indeed. Unfortunately, Dr. Fox had a stroke in '66, and since then practically no one has gone back, mainly because it's in a restricted area."

"Restricted?"

"Yeah. There's two reasons. One is to protect the indigenous Batak. But more importantly is because Abu Sayyef, the terrorist group linked to al-Queda, were believed to operate there, and because it's jungle, the military has little control. Abu Sayyef are the militant Islamic group that in '95 tried to launch a Manila based plot to blow eleven passenger planes out of the sky, crash another into CIA headquarters, and assassinate the pope."

"Jist a minute, they're not the group thet kidnapped a bunch of tourists at a Palawan resort fer ransom in 2001?"

"That's them. There were twenty hostages, including three Americans. They claim to be fighting for a Muslim homeland in their southern stronghold of Mindanao, but they're really more interested in kidnapping for ransom. 5,000 Filipino troops chased them there. Several hostages were beheaded, including one of the Americans. In a shootout, another American, a missionary, was killed and his wife wounded. Because there haven't been reports of them in the Palawan region in a few years, we wrangled a Writ of Permission from the government to enter. But we'll have to be careful."

Chase watched for a reaction from Liana but she merely checked her watch, made a face, and whispered a polite 'excuse me.' Easing back to the case, she bayoneted a lens into a camera. He was impressed. She was fearless indeed.

"Sounds like it could be a mite dangerous," Ben replied, his eyes brightening again. A disposition to flirting with danger was a common bond among club members. "You'll be packin' guns?"

Chase shook his head while he looked for a diplomatic exit. "The government insists we don't. I was hoping to argue the case when we reached Manila but because of delays, we'll be flying directly from Ninoy Aquino International to Palawan to catch up with Dr. Quinn in the field. Now, if you—"

"Dr. Quinn?"

"He's a Canadian anthropologist who's been living in a remote part of the Philippines for years, but recently moved to Manila and is expanding his interests. We know there's caves there because of aerial photos he sent. Whether or not there'll be burial jars is another matter, but the magazine is confident enough there is to go for it. We'll do a story on him doing a survey."

"I remember we once came across underwater caves off Cartegen—"

A tapping of glass behind the writer saved him. It was Liana making a face as she pointed from her wristwatch to the locked cabinet.

"Right! The key!" Chase said, setting his book aside and turning toward the door. "Ben, excuse us. We're leaving tomorrow morning and we're up to here. I'll see the concierge."

Ben stared at his dead pipe. Minutes later Chase returned waving a key. While Ben looked on, Chase and Liana removed the jars and placed them on the table beside the *bolul*. He studied her efficient shooting style with admiration. Twenty minutes later, the heads were bobbing back in their positions, and the photographer was cinching the straps to her camera bag.

"The bag lady has to be running," she lilted. She stuck a hand out to Ben. "I hope to see you again."

"Mind them Manila Galleons," Barnacle Ben said.

9

She bobbed her eyebrows at Chase. He grabbed his book and their Scotches and they strode out the door and skipped down the stairs.

"So that's what happens to old divers," she said *sotto voce*. "They don't get old—they just run out of air. He's such a sad looking man, but has such character in his face! I'd love to shoot him sometime."

So would many club members, and don't be so sure about Ben running out of air, Chase thought, but bit his tongue. But perhaps the old crocodile was finally going to bite his own. Then Chase remembered that cough. Maybe the old guy *was* running out of air. . . .

Moments later they stood on East 70th, the air laden with the fullness of Indian Summer.

"Meet you at Philippine Airline's check-in?" Liana backed toward Madison.

Chase shot her a thumbs up before turning toward Park Avenue and a cab back to his Tribeca flat. He was pleased. They seemed to be a good match. He expected the expedition would go without major hitches, just another straight forward little adventure.

Certainly less dramatic than the one the young couple in the jars had, he was certain.

2 The Boy in the Bottle

_____

Jan Van Larmancaller crouched behind a windmill beside Fort George panting, his trembling caused less by the crisp October air than by fear. He took in his breath as something screeched above his head. It was the proprietor's new sign swinging in the wind.

"John Miller, New York, 1703" it read.

Brushing a blond lock aside, Jan squinted through moonlight across Bowling Green to the homes and farms beyond, searching for his pursuer. A large figure charged out of Beaver Graft, his head swiveling up and down Broad Way. Flickering light from a street lamp enhanced the size of the flintlock in his hand.

The young man's blue eyes widened, and he ran down De Perel Straet. A cobblestone caught his bare toe, and he sprawled into the open sewage trickling down the center of the lane. Instantly, he was up and limping down the street. He tried to will away the lanterns illuminating the brick buildings, all built in Dutch style.

Hopping on one foot to the entrance of one of them, he pounded on the door. The top half of the door swung open and a red face peered out. Behind him in a neat, candle lit parlor sat a table of young men. One of them threw down his cards and sighed. Moments later, Jan was tugging his brother down the street. Reluctantly, Guert broke into an awkward clack in his wooden shoes to keep up. Jan bellied over a fence into a corn plot.

"What have you done this time, Jan?" Guert whispered in their native Dutch as he crouched beside his shaking sibling.

"You've lost your wooden shoes. Someday you're going to lose your wooden head, the things you do!"

Although senior by only five years, twenty-two-year-old Guert had always treated his brother paternalistically. Partly it was because Jan was so young and sensitive for his age. Mostly it was because their father had been massacred by Indians four years before. Shortly thereafter, their heartbroken mother had succumbed to one of the yellow fever plagues that periodically decimated the frontier settlement.

"De Peyster is after me," Jan blurted.

Guert froze. Old Abraham de Peyster was a developer, their boss, and Guert his foreman. After they had been orphaned, de Peyster had installed them in an outbuilding and, in return, had indentured them as apprentice carpenters at sharply reduced wages, taking advantage of their desperate circumstances. He was a demanding man with a temper when he felt his workers were not giving their due—and Jan regularly ran afoul of that temper, and fist.

"*What* have you done?" Guert repeated.

"It . . . it's M . . . Margaretje."

Guert blanched. Margaretje was the stolid de Peyster's fifteen-year-old daughter. Blossoming into a fair haired beauty.

". . . *Ja*. . . ?" Guert said, unable to disguise a note of pain.

"Sh . . . she is going to have . . . a baby!"

Guert reeled. It was one thing for the despised English and the pirates swarming up and down the coast to carry on with the strumpets that filled the taverns of nearby Dock Street. It was quite another to become awkwardly involved with the daughter of one of the town's leading citizens!

And there were other reasons, when Guert thought of the beautiful young Margaretje, which he didn't want to speak about. He wanted to lash out at his younger brother, but when Jan looked up and Guert saw moonlight glistening off tears on his muddy face, the thought vanished. Nature had bestowed Jan with handsome good looks and an athletic body that caused many a girl to look softly his way. That same nature hadn't been as kind to Guert with his lanky frame and prominent ears, his knotted dirty blond hair to Jan's tousled gold.

". . . When? Where?" Guert asked.

Jan looked sheepish. "When I checked our rabbit snares . . . Margaretje would meet me. Wha . . . what do I do?"

Both knew there was no place to hide in a town of 4,500 people. The thought of sending Jan to find employment in one of the rough communities, like Boston or Philadelphia, passed through Guert's mind but just as quickly left. The seven years in Jan's endenture weren't completed, and de Peyster would track him down.

"Perhaps tomorrow—when Mr. de Peyster is calmed down— we should talk to him. . . ? He's Christian and perhaps he'll find it in his heart to forgive—"

"Christian! He's as bad as those hypocritical Papists with their Indulgences and Inquisition! He doesn't represent any god I want to have anything to do with!"

Guert was sorry he had brought up the subject. They had had many arguments about Jan's stand that the Dutch Reformed Church—of which de Peyster was an Elder—was harsh, cruel and unjust. He was especially disgusted with its Calvanist doctrine of predestination, that man was born to suffer except for a chosen few. That Jan was in the former group, de Peyster had impressed upon him many times.

It had been Jan's relationship with de Peyster that had taught him to revile Christianity. Guert would have to worry about his younger brother's spiritual vacuum later. Shadows falling across Guert's face deepened when he acknowledged there was only one way out. It lay in the direction of rum filled laughter on Dock Street.

"Jan. . . ," Guert said, wiping muck from his brother's face, "I think you must leave New Amsterdam for awhile." He used the preferred name among the Low Landers for the now English garrisoned settlement.

"Bu . . . but where can I go?" Jan asked, snuffling back his freckled nose.

"I know a ship that needs a carpenter."

Jan looked crestfallen, but it was the only alternative. Governor's Wharf was a forest of masts.

"You've seen the *Raid*?" Guert asked.

The British ship had been the subject of rumors. What was known was that it was a privateer holding a Letter of Marque, empowering it to attack enemy vessels. Speculation centered on why it was loading so many supplies—depleting the food shops of New York—if it was only going to be operating in the Caribbean.

The War of the Spanish Succession, known in contemporary times as Queen Anne's War, was barely two years under way with the Grand Alliance of England, Holland, Austria, and most recently the Germanic states and Portugal teaming up against the Bourbon Sun King, Louis XIV. He had proclaimed his grandson, Philip V, successor to the Spanish Hapsburg throne. The idea of France and Spain united under the same roof was cause for alarm among the other houses of Europe, and they were determined to kick the Hapsburg door down, and restore a more equitable balance of power.

Jan nodded. The *Raid* was the finest vessel he had ever seen. She was a sleek, triple-masted greyhound of 1,400 tons, 165 feet and with a crew of 640. He had counted the gunports in the single row along one side—thirty-four. Both knew that the dangers there could be no worse than those offered by the enraged de Peyster.

"The first mate ordered spars from us, that's why I know they're short a carpenter. They're sailing tomorrow. Come, he mentioned Nelly's Tavern."

They hurried toward Dock, Guert checking behind for de Peyster. The thought that he would have to face his boss alone the next day knotted his stomach, but de Peyster favored him because he was a hard, obedient worker. They skirted bales of beaver pelts on the wharf, then gave a wide berth to a drunken brawl which a clutch of redcoats were trying to break up. In the harbor bobbed a flotilla of barks, brigs and bilanders. Jan caught a glimpse of the *Raid*. Suddenly, the magnificent ship he had so admired took on an ominous appearance.

Guert gave an equally wide berth to other taverns before tacking toward Nelly's and pulling Jan inside. The Dutch boy looked wide eyed through flickering candle light, finding it hard to believe that a first mate would be found in a dive like this. A drunken rowdy of seamen from all over Europe sprawled around sailor proof-tables. Many had trollops on their laps. More than a few were inspecting their mammarian wares to the hoots and hollers of their mates. The stench of rum and homemade whiskey, unwashed bodies and tobacco was overwhelming.

14

Guert nudged his younger brother when a huge, disheveled figure with wild, red hair and a wilder beard staggered out from behind a dirty curtain pulling on a tricorn cocked hat. He was probably forty, but his enormous belly made him look older. Behind followed a frumpy figure straightening her stained dress. A drunken grin of rotten teeth spread across the first mate's sweaty face as he dropped coins down her ample cleavage.

"H . . . him. . . ?" Jan gulped.

"*Ja*," Guert replied, closing his eyes. "He's not like any first mate I've seen before either."

Guert wormed through the crowd, Jan in tow, as the sailor grabbed a tankard from a passing serving wench. It took several blinks before he recognized the lanky young man.

"Well, if it ain't!" The Englishman roared in an accent forged in the taverns of Liverpool and Portsmouth. Slapping a beefy arm around Guert's shoulder, he tried to draw him to his table. It seemed to take forever before the Englishman grasped that Guert needed to speak to him privately.

"John Hoogley, this is my brooder, Jan," Guert said, slipping into English. "He is a very goot carpenter and would like to join yoor ship."

". . . A carpenter ye say?" A serious squint entered Hoogley's red eyes as he extracted a clay pipe from an elaborate wooden case with drunken care. While he loaded it, Hoogley tried to focus on the boy, trying to fathom why his face was muddy.

"What's 'e done then?" Hoogley demanded, no fool even if he was three sheets to the wind.

The brothers exchanged glances, then Guert told him. Hoogley roared until he doubled over.

"We cin always use a carpenter who's good with the blocks!" he thundered, tousling Jan's hair. "'e reminds me of me own lad back in Rye!"

A huge, hairy hand reached out and gripped Jan by a buttock. He jumped away and pivoted to see a dark hulk about thirty with a black, pointed beard and long, matted hair sticking out from beneath a strange bucket-shaped hat. He was grinning lasciviously through two missing front teeth. The man was of a nationality Jan had never seen before, in bare feet, a shirt that reached to his knees and billowing, black pantaloons. A loud *craump* followed as the barrel of Hoogley's pistol connected with the man's head, knocking his fez off, and sending him sprawling to the hoots and applause of his mates.

"Ye don't touch the lad again Mustafa ye bloody Turkish pervert!" the first mate growled at the dazed figure. Then he offered Jan the Ottoman's spot at the table.

Guert grabbed the first mate's arm. "Yoo doon't oonderstand. We must get him aboord *now!*"

Hoogley eyed the restraining hand. Guert jerked it away. Seeing the Turk skulking away massaging his head, the Englishman's good humor returned.

"Ahhhhh, it cain wait. I still 'ave a few cobs left to spend. Tomorrow we sail. Tonight we tars scupper grog!"

But Guert was persistent. While Hoogley weighed the matter, his thumb caressed the pipe bowl. Jan glimpsed a small anchor and personalized initials—J.H.—embossed on it.

". . . Aye, all right," First Mate Hoogley slurred, putting the pipe away with a delicacy surprising in a man as large and drunk. "I'll 'ave me lads row 'im out."

Jan and Guert followed the inebriated Englishman out the door. After checking for de Peyster, they followed along the half moon breakwater of Governor's Wharf. As Hoogley stumbled closer to a longboat, two sailors guarding it hid a jug. Hoogley barked an order. One fell to the ties while the other fitted oars.

The two brothers stood, eyes locked, not knowing if they would ever see each other again. Then Jan gripped his brother to his breast and both fought back tears. Hoogley scratched his belly and glanced back toward the tavern.

"I'll leave ye two lovebards," he muttered and stumbled off.

Guert and Jan remained embraced while the coxswain and his mate looked on bored. They had witnessed the scene before. They had probably been a part of it at one time.

"Go, Jan," Guert said, pushing Jan back. "And may Go . . . may luck go with you."

"S . . . say goodbye to Margaretje for me," Jan implored, gripping his brother's arm.

Guert felt uncomfortable, but nodded. Jan clambered into the bobbing boat and the sailors leaned back on the oars. He sat listening to the creak of the oarlocks and laughter drifting from taverns, his eyes fixed on the lone figure of his older brother receding in the distance. Neither waved.

After climbing the ship's sidesteps, Jan stood at the spardeck rail and watched as Guert turned and was swallowed up in the gloom.

The only other time Jan Van Larmancaller felt so alone was when his parents died.

3 The Bobbsey Twins

"Well, I'll be!" Chase exclaimed, looking up from Dr. Quinn's book. Five miles below their seats lay the Pacific Ocean. "I just learned that *bolul* rice god in the Trophy Room is from Banaue too—like Hansel and Gretel!"

He and Liana had emailed the article to Liana's agent.

"No kidding? That's a coincidence!"

Chase felt a passing aura of déjà vu. "Many are also squating." Closing the book, he took a sip of Scotch.

"So, what would you like to be doing in five years?" Liana asked.

He raised his eyebrows. "Boy, you sure cut to the chase, don't you?"

"Well, that's your name, isn't it?" she laughed.

". . . Actually, I'd like to cut back on assignments. And I'd like to buy a dog. A Rhodesian Ridgeback."

It was her turn for eyebrows to raise. "You're kidding? You have the ideal life—ranging over the planet, living an adventurous life. It's everyone's fantasy!"

"Hey, believe it or not, it loses some of its appeal after twenty years. Try living out of a packsack that long." He wasn't used to exposing himself to virtual strangers, and he knew it was indicative of how little contact he had with his friends that he was doing so. That and because something indefinable had been niggling him all day. "Don't get me wrong, I love what I do, but there's no balance to my life. I didn't even have time to unpack this time between expeditions. How do you keep up relationships living like that? Oh, I make friends all over the world, great, fascinating

18

people, but I rarely see them again. . . . I don't really have a home?" He didn't know why it came out as a question.

She swirled ice in her Scotch. "And that's why you want a dog. A dog. Home. They go together."

"Something like that. I love dogs but I haven't been able to have one since I grew up in Colorado on a farm. It wouldn't be fair to the mutt, me being away so much. Do you know the only plants I can keep are cactus because they can go so long without water?"

"You're a good looking man. You must have a girl friend. Or a string of them."

"That's where a dog would come in handy, for meeting women in parks. Look at my last girl friend—because I'm away so much, she moved on. I couldn't blame her. Oh, we've remained friends. She waters my desert when I'm away and forwards mail but that's it." There were the bargirls and one night stands, but he wasn't going to mention them.

"But what would you do? Besides putter around the house and walk Rover?"

"Oh, I'd still do an assignment or two annually in areas that particularly interest me. But, like everything in life, it's time to move up to the next level."

"Ah! There is another reason! And that is?"

"Get ready to be bored. I'm fascinated by the debate between the Isolationists and Diffusionists, and in my travels and research I've gathered an enormous amount of data. I'd like to write a book."

"I don't find this boring at all. Go on."

That's what a man likes to hear. "Basically, the Isolationists believe that cultures in diverse parts of the world developed in isolation. For example, they believe that no Europeans were in the Americas before Columbus and the Vikings. For example, they see it as coincidental that pyramids appeared in both Egypt and Mesoamerica. On the other hand are the Diffusionists who find evidence that cultural seeds traveled across land and sea, one culture influencing another."

"And your take?"

"Diffusion hasn't been given its due. Even some of the Isolationists have found over sixty points of similarity between Mediterranean and Mesoamerican cultures, but still stick their heads in the sand. Besides the building of pyramids with burial chambers, there's the cutting of colossal stones with fittings so exact razors can't be wedged into the joints, mummification and the placing of gold masks over faces, the use of the same type of reed water craft—even circumcision. Thor Heyerdahl found more than a *hundred* points of similarity. Like Thor, my major interest is trans-oceanic diffusion."

Chase thought of adding that a huge globe in the Explorers Club is the one Heyerdahl had plotted his Kon-Tiki adventure on, but let it pass.

"Why don't you just do it then?"

He wondered if he should tell her. It was personal. Ah, what the heck, he'd already told her too much. "I was about to a year ago when my stocks crashed. It takes money to live in Manhattan, and I don't want to live anywhere else." The pain of that loss was still with him. "What about you, Liana? A boyfriend?"

"I had one once. I gave it away."

Chase laughed so hard other passengers looked up from their reading. "Independent, aren't you? In five years?"

She saw no sense in telling him about her one shot stands. Her eyes brightened. "Actually, I want to be doing what you're doing right now—on the road internationally shooting full time. But freelance assignments and coffee table books don't pay that great either. San Francisco hasn't gotten any cheaper since I grew up there."

Chase raised his drink. "Well, good luck. We're going in opposite directions, but one thing we have in common is that we both like Scotch."

She laughed and clinked glasses. "Another thing we have in common is we're heading into an area that's had Islamic terrorist problems. Do you think we're going to have any?"

So she had concerns about Abu Sayyef after all. "Everything's a risk in this business, but I think it's low. Certainly the Philippine government thinks so too or they wouldn't have given us permission to go in."

"Good. I've covered a few war zones, but Islamic fanatics are one hazard I prefer skipping." She paused. "Isn't it terrible how religion has always been one of the greatest causes of strife? These spiritual leaders—Christ, Mohammed, all of them—carried the same message of goodness, and it has so often been perverted

20

by their followers. The Crusades, Islam spreading the faith by the sword, car bombs—*wars* in the name of religion! And now they've escalated to where we are now fighting the first Religious World War. It's so, so out of frame."

"And now that Pakistan has opened the nuclear Pandora's Box, how long will it be before New York, San Francisco, Washington, London and Paris disappear in mushroom clouds—and in the name of God?" More reason to live one's dreams.

"It's sobering alright. We're nearing a cataclysmic climax. . . . ”

"And some of them have been battling since they were at the cult level, before their populations grew large enough to be considered religions." Another thought struck him. "I wonder if any of these early warring cults-slash-religions ever wiped another out so completely that we lost a Jesus or a Mohammed or a Buddha along the way." They flew on for several minutes lost in thought, his mind drifting back to his indefinable feelings.

". . . Liana, do you believe in destiny?"

"I thought that New Age stuff was for those of us from the Left Coast, not a farm boy living in Manhattan?"

Chase chuckled. "No, it's none of that. I know it sounds silly, but when I woke this morning, I felt something . . . strange. I've been on tons of expeditions, but there's something . . . different about this one. As if it's driven by . . . destiny. I can't think of another word."

He was about to joke it away when she turned to him. "You know, I had the same feeling—almost like déjà vu. Isn't that peculiar?" They flew in silence for some time again. "Destiny . . . the Great Mystery . . . do you ever think about it?"

"Where my socks go when I throw them in the laundry? All the time."

She laughed. "You know what I mean."

". . . I think whatever is going on is so far beyond what our infinitesimally small minds can imagine, that all our attempts at guessing are crude at best. What could be cruder than the symbolic cannibalism of Catholics with wafers and wine? But I also think that because that Great Intelligence gives us so few clues, that all attempts to communicate are legitimate, even those of your California crystal gazers. If one feels that they're connecting, who's to say they're not? What about you? Your thoughts?"

"I don't know. That's why I asked you."

21

4 The Manila Galleon

"Now son," John Hoogley said, drawing on one of his monogrammed clay pipes. "All we 'as to do is wait—and 'ope we're not spotted."

Jan wiped sweat from his forehead. He couldn't believe how hot it was. Nor could he believe that the dry hills on the eastern horizon four cable's length, or about a half mile, away belonged to the Philippines either, but they did. The *Raid* had sailed from New York three days when Captain Seagrave had announced the ship's real mission: the seizure of the greatest prize on the Seven Seas—a Manila Galleon. While the crew cheered, Jan had gulped.

"How did Captain Seagrave learn aboot the galleoon's schedule and route?" Jan dared. The crew had never been taken fully into the owners' confidence. "Was that from Vigo too, Mr. Hoogley?"

It was common knowledge aboard how Captain Seagrave and Hoogley had raised the money to purchase the *Raid*— which explained the unorthodox first mate. They had fought in the Vigo Bay engagement two years previous. It was the first major naval confrontation of Queen Anne's War and involved one of the greatest takes in maritime history. The British had ambushed the Spanish treasure fleet in one of its home harbors, seizing seventeen of the twenty-one galleons—with some 13,000,000 pieces-of-eight aboard. Besides their share of the spoils, they had seized Spanish colors, and a brace of their freshly cast demi-culverins—state of the art artillery. Indeed, ninety percent of their cannons were Spanish.

"I giss I cin tell ye now," Hoogley replied as he put his arm paternalistically around the boy's shoulders, "since there's nay danger of it jumpin' ship at this late date. Aye, it was at Vigo. Ye see, Seagrave and me 'ad gotten our 'ands on the Don flagship's navigator. We showed 'im a ball—'is ball. Then 'e was kind enough to draw us a map of the islands." Hoogley smiled a black stumped grin. "Aye, we showed 'im such a proper time thet when we left 'im 'e was grinnin' from ear to ear!"

Jan swallowed. He knew what that meant, and tried not to picture the bloody sight. But he was impressed—seizing the Spanish navigator had been a stroke of the greatest fortune. The information he had imparted was one of the best kept secrets of the eighteenth century.

Jan studied Captain Seagrave striding across the poop, occasionally shouting orders down a hatch to the man operating the whipstaff, it being a few decades before the more practical helm appeared. Seagrave was dark and nattily dressed in a blue tricorn hat and matching serge with brass buttons. It was he who proposed sailing into the very maw of the Spanish monster and plucking out its silver teeth.

"Mr. 'oogley!" a man shouted from a hatch. "We need 'elp on the pumps!"

The first mate scowled and ordered men below. "Curse those toredo worms! The captain planned to set our trap by the Pasa de Acapulco"—he named the narrow Straits of San Bernardino on the Philippine's eastern and windward flank where the treasure galleons entered the Visayas Islands, before sailing around the chin of Luzon and up into the yawning mouth of Manila Bay—"but the sea would 'ammer this worm eaten tub into sticks! We don't 'ave time to careen—and the galleon is due any week!"

Toredo worms had played havoc on the eight month voyage. Captain Seagrave had chosen instead to wait off the chin of Luzon, praying that the Spaniards concentrated their few men in Manila—as the loquacious navigator had told them was the case in his newly tenored voice.

"Woon't we be outgoonned by the galleoon?" Jan ventured, pausing from hoisting a jug of beer. He couldn't believe how his tolerance had increased, but that's all there was to drink.

Hoogley scratched his red beard. "Our navigator friend said thet they carried most of their cannons below as ballast on the crossing. Let's 'ope so. The crap eating Dons still think the Pacific is their other Spanish Lake. I'm content to let them go on thinkin' thet for the time be. . . ."

He trailed off as Mustafa, known behind his broad back as the Terrible Turk, slouched by, exchanging a cold glance with Hoogley. The animosity between the short tempered first mate and the brooding Asia Minorite in the fez was palpable. Nor could it be said that he sailed with a full compliment of canvas—but in battle, all wanted him on their side.

"I'm sorry I 'ad to assign ye to his gun, son," Hoogley said quietly, "but there was nowhere else to fit ye in. As long as 'e keeps 'is 'ands to 'isself."

Jan nodded—and thanked his stars the first mate had taken him under his wing. Shipboard life had had a sobering effect on the Dutch boy—but nothing more so than his relationship with the Moor. In an environment where the practice of *matelotage* was the norm—many of crew members taking mates, a term that went far beyond the mere nautical—the silent Turk was left out in the cold. Unfortunately, he had the most evil of eyes for the golden boy. It was an attraction Jan deflected as diplomatically as possible—as he did all of them. Indeed, he found the affections between crew members abhorrent. Seldom did his thoughts stray from Margaretje—nor from more recent thoughts that he must now be a father.

To take his mind off his distant family and home, Jan looked up at Spanish tri-color snapping from the mainmast. For the last few days a strong nor'easterly had been brewing under gun barrel skies.

"Aye, I 'ope the weather 'olds too," Hoogley worried as he tapped ashes from his pipe and returned it to its case. "Typhoon—or *baguio*—season, as our navigator friend called it, is jist around the corner." He forced a smile. "We jist 'ave to wait, and 'ope the Don basterds sail into our trap. . . ."

* * *

"*Fire!*"

The ship shuddered and rolled back on her beam ends as all thirty-four guns roared. Smoke blew back through the gunports, stinging Jan's eyes. Their wait had only been a week before the

24

Manila Galleon rounded the chin and into sight. She had tried to turn and run—but the much faster greyhound had run her to ground.

"Worm and sponge! Fresh charges! Wadding! Drive 'er 'ome!"

Jan plunged the tamper down the barrel. Once the huge demi-culverin was reloaded, the gun crew hauled it out again with block and tackle. Jan risked a glance out the gunport, and his heart caught in his throat. The mighty port hull of the prize lay only fifty yards away! He could even read the ship's name on its bow—the *Santa Maria de la Immaculate Concepcion*!

Topside, as the blinding smoke blew away, Captain Seagrave watched with nervous satisfaction as spars and blocks crashed onto the galleon's crowded waist, crushing scores of people who hadn't been hosed off by grape shot. Most of the rail no longer existed. Screams rose above the shouting and shooting.

Seagrave spotted his opposite gesticulating and shouting orders. He appeared to be hampered by a tall figure in black, his enormous blond beard fanning out like a flag in the wind, who seemed to be issuing orders at cross-purposes. Seagrave had no time to question why the captain-general would tolerate a Jesuit at a time like this, but he was delighted he did.

"Thunderation!" Seagrave exclaimed as the smoke cleared.

The *Raid's* nine pound balls had merely bounced off the thick sides of the great ship. The hair on his neck bristled when first one, then six, then two dozen cannon ports on all three levels fell open, and their demi-culverins and sakers rolled out.

"'ell's bells," Hoogley muttered. "The Dons didn't lower all their artillery into the 'old."

The galleon's powerful guns fired in an enormous explosion. The *Raid* groaned from the terrible blow. A mizzen yard snapped and crashed to the poop, crushing a half dozen sailors.

Below, Jan stood in shock surrounded by a screaming hell. Men groaned and cried out and bitter smoke filled the gundeck. Limbs and intestines were spread everywhere. At his feet lay his gun captain's headless, twitching body. The Terrible Turk, slipping in blood, pushed Jan aside and grabbed the smoldering taper from the deck.

Above, Hoogley shouted, "Ready Captain!"

Seagrave almost fell when he stepped on a severed arm. He recognized the tattoo. His second mate's. "*Fire!*"

Their second broadside slammed into the galleon, tearing more rigging away. The top of the mainmast crashed onto the Spaniard deck, crushing screaming passengers, sailors and soldiers. The *Concepcion* wallowed like a water buffalo in the rough seas, but the *Raid's* nine pounders again had merely bounced off her sides.

"Captain Seagrave! They've sprung our 'ull! We're taking wat—" a sailor shouted from a hatch before a shot tore his jaw away.

"Mr. 'oogley, we can't tolerate another broadside!" the captain shouted. He was about to issue an order to his third mate when the man doubled over groaning. "Mr. 'oogley! Prepare to board! Gun crews topside! Whipstaff to starboard!"

The wounded *Raid* lurched toward the galleon. The captain-general tried to turn away but his ship wouldn't respond. A terrible crunching filled the air as the hulls ground together. Grappling hooks flew. Flintlocks cracked like Chinese firecrackers.

Captain Seagrave glanced at the galleon's bridge. The captain-general waved his arms, but to little avail. The Jesuit was also still shouting orders and gesticulating, adding to the confusion. Seagrave was startled to see that the man of the cross had taken up a sword. He caught the gaunt figure's eye and the Jesuit glared at the *Raid's* captain, the venom in his eye unmistakable.

Seagrave suddenly cried out and spun as a shot slammed into his elbow, leaving his forearm dangling by skin and a tendon. He leaned back against the hurricane rail, hyperventilating, blood staining his tunic. A battle cry cleared his senses as Hoogley led the boarding party with a reluctant Jan in tow, flintlock pistols in hand. The Terrible Turk, sporting a rare smile, was right behind. Then the shock and loss of blood had its effect and Captain Seagrave's knees buckled.

The privateers swarmed over the ship. Women screamed as raiders climbed rigging and fired down into the mass of people. Horses whinnied and reared, crushing passengers. Cattle churned, sweeping sailors off their feet. Despite their numbers, the Spanish soldiers were of little use.

A terrified Jan was in the midst of the mayhem as Hoogley and his company slashed and shot their way toward the bridge. A Spanish soldier leaning over the quarterdeck rail took aim at the Englishman. Jan reacted, his flintlock cracked. The Spaniard's head snapped back, but his body fell forward into the waist, landing on a bleating goat.

Hoogley wheeled around, his eyes burning into Jan's. The Dutch boy stood as if in a trance, stunned by what he had done. Then the first mate turned and led the charge up the companionway. The Spanish officers' guards fell on them in a frenzy with swords, their arquebuses rendered useless by rain that began to fall. Hoogley cut two of them down, while Jan managed to fend off a third before the Terrible Turk charged howling into their midst, scimitar flashing.

In less than a minute Hoogley, face splattered with blood, stood before the frightened captain-general and the Jesuit, his sword stained crimson. He threw it aside with contempt but stood defiant.

"*Strike the colors, ye Don basterd*!" Hoogley thundered at the captain-general, shoving his cutlass into the man's portly middle.

The galleon's master looked to the man in black. His blue eyes were cold chips of ice as he nodded. It was all over but for raping and pillaging, and both were taken up with gusto.

"Jan, search thet blackguard," Hoogley ordered, thrusting his bearded chin toward the seething Black Robe. "The spot 'e's in and 'e's still got wind in 'is sails!"

The Spaniard's eyes burned into Jan as the boy stuck his pistol into his belt, and gingerly reached into the pocket of the Jesuit's robe. He lifted out a large gold and emerald crucifix. He had never seen anything so valuable in his life. Hoogley grabbed it and turned it over in his hand.

"What this Papist son-of-a-dog was doing manning a cutlass, I'll never know—but I *do* know jist what to do with this 'ated basterd! Turk—let down one of their punts—we'll cool off this 'ot 'eaded, dung-eating Don in the soup!"

A scowling Terrible Turk shoved the Spaniard toward the companionway. The insolence in his Iberian eyes barely dimmed as he strode toward his fate. A punt was lowered into the sea where it bobbed like a cork. He was thrown over the rail in a tangle of arms and legs, plunging below the angry waves. Fighting to the surface, he scrambled aboard the small boat where he sat, his rages lost in the rain and wind, until a laughing tar threw a wooden bucket at him. It missed by inches, crashing into the boat's bottom. To the taunts of the privateers, the castaway lined his oars.

Despite his disgust for Christianity, Jan felt a twinge of pity for the brave Jesuit rowing into oblivion. Jan had seen all the death he wanted.

"'ere, son," Hoogley grunted, slapping the heavy crucifix back into the young Hollander's hand. "Ye found it, ye keep it. The first of yere spoils."

Jan stared again at the cross while Hoogley scanned the scene. Jubilant privateers moved among terrified passengers stripping them of valuables, with the women being stripped of more. The two ships, their canvas cut to ribbons, ground and thumped against each other. The first mate's eyes gleamed as he turned toward the officers' cabins.

"Now, let's see what we 'ave 'ere!"

Jan slipped the cross into a pocket and followed. Hoogley was about to enter the passageway when a sailor ran up.

"Mr. 'oogley! I 'ave a message from the captain. He's been wounded and—"

"Thunder and lightning! How bad?"

"'e's slipping in and out of consciousness," the sailor shouted over the rising storm. " 'e wants ye to take command. He also says to tell ye thet thar's three feet of water in the 'old and the pumps can nay 'andle it. He says to move the Dons to the *Raid* and we'll take over this tub. It's our only chance. Captain Seagrave 'as ordered our breechlocks spiked."

Hoogley cursed. He stepped to the waist, swept up the captain-general's speaking trumpet, and bellowed the order. Sailors froze—then sped their stripping of passengers before beginning the mammoth job of exchanging ships. Hoogley swung toward Jan, his face full of concern.

"Son, take this Don captain across to the *Raid* and while you're there, do me a wee favor. Fetch me pipes."

By now Jan well knew of Hoogley's attachment to his embossed pipes. In double time, he was back with the cigar box-sized container. Hoogley paused from shouting orders to smile.

"Thanks much lad," he said. He lifted the signal flag chest lid and placed the pipe box inside, then turned to the *Raid*'s quartermaster. "Take the trumpet. Yere in charge. 'ave Captain Seagrave brought over. The rest of ye, follow me."

He threw open the doorway and thundered down the dark passageway to a door at the end, next to a short companionway leading upward. Hoogley shouldered the door open, and barged into the captain-general's great cabin. Jan and the men were on his heels.

They came up short, thunderstruck.

The room was stacked to the ceiling with wooden strongboxes, leaving just enough room for the captain-general's table and cot. Hoogley seized a pike, snapped a lock open, and threw back the lid. They stared at a chest full of freshly minted pieces-of-eight. While the men broke out in cheers, Jan was stunned. There were *tons* of silver in this room!

The jubilant first mate barged out of the cabin, charged up the side companionway, and shouldered the door at the top aside. His men scurried behind like puppies. It was the admiral's cabin, when such was aboard, and even grander than the captain-general's. But it was virtually empty. It was obvious from religious paraphernalia that it had been occupied by the Jesuit.

"Aye, and what do we 'ave 'ere?" Hoogley growled.

In the center of the room sat a single, iron strongbox. Over it was spread a linen cloth, and atop this a Christian altar. Hoogley swept the chalice and candles aside and gripped the handle to test its weight. His expression registered surprise as, with difficulty, he lifted the end four inches off the floor. When he let the handle go, the chest landed with a solid *thump*.

"I know what's in *this* one!" he roared.

The men's blood quickened. It could contain only one thing. *Gold.* Gold doubloons!

"Mr. 'oogley! Where are ye?" a voice shouted from the corridor. It was the coxswain's.

Hoogley was about to lever the heavy lock off the chest, but paused. "'ere! What the 'ell is it then?"

"The weather is turnin' fer the worst! Ye's needed on deck!"

Hoogley cursed. "Jan—all of ye—follow me. We'll need all our carpenters to make this tub fly."

Outside, the sky was leaden gray and the wind was up, slashing rain across the decks. Rising seas and differing freeboards of the two ships made evacuation dangerous. More than a few Spaniards were crushed when they slipped between the ships, while others fell screaming into the churning water. Hoogley led Jan to the spardeck where the remaining passengers aboard the *Concepcion* were, not coincidentally, female. At Hoogley's angry orders, the last few of his crew still enjoying the charms of the Spanish women hiked up their britches, and turned to brooming bloody limbs overboard and transferring supplies. Jan spotted the Terrible Turk tossing barrels of provisions from the *Raid* to the *Concepcion*.

"Son, grab yere 'ammer and . . . aye, what's this then. . . ?"

Hoogley had spotted a slippered foot sticking out from under burlap covering a large box. He ripped the material back revealing a beautiful, olive skinned young woman in burgundy and lace. In her arms was the lifeless body of her husband. She crossed herself as she beheld the monstrous, bloody sight before her. As the Englishman yanked her into the open, her husband's body slipped to the deck.

"No sense the other tars 'avin' all the fun," Hoogley grinned. "I 'aven't blown me wad in months!" He grabbed the bodice of her billowing dress and ripped it down to her thighs in one motion, then slammered her down on the deck.

Jan's stomach tightened. The young woman had large breasts, between which hung a gold, two inch crucifix inlaid with cabochon rubies. Below swelled a large, rounded abdomen. As Hoogley fumbled with his belt, Jan gripped his arm.

"Go git ye's own woman, son," Hoogley snarled, swatting his hand aside.

"Mr. Hoogley! She's gooing to have a baby!" Like Margaretje.

The terrified woman gripped her crucifix between both hands.

"Thet's not *all* she's gonna 'ave!" Hoogley dropped his pants.

The woman gasped at the sight of his erection. Her hands flew to her face.

"I saved yoor life! Yoo owe me a favoor!"

"I already gave ye thet crucifix, Jan! How much is me bloody life worth! Butt out now!"

Jan dug the cross out as Hoogley dropped to his knees, and forced her legs apart. She closed her eyes tightly, her lips trembling a prayer.

"Here Mr. Hoogley! Take it back!"

The first mate hesitated and looked up into the boy's eyes. The Englishman hadn't seen the lad so upset since they had sailed from New York. "It really bothers ye, eh, son?"

She opened her eyes and blinked at the unintelligible, to her, argument. A shout came from behind them.

"Mr. 'oogley! The captain's coming aboard!"

Captain Seagrave was being carried aboard the galleon on a stretcher. He weakly issued an order. Sailors sought buckets and tossed them aboard the doomed *Raid*—a humanitarian gesture. Not so humanitarian was the distant sight of a skiff bouncing on the high seas, a black silhouette in its center. Hoogley cursed and pulled his pants up.

With the first mate gone, Jan pocketed the cross, helped the woman up, and pulled her torn dress over her. She looked at him with confusion, then pointed at the *Raid*. The frigate was packed far tighter than the galleon had been. The captain-general was organizing bucket brigades.

"*Baguio* cooming," Jan said, drawing his finger across his throat. She understood. While she held her bodice in place, he grabbed her hand, led her to the hatch, and down into the unfamiliar lower decks.

They descended to the pitch black, reeking hold. She cried out as rats squealed. They waded through the sloshing bilge to the ballast pile. Atop it lay the other half of the ship's cannons, lined up in a row. They crawled over each in turn, picking their way forward until they reached the bow where he led her up the see-sawing keel until they were high and dry.

She cried out again when the bilge pumps started up, but her sobs stilled when he pressed the only food he had into one hand—a moldy hardtack. Wondering what else he could leave to comfort her, he wrapped her other hand around the Jesuit's large crucifix. She dropped the biscuit onto her lap and grasped his hand, kissing it again and again, speaking in a choked voice. He

31

didn't need to know Spanish to understand her gratitude, but it embarrassed him. He also felt jealousy that, in the cross, she had something providing strength and reassurance while he had nothing. Jan pulled free and fumbled back to the hatch.

He reached the spardeck just as the typhoon struck. It slammed down on the two ships with the fury of a Banshee, snapping the threads securing the vessels like cobwebs. Hoogley whistled his men aloft into the damaged and unfamiliar rigging. They managed to set the bowsprit, which tugged them on a south-westerly heading. Further repairs were impossible.

Aboard the *Raid*, the Spaniards fought to storm rig their canvas. She disappeared into the haze as squalls flailed the sea like cat-o-nine tails.

Triumph dissolved to fear on the faces of the privateers aboard the *Concepcion*. The ship was dangerously slower to respond than the sleeker *Raid*.

"*Jan!*" Hoogley cried, his tricorn torn away by the wind. "Grab all the men ye can and lash the cannons down! I'll 'ave men batten the spardeck 'atches! We'll use the whipstaff 'atch to git below. *'urry son!*"

Frightened by the look in the first mate's eyes, Jan slipped and slid across the deck, shouting into as many sailors' ears as he could. Ashen faced men scuttled down hatches like sand crabs. Others tried to reef and set storm anchors.

"Thank God," Hoogley said under his breath an hour later. After an enormous effort, the cannons were secured. They now had a fighting chance of outrunning the tempest.

"Mr. 'oogley! The worms 'ave been at this 'ull too. We've shipped a foot in the 'old!"

"The pumps! Change men every quarter glass!"

Jan was moved to try mouthing a prayer that the woman would be safe, but trailed off when he couldn't feel a connection, a communication. Worse, he felt like a hypocrite—and never so frightened, weak and empty in his life.

* * *

For three days and nights the South China Sea foamed at the mouth. Exhausted tars manned the pumps, broke the chains, and repaired them only to have them plug again. The water in the hold continued to rise.

Every chance Jan had, he slipped down with food and comfort, and on the first with a needle and thread to repair her dress. Each visit, she gripped his hands, but had stilled her sobbing. Because of water now surging up into the bow each time the *Concepcion* nosed into a trough, she had been forced to descend to a wretched location in the middle of the unstable ballast pile. There, the rising water often surged over her, but she held her position by wedging between two cannons. So dark was it that sailors descending to clean the bilge pumps didn't discover her.

By the third night, the typhoon gave signs of breaking. The shroud of clouds swept away revealing a full moon. Liquid canyons and white tops still resembled a liquid Andean range but the lashing rain departed. But just when the exhausted sailors thought they might survive, the wind began to alternate over several degrees of the compass.

The tugging from side to side snapped the anchor cables and the top-heavy galleon turned, quartering the waves, threatening to lay over onto her beam. Men shouted and grasped at anything to keep from sliding down sloping gundecks.

"The guns are breaking free!" someone shouted.

With a great screech, one of the huge sakers charged across the middeck, crashing into another gun, breaking it free. Before the Terrible Turk and others could lash the renegades down, the ship lurched to her other side, sending both guns careening back across the gundeck. Terrified seamen abandoned booty and scrambled for hatches. One, then two screamed when they were crushed as the cannons raged back and forth.

Jan was the last to scramble up to the top gundeck and he did so an instant before a gun truck tore away the companionway below him. As he lay sprawled, trying to still his terror, a voice shouted.

"The accursed Don pumps are plugged again!"

The man ran to the hatch beside Jan. He paused at the sound of the rebel guns freeing their iron mates, then dropped into the darkened hole. The rumble of a gun truck masked his cry and the crush of bones. Bile rose in Jan's throat. The woman was below that.

A voice topside rang out. It was First Mate Hoogley's. "*I said—carpenters topside with axes! Quick!*"

Fighting fear, Jan grabbed an axe and a retaining line and clambered with the other surviving carpenters to the quarterdeck. The full moon, surrounded by stars, cast the watery landscape with an eerie, iridescent light. The ocean was a boiling stew. Hoogley, eyes black from lack of sleep, stood securing himself to the rail with a line.

Just as they reached him, the thing they feared most happened. A wall of wind curled the great ship around—laying her length along the troughs. The titanic vessel lurched onto its port beam at a forty-five degree angle, forcing them to grasp the rail but this time, instead of rising, the galleon lay moaning like a drunk in a gutter. A great tearing sound rended the air as the bowsprit flew off into the darkness like a ghost. In horror, Jan watched two sailors slip down the deck, clawing for holds, only to disappear into the foam.

More ominous was a stupendous rumbling and crashing below deck. The men exchanged terrified looks. The remaining cannons were breaking loose and piling up against the port bulwark.

"Fell the masts before they blow us over!" Hoogley bellowed. "It's our only chance!"

Jan was the slowest to react, and for his tardiness was rewarded with the mainmast. They roped themselves to the trees before they were swept away by surges breaking over the deck. Axes beat out a disjointed tattoo against pine.

First the mizzen, then the foremast snapped and plunged into the sea. Just when Jan was sure he didn't have another ounce of strength left to raise his axe, the mast *craaacked* with the sound of a thousand flintlocks and crashed into the sea. His chest heaving, Jan watched it swept back alongside the hull with the others.

With the masts gone, the ponderous vessel fought to right itself, but failed. A terrible splitting sound rose aft, followed by the thumping of timber against hull. A head popped up through the whipstaff hatch and shouted something to Hoogley before the first mate turned to Jan.

"Jan! 'ere!"

Jan groped to the bridge. The fear in the Englishman's eyes filled the Dutch lad with even greater dread. The first mate wrapped an arm around his shoulders.

"Son," Hoogley shouted, "one of the drifting masts 'as snapped the rudder. I'm afraid we're nay gonna make it. I jist wanted ye to know, fair to fair."

Jan was too exhausted to reply. His stark thoughts galvanized around the mother and child in New York he would never see. And to the helpless mother and unborn child below.

"Wait! Do ye 'ear thet?" Hoogley barked, cocking a hand to an ear.

All Jan could hear was the ship's death rattle, but Hoogley was incredulous. His grip on Jan eased.

"Breakers," the first mate mouthed.

Jan squinted downwind, but could make out only the most violent meeting the most calm of blues. Then he noticed a different kind of roar above the wind. It was distant, threading through the main thundering orchestra like a motif of drums.

A spark glinted in the Englishman's eyes. A single longboat hadn't been swept away, its prow pointing down the sloping deck. It tugged against its bonds with each oceanic thrust across the waist.

"I nay ship out all these yars to 'ave some bloody storm in some bloody foreign soup take me without a proper fight!" Hoogley sliced through his retaining line. "And if I go to 'ell, I'm takin' blunt with me to pay the devil for a dry room! Ye with me, son?"

Hoogley lunged down the steeply angled, dark passageway leading to the officers' quarters. Jan, hope igniting, followed. The door to the great cabin was jammed but Hoogley threw his shoulder against it, tearing it from its hinges. Moonlight seeped through leaded windows.

The cabin was a shambles. Like the cannons, the treasure chests had slid down to the leeward bulkhead, although none appeared to have broken. A limp hand stuck out from beneath them. Hoogley's face tightened. The ring belonged to Captain Seagrave. The first mate gripped the handle of the closest strongbox.

"Here Jan—grab the other 'andle. There's nay a thing we cin do fer the poor basterd!"

Jan didn't move. His concern was for the woman.

"*Come on* son! If we make it, we'll need it to pay for our passage back from the new English factory at Canton, or on a Dutch trader from Batavia!"

Jan gripped the handle, but so drained was he that the heavy load slipped from his grasp after only a few steps. Hoogley glared at him with the contempt of a father for a weak son.

"All right, go git thet big basterd the Turk—but thet means we 'ave to take 'im too! I 'ate his guts, but at least 'e 'as the strength!"

It took ten minutes to locate Mustafa below. When they popped up through the whipstaff hatch the Terrible Turk paused, cocked his ear, and a rare expression of fright swept across his dark features. The crash of breakers was louder. Jan led the Ottoman to the captain-general's salon. When the Turk saw who was there, he glared.

"Forgit the business between us Turk. We're gonna try to save ye's useless life and make ye a little booty besides. This ship is doomed. We're gonna take a kit of cobs and try to make shore. We need ye's help."

The Terrible Turk seemed to understand, and put aside his animosity. At Hoogley's direction, they lugged the wooden chest down the hall. They waited until a huge wave slammed over the waist before staggering to the longboat. Grunting, they splashed the box into the boat's water filled bow, then scrambled up the sterncastle companionway just ahead of another great wash of water. Jan, trying to be useful, had dragged another chest close to the door but Hoogley shook his head.

"Nay, not thet one. We'll grab the little one out of the Jesuit's cabin. Two is all we have time to take—may as well be a rich one. The devil is a greedy basterd."

He led the way to the admiral's cabin. With great effort, John Hoogley and the Terrible Turk grunted the iron chest down the heaving companionway and passageway and onto deck. They waited until another wave swept across the waist, then waddled it to the longboat. Another enormous tongue of water licked at their heels as they scrambled back to the quarterdeck. Each surge now lifted the longboat before slamming it down. Even the Terrible Turk recognized that they didn't have much time before it broke loose or apart.

"*Look!*" Jan cried.

Moonlight glistened off a jagged white line leaping across the horizon. They were drifting towards the reef fast.

"Turk and I'll bail 'er out," Hoogley shouted to Jan as he reached into a storage locker for buckets. "Get hardtack and salt pork. And grab one of the stronger lads—we'll need another tar to oar! Hurry—if this line breaks we'll be rollin' dice with the devil for sure!"

Jan slipped down the hatch. Barrels of supplies were piled in a broken heap against the bulkhead. He stuffed a canvas bag and set it aside.

He didn't recruit another sailer. Instead, Jan slipped down the levels until he found himself in bilge water up to his armpits. Rats squealed in the darkness but the pumps were silent, the men having given up. Jan tripped over a cannon. In shock, he realized they had slipped down one side of the ballast pile.

"Are you there?" he cried in Dutch. He was terrified that she had been crushed or drowned.

"*Aqui!*" a female voice called in Spanish.

"Thank Go . . . thank, thank . . . come, we're going."

Hand in hand, they groped to the top gundeck. Early morning light seeping through the whipstaff hatch illuminated huddles of men, many *matelots*. Several were in drunken stupors, some had gone mad and were raving, most prayed in voices that bespoke imminent end. The breakers could be heard over the angry sea. Few noticed, or cared, that Jan had a woman with him. None paid any attention to the duffelbag he heaved through the whipstaff hatch.

Hoogley and the Terrible Turk had just rushed back to the quarterdeck after bailing the boat when Jan pulled the woman up onto the bridge. The Turk looked confused. The first mate stared in disbelief, then his temper flared.

"Doon't say anything Mr. Hoogley," Jan shouted over the wind. His voice carried a determination he rarely felt before. "She coomes or I stay!"

"The wench better be able to 'andle a bucket!" he snarled. They didn't have time to argue.

As the next surge poured off the lee side, they ran to the longboat. Hoogley and the Turk dived inside. The first mate yanked the woman into the bow. Jan had no sooner clambered in beside her and had secured the duffelbag to the seat before another great wave surged over the ship's waist. The first mate scrambled to the stern and slashed the retaining line with his cutlass. The sword clattered to the bottom of the boat as he grappled for something to hang onto as they were swept bow first down the deck and into the sea, shipping a foot of brine. Hoogley and the Turk wrestled oars from their housings while the long-boat bounced in the maelstrom below the galleon. If they didn't pull away, the next river of water cascading over the deck would crash down on top of them like a waterfall.

"Bail Jan! Bail!"

Jan grappled for buckets Hoogley had secured to seats with lines and shoved one into the woman's hands. Water leapt in over the gunwales as fast as they threw it back. The breakers were a half league away, the *Concepcion* approaching with her low port side still lengthwise in the trenches.

Cursing in English and Ottoman, Hoogley and the Turk strained on the oars with all their great strength, pulling them forward of the deck moments before the next surge broke. After several more curses, they bobbed ahead of the galleon. The two men fought to keep the boat from flipping each time it was swept to a spindrifting crest. Wind pushed them inexorably closer to the coral.

The next time Jan looked up from bailing, he froze. Seething white foam danced and hissed only two cable's length distance! Through dawn's early light, a high silhouette stretched from horizon to horizon. Land!

The galleon was now well astern—a dark, dying outline. The longboat and ship were being separated by a riptide sweeping them horizontally in opposite directions.

Seeking a break in the reef was out of the question. The longboat's only hope was to ride a wave over the dagger sharp coral and into the calmer water beyond. There was no hope for the *Santa Maria de la Concepcion*. Her thirty foot draft doomed her.

The South China Sea boiled as wind and waves swept them closer. While Jan and the woman bailed, the rowers wrestled to keep the bow pointed toward the forty-foot-high wall of churning foam. An instant before they reached it, the woman pulled out the Jesuit's crucifix and gripped it before her as if the storm was the devil himself. Jan tore it from her hands and threw it overboard. Wrapping her arms around his waist, he held onto her and the seat with all his might.

Hoogley was cursing into the wind, the Turk shouting to Al-lah, the woman praying aloud, and Jan shouting his love to Mar-garetje as a great wave fired them into the seething foam.

A peace in that sizzling insanity descended over the Dutch boy and he felt his spirit leave his body and rise until he was hovering, looking down on the longboat and its battered occupants, including himself. Music—like babbling brooks and wind lowing through pines, and birds, and beautiful beyond description—filled his ears and bliss filled his being. He watched with calm detachment the crisis unfolding below, then became aware of a tunnel with a brilliant light at the end. He was drawn toward it . . . floating down its length . . . the light growing brighter, purer, more inviting . . . but, to his disappointment, he was stopped by vague Figures in White.

No, they told him with lips that didn't move—you haven't fulfilled your destiny. You must return.

The music faded and Jan, with reluctance, drifted back down the long tunnel, the light darkening as his eyes closed.

When he opened them, he was hacking and gasping in the bottom of the longboat, and the woman was holding him and beating him on the back. Hoogley and the Terrible Turk, his fez missing, were untangling from the bottom of the boat and clambering onto their seats.

They had reached the relative peace of the inner reef but the boat was swamped and still shipping water. The weight of the treasure chests was going to doom them. Hoogley shouted to the Terrible Turk and they waded forward and plunged up to their shoulders. Hoisting the larger of the two chests onto the stern, they dumped it overboard—but the longboat rose only an inch. Jettisoning the other would be a waste of time.

"*Bail!*" Hoogley bellowed as he and the Turk waded back. "Bail!"

All four bailed in a frenzy, and the boat slowly rose until the Turk was able to line the oars and beat toward the mouth of a river. To its port, a long, undulating beach fringed by coconut trees stretched into the darkness. To the river's immediate starboard rose the silhouette of a 300 foot high, whaleback promontory. Never had land looked so beautiful.

Their attention was diverted by a nauseating crunnnch in the distance as the Manila Galleon ground onto the reef. With the exception of the single minded Mustafa at the oars, they paused from bailing to witness the final drama of *Santa Maria de la Immaculate Concepcion*, little more than a dim shadow. She surged back and forth onto the coral, beating herself into sticks.

Jan closed his eyes and held the woman who was racked by sobs. Somehow, he couldn't muster the same feelings of tragedy as she and the grim faced Hoogley. Something profound had happened to him minutes before when he was drowning. Something that had awakened him to a belief in an afterlife.

When he edged open his salt-stung eyes again, the world around them, almost like magic, had become peaceful, but for the flutter of leaves and the rhythmic complaining of oars. As if to put as much distance between themselves and the sea as possible, the Turk had rowed up the jungle river. Rising ahead alongside the banks were soaring limestone karst formations. Beyond rose a chain of rounded, jungle shrouded mountains.

The woman slipped to the bottom of the boat, Jan sliding down beside her. While the Terrible Turk took up chanting his *Allah ak-bars* and continued rowing as if in a trance, the other three members of the vessel drifted into the deep sleep of the utterly exhausted.

The nightmare was over. A worse one was to begin.

5 The River With No Name

The island of Palawan, looking like the back of an enormous dragon snoozing in the turquoise waters, lay off the port wing of the Cessna 185 floatplane. Off the starboard shimmered the languid South China Sea. It was a glorious morning, a few popcorn cumuli setting off the robin's egg sky. The *National Geographic* team was nearing the field for its burial cave expedition.

Liana's eyes weren't on the scene. She studied, with amusement, the back of the greasy, gray head of the fat, sixtysomething pilot in front of her. On it was perched an Atlanta Braves baseball cap. Earthquake McGoon—as he had jovially introduced himself after they had cleared customs—stood six-foot-two and crushed the scales at 350 pounds. When he had flip-flopped before them in rubber sandals and Hawaiian shirt to their awaiting van, leaving a trail of peanut shells, Liana couldn't resist snapping a picture. The pilot's blue jeans slipped so far down that the Grand Canyon of his hairy butt half mooned the terminal. The van had been chauffeured by Dr. Garnet Quinn's driver, a wiry Filipino named Jesus Cabez. He had driven them to McGoon's floatplane in nearby Manila Bay.

Liana was bemused because the pudgy hand that rested atop the yoke also held an eight inch Manila cigar and a can of San Miguel, the second he had snapped open since lifting off. The other hand made continuous excursions into bulging breast pockets for peanuts. Debris littered the floor.

Beside him, Chase stifled a jetlagged yawn. He wasn't worried about the pilot's flying ability either. He recognized the thick, gold link bracelet on McGoon's wrist as the trademark jewelry ex-Air America pilots wear. He had met several on expeditions around the Far East, leftovers from the CIA's various secret wars. He had never met one who couldn't outfly a barn swallow. He also had never met one who couldn't out drink an elephant either—and Earthquake McGoon appeared to be that league too in more than his penchant for peanuts.

Liana turned to snap shots of the mountains, but lowered her Nikon, puzzled. "Earthquake, what happened on the other side of the mountains? This side is jungle, but over there it looks like it was clear cut."

"It was. Illegal logging." Earthquake's Southern drawl was so resonant he didn't have to raise it to be heard over the engine. "It's only a matter of time before this here side gets skinned too—fuggin' Abu Sayyef and protected area or not. The whole world's screwed up. We all can only do our small part," he said, pushing his side window open and tossing his empty beer can into the slipsteam. The action whipped peanuts shells into a tornado.

"Yes," she said, plucking a shell from her khaki blouse as Chase frowned. "We can all only do our small part. Like the loggers." At least the cigar smoke had been sucked out with the can.

"Actually, logging is a reason *National Geographic* sanctioned the expedition," Chase said, turning back to her. "Before it's too late. The Philippines has less than twenty percent of its original jungle left."

She had changed into shorts aboard the jumbo, just before it touched down, and those legs, indeed, did reach right up to her earlobes. Their eyes met and he sensed a path of light bridging them. Despite their different goals, their chemistry was good and both were aware of it.

She pointed her camera toward the island again. "I didn't think Abu Sayyef was a problem here anymore."

"It's not," Earthquake replied, snapping open another beer. "The army keeps them pinned down in the deep south since thet last kidnapping."

"Good," Chase said. "You been here long, Earthquake?"

"In the Far East since '68." The fat pilot wiped foam from his lips. "Flew Hueys in 'Nam, and when my tour was over, I decided to stay."

"I see you were with Air America," Chase said, indicating the bracelet.

"Oh, you know about these, huh?" Earthquake grinned. "Yeah, I did my share of dropping hard rice to Hmong in Lao."

"Hard rice?" Liana asked, leaning forward. "What's that?"

"Guns. Ammo. Thet sorta thing. Now I jist haul a lot of TNT—tourists and trash—around the islands. Not as excitin', but I don't get my butt shot at. And business is good. Matter of fact, I'm lookin' fer a bigger plane. I need somethin' with more seats—and more room in the cockpit. Y'all probably noticed it took a good bit of water to take off."

Chase chuckled. Earthquake had been unable to pull the yoke further back than his beer belly. He cracked open another peanut and checked the chart. Ahead off their port rose the highest backbone of mountains, the monotony of jungle broken by limestone cliffs as white as the narrow beach that hemmed the coast. The mountains were high enough here that the devastation on the other side wasn't visible. Liana bayoneted a long lens into a camera and zeroed in on a karst formation.

"What can you tell us about Dr. Quinn?" she asked.

"Not much," Earthquake shrugged. "Polite like all them Snowbacks. His place looks like an anthropological museum—spears and shields and all kinds of tribal crap."

"He seems to have enjoyed living among the natives more than publishing because he hasn't written much," Chase said. It was on the strength of his only book, that had been published years ago and didn't make a splash, that the magazine agreed to go ahead with the project. "How long have you known him?"

"Jist a week! He rented a flat next to me across from Intramuros. When he found out I charter, he had me over fer a beer and offered me this gig."

"Intramuros?" Liana asked. "What's that?"

"The Spanish word for 'walled ciiiiiity,'" he replied, belching so loud he almost blew the windshield out. "Inside is Fort Santiago. When the Spanish was here, Intramuros was surrounded by a moat on two sides, with the Pasig River on the north. The moat's been filled in and a big park, Rizal, sits just south of Intramuros. Manila Bay used to lap at the front door, but it's been landfilled too back a quarter of a mile."

"I'm sorry there wasn't time to play tourist, Liana," Chase remarked. It was one of the few countries he hadn't visited.

"Y'all'll have time after yere li'l expedition," McGoon shrugged, wiping the windshield with a dirty rag that hung on the throttle. "Typical Asian mega city—overcrowded, noisy, polluted, horrific traffic jams, bars and bargirls everywhere. I love it."

Chase belly-laughed and Liana suppressed a smile. She prayed the pilot wouldn't break wind next. No, please, please, anything but that.

"Anything else you can tell us about him?" she asked, fanning smoke away with her bush hat.

"Why don't y'all ask him yourselves?" Earthquake drawled as he butted his cigar on the dash and shoved it into a breast pocket with the peanuts. "See thet fan of muddy water jist this side of thet huge promontory ahead?" It was unmistakable—like the back of an enormous whale jutting 600 feet out to sea. "Thet's the river we're meetin' him, and thet's the sucker standin' in thet *banca* jist off the mouth. Hang onto your hats y'all!"

The double outriggers of the narrow vessel made it appear like a daddy long legs. Earthquake rammed the throttle and yoke to the instrument panel, causing Liana to grab her camera bag before it hit the ceiling. While Chase felt sloppy *adobos* flashflooding up his gorge, Earthquake dived like a Kamikaze. The writer looked at the pilot askance as he sucked his beer dry while the South China Sea rushed up at them like a liquid anvil.

"Just what are you doing?" Liana demanded through a fog-bank of peanut shells, empty potato chip bags, and smoke. She was having second thoughts about Earthquake's beer con-sumption.

"Keepin' in pracccccctice!" McGoon belched as he buried the yoke into his stomach. The nose lifted, the Cessna pulling up feet above the water.

"Geez McGoo—" Chase gritted as the *adobos* sloshed to-ward another exit and debris crashed down around them. Liana held onto her camera bag like it was her first born.

"Relax," Earthquake cackled while fingering the catch to his window. "Extras aren't extra when you fly Air Earthquake."

44

While the slipstream whipped cigar smoke and peanut shells into another tornado, he stuck the hand holding the beer can out. Chase hung onto his Explorers Club ballcap, jetlag forgotten.

"Me and Quinn did this to thet little island comin' in and he got a kick outta it." Below them was little more than a cartoonesque deserted island, though instead of a single coconut tree, there was a dry flower arrangement of them with foliage at their base.

The sea was a silvery streak as they rushed toward the motionless *banca* at 175 knots. The figure in it dived forward for cover.

An instant before the Cessna rocketed over him, Earthquake released the can. The plane banked hard to port, parting the hair on the coconut trees lining the shore, while the pilot strained to see over his shoulder. The can tumbled once before bouncing in the bottom of the *banca*.

"Right on the ol' drop zone! Ain't lost the touch after all these years!"

After completing the 360 degree turn, McGoon throttled back and leveled out. Everyone was covered in peanut shells. Chase was relieved to see the figure in the *banca* standing again.

"McGoon, that could have put a fast end to our expedition!" Liana said.

"Don't worry your li'l ol' pea-pickin' heart out," McGoon chortled as he fumbled at his feet for a fresh beer. They had rolled around like loose cannons. "He had the patron saint of the Philippines—San Miguel—lookin' over him."

"That's what I was afraid of," she muttered, realizing protest was useless. "And I wish you wouldn't throw those cans into the sea."

While Liana slapped peanut shells from her hair, Chase bit back a grin. He always found something attractive about a beautiful woman who spoke her mind. He just hoped Earthquake was right about Dr. Quinn's reaction to being dive-bombed.

McGoon set the Cessna down and taxied up to the *banca*. The grin on Dr. Quinn's face put Chase's concerns to rest.

"If you're gonna launch a darned Mig at me, Earthquake," the figure in the bow called, staring at a bent joint, "at least please leave something *cold* in it, eh?"

"Told you he weren't a bad guy," Earthquake grinned before flipping an unopened can to him.

The anthropologist caught it, threw his joint away, and snapped off the tab. He allowed the foam to explode away, then took a long draw. Chase liked him already.

Liana put aside her anger as she prepared to meet the expedition leader. In a Tilley hat, red checkered shirt, jean cutoffs and work boots, he looked like a Canuck lumberjack who had gone bamboo. Tanned, fit and of average height, he looked less than the forty-eight years the magazine's background kit said he was—an impression reinforced when he raised his hat in greeting to reveal a head of black hair.

"Dr. Garnet Quinn, I presume," Chase said, stepping down to the pontoon. He set aside misgivings about the joint. It wasn't the grass so much as the legal hassles it could cause.

"*Mabuhay*, you must be Chase." He stuck out a hairy hand. "Please forget aboot the formal stuff, eh? Friends call me Quinn."

His grip was full and strong. Quinn grabbed Chase's knapsack and tossed it into the narrow hold, then handled the writer's laptop with greater care while he climbed into the bow. Quinn flashed a smile at Liana as she appeared at the door. "You must be the lady with the lens—Liana."

"Hi," she said, patting her camera bag, "but Chase calls me the bag lady."

"'Bag lady!' I like that!"

Transferring supplies didn't take long. Jetlag was jettisoned for good as Chase studied the river mouth. He might want to reshuffle his life, but he had to admit there was nothing like just arriving in the field for an expedition. The river was a hundred feet wide, the dry season current lazy.

"Well, folks, y'all have a good un, I've got an army of Germans to ferry to Cebu." McGoon named the Philippine's second city and a major tourist destination. "I'll be back with supplies in ten days."

He cranked the propeller into a blur and, to Liana and Chase's chagrin, tossed the tab from a beer can out the window before shoving the throttle in. It took the Cessna several hundred yards to lift into the air.

Quinn sat in the stern and maneuvered the *banca*, the inboard coughing and shuddering, into the river mouth. Liana, perched atop the mound of gear, snapped off shots with one of two cameras she had strung around her neck. Along the banks, jungle dipped its fingers into the tan flow.

"Sorry for not meeting you in Manila. I was just aboot to walk oot the door when I received the magazine's email that you were coming after all." Quinn raised his beer. "While you were on your way, I stocked up on provisions in Puerto Princesa and rented this *banca* in Ulugon Bay." The large bay, almost dissecting the island, was seventy-five miles down the coast. Across a sliver of land holding both sides of the island together lay the sleepy capital.

"Good thing there's only three of us," Chase joked. "This boat wouldn't hold more, but it's the right size for the river."

"Hey! Good things come in threes!" Liana exclaimed, her mood soaring now that they were underway.

From Chase's experience, it was bad things that came in threes, but he didn't say so. Liana snapped pictures of monkeys watching them with curiosity as Quinn guided the boat around a long curve.

She called back, "These burial jars we're looking for, Quinn, how old are they?"

"1,000 B.C. until the sixteenth century, shortly before the first Spanish settlement at Cebu in 1565."

"Most caves around the Philippines have been looted by antiquity poachers, except for this region," Chase added. "Which is another reason why we're coming—"

"Looted? Of what?"

Sweat patches had already formed under their armpits to match Quinn's.

"Lots, but Quinn can be more specific. A number of jars found at Tabon Cave were declared national treasures. Priceless in other words."

Quinn's expression had gone grave. "The antiquities black market is a major problem, eh? The grave furniture is often Chinese porcelain—Sung and Yuan primarily, pre-Ming stuff. Occasionally gold is found. Because Palawanians believe the grave sites are occupied by malevolent spirits, this area is virtually uninhabited."

"Virtually?" she repeated. "That's the Batak then?"

"Right. There's a few bands, hunters and gatherers, but they're shy and harmless. They protect the sites, which is a reason I'm convinced we'll have luck."

"You sound awfully confident," Liana said, then swiveled

to capture a pattern of parrots flashing by.

"I was flying back from Puerto Princesa a few months ago when I spotted the caves." He rummaged in a knapsack with a Canadian flag sewn to it and pulled out photographs. "The only reason I did was because we'd had an unusually long dry season and the leaves were dead. I'm sure you can't see the caves from ground level, which is another reason I'm so excited. We dropped down for a closer look and I counted fourteen of them. One is enormous. That's what I'm looking for." He passed the pictures to Liana.

She glanced at them, noting their utilitarian quality, and handed them forward. Chase recognized them; they were central to Quinn's proposal to *National Geographic*. As in the pictures, they were now among the higher foothills before reaching the mountains proper. Limestone ridges were sliced off the sides of many like Christmas turkey, some dropping to the water's margin. Chase passed the pictures back down the line to Quinn who eased the *banca* around another bend. As he did, he drew close to the outer bank.

The staccato clicking of Liana's camera drew their attention. A broadening V sliced from shore toward them.

"Croc," Quinn cautioned, his hand slipping back into his pack. It emerged with a Beretta 92F pistol. He opened up the throttle; the engine sputtered and banged but sped the craft into the middle of the river, leaving the crocodile behind. Quinn held up the 9mm before putting it away. "I have a collection—mostly flintlocks, arquebuses and so on—in Manila. Permits for foreigners are impossible to get"—he gave them a meaningful look—"so please keep quiet aboot this, eh?"

Both shot him thumbs up, happy to have it along. It was several minutes before anyone spoke. It was Chase.

"You wrote your Igorot book twenty years ago. How did a Canuck ever come to live in the Philippines? Good book, by the way."

Quinn chuckled. "Thanks. Ever been to Canada? We have two months of summer and ten of bad canoeing. I didn't know what it felt like to be thawed oot until I came here on an expedition—"

"Hey, guys, these karst formations are as riddled as Swiss Cheese!"

Their blood quickened. Quinn drained his beer and dropped the can into the bottom of the boat. His eyes darted from the airborne pictures to the rising terrain.

"I think this might be it!" He pointed toward a jungle-enshrouded cliff ahead off the port bow and fifty yards inland.

They squinted but were unable to penetrate the thick foliage. No caves were visible, but then Quinn had said that they wouldn't be from this level. The *banca's* bow crunched against a patch of sand to the left of a stream. After checking for crocs, they alighted. While Chase tethered the boat to a mangrove root, Quinn strapped on his holster and a machete.

"Watch the boat please," Quinn said. "I'll do a reconnaissance."

The anthropologist hacked his way into the jungle, leaving them to be swallowed up by the pristine calm. Chase judged the lazy river to have narrowed to seventy-five feet. The gurgle of the brook mingled with bird calls echoing in the jungle. He opened his laptop, sat with his back to a tree, and began translating the view into apt words and phrases.

Other words sprang to mind when he glanced up and admired the other attractive vista. Liana was bending over, digging for something in her camera bag, with her back to him. Further admiration was cut short by the jungle rustling. It was Quinn and his face was flushed.

"It's the cave alright!" Oblivious to crocodiles, he waded into the river and scooped up his field pack.

Liana and Chase grabbed their daypacks and hurried to catch up to the anthropologist. He moved through the tangled undergrowth, widening the path he had forced with his machete. They burst into a small clearing. Before them skyscrapered the limestone cliff, its face melted into Gaudian shapes thanks to a millennium of monsoons. Jungle grew in a long, thick tangle along a horizontal line fifteen feet up the wall.

"Where is it?" Liana asked, a camera at the ready.

"If you step back to the edge of the clearing you can just see the top over the vegetation, but this is what I spotted first." Quinn pointed. A pile of overgrown potsherds lay around a rock a dozen feet out from the base. "And when I looked up. . . ."

Pushing aside jungle, Quinn revealed weatherworn footholds cut into the wall. Adrenaline flashflooded through their veins as Quinn climbed, slashing through thick vegetation to create a wide path, along which they followed. At the fifteen foot level, they joined him on a broad shelf, beyond which yawned a cavern fifty feet across and twenty high, its depths lost in shadow. What could be seen of the cave was clean and dry, but for a few fallen stalactites. Quinn flicked his flashlight on.

". . . My gawd. . . ."

Positioned around the walls were terracotta burial jars. Most were two feet high, and many had geometric designs incised into their sides. A few had collapsed revealing human bones, porcelain and bits of jewelry. Quinn's light reflected dimly off the rear of the cave 150 feet back.

"Fantastic!" Chase exclaimed as he feasted on the archaeological buffet. He hadn't yet been jaded by the thrill of discovery either, despite his being on many. That this one came so soon into the expedition was a rare treat.

Liana shook herself free of their reverie and fired off several rounds, breaking the spell. Chase again pulled out his laptop.

"This is a *major* find!" Quinn gushed, swinging his pack to the ground. "There has to be over 200 jars—more than at Tabon! And the lids are all still on, eh! This one hasn't been looted!"

"What do you think caused that scooped effect," Liana asked, looking up. The walls and ceiling were connected by large concave depressions, like cupolas.

"Sea water plunging in and oot of the cave," Quinn replied. "The Philippines is on the Ring of Fire. Because of tectonic plate action, the islands have been bouncing like rubber balls for eons."

He hurried to a jar and troweled a lid free. Their three heads almost banged together Three Stooges style as he beamed his flashlight into the jar. A skeleton sat with its arms huddled around its shins. Around it lay dusty Chinese ceramics, the glitter of gold and silver ornaments, and the twinkle of beads which had fallen off the neck and tinkled down ribs.

"My gawd, if they're all like this, this is an incredible find! The ceramics alone! The pictures are going to be great!"

"Indeed." Quinn's voice quivered with emotion.

"It makes you wonder why the authorities want to leave it," she worried, "when the logging is going to eventually reach here anyway. It would be a disaster to lose this to the black market!"

"I wouldn't be concerned," Chase replied. "Once we report back to the National Museum in Manila, they'll surely sanction a major expedition and retrieval."

"*Exactly!* And you can guess *who* they'll be sending in, eh?" Quinn's face lit up like a Christmas tree. "It's finds like this that make an international reputation!"

Liana slipped a flash unit onto a camera while Quinn pried open another jar, and Chase slipped into his writer's trance. With his flashlight, he began to explore the shadowy netherworld of the cave. He didn't go far. His trance didn't last long either.

"Uh, Quinn, have a look at this. There's three piles of bones a few feet out from the wall—but I can't find any trace of jars."

Quinn and Liana hurried to his side. There was a break in the line of jars wide enough to accommodate three missing vessels.

"Hmmmm," the anthropologist pondered as he squatted. "Appears to have been dumped. Just a minute—it might explain the broken jar ootside the cave."

Chase shone his flashlight around. "But what happened to the other two?"

"Darned interesting, whoever took them left these Sung noodle bowls and that gold pendant. Why would they do that?"

Seeing an opportunity for a dramatic shot of the pair absorbed in the mystery, Liana set her flash at its greatest range. She walked backwards into the darkened interior. Her foot stepped on something that rolled and she cried out as she crashed down in a clatter of cameras, her flash misfiring against the ceiling. She had already scrambled to her feet by the time Chase and Quinn reached her.

"You okay?" Chase asked, gripping her arm.

After checking her cameras, she let out a breath, nodded, and returned the touch. "We can't say the same for this hoser," Quinn said, shining his light onto the ground. "The bag lady stepped on someone's thigh bone! And this one isn't out of a jar."

They stared down at a skeleton lying on its back. Chase's light illuminated the skull. A gap-toothed smile, two front teeth missing, grinned back at them. Matted long black hair and remnants of a pointed, dark beard clung to the skull.

In the middle of the forehead was a hole. Ice water trickled down their spines.

"Large caliber," Quinn muttered, his whisper eerie in the cathedral silence. "Aboot thirty years old I'd say from the teeth. From the beard, male, and a sturdy one." His brow knit. "He wasn't a native. Not with a beard like that."

"Hey guys! Here's a belt buckle! But what's it doing at his knees?"

Any clothing had long since rotted away. Chase picked it up. "From the style, it's two or three hundred years old!" He also picked up the skull and turned it around looking for an exit wound. There was none—but something rolled out of an eye socket and thumped to the ground. They stared at a musket ball.

". . . Oh, my gawd. . . ."

Chase zig-zagged his flashlight over the floor. "Wait! There's *another* skeleton!"

His beam splashed over a jumble of bones ten feet away. Chase pocketed the ball and buckle as they rushed over.

"My gawd, what happened to him? The skeleton's broken into pieces and scattered all over! Do you see the head anywhere?"

"*There it is!*" Quinn shouted, hurrying to where his circle of light captured it fifteen feet away. Liana and Chase were right behind him, their hearts beating like jungle drums.

It lay on its side. Snatches of red hair and beard clung to it and the teeth were badly decayed. Quinn rolled the head over with his boot.

"No musket ball in this one. Check the skeleton."

They returned to the skeleton and Quinn and Chase squatted while Liana remained standing, looking over their shoulders.

"The guy's ribcage looks like spareribs on a discard plate," Chase said. "It's broken into pieces!"

"Could an animal have done this?" Liana asked.

"A four legged one, I doubt," Quinn said. "One couldn't get in here."

Chase picked up a forearm bone. "This has been *cut* through! Look!"

The bone was sliced through at the wrist. Quinn shone his light around until he spotted the skeletal hand several feet away. Chase picked up pieces of ribs and leg bones and studied the ends. Liana's voice ran cold.

"He's been . . . hacked . . . to pieces."

Chase shone his flashlight around the cave floor again. "No, uh, cutlasses or flintlocks that I can see," he said, knowing he sounded ridiculous. Cutlasses? Flintlocks? Long John Silver? "There had to have been be a third party."

They tried to reconstruct the grisly scene that had once taken place, but it was impossible.

"What's this?" Chase asked. Something white that wasn't a rib had caught his eye. He picked it up. "It's a clay pipe . . . or rather just the bowl. The stem is broken into pieces. Look! On it is embossed the initials J.H. and an anchor!"

"My gawd! We have a clue to who this poor man was!"

They scanned the cave with their flashlights, looking for anything else. Something caught in Chase's beam. "What's that?" He rushed towards it, Quinn on his heels.

Liana composed a shot of them squatting with the cave's depths in the background. Her flash captured the look of amazement on the men's faces as they studied a rusty, broken, centuries old padlock. Then she lowered her camera and squinted into the darkness behind them.

"I think we better have a very thorough look around," Quinn rasped.

She stepped to one side, the camera at her breasts, and fired the flash again. "Hey guys! There's something way at the back!"

Chase pocketed the pipe and padlock, and they rolled out a carpet of light before them. They came to a halt before something behind a stalagmite. It was a rectangular block made up of small, blackened columns. Rusting iron straps bound the block. On top rested a two inch crucifix.

"Geez," Quinn gasped, falling to his knees and grabbing the relic, leaving Chase wondering if he was having a religious experience. The anthropologist swept dust off the cross with a paintbrush. Cabochons glistened in the light. "Rubies! And it's solid gold!"

They fell to their knees on either side of him, their eyes nailed to the cross, the original purpose of the expedition forgotten.

"It must be worth a small fortune!" Liana gasped, photography forgotten for the first time in years.

"You said it," Quinn said. "It's Spanish, a woman's crucifix."

Chase dropped the beam of his light and ran a hand over the rough surface of the block. "The wood from the chest has rotted away. Wait. . . ." He shone his light on an end where his hand found an abnormality. The corner had crumbled away. Chase picked up a blackened column and struck it against the stalagmite, fracturing it into numerous disks. He picked one up. Although the edge was black, only a thin layer of oxide covered the surface. On it was a large cross with little castles. "Just as I thought. Pieces-of-eight. They're fused from being in salt water!"

Quinn grabbed it. "I think we're onto something that just might make us very rich!"

Liana and Chase stared at the coin, at Quinn, then at each other.

"But how did it get here if it was in salt water?" Liana said. "And who were these two guys? They had to be Spanish. And a *woman* may have been here—"

A shout from behind them cut her short. They spun around. Angry voices in an unintelligible tongue drifted up from below the mouth of the cavern.

6 The Treasure Chest

The chirp of birds and the babble of a brook nudged Jan from his dream of playing with Margaretje in the forests of mid Manhattan. Then a sharp pain in his side jabbed him into reality. He had been lying across one of the longboat's ribs.

He scrambled to his feet, wobbling the boat and awakening the woman. The Terrible Turk lay snoring in the bow, having collapsed after tying the boat to mangrove roots. The craft had nudged against a small, sandy beach, just to the left of a stream. Fifty yards inland rose a vertical cliff.

"Are yoo alright?" Jan asked the woman, forgetting she didn't speak English.

She wordlessly understood and nodded. Jan helped her disembark, while a grunt issued from Hoogley in the bottom of the boat. Jan had never been in a jungle before and while he normally might have felt threatened by its foreignness, now he found it beautiful. He had lost his fear of death—though not his desire to survive. He knew it related to his experience shooting through the foam, but he didn't have time to think more about it.

He checked for weapons and realized that he possessed the only flintlock, and that the contents of his powder horn were dry. Turning his back to the boat, he loaded the pistol. By the time he had finished—and passed it to the startled woman to conceal in her dress—a sour looking John Hoogley tried to stand, lost his balance, and fell back with a crash.

The Moor groaned up onto his bare feet, checked the position of the sun, and grimaced. It was low in the sky; they had slept all day. Realizing he had missed his prayer calls, he stumbled onto the beach, dropped his scimitar and dagger, found Mecca, and began pounding his head into the sand. The white powder clung to his tangled hair and low forehead.

A disheveled John Hoogley slapped his sides looking for his sword and swore. He searched the vessel, his face turning the color of his beard when it was nowhere to be found. Jan had slipped his gun to the woman just in time; Hoogley eyed him for weapons. The big man would demand any he had.

Hoogley also eyed the Terrible Turk, his chanting irritating him.

"Ye took it ye filthy backside bandit!" Hoogley cursed as he booted Mustafa in the side, sending him sprawling. The Ottoman scrambled up and lunged at the Englishman. They tumbled to the ground shouting, swearing and punching. Jan ran to them.

"Stoop! Stoop! We moost save our strength! We need each oother to survive!"

Jan's argument finally sank in and they separated, but sat regarding each other with unbridled hostility. Before something sparked a second round, Jan grabbed the duffelbag and distributed breakfast. As Hoogley bit off a piece of salt pork, he eyed the Turk's sword with a mixture of envy, caution and hatred.

"I'll spy around," the first mate grunted as he stood and disappeared into the foliage.

With Hoogley gone, the Turk softened and grinned his gap-toothed smile at Jan. He tensed. Their predicament hadn't lessened the Terrible Turk's terrible affection for him. The situation was dangerous. The pent up feelings between the two large men could explode again. It would be just a matter of time before Hoogley pressed his interest in the woman and the Turk pressed his in Jan. There weren't the same constraints on the Turk as aboard ship.

"Ahoy lads! I've found a cave!" Hoogley shouted as he exploded from the underbrush. "And it's full of strange jars! There must be people around! It's a good defensive position. We'll store the booty there til we see if they're friendly. Perhaps they can supply us with grub and take us to either Batavia or Canton. Come on you bloody head banger—up! And Jan, bring the line from the punt."

Jan pulled the bow up onto the beach and untied the mooring line while a glowering Turk helped Hoogley manhandle the chest through the foliage. Jan followed with the woman close by. They broke through the jungle into a small clearing before a limestone cliff. Steps, like a ship's sidesteps, were cut into it leading to a yawning cave with light shrubbery along the lip. With much sweating and swearing, they hoisted the iron case by rope, and dragged it a short distance into the cave while Jan helped the woman up. The late afternoon sun reached deep into the cavern, lighting jars all along the walls.

"Jan, me lad, see what they are while I open this thing," Hoogley panted as he turned to the chest.

Jan pried the lid off one. Dipping his hand into the darkened interior, his fingers formed around something shaped like a smooth cannonball. He lifted it out—and his face drained when he found himself staring eyeball to eyesocket with a grinning skull. While the woman crossed herself, Jan dropped it back into the jar like it was a hot coal. He returned to where Hoogley had smashed the padlock off with a piece of stalactite. The three privateers stared down at the strong box. The woman stood behind Jan, trying to allay her fears. Hoogley licked his lips.

"Let's 'ave a look, then lads." The lid creaked open—and the light snuffed out of their eyes. "What in 'ell's name?"

Instead of the expected gold doubloons—an elaborate headdress with long, brightly colored feathers lay atop a neatly folded white robe.

The headdress and robe flew in opposite directions revealing burlap wadding protecting a large object. Hoogley dug the padding out by the handful. An uncertain smile ebbed and flowed along his thick lips.

They stared at a glistening statue over two feet long of a naked man with slightly bent knees. The figure was stocky and had a long beard. But the figure wasn't the yellow of gold either.

"Sil . . . ver," the Turk mumbled.

Hoogley frowned. He tried to lift the statue out of the chest, but had to let it fall back.

"Help me ye bloody carpet beater!"

With the Ottoman's help, it *thunked* onto the cave floor, right side up. Jan couldn't understand why the small figure weighed so much. Neither could Hoogley. He fingered a piece-of-eight out of his money bag and tapped it against the statue's beard. The first mate's red face turned white. He tapped it again, cocking an ear to the dull sound. Leaping to his feet, he raged around the cave cursing, striking the air and kicking at the floor. The terrified woman retreated into the shadows.

"Woot's the matter Mr. Hoogley? It is silver, ain't it?"

"*Nay*! The bloody thing is *platinum*! Couldn't ye tell by the sound! *We threw the wrong bloody box out*! What the 'ell was that Don dung eating Jesuit doing?"

Jan gulped. Platinum was worthless. They had no money to pay for their passage from Batavia or Canton—if they even reached them. They would be indentured to the ship for their passage, and would arrive back in England destitute. The slip from grace was too much for First Mate Hoogley.

"That son-of-the-devil Jesuit! I should 'ave boiled 'is butt in oil and made him eat it before I threw 'im in thet punt!" He swirled toward Jan and stuck out his hand. "The Don crucifix! The big gold one!"

Jan told the Englishman what had happened to it. The first mate's face now turned redder than his beard.

"You threw it away to save 'er life!" His inflamed eyes fixed on the woman. "She 'ad another—a smaller one—around 'er neck!"

He lunged at her, throwing Jan aside when he tried to stop him, causing the Turk to look upset. The woman shrieked and tripped as she jumped back and fell. Hoogley crashed to his knees between her splayed legs. One hand jammed down onto her face, smothering her cries, while the other tore at her bodice again. The threads holding it snapped and it came away, again revealing her swollen breasts and abdomen. The flintlock was tangled somewhere in the folds of her dress.

"*Where is it ye bloody wench?*"

Her hands flew to her neck. It was gone! Unknown to them, it had come away with her bodice and lay in the shadows.

"Ye'll pay for this ye Don daughter of an 'arlot! I'm goin' to get something for me bloody troubles!" His shoulders trembling with rage and sudden violent desire, he tore at his belt.

"*No, Mr. Hoogley!*" Jan shouted as he tackled him.

The enormous Englishman swept him off. Both scrambled to their feet. The woman scuttled like a crab into the darkness, where she retied her bodice as best she could.

"*Jump me will ye, ye little Yankee sea beggar!*" Hoogley roared as he descended on the boy. "I treat ye like a son and what do I git—the poor 'house! Throwing the crucifix away!"

Jan slugged him with all his might. Hoogley's head flinched but he didn't even stagger. Wiping his mouth with the back of his hand, blood came away. The Englishman's eyes flared. Jan swung at him again, but Hoogley blocked the blow and haymakered him. The Dutch boy spun and collapsed in a senseless heap face down. The woman stifled a scream and tried to crawl deeper into the cave but the wall stopped her.

"You . . . hit . . . Jaaaan!" a gutteral voice said.

Hoogley whirled. The Terrible Turk, his face a dark mask of outrage, gripped his scimitar with both hands, and with a great roar of something in Ottoman leapt forward. The first mate threw up an arm to protect himself, but the blade sliced through his wrist, and his hand twisted through the air and flopped to the ground. Hoogley bellowed and grasped his wrist, blood pulsating from the stump in a red fountain six-feet-long. With another great shout, the Terrible Turk's blade blurred again.

John Hoogley's head flipped backwards and *thudded* to the ground, his body crashing beside it. Blood now also spewed from the severed trunk. With a third savage shout, Mustafa kicked Hoogley's head toward the rear of the cave—then chopped up the body, oblivious to the woman's screams. As a final gesture of contempt, he jumped up and down on the butchered corpse, the few intact ribs snapping like sticks. Only when he was exhausted and nothing recognizable remained of John Hoogley did the raging fire die down in his dim eyes.

Turning to the still body of the Dutch boy, concern streaked across his dumb features. Throwing aside his dripping sword, he strode on bloody bare feet to Jan and fell to his knees and shook him, blathering tender mercies in Turkish.

The woman bit back sobs and pressed her back to the wall. She wanted to run to Jan, to help him, but she was terrified of the huge madman.

The Turk's voice quietened to a whisper as he stroked Jan's blond, tousled hair and seemed to enter a dream world. She watched with lack of comprehension as he caressed Jan's back, then his hands slipped down to his buttocks. His chest beginning to heave, he tugged at Jan's pants, yanking them down and off one ankle. The woman whimpered as the Turk spread Jan's legs and fumbled at his pantaloons. They fell away revealing his primed demi-culverin. He shifted between Jan's legs while muttering.

The woman pulled herself together. She had to help the young man who had risked his life for her. She fumbled through in her dress, then scrambled to her feet, flintlock in hand. With terrified determination, she crept up behind the Turk. He was lifting Jan by the hips when she wrestled the hammer back with both thumbs.

The Turk tensed, the familiar *click* signaling danger deep in his Neolithic skull. He spun and was about to leap when she pulled the trigger.

The explosion boomed off the cliffs across the river. The tiny lanterns behind the Terrible Turk's eyes smudged out as the lead ball hammered a hole in the middle of his forehead. He collapsed in a heap on top of Jan.

She dropped the weapon and tugged at the Turk's heavy body until it rolled off. She fluttered over Jan, her fears hardly calming when he groaned. Jan staggered to his feet and raised his fists but no adversary lunged at him. As his vision cleared, he made out a dark heap a few feet away. His mouth fell when he recognized the body of the Terrible Turk—his enormous erection still standing like a stalagmite. Nearby lay his flintlock. The smell of gunpowder hung in the air.

Turning, he gaped at the butchered body of John Hoogley. The remains lay in an ocean of blood and guts, the head nowhere to be seen. Jan's eyes seared into hers. She was hyperventilating, on the edge of collapse. He wanted to get out of the cave before his rising nausea choked him. Jan stepped forward—but stumbled on the pant leg flagging out from his ankle. He looked down—then a greater horror filled his mind as he beheld the Turk's erection again. He yanked up his britches. Fighting revulsion, he swept up the weapons and reloaded the flintlock. Grabbing the woman's hand, he led her down the steps, back to the longboat, and was about to push off when he paused.

The strongbox's strange contents seemed worthless, but when you have nothing, everything has value. He returned to the cave for the chest. Then, with a supreme effort, rolled the platinum statue out the cave's mouth where it landed with a *whumph* on the soft ground. Thankful for the sail's block and tackle, he dragged it to the dory, up an incline of driftwood, and into the chest in the boat. Bathed in sweat, he trudged back to the cave for a last look around.

His eyes had hardly accustomed to the dark when a scream and the rustle of bushes seized his attention. Yanking out his pistol, he ran to the mouth of the cave in time to help the woman clamber up the steps. She gripped the back of his shirt while his eyes raked the foliage.

"Savages," he shuddered as two dozen short, dark men in indigo loincloths, and with swirling tattoos covering their chests and arms, burst out of the jungle. The report of the pistol had attracted them.

Spotting Jan, they stopped short—the look of shock in their eyes only equaled by that in Jan's. Some wielded longbows, others spears and shields, and still other poles that he couldn't know were blowguns. Fear and dismay in their eyes, they babbled among themselves and pointed. Although they made no aggressive motions, Jan trembled. It wasn't only because his father had met his fate at the hands of natives with bows and arrows— aboard the *Raid*, stories of headhunters and cannibals on these islands had been rampant.

He motioned the woman into the interior and crouched back of the lip. Jan stiffened as the natives gesticulated to him to come down. Although their voices were soft, and none had lined their bows, Jan was convinced it was a ruse. He looked behind him for something to build ramparts with. Crouching back to the row of jars, he dumped the contents of one in a clatter of bones, beads and bowls. When he pushed it to the lip of the cave, the natives' babbling cut short and they stepped back as one. Jan furrowed his brow, unable to understand why, but wasted no time rushing back for another jar. As he set it beside the first, the natives broke and ran. Jan's spirits rose—then sank when foliage rustled. Some had retreated only a few feet into the jungle.

An idea lit up like a candle. After fetching a third jar, he rolled it over the lip. As the jar smashed against a rock, the remaining natives screamed and ran pell mell. Grabbing the two jars in turn, Jan quickly ferried them to the ground.

"Come!" Jan hissed.

Once she joined him, he shoved one of the jars into her arms and, with the other, they hurried toward the longboat. Halfway there, Jan slowed when he spotted a pair of horrified faces behind coconut trees. To Jan's relief, they retreated as he pressed forward. Why they were frightened of the jars, he had no idea, but he thanked his stars they were. He sighed with relief when they found the longboat intact.

"Get in!" he ordered, clunking his jar on the stern ledge, then grabbing hers and setting it beside it.

She scrambled aboard. Two hundred feet down river, the natives regrouped and conferred as Jan pushed the heavy boat out into the current and lined the oars. Then a cry rose as the natives attacked.

7 The Batak

"Let's hope they're not Abu Sayyaf terrorists," Liana whispered as Chase and Quinn snapped off their flashlights.

Quinn cocked an ear. "No, they're not speaking Tagalog. My guess is it's Batak." He shoved the cross and coin into his bag. "They must have heard our darned *banca.*"

"They don't sound too happy about us disturbing their graveyard," Chase said. "This is your turf, Quinn—how do we appease them?"

"The mirrors and knives I brought for just that reason are in the boat, but I'll give it my best shot." He pulled out his 9mm. "Liana, stay back and Chase and I will make sure they're just natives."

"Forget it! I'm not missing this for the world!"

"Suit yourself."

Liana scooped up her camera bag as they passed by it and followed to one side, camera at the ready. Quinn motioned to drop down. They crawled to the lip of the cave, and peered through their cut in the foliage.

"Thank God—Angela Davis haircuts," Chase said *sotto voce*, relieved that they indeed weren't Islamic kidnappers. "Batak?"

Along the far side of the clearing stood a half dozen agitated warriors in indigo loincloths. They were short and adorned with whirling tattoos. All carried machetes in wooden scabbards, some were armed with strung longbows, while others had blowguns or spears and carrying shields. They pumped their weapons in the air and shouted when the trio's heads appeared. Liana stood on a fallen stalactite peering over the foliage.

63

"Yes," Quinn replied, "and, as the saying goes, dressed to kill."

"And, as the other saying goes, the natives are restless," Chase said. "I thought you said they were shy and harmless?"

One of the Batak stepped forward and motioned in no uncertain terms to descend. Neither had to say that they didn't like the idea.

"That's their reputation, but I sure don't like the feel of this."

The Batak leader gesticulated with greater force.

"What choice do we have?" Chase asked.

Quinn indicated the pistol and nodded toward the tree tops. "I said I'd give it my best shot. It should scare them away."

"If we do that," Liana retorted, "it'll be the end of the expedition!"

"My dear bag lady, is the expedition really relevant anymore? Eh?"

She thought of the trove they had discovered. "No . . . I guess . . . not. But how will we be able to search other caves for more, uh, treasure?"

"Our first priority is getting this stuff out with us in one piece. Do you want to go down and discuss it with them?"

"Uh . . . no."

"Chase?"

The writer'd been in enough tough spots to not like the feel of this one either. And he also thought of being able to write his book in his flat, with real flowers, and his dog at his feet. "Do it."

Three explosive reports from the pistol shattered the calm of the jungle, the echoes booming off the cliff on the other side of the river.

"That should take care of them," Quinn said, raising his head. Jungle tops shook as monkeys screeched and scrambled for safety. "But we'll have to be fas—"

He was cut off by a barrage of bullets that ricocheted off the cave walls, the thundering echo from the opposite shore threatening to shake loose more stalactites. Quinn's cheek slammed against the ground, his eyes the size of the Sung bowls. Liana continued shooting pictures.

"Get down!" Chase shouted as a bullet whipped her hat off.

She dived for cover. "Some blowguns!"

"AK-47s!" Quinn sputtered. "There must be more men hidden in the jungle!"

"Who could supply them except Abu Sayyaf?" Chase said, pushing aside images of their hostage pictures—or worse—being flashed around the world. "The Filipino military uses M-16s."

A tense silence followed. Liana grabbed her hat and crawled to Chase's side. She checked her cameras, her green eyes dimming as she inspected a scratched lens. Quinn peeked over the edge again.

"They're behind foliage but I see muzzles. Kidnappers or not, I don't think they'll charge us because of their fear of the dead."

"Great," Chase said. "What are we supposed to do? Eat limestone?"

A twig snapped. Quinn gripped his 9mm.

"Surren-dor! Throw your weap-ons out! Do eet!"

It was a Filipino accent, with that peculiar way of breaking up words. Liana brushed a feather of red hair from her eyes and peeked over the rim with Chase and Quinn. The leader stood at the edge of the clearing with a Russian RPG. They dropped down again.

"I guess we can forget about a siege," Chase said.

Quinn reluctantly tossed his gun over the edge. It landed with a thump. The warrior snatched it up and shoved it in his loincloth. The trio rose, hands reaching for stalactites. Jungle foliage rustled as the Batak emerged. There were now two dozen, most wielding Kalashnikovs. The original half dozen held bows, blowguns and spears at the ready as the trio climbed down. The leader, holding the Beretta, passed his RPG to a sharp-eyed young man and issued an order in Batak. Three warriors set spears aside and stepped forward. The contents of pockets and field packs piled up on the ground.

"Easy with that!" Liana protested as they dumped her camera gear, her motion forward checked by a phalanx of spears. Chastised, she stepped back beside Chase.

The leader sifted through their gear with his foot. His face darkened as he stooped and picked up two objects. One was the crucifix. The other, the piece-of-eight. He was lost in

65

thought as the captives studied him. He was about thirty, well built and intense.

At an agitated motion from him, the prisoners braided fingers on top of their hats. Spears nudged them down the crude path Quinn had hacked. Liana looked back and swore. The natives were shoveling her camera gear back into her bag, while others swept together the rest of their belongings, and formed a sullen rear guard behind the sharp-eyed one with the RPG. The leader appeared filled with turmoil. Dr. Quinn stared ahead, his face dour.

They were halted before their *banca*. Guarding it was a skinny, wrinkled old warrior with a betel nut stained mouth. Longbow in hand, he eyed them with the bemusement of the senile. From out of the jungle ran a naked child, his little dangler flip-flopping like a metronome. He stopped cold and stared in awe at the white captives. While the explorers barbecued in the sun, the Batak emptied the boat. Clothes and gear flew. Hand mirrors spilled out of one of Quinn's packs.

A *National Geographic* crashlanded not far from the leader's feet. Chase knew it contained a story of his on the Aztecs— and that his picture was in the index.

"We're on an expedition sponsored by *Nat*—"

"Shut up!" the leader barked.

Chase bit his lip, tasting salt from sweat trickling down his face. The leader picked up the Writ of Permission. Liana caught Chase's eye. The native was studying it, and holding it right side up—he could read! Scooping up the magazine, he ran his finger down the index. His black eyes searched out Chase. The writer nodded.

"You are not grave rob-bors," the leader said with disappointment.

Chase hastily introduced his partners. The warrior didn't care, but let the Writ and magazine flutter to the ground. "What am I going to do with you? There is also the problem of you finding these."

The cross and coin landed atop the Writ and magazine. You could cut the tension with a machete.

"You're . . . not . . . with Abu Sayyef?" Liana ventured, her arms drifting lower.

They shot back up again as the Batak's dark face curled into a fist. "Those scum tried to come through here to attack Puerto Princesa from the rear but we ambushed them. Where do you think we got weapons? To defend our territory from them, loggers and intruders, we have had to learn to *fight*!"

The trio exchanged glances. At least they weren't kidnappers.

"While you're deciding, " Chase said, "remember it'll be worldwide news if anything happens to a *National Geographic* team."

The leader's lips tightened. Chase was about to take another step with his thesis when Quinn stepped forward and swept up the crucifix and piece-of-eight. A quick gesture from the leader was the only thing that saved the anthropologist from being pincushioned.

"We're not only going to leave," he said, "but we're taking these with us."

"*Quinn*!" Chase hissed.

"Shut the hell up, Ballantyne. Our friend here doesn't have a choice."

Chase, Liana and the native stared at the anthropologist like he had lost his mind.

"You have a big mouth for someone miles from anywhere," the native said.

"If the military didn't know we were in here, I'd be worried. If you obviously hadn't spent time in civilization, I'd be worried. But you know my colleague is right—if anything happens to us there'll be a major search! And you know that the Air Force'll napalm your lousy village." He indicated the child. "And it can't be far."

The ancient warrior pointed at them while he carried on a conversation with an imaginary friend. The leader shifted uneasily.

"We just want to be left alone—from them, from you—from *everyone*!"

"And that's just what we want to do," Chase said, trying to maneuver the debate back along more conciliatory lines.

The Batak leader snorted. "If I let you go, what guarantee do I have that you will keep quiet about these things?" He indicated the objects in Quinn's hands. "It does not take a genius to figure out that there might be more in the sea. Then there'll be treas-ure hunters everywhere! I'm sorry."

He wasn't at all. Chase exchanged glances with Quinn. Both noted that the warrior said it came from the sea. That meant a shipwreck.

"We're not treasure hunters. We have no interest—"

"Bull Ballantyne," Quinn interrupted. "I have a better way of solving his problem." He pointed at the Batak leader. "*You* are going to help us find it!"

"Quinn, you really *do* have to be out of your mind!"

"He doesn't have any damn choice, Ballantyne. We *do* want to find out if there's more. At least *I* do—and if you two don't, you're nuts!"

Chase and Liana wondered what had happened to their polite, easy going anthropologist. He was going to get them killed!

The native leader stared open mouthed at Quinn. Then he laughed a laugh as bitter as betel nut. The old man took up the laugh with him. It sounded like a high pitched echo. The leader suddenly stopped.

"'There is something about a treas-ure that fastens itself upon a man's mind. He will pray and blaspheme and still persevere, and will curse the day he heard of it.'" Sarcasm dripped off each word.

"Pardon?" Liana said.

"Joseph Conrad. Some call it Conrad's Curse."

Another treatise from Conrad flashed through Chase's mind. One about an expedition up a jungle river with a madman at the end. "Quinn's right," he said, sensing that this was not the time to split the vote. "Be our guide. You know the area. We can put together another—small—expedition to search the coast. With your help, it won't take long. You could share in the profits."

He scoffed. "Thanks, but I want *nothing* to do with your corrupt world. Besides, an expedition means more people."

Chase glanced at Liana. She read his thoughts.

"We only have to bring in two people," Chase said. "A pilot and an expert treasure diver. Keeping secrets is second nature to both—and it's in our best interest to keep this small and quiet too."

". . . The article you are writing will attract attention. Others will come—the grave rob-bors."

"I'm spiking the story. It's against the magazine's philosophy to disturb archaeological sites that are actively treated as sacred."

The Batak spokesman gripped the handle of his machete, wavering. His men eyed them with cold eyes.

"Where were the coins found?" Chase pushed. "You mentioned the sea. . . ?"

". . . It . . . it was after a *baguio* several years ago. I was fishing north-east of the river mouth. The typhoon had cleared the sand off. It was in eight meters of water. . . . I don't know why I am telling you this. . . ."

"What about the crucifix?" Liana piped in.

"It was in the cave already, near two skeletons. We found it when we stored the coins there." His voice grew as dark as his face. "I should never have kept them. I saved them because I thought they might benefit my people, but we don't want change."

"Have you come across wreckage where you found the coins," Chase asked.

"Bits of metal. Rusty spikes and bar-rel rings all along the coast for kilometers."

Their questions were clearly intruding on his thoughts of what to do with them.

"Sounds like a shipwreck alright," Chase said. Despite their predicament, he was having trouble tempering excitement.

The leader searched their eyes. The old man looked on as if it was an exciting puppet show, if in a foreign language.

"And that is *all* what you want from me? To help you? Before you'll leave my people in peace?"

"Yes!" Chase and Liana chimed.

The warrior gripped and ungripped the handle of his machete.

"Make up your mind," Quinn demanded. "Help us find that treasure—or shoot us. One way you get to be left alone—the other, you'll be hunted down like dogs."

Rage flared on the Batak's face.

"*Quinn!*" Liana exclaimed.

"*Well?*" Quinn repeated.

The warrior swept his machete from its scabbard and took a step forward. Chase dropped his arms, ready to move in and sweep the man's hand aside. Quinn stood his ground. The warriors raised their weapons. The Batak leader's face was a mirror of frustration as he slammed his machete back in its scabbard. "Yes! Now get out of here before I change my mind!"

Turning, he spoke in Batak. His men lowered their weapons and four disappeared in the direction of the cave. Chase and Liana's shoulders sagged with relief. Quinn shoved the crucifix and coin into his pockets, then they crouched to repack their bags. Hurrying them along was the leader's expression—that he was unsure if he had made the right decision.

Quinn reached for the spill of mirrors and knives.

"Leave them, Quinn," Chase said *sotto voce*, hoping that the anthropologist would keep his mouth shut for a change.

Dr. Quinn nodded and heaved a bag of rice back into the boat. They had almost completed loading when the four Batak wobbled out of the jungle carrying the block of silver, which they lowered into the *banca*

"Since we're going to be working together," Liana ventured to the Batak leader as she climbed aboard, "we should know your name. You're obviously educated."

His reply came with the enthusiasm of pulled fingernails. "My Batak name is . . . Batuta! When I was a boy, I got dengue fever. My parents took me to Puerto Princesa where a Filipino missionary couple cared for me, promising to return me when I was better." His lips tightened. "Instead, they took me with them to Manila. I never forgot my real family, but I was attending university—"

"University!" Liana exclaimed. This was no ordinary native.

"—before I pried from my stepmother where I had come from. I returned home ten years ago . . . but my parents and most of my family had been killed in a fight with log-gers. I have had enough of evil—your world." His face tightened as he tossed the Beretta before them. "Get out!"

Quinn slipped the pistol into his holster and climbed into the stern while the old man cackled and clapped. After pushing off Quinn fired up the engine and the *banca* putted out into the river. The warriors' eyes bored holes, like AK-47 slugs, into their backs. No one spoke until they rounded a bend.

"Quinn, you've got more guts than a slaughterhouse," Chase said. "You were doing a good job on the blaspheme part of Conrad's Curse."

"The best defense is a strong offense, eh?" he said with embarrassment. "But please—*please*—excuse my behavior. After living hand to mouth with Igorots for years, the thought of losing it caused me to lose it!"

"I was more afraid about losing our lives," Liana said, fingering the hole in her hat. Relief was replaced by excitement. "I guess we take the silver and crucifix to Puerto Princesa and radio Earthquake to pick us up. Then what?"

"Then we organize this treasure hunt!" Dr. Quinn exclaimed. "I see everyone wears dive watches—I presume you dive?"

They flashed him A-OK signs.

"Dive gear and a compressor are easy enough to find," Quinn said, his mind flying. "But we need a lot more—a magnetometer for one, eh? You mentioned some treasure hunter, Chase?"

"Yes—Barnacle Ben Gordon. He has everything, and he'll jump at the chance to join us." He suppressed worry about the old man's health. "What about financing? Treasure hunting isn't cheap, and the two of us aren't flush either."

"We can sell the silver and the cross!" Liana chirped up.

Quinn pushed back his Tilley hat. "If we put them all on the market right away, Bag Lady, not only the Filipino government—but every two-bit treasure hunting hoser in the Far East will be circling us like timber wolves. I'd suggest Chase sell the crucifix in New York. And you can flog my Igorot collection too."

"You'd do that?" Chase asked. "They must mean a lot to you."

"Did. I'm wanting to change my life, to move up to the next level. Why do you think I left Banaue? I'm sick of being broke. We can balance it oot when we hit paydirt."

"I can relate to that," the writer said. "That's generous of you."

"But this"—Quinn patted the block of pesos—"we should store at my place for the time being."

Chase thought about it, and nodded. "What about a boat?"

Quinn eased the *banca* around another bend.

"Old scows are a dime a dozen in Manila Bay, eh? Wire me the money. Liana, you may as well play tourist in the meantime. Everyone can use my apartment as a mail drop and Earthquake can deliver it with supplies. If we cut him in for one percent, that'll guarantee the hoser's silence and service."

Chase tried to throw a blanket over his displeasure that he'd have to be away from Liana. She looked away in an effort to hide her own disappointment.

Quinn held up his finger. "It's best that Jesus, my houseboy, doesn't know a thing aboot this, eh? I'll lock up the pesos so he doesn't see them. As for the boat, we'll say that we're ootfitting it to do underwater archaeology, which isn't uncommon around the islands. We don't want any leaks. Got it?"

Chase shot him the A-OK sign, then winked at Liana. "You're right—good things do come in threes. Quinn, you and I."

8 The Young Cannibals

Jan hadn't rowed fifty feet out into the river before the attacking warriors reached the bank opposite them. Chase pushed the woman into the bottom of the boat, and fell on top of her an instant before arrows whizzed by, thunked into the stern and twinged off the two jars. Jan jumped back onto the seat and had time for only two strokes before the next broadside sent him diving again.

When he rose, the natives were rushing into the water, leaving two men on shore to keep him pinned down. The current was so slow Jan had no choice but to expose himself to row. Another arrow thudded into the side of the boat as he leaned back on the oars—but in his haste they didn't bite and he tumbled backwards. By the time he had scrambled up, the first swimmer, knife between his teeth, was only yards from the stern.

The report of Jan's flintlock sparked an explosion of birds from the surrounding foliage, and the native went motionless, blood staining the dirty water. The others stopped swimming. The pair on shore paused. All looked shocked.

Jan grappled with the oars, making certain they bit this time. Another war cry rose. So close were the swimmers that their colleagues on shore held their fire. Before Jan could gain any speed, two natives gripped the stern. He abandoned the oars and chopped off an arm with the Terrible Turk's scimitar. With a cry of pain, the man slipped back into the water. Jan swung at the other, decapitating him. Twenty were almost at the boat, several already grabbing the gunwale. Jan knew only a miracle could save them. A vision of Margaretje and the baby flashed before his eyes.

The miracle came in the form of thrashing in the muddy water. A huge, reptilian tail rose out of the boiling brine and smashed the two jars, then disappeared in an eddy, taking a native with it.

Shouting, his comrades struck for shore. A half dozen Vs streaked toward them. A man cried out and disappeared in a maelstrom. Then another. Their limbs beat the water as the huge crocodiles rolled over and over.

Jan grabbed the oars again. One dug into the water but the other bounced off a crocodile's back. The next pull bit and with strength he didn't know he possessed, Jan oared away from the mayhem. He didn't stop until they were around two bends, and in the deceptive quiet and beauty of the lower river. There his rowing slowed, weakened, until his arms fell between his knees. He wasn't aware until then that he had been crying. After catching his breath and wiping his tears, he looked behind him.

"Nooooo!"

The woman lay motionless in the bottom. Scrambling to her side, he lifted her head onto his lap. Her eyes rolled back. He searched frantically—and in vain—for the arrow. All he found was a six inch dart stuck into the fabric of her shoulder. A nick marred her skin. He couldn't imagine how it could cause this reaction—as he couldn't imagine how it even got there—but he could see no other explanation. He tossed it overboard.

Blubbering, he pressed his ear to her breasts. Her heart beat irregularly. After checking for the monstrous water lizards, he palmed water onto her face and washed the scratch, but it did no good. While he sobbed and rocked her, the gentle current twisted the longboat in circles until it carried them to the sea.

Finally out of tears, Jan calmed his wild thoughts and assessed their situation. It came down to one thing: she and her baby had only one chance for survival—and that was to take them to Manila. He had no idea how to find Canton or Batavia anyway, and cannibals were everywhere. He had no choice but to throw himself on the mercy of the Spaniards . . . where he knew he could expect none.

His eyes drifted to the bottom of the boat. The iron chest with its strange contents sparked hope, and he was glad that he had made the effort to bring it. There had to be a purpose—even an important one—for it being aboard the galleon. Perhaps it offered something to bargain with.

With strengthening resolve, he broke open the boat's survival kit and fingered through flint, steel and a tinder box, as well as hook and line. They shouldn't go hungry. If he tacked into the now light trades, he should bump back into the chin of Luzon in not too many days. Hoogley had intimated that Manila bay's mouth—with its teeth—was only a day or two's sail further. He made the unconscious woman as comfortable as he could.

With the huge promontory to his port, he rowed to starboard, out of the river's muddy flow, and into the now calm water of the inner reef. Beyond, great rollers, leftovers from the typhoon, bellied over the outer reef. Rigging and wreckage floated everywhere, but the galleon was nowhere to be seen.

His heart heavy with the knowledge of what he must do, he stepped the mast and tacked into the breeze, skirting the shoreline of an island he couldn't know was named Palawan.

9 Sea Hunt

The soaring bow of the converted seventy foot inner island passenger scow plowed through the languid South China
Sea along Palawan's coast. It had been Ben Gordon's suggestion to slap fresh paint over the battered vessel's peeling name
plate identifying her as the *Wracker*, rechristened after six-
teenth-to-nineteenth century shipwreck salvagers. The name
was also appropriate because of her appearance. She looked
like a wreck.

Off her port, the crocodile's back of mountains slithering
along the island were turning brown in the dry season sun. Just
a couple of hundred yards away also lay the long, low reef. It
rested just below the surface, causing gentle waves to rise,
sometimes breaking into whipped cream.

Chase, Liana and Quinn were high in the middeck bridge.
The crackle of the radio on the open channel, 16, provided
backup for the anthropologist, smoking a joint, and humming
Rose Marie. Before him on the dash rested the clay pipe bowl,
broken lock, musket ball, belt buckle, two pairs of binoculars
and a can of San Miguel. Quinn wore only his ragged blue jean
shorts and Tilley hat. The patches on his back looked like a
collection of the worst of Frank Sinatra's greatest hair trans-
plants.

Ben Gordon, sitting in his familiar work clothes, sucked on
his pipe and fingered the piece-of-eight while staring out to
sea. When Chase had shown him the crucifix, coin and pictures of the silver block, he had undergone a transformation.
Five minutes later he had been shouting into the club's tele-

phone to Key West, rounding up his equipment. With a sense of purpose, gone was his neediness, replaced by a buoyant confidence.

Chase, leaning with Liana against the bulkhead opposite, looked at Ben and grinned. It had been a successful trip to New York, if somewhat longer than planned. Chase had made a quick sale of the crucifix to an antiquity dealer for 50,000 dollars. The sale of Quinn's Igorot collection brought so much that even after covering the *Wracker's* price, refitting and their expenses, there was over 1,500,000 dollars left. Quinn was no longer poor, something that brought him a huge smile.

And it had been a successful homecoming. Chase had returned only a week before to a lingering hug at Ninoy International from Liana. That special electricity arching between them had grown stronger during the time apart. The shared sense of adventure hadn't hurt in kicking it up higher either.

When she leaned back beside a searchlight to focus a shot on Ben, Chase's eyes flickered down her red bikinied form. Then he had to look away, towards the stern. The sight turned his blood into sperm.

The aft had been stripped of railing, sunroof and chairs and replaced by salvage equipment, protected from curious eyes by tarpaulins. They would be kept ready to throw over the gear if an Air Force's F-5 on patrol flew too low. The military had been informed that the boat would be anchored off the river as a staging platform for the cave expedition . . . and they might even take in a little pleasure diving.

One of the few pieces of equipment that didn't belong to Ben was a large rattan basket stuffed with a nylon bag, propane tank and blaster. At Ben's suggestion, they had borrowed a spare balloon from a club member who had set a record soloing around the world. The view from a towed balloon is an excellent vantage point to spot abnormalities beneath the surface. Behind the *Wracker* skimmed a small Zodiac.

Feeling his testosterone levels subsiding, Chase turned his attention forward. The main deck cabin, entered by a door just to the right of the companionway leading up to the bridge, had been converted into living quarters for the men.

In it was an armory—three M-16s and a Remington 870 12-gauge pump shotgun, in addition to the 9mm pistol. It was from Quinn's gun collection—one, it was apparent, that held more than flintlocks.

A few feet to the left of the bridge companionway was a broad hatch with another set of stairs leading to the hold. There, forward of the diesel engine, Liana had laid out a futon and set up a laptop and color printer.

She lowered her camera and tried to hide a smile. Chase's appreciative inspection hadn't gone unnoticed. If he hadn't looked so delicious in his own red bathing suit she might not have teased him by leaning back like that. She liked the way his broad shoulders tapered down to a stomach you could play chess on. She brushed her shoulder against his.

"Isn't it great to be underway? With your help, we got away two days ahead of schedule."

"I was wondering if we ever *would* get going," Chase laughed. "I didn't expect to be gone six weeks, but Barnacle Ben and I had to wait, literally, until our ship came in to Key West before we could collect his gear. It wasn't easy waiting. How'd your sightseeing go, Liana?"

"Great! Did you know there's still a dungeon in Fort Santiago? The Spaniards were a mean bunch. They had a grill connected to the river so that when the water rose, it would fill, leaving prisoners little room to breath. And I hit a few beaches. Great beaches!"

"Which explains your tan."

"Hansel and Gretel and Quinn's book got me interested in traveling up to Banaue. Man, those Ifugao haven't changed their lifestyle in centuries! I can see why you lived with them, Quinn. They're fascinating—intelligent and incredibly artistic. I don't think I even saw two wooden spoons carved alike! I got incredible photos."

"If the Guinness people had records," Dr. Quinn said, "for the most anthropological articles ever written about a tribal group, it would go to the Ifugao. There's been over 600."

"I'd love to go up somet—" Chase began.

"It's a bloody excitin' find," Ben interrupted. "There's a reasonable chance thet what we're lookin' for is a Manila Galleon—one that possibly blowed here in a typhoon."

"You're kidding!" Quinn exclaimed, pushing aside the chart. "Why?"

"There wouldn't be a whole lot else thet would carry pieces-of-eight and a crucifix like thet. Once I dipped the coin in acid, I could make out the year—1703—so we was able to date the wreck right off. I contacted Jose Fernandez, an old friend in Seville who has researched for me in the past, and put him back to work. Bad as his eyes are, he was happy as a pig in doo-doo to go on one last hunt too, pardon my French. Even if it's not a Manila Galleon, there's enough evidence of a wreck to justify an exploratory trip before we hear from him."

"Did Jose dig up anything yet?" Quinn asked.

"Bloody little, but it ain't unusual. There's 250,000 ledgers in the Archives of the Indies. Most of the boogers ain't been catalogued, and only about twenty percent have ever been opened. They're handwritten and thet makes them tough to go through too. Education weren't very good and spellin' mistakes are frequent. But if it were a Manila Galleon thet sunk around 1703, we should be able to identify it. They're well documented. And if anyone can find it, Jose will—he's so respected he's one of the few researchers allowed to sign out original documents. The moment he finds anything, he'll courier the info to Doc Quinn's address and thet pilot, uh, Earthquake, will fly it out." Ben suppressed a cough. Chase had noticed that it was more frequent.

"Quinn, what can you tell us about this part of the world around 1700?" Chase asked.

"Well, Intramuros was already built, eh? But there were no more than 1,500 Spaniards, and less than 600 homes. Several hundred were priests and several hundred more were itinerant trader-adventurers. They could rarely muster 700 troops at the best of times—which was a bit sticky because there were aboot 35,000 *Sangleys* living ootside the walls in an area called the Parian."

"*Sangleys?*" Liana asked, fingering aside a strand of red hair.

Quinn raised binoculars. They weren't far off the river mouth. The whaleback promontory was less than two miles ahead.

"Chinese. The word is an Anglicization of *xiang ley*, the Cathay word for 'traveling merchant.' Each year the *Sangleys* sailed to Manila Bay from Canton with trade goods. The *Sangleys* often settled, despite severe restrictions and frequent expulsions. They virtually handled all the trades, even building the galleons themselves. The Spanish were an indolent lot who did little but enjoy the good life, except for one or two months a year when they prepared the galleon for her journey."

"Sounds like it was a good arrangement for both parties."

Quinn laughed. "As long as everything went smooth. Everyone depended on the annual Manila Galleon. Profits were in the range of 100-200 percent, making business good—when the ship came in, but just let one not arrive and all heck broke loose. When the *Sangleys* found they weren't going to be paid after extending credit for a year, they got seriously peed off."

"What would happen?" Ben rasped.

"The first insurrection was in 1603, but don't feel sorry for the Spaniards. They may have been lazy, greedy and corrupt—but they knew how to fight! They wiped oot over 23,000 Chinese."

"No kidding!" Ben exclaimed.

"Yes, Chinese," Quinn chuckled. "Jesus is my driver and houseboy. Every fourteen years on average after that there was an uprising, but the Spaniards always managed to put them down. The relationship was always tense, eh?"

Ahead off the port bow, the small island with the sprig of coconut trees where Earthquake said he had dropped hard rice—a beer can—rose from the sea. Quinn gave it a wide berth. Chase glanced at the Admiralty Chart. Shoals were marked.

"Ben, what all did they carry to Acapulco?" Liana asked.

For once, Chase didn't mind when the old treasure hunter paused to refire his pipe before letting loose.

"Silk and spices were the staples, silk mainly, but there was also gems from Ceylon, ivory from India, and even carpets from Turkey. The *Sangleys* would only accept silver in payment. So precious was silver to them—they had few mines of their own—thet they called the Spanish king the Silver King. This caused a drain from the King's coffers. Because of this, the galleon wasn't officially allowed to bring more than about 750,000 pesos during this period, but Spanish corruption being what it was, a heck of a lot more was smuggled. One ship in 1597 carried 12,000,000 pesos." His eyes twinkled. He knew he was broadcasting the kind of news they wanted to hear.

Liana whistled. "Three cheers for corruption!"

Familiar limestone peaks rose ahead. Quinn reached for his binoculars again. "Ben, you're the expert. The river mouth is aboot a mile and a quarter ahead, just this side of that big promontory. Batuta said he found the block of coins in that area. The chart says the reef ends at that point."

"Anchor there, then fetch your native friend," he said, pocketing the peso. "We'll do a general survey first. Jist because the coins was there don't mean we'll find a ship. In a storm, debris can be scattered miles."

They were swept up in a flood of anticipation as they closed the final ten minutes to the river's mouth. Liana dropped to the deck and took up position on the starboard while Chase skirted the cabin to the bow. At first all they could see through Polaroid sunglasses was the tan river water but it cleared as they circled back behind the reef. There, light danced on coral heads and puckered white sand.

"Chase! Let the hook go!" Quinn shouted while leaning around the bridge.

The plunge of the anchor followed. It caught on a chunk of coral and the *Wracker* swung around.

* * *

Three-quarters of an hour later, Chase cut the outboard as the Zodiac nudged up to the *Wracker*. To no one's surprise, Batuta looked sour. Not so his companion. The addled old warrior smiled cavernously and waved his longbow in greeting, delighted to be on an outing.

Liana returned the greeting and reached down to help him board. He accepted, standing and spilling arrows from his quiver. Only quick action by Batuta kept him from tumbling into the water. Once up the squeaky dive ladder, he stood on spindly legs using his bow as a staff, his small, wrinkled potbelly hanging over his loincloth. He stared with childlike wonder at the oddities on deck, the tarps having been rolled up.

Batuta waved away Quinn's hand when he reached for the native's AK-47. Once aboard the Batak leader, with visible respect, helped the old man shuffle to a lawnchair. Batuta's expression hardened when he turned to the crew.

81

"Batuta, this is Ben Gordon," Chase said. The only response to the writer's attempts at conversation since he had picked the pair up had been sullen grunts from Batuta.

He ignored Ben's proffered hand and the old treasure hunter let it drift down with no sense of disappointment. He had been warned not to expect a warm reception.

"No one else was to know about this but you?" Batuta spat.

"What are you talking about?" Quinn asked.

"There was a wide bodied *banca* with men diving here!"

Blood drained from the faces of the original three crew members. Their reaction was so spontaneous that doubts cracked the concrete bunker that was Batuta's face.

"How long? When did you last see them?" Quinn demanded.

"Two days, and they left four days ago, Dr. Quinn." His formality was less out of respect than to keep a strict, formal distance. "But that might be because they were having engine trouble. My guess is they headed back to Ulugon Bay for repairs."

"Sounds like sport divers," Chase said, "though they're taking a chance diving in a restricted zone. The Air Force would spot them."

"It looks like a beat up fishing *banca*," Batuta said. "The F-5s would ignore it. They only fly by every four to six weeks anyway."

"How many were on it?" Quinn pressed.

"Nine."

"Nine! What did they look like?"

The old man tapped the airlift with his bow, then looked around for the darts the huge blowgun used. His rheumy eyes widened when they settled on the sharksticks.

"They camped on a small island so it was impossible to get close. But they're Filipino."

"Let's not git our shirts in knots," Ben advised. "We often had to contend with curious sport divers in my Caribbean days. Jist displayin' a rifle is enough to send most of the boogers packin'." Pulling a battery operated alarm clock out of a pocket, he held it at arm's length. "10:00 a.m. We should git the lead out. Chase, haul the balloon to shore and fire 'er up. Doc Quinn cin tow it behind the Zodiac."

A rising breeze sandpapered the water's surface.

"The balloon will not be necessary, Mr. Gordon. We know where the wrecks are."

"*What?*" someone sputtered.

Batuta studied them with distaste. "Lolo"—at the sound of his name, the old man's mouth gaped in a toothless smile—"here is our oldest and best fisherman. When he was a boy, he and his father discovered things they couldn't explain on the bottom after a bad *baguio* had swept the sand away. Another a month later covered them again. He never knew that they had found rows of cannons and bal-last until I offered an explanation."

"What do you mean 'wrecks'?" Liana exclaimed.

"There are two, Mis Eastlake. Close together and lying parallel."

"It's probably a single wreck thet broke its friggin' back, pardon my French!"

The old man tapped his bow against the three-foot-long blade of an air-driven underwater chainsaw. Strange looking machete.

"Ben, why didn't you tell us this when we were here before?" Quinn asked. "We wouldn't have needed a lot of this equipment!"

"I didn't want to encourage you, Dr. Quinn. But since you're here, let's get this unpleasant business over with."

"Where's the sites?" Ben asked, his gray eyes gleaming. "Here? Where you found the block of eights?"

Batuta turned to old Lolo and spoke in a raised voice, though his tone carried a such a high degree of respect that Chase and Liana exchanged looks. The old man opened his mouth in another toothless smile, creaked to his feet with Batuta's assistance, and stumbled around to face up island. The ancient warrior lifted his bow, croaked something, then faced them, his face shining with satisfaction that he was still useful.

"They're two kilometers up the coast," Batuta said in the clipped tones he reserved for them. "About 400 meters off that small flat peninsula, not far from the reef."

"The side scan radar and magnetometer!" Barnacle Ben rasped, hammering tobacco from his pipe into his palm.

With Liana's help, he hooked up the rocket shaped devices' umbilical cords while the writer ran forward to deck the anchor. Quinn flew up the companionway and cranked over the diesel while Ben pulled on his demi-tasses and fiddled with knobs on the profiler. Batuta watched their frenzy with a grim expression, then placed his hand on the sunburned shoulder of the smiling old man who had returned to his seat.

"What the heck is the matter with this thing?" Quinn cursed as the diesel chugged over without catching. "We paid enough for that overhaul, eh!"

It hacked like an old smoker, the exhaust rattling and coughing black clouds out the stern, until it finally caught. Quinn blew its lungs clear by revving up the engine.

"Sounds like a dirty bloody fuel line," Ben offered before fitting earphones.

Exasperated, Quinn shoved the gear shift into Forward and they plowed ahead, Liana stringing the instruments out behind.

"How we doin'?" Quinn shouted around the corner of the bridge as they approached the point opposite the small peninsula, really no more than a spit of sand.

Chase hung over the bow while Liana leaned over the port gunwale, trying to see through the roughened surface. The old man indicated with his longbow to move closer to the reef. Quinn spun the helm.

"We've got an abnormality folks!" Ben croaked as wavy lines emerged from his ancient paper profiler. "Wait! Two parallel readings 200 feet apart off the starboard! The first of 'em is about thirty . . . five feet long, and the second . . . forty. Looks like a ship thet broke its back alright! Turn and drive right over 'em!"

The crew was electrified. Ben's face pinched with concentration as Quinn chugged over the area. The old diver pressed his earphones tighter.

"*A hit! Metal!* This is Site One." He noted the reading on a GPS. "There . . . it's fadin'." Two tense minutes later his bushy eyebrows bounced. "*Another hit! Hold it!* We're gettin' out of the area! Reel in the tackle and reverse engines back to this last one—Site Two!"

Chase ran back to help Liana pull in the magnetometer and side scan while water at the stern churned as the *Wracker* groaned to a stop. Once the gear was aboard, Quinn backed up.

"Who woulda thought we'd hit the sites jist like that!" Ben laughed after Chase dropped the anchor. "I've been doin' this since Noah was whittling a mast—and it's a first!"

Liana and Chase were already leaning over the woodpile of dive tanks when Quinn joined them. The writer was about to rip the tape from a K-valve when he paused.

"Do you want to go down with the bag lady, Ben? I can stay up here if you want."

"Thanks fer the courtesy, but Cousteau was the only old geezer I knew who still dived at my age, but thet's because he was a Frog. Liana's Nikonis cin be my eyes."

She disappeared below. By the time she emerged with the underwater camera, Chase had pulled on his red wetsuit. Seeing that she was behind, she decided to forego her matching suit. There didn't appear to be much coral to get scraped on anyway. She had another concern though.

"Quinn, any sharks? I just don't like sharks. I was diving off La Jolla with a friend who was attacked by a Great White and lost an arm."

"Maneaters aren't a problem in the Philippines," Quinn grunted as he pulled on a yellow suit.

"But there's sharks. . . ?"

"Oh, yeah, of course."

". . . Any shark can turn savage if there's blood around."

"We've got sharksticks," Chase said.

"I wouldn't worry," Ben added, noting her apprehension. "A salvage rig makes so bloody much noise it scares the boogers away, pardon my French."

"Good," Liana said, screwing a regulator onto a tank and cranking it open. 2500 psi. Full. She attached the tank to her matching red vest.

"There's Crown of Thorns starfish everywhere though." Quinn spit into his mask. "The black spikes are toxic, so mind them. And there's the usual scorpion, stone fish and cone shells to watch for."

Chase and Liana shot him A-OK signs.

"Ready?" Quinn asked after Ben passed out markers and hooked a writing slate and grease pencil to Liana's vest with instructions to draw a diagram of the sites too. The anthropologist held a metal detector.

"I gotta warn you I've got rice paper eardrums," Chase said, grabbing an eight-foot-long, stainless steel rod. "It'll take me longer to reach the basement than you, but don't wait."

The explosion of bubbles on entry dissipating, they set their watches and sank into the silent, calm world below the agitated surface layer. Light shimmied on the corrugated bottom and thin coral. Quinn hadn't been exaggerating about the starfish—they were scattered like a grade-B movie invasion force over the sand in all directions to the underwater horizon 150 feet away. They were burgundy and deceptively beautiful, many a foot across, and the black spikes at the center protruded several inches.

There was no hint whatsoever that the remains of a ship rested below the sand and coral heads.

Above, Chase's eyes were squeezed shut as he pinched his nose and blew. Grudgingly, his ears cleared and he drifted down, being careful not to step on a Crown of Thorns when he landed. He checked his depth gauge and would have grinned if the regulator wasn't crowding his mouth. Twenty-four feet. At less than one atmosphere, they could dive all day without being bent into pretzels when they surfaced. He corkscrewed looking for his dive buddies.

Quinn's was moving the detector back and forth over the bottom like a hammerhead shark in a feeding frenzy. Chase kicked over beside him, his eyebrows raising when he saw the dial swing over and tap the pin. The men looked at each other, eyes round.

Chase pushed the rod four feet into the sand. The ding he felt through his hands was unmistakable.

Metal!

Adrenaline coursing through his veins, Chase finned over a couple yards. The shaft sank down only two feet before hitting something solid.

Ballast!

He booted on farther, and worked it back into the sand. This time the entire rod disappeared without striking anything. He guessed that he had crossed the ship.

Using the markers, they outlined the ballast's cigar shape. They couldn't make sense of one thing though—spread out twenty feet on one side only lay a wide 'outrigger' giving strong readings on the metal detector. They would leave the evaluation to Ben.

That completed, they kicked over to Site One. When they had finished marking it, they found double 'outriggers' buried on either side of the ballast.

By this time, it was late afternoon and they had sucked several tanks dry. A weary Chase corkscrewed looking for Liana and spotted her fifteen feet above them, finning to the south-west, Nikonis in hand. He paused to admire the bikinied view, wondering why women looked so much sexier underwater.

He also wondered why she suddenly kicked off to the edge of his visibility. Puzzled, he watched her twist to face all four points of the compass, her camera to her mask. Spotting Chase looking at her, she urgently waved him over.

Chase grabbed Quinn's arm and pointed towards Liana's animated figure. Dropping their equipment, they swam toward her. They had only kicked half way when they saw what had caused Liana's excitement. It was startling enough that they both sucked in their breaths.

Cone-shaped holes six feet across appeared.

They pulled up beside her, huddling as if for protection. The pattern of holes was haphazard, and spread to the limits of their vision in the direction of the river. Chase pointed at a long, plastic tube.

An airlift lay on the sand.

10 Corregidor

Jan pretended not to see the semaphore flags trying to attract his attention from the island of Corregidor. To the young Hollander, tacking into the mouth of Manila Bay was like sailing into the mighty maw of the Iberian monster, and the large rock was the first of many molars that would chew him up. He was resigned to his fate. But it wasn't one that looked entirely bleak.

He had had time to reflect on the experience of rising above his body when the longboat had shot over the reef. He couldn't find words to describe the experience—it was that overwhelming—but it had convinced him that there was something beautiful beyond. The Experience had placed the present into a different, well, light.

Ironically, although the Figures in White spoke about his "destiny"—which validated his church's teachings on predestination—he felt no closer to the harsh god they espoused. He had tried praying to it the last twenty-four hours, but there was still no connection, and he was left feeling largely as empty as ever. The Experience had given him hope and strength—but he needed more. Especially for what lay ahead.

He was committed to seeing the pregnant Don woman home and was prepared to take his chances, slim as they were. And if he was wrong in believing the worthless iron chest had some other value to the Dons, well, at least he had done something good, something worthwhile, in his so far worthless life by saving hers. Perhaps that's what the enigmatic "destiny" was that the White Figures had told him was his to fulfill.

She sat forward, now recovered from the inexplicable effects of the dart. She tried to penetrate the inscrutable face of the boy who stared past her. He had fed and protected her from the sun, and made leaf beds for her on islands where they tied up nights. And he was taking her to Manila.

He had offered no explanation, but she could see by his haunted look that he knew he was sailing toward his doom. All her life she had done as she was told—but now she must learn to think for herself—and for him. Her Catholic conscience was in turmoil, but she knew she had to somehow protect him. He may have been a Protestant heretic but, like the Christian son-of-God she prayed to, he was sacrificing his life to save hers.

She crossed herself and lowered her head. The iron chest was missing. He had either dumped it overboard, or hidden it when she was unconscious. She suspected the latter because there was now a cord necklace with a pendant made from coconut shell around his neck. On its surface were strange scratches.

Jan glanced back at Corregidor. The officials apparently concluded that his small craft—clearly Spanish—wasn't worth the effort of intercepting. His tension hardly eased. He knew the teeth would be closing soon enough.

11 The Airlift

"Do you have the sites marked ou. . . ." Barnacle Ben's voice trailed off when Chase tossed the airlift onto the deck. The plastic tube bounced with a hollow sound.

Ben grew solemn as he creaked down beside it. Even Batuta's interest was peaked enough to stand. Lolo looked at the dripping blowgun with admiration. It was even bigger than the one on deck. The three divers climbed up the squeaky ladder.

"Some sports divers!" Quinn growled as he wrestled out of his yellow vest.

"I told you so," Batuta snarled. "They're being supplied by a Beaver floatplane."

"Why didn't you tell us this earlier?" Chase demanded.

"You didn't ask."

The writer rolled his eyes. After Ben pulled on demi-tasses, Liana clicked through digital images on her camera of the blasted holes.

"Looks like we got Beagle Boy problems," Ben said. "Thet's what we called 'em in the Carib."

"It also looks like we have what Batuta feared most—a leak," Chase said. "Where did it come from?"

The crew searched each other's eyes, but it was evident that the airlift was a revelation. None could bring themselves to look in Batuta's direction. Muttering under his breath, he stalked away.

"Earthquake?" Chase said. "Drunk in a Manila bar?"

". . . I'd be darned surprised, eh? He's been in the business of keeping secrets all his life."

Gloom fell over the boat.

"I cin tell you one thing," Ben said, toeing the alien airlift. "These boogers ain't pros. This has an eight inch opening. It would buck like a mustang hit with an axe handle on its butt, pardon my French. We only used six inchers."

"Possession is nine-tenths of the law," Quinn said, reaching into the cabin for an M-16. "We'll mount watches, make sure the dive ladder is pulled up at night—everything!"

"I agree," Ben said. "let's not let 'em stop us."

"Fine with me," Liana said as Chase nodded.

Taking Liana's Nikonis, Ben held it at arm's length and clicked through the rest of the images. Then he studied the diagrams on her slate. "Strange, Site Two seems to have its cannons spilled off one side of the ballast, but on the smaller Site One the boogers are scattered evenly on both." He surveyed their cluttered deck. "I know everyone is pooped, but we should set up for tomorrow. We'll lower the mailbox and show them claim jumping mongrels how to blast holes." He referred to a boxy sheet metal device designed to direct water from the propeller downward. "If we git rid of the balloon, we'll have a lot more room on deck."

"We can set it on the beach," Chase said. "Quinn, you wanna gimme me a hand?"

They stripped off their wetsuits and eased the basket into the Zodiac. Chase clambered into the craft, and centered the load.

"Since you're heading that way, gentlemen," Batuta said as he squinted at the late afternoon sun, "take Lolo and me back to our vil-lage. I have lived up to my committment. Now you do a better job of living up to *yours.*"

Chase nodded. "Bag Lady, best you come. We'll be overloaded with Quinn. We can manage the basket."

Quinn passed his M-16 to Chase.

"If I have to shoot anyone, I prefer using a camera," Liana said, bayoneting a lens the size of a small bazooka. She climbed into the bobbing boat's bow, then helped the always smiling Lolo aboard and onto the center seat facing forward. The unsmiling Batuta sat opposite her on the bow's tubes, and the laden Zodiac plowed toward the small peninsula. True to form, Batuta offered no assistance while Chase and Liana wrestled the basket out of the boat. Instead, he shifted to the seat beside Lolo and waited while they walked the basket up to the coconut line where they left it.

The lightened Zodiac sliced towards deeper water before

pounding over waves parallel to the beach. As Chase began to ease the craft toward the river mouth, Batuta craned forward. Liana turned to follow his line of sight.

Appearing around the point of the whaleback promontory was a large, beatup *banca*, looking like a giant crab on water skies. The body of the crustacean had to be ten feet across and thirty long.

"That's it!!" Batuta cried. "They must have gotten their motor fixed!"

The Zodiac wallowed as Chase twisted the throttle back. The *banca* spun on its axis and began to retreat, but not before several figures were silhouetted against the sun. As the *banca's* throttle was cranked open, the roar of the engine skipped across the water, audible now over the Zodiac's burbling idle.

"They spotted us!" Liana shouted. "This is our chance to find out who they are! We can easily overtake them!"

The old man, sensing action, fumbled the string onto his bow.

"We can't risk it with Batuta and Lolo aboard," Chase said as the Zodiac twisted in the river's outflow.

Liana stared in frustration as the *banca* disappeared around the corner. The old man glowered in its direction and said something that drained Batuta's face of color. He tried to argue with the ancient warrior who was trembling an arrow onto his bow. Lolo's voice, although cracking with age, snapped with authority. Batuta sat up like a reprimanded school boy.

"Lolo insists—go after them."

Batuta looked at the old man again, searching for a sign he would change his mind. A sharp backhand was his answer. Chastised, Batuta set his AK-47 down, rolled over the side, and began swimming across the river current toward calmer water before turning to shore.

"What was that all about?" Chase mumbled as he twisted the throttle open, and the Zodiac sped after the *banca*, the outboard screaming. Liana knelt in the fat bow, facing forward, her long lens bobbing.

"There they are!" she shouted as the Zodiac skipped around the promontory.

Chase steered into the wake of the fleeing vessel and rapidly narrowed the gap. Liana squeezed off several shots of dark skinned figures staring at them, and cursed because the sun would flare them. A menacing looking Lolo leaned forward, bow and arrow at the ready, oblivious to the bashing his bony buttocks were receiving.

"They're Filipino all right!" Chase shouted when they had closed to a hundred feet. "Liana! Wave! Let them know we want to pull alongsi—"

A small geyser of water burst up six feet to their port. It was followed an instant later by the sharp *crack* of a rifle catching up to the bullet.

"My gawd! They shot at us!"

Chase veered away to the starboard and took evasive action until they were 200 yards away. "It was a warning shot. Maybe we better back—"

"Go after them! Show them your M-16 so they'll know we're armed too!"

"You're crazy!"

"We need pictures! The sun is in my lens! Run parallel to them! You don't need to go as close! With everyone bouncing around, they can't aim well."

Seeing Lolo waving him forward, Chase cranked the throttle open. They drew opposite and a hundred yards apart. A row of scuba tanks and a compressor dominated their deck. Chase picked up the M-16 bouncing on the floorboards. A row of AK-47s appeared. Blanching, Chase lowered his weapon and was about to veer away again when Liana shouted.

"Don't! Just a little longer! It's hard to get them in frame!"

"Hurry up!" Chase shouted since they were holding their fire. He held their heading while Liana clicked like crazy. "I just hope they don't think your lens is a rocket launch—*Lolo!*"

Before Chase could stop him, his arrow arched high through the air. As it thudded into the *banca's* side, the Beagle Boys let loose with a broadside. Bullets plowed into the water around them and whizzed past like hornets. Two of the Zodiac's air chambers collapsed. Chase fingered off a wild burst as he shoved the handle to port and cranked it open.

At the same instant, the back of Lolo's head exploded and he collapsed across the rubber gunwale.

"*Lolo!*" Liana screamed.

Just as suddenly as the typhoon of bullets began, it stopped. Chase didn't though—not until they were safety around the promontory and in sight of the *Wracker* bearing down on them at full speed, and then only because the Zodiac was swamping because of the collapsed bladders. Chase and Liana stared at Lolo's motionless body, gnarled fingers still clutching his bow. All that remained of the back of his head was hamburger, his blood and brains mixing with seawater sloshing in the boat.

Liana's hands flew to her face and huge, horrible sobs burst from her.

* * *

"Where is Lolo?" Batuta shouted from shore as the waterlogged Zodiac plowed toward him. "I heard shots!"

His dark face turned ashen when he saw the expressions on Chase and Liana's faces. He ran into the water to meet them.

"*No!*" he screamed. Clambering aboard, he rocked the old man's limp body, oblivious to the gore. His unseeing eyes were still open, and his hollow mouth smiled at the sky. "*Noooo!*"

Numbed, Chase guided the Zodiac toward the oncoming *Wracker* while keeping an eye on the promontory. Liana reburied her head in her hands and continued sobbing.

"We heard shots," Ben called as they pulled alongside the mother ship, now idling just north-east of the river's outflow. "Oh, my gawd. . . ."

Chase and Liana climbed aboard the *Wracker* where she collapsed into a lawnchair. Quinn placed his hand on her shoulder.

"It's my fault!" she sobbed.

"I didn't even get a proper shot off," Chase muttered, wishing he could block out Batuta's pitiful sounds. As Chase gravitated to Liana, she jumped into his arms, tears wetting his shoulder. "We might have to abandon our treasure hunt. We're seriously outgunned." A fleeting image of a Rhodesian Ridgeback trotting away passed through his mind.

"I'll solve *that* darned quick, eh! I'll get Earthquake to fly us oot more artillery."

"Come on, what could you have that'll even the playing field?" Chase asked. "We're outnumbered too."

Liana choked back sobs, getting control of herself, and

looked at Quinn.

"How aboot an M60 machine-gun, eh? And M203 rockets for our M-16s. I know—they're illegal too," he said, raising a hand when they looked at him strangely, "but they're easy enough to come by in this part of the world. I'll have to radio Earthquake in code, but I think I can make him understand what we need, and to see Jesus for them. I'll tell McGoon we're having trouble with pirates, and that's not a lie, eh!"

"You certainly are some gun collector," Chase muttered. His eyes flickered to Ben and Liana. "Still. . . ."

"Still, there's only two able bodied men and an old geezer and a dame," Ben retorted, his color rising. "Well, gimme me a rifle and I'll show you—and them—where the bear crapped in the buckwheat, pardon my friggin' French!"

"I didn't mean it that way," Chase countered lamely as Liana pushed him away and strode into the cabin.

She returned with the shotgun and a box of shells. "Three inch Number Fours. Good for goose—and anything that comes within range to be goosed." She thumbed five shells into the weapon, pumped a round into the chamber, and flicked on the safety. "You've got a lot to learn about me farm boy. My daddy made me a tomboy."

"Good," Chase said, relieved. The Ridgeback trotted back, tail wagging. "The *Wracker's* built like a brick outhouse and gives us the advantage of height. We should be okay." He studied the mile of water separating the whaleback promontory from the dive site. "As long as we take precautions, we can continue diving while waiting for the machine-gun. If the Beagle Boys wanted to wipe us out, they could have done it while we were in the Zodiac. But they well could change their mind when they see we don't scare easy, and want the dive site back. Only two should dive at one time. If they appear, whoever's aboard can signal those below by shutting down the diesel and the compressor. They'll have lots of time to surface."

"Good!" Ben beamed. "I'll tell ya, a few bloody guns ain't puttin' no end to my last treasure hu—!"

"I knew something like this would hap-pen! And all over *trea-sure*! I never should have let Lolo go with you! But how could I stop him? Do you know who he was? *Do you?*"

They looked down at him, still in the rubber boat.

"He was my *grandfather!* That's what Lolo means in Tagalog."

It was some time before anyone spoke, and it was Chase in a quiet voice. "Quinn, I think you better move us away from the promontory. In an hour, the sun'll be history. Best park over Site Two—it's furthest."

Quinn climbed to the bridge and towed the Zodiac and its grisly cargo to the site, where Chase heaved the hook.

"It wasn't worth it," Liana said as they gathered on deck again, "but I got pictures." Her eyes were raw, but her voice carried determination. She clicked through them on the camera's screen. "Sorry about the compositions, but it was a bouncy ride. Still, there's one fair group shot—there's nine alright—and a few good close ups."

One of them had a nose with nostrils the size of a water buffalo, another with more craters in his face than the moon. Most appeared to be in their twenties and thirties.

"Go back to the group shot," Chase said. ". . . This one, the middle aged, heavy set guy has to be the alpha beagle. But who are they?"

"I'll make prints and we can send them back with Earthquake," she said. "Maybe he can find out."

Hearing the dive ladder squeak, they turned. Batuta had mounted the deck. Lolo lay alone in the Zodiac, awash in his blood.

"Repair the rubber tubes and take us back to our village before dark." His hatred was palpable. "Like it or not, I now need you. My people will demand revenge. A good chance to get it will be by having men on board with you. . . . But we will not be able to do anything until after Lolo's f . . . funeral. In the meantime, I'll station men on the promontory with mirrors so they can signal if the *banca* appears. It would help if they could use binoculars."

"Hey, you got 'em," Ben coughed.

Batuta displayed no gratitude. Instead, he faded into the shadows beside the cabin where he sat, head down.

Ben hobbled to a toolkit. "Doc, while Chase and I work on the Zodiac, best bring up this Earthquake feller on the radio."

Quinn returned to the bridge. It wasn't long before he slipped back down and slapped a fresh clip into Chase's rifle. "Caught him on his way to Cebu. He'll squeeze in a flight here tomorrow."

Twenty minutes later, the Zodiac's tubes were turgid again. Chase tossed a bucket onto the deck and Quinn handed him his M-16. The heartbroken Batuta, binoculars and AK in hand, crawled down into the rubber boat beside his grandfather's body.

"Be careful," Liana said as Chase started the outboard and she threw the line in the bow. "And sorry about losing my temper. I'm stressed out. I'll help you setting up for tomorrow when you get back."

"We're all stressed. Don't worry about it."

Chase pulled away. She watched the Zodiac disappear up the river. Then she looked down and her stomach turned. The choppy water was pink. Liana turned away.

A shadow glided just below the surface.

* * *

"Ben insists he's handling a watch," Dr. Quinn said as Chase and Liana slipped out of their dive gear. The *Wracker* was now secured over Site Two not unlike Gulliver, by anchor lines leading from the corners of the boat. "Says he doesn't sleep well at the best of times. He also insists he and I take them all tonight. You two need rest, eh."

The couple muttered their thanks. Chase stared across the quieting waters at what he ordinarily would have admired as the spectacular, watercolor sunset it was, but turned away. The reds bleeding across the sky reminded him of Lolo's blood. The old man's bow and quiver had been forgotten in the Zodiac, and now lay inside the cabin until they could be returned to his grandson. Chase felt a touch on his arm.

"Chase, I . . . I don't want to be alone tonight."

He nodded. After checking that the dive ladder was pulled up, he picked up his M-16. The odor of diesel fuel filled Chase's nostrils when he reached the bottom of the companionway and fumbled on a dangling, low cholesterol bulb. The futon lay on the floor. Pictures of happier times—of *jeepneys* and sunsets over Manila Bay and Ifugao children playing with rice terraces behind them were pinned against peeling bulkheads. Two portholes allowed in a whisper of a breeze, caressing her few changes of clothing hanging from electrical conduit running along the ceiling.

"It's not exactly The Manila Hotel," she said as she lay her camera on the bilge hatch she used as a table. Crouching, she lit a candle and tried a weak joke. "But bag ladies aren't welcome there anyway."

Chase laid his weapon on the floor and himself on his back while she flicked off the light and discretely changed into a sarong. He felt the futon sag beside him. They lay watching ominous shadows cast by the candle weaving like giant cobras. Listening to the irritating rattle of metal somewhere on the boat, and the lazy slap of waves against the hull.

"Chase?"

He turned his head to her. They slipped into each other's arms and held each other for an eternity, until their tensions melted. Neither had gone to her quarters expecting to make love. Even when their lips brushed, then closed, it wasn't a kiss given or taken with passion in mind. It was for the need to seek comfort with someone you had shared a terrible, deadly intimacy with.

But a different need replaced it—that of renewing life in the face of death, pleasure in place of pain. The need consumed them and they made love with desperation and a celebration of life that denied death. Then, when the coming was gone, they lay in each other's arms feeling a beginning to healing. The love making had put distance between them and the dark events of the day.

The shadows against the bulkhead were now friendly, weaving a slow belly dance. The metallic rattle seemed now musical. They listened to the light wash of waves against the hull, the murmur of Quinn and Ben in conversation, and the occasional ethereal voice crackling out of the radio. The smell of Dr. Quinn's grass drifted in the porthole.

"Wh . . . where do those voices come from?" Liana whispered. "The ones on the radio?"

"Ships passing in the night. In the Palawan Straits. Just over the horizon."

". . . Ships passing in the night. . . ." Her voice was as detached as those on the radio. "That's what we are, you know . . . so don't make too much of tonight. It can't work out. You're heading to one port, I'm steaming to another."

Chase studied her emerald eyes. "I know. But if those ships keep sailing, they'll eventually meet again, and possibly they'll be carrying different cargos."

". . . Hmmm!" she said, smiled, then snuggled in and closed her eyes. A pact had been signed on the waters of love. The candle flickered out.

* * *

"I hardly got any sleep between watches last night," Ben complained between coughs.

"No wonder, eh?" Dr. Quinn said with a wink. "From all the banging below last night, I thought the diesel was throwing a rod! Then I realized it wasn't running!"

Liana's response was to blast her regulator at them, then sneak a look at Chase. He failed to hide a smile as he zipped up his wetsuit. They were thankful to Quinn for picking up morale—and it was hard not to see the bright side. Besides the deepest sleep Chase'd had in months, and Liana's lingering scent, it was a travel brochure morning. The sun shone down from a spotless sky onto a mirror sea.

"I don't mean thet." Ben hawked his throat and spit overboard. "There's a bloody rattle off the stern worse then thet bloody dive ladder's squeak."

"I heard it too," Chase said. "Did you locate it?"

Ben inched to the stern. Chase finished strapping his dive knife to his calf, then followed. The old treasure hunter jabbed a finger over the deck's edge. The writer dropped to his belly and peered over. The exhaust pipe stuck out three inches and when he wiggled it, it rattled.

"Ben, a hammer, wire, and a couple nails will fix this," he said. After dropping the dive ladder, he slipped into the water, wrapped wire around the pipe and secured it to nails he drove into the stern. He wiggled the pipe again. "Quiet as a church mouse now."

"Thanks, son. You have no bloody idea what a pain in the butt thet was. Like fingernails on a blackboard."

Chase had no sooner climbed back aboard to finish gearing up when Quinn shouted, "I hear a jet! Cover the gear!"

They had hardly yanked tarps over the equipment, and Chase and Liana, in their wetsuits, had ran into the cabin before an F-5 streaked overhead along the coast. Quinn waved as it wobbled its wings.

"They know we're here alright, eh? Okay, the hoser's gone and not due back for weeks. That gives us a big window of opportunity. Back to work!"

After helping removed the tarps, Chase slipped on his dive vest. Quinn studied their matching red suits. "You look like the Bobbsey Twins. Since you're going to be indulging in a little, uh, cabin fever down there, I think you should take my pistol. It's better than an M-16 if you have to run up the hatch."

Chase hid a small smile as he threw him a bird, before slipping on flippers. "The mailbox ready?"

It had been lowered on its hinges over the propeller.

"Yep," Ben wheezed as he trembled a wrench onto a bolt, and Quinn climbed to the bridge. "The first thing we gotta do is date and identify the wreck, and hope it comes in at 1703 like the pesos. Since the stern is where the boogers kept their loot, we'll do preliminary blasts on the ends. Watch fer anchors—galleons carried smaller storm anchors in the stern. Jist about everything provides clues—and the ballast is full of 'em—so stick everything you see into your goody bags or into the basket."

"And be mindful of those Crown of Thorns, eh?"

"Ready to go down?" Liana asked.

"Anytime," Chase winked.

She hit him across the stomach, but couldn't hide a smile.

They took the plunge. She dropped to the floor but Chase, as always, had to take his time because of his plugged ears. No sooner had he reached bottom than Quinn kicked in the diesel and juiced up the revs. As the mailbox channeled water in a clockwise flow downward from the prop, the anchor chains fought a tug-of-war for the boat. Small, brightly colored fish flitted about seeking sand worms as sediment scattered in a sandstorm outward from a central vortex that spread to a twenty-five foot diameter. Both divers flattened against the bottom, thankful for the extra weights they had added that prevented them from joining starfish cartwheeling away.

Liana hoped Ben was right about the noise keeping sharks at bay because visibility was restricted by a huge, swirling doughnut of dirty water—something that didn't build her confidence. Her anxieties disappeared when something long and pitted began to emerge. A cannon. Iron. Then another. Bronze.

Something round and smooth appeared beneath the cannons. A river rock. Then another. Soon there were more smooth white tops than at a Shriner's convention. Ballast.

As the tip was exposed, the muzzles of more cannons of varying sizes appeared. All had slipped down one side of the ballast pile. As Chase grabbed the trunnion of one to anchor himself, he noticed a broad arrow mark near the powder hole. Pulling himself from cannon to cannon, his heart soared when he saw Spanish lettering on the next. It sank when the third was German, then French, the next Scandinavian of some kind. But predominating were British.

They snatched up pieces of porcelain, much coral encrusted. The stripping action slowed as the liquid drill reached the limits of its range—but not before laying bare keel and ribs with jagged ends. Chase signaled Liana with a double thumbs up and they surfaced.

"No anchors," Chase shouted over the engine and compressor. "Nothing but cannons and cannonballs, and we're down to timbers. *Ptttew!*"

"Wood you say?" Ben shouted as Quinn throttled back. Ben grabbed the chainsaw and hooked its long hose to the compressor. He passed two Ziploc bags to Chase. "Saw sections of beam and bulkhead—they're often from different trees. Liana, start hauling the rear anchors forward so we can reposition over the other end."

Chase sawed samples and placed them in the metal basket Ben lowered by rope from a power winch on the starboard sterndeck. By the time the boat had crawled forward, they were already feeling fatigue but were too excited to take a break. Liana surfaced and signaled Quinn to kick in the engine.

No sooner had the first Shriner appeared than something yellow tumbled before Chase. He snatched at it like it was a fly, managing to grab it on his second try. He couldn't believe his eyes. A gold coin! Liana shook an A-OK at him. He slipped it into his bag while she returned to the search with renewed vigor.

Their heightened expectations faded as the other end of the ballast pile was cleared. The cannons here too had slipped down the same side of the ballast.

Chase checked his air gauge. Seeing it was down to 200 pounds, he drew his finger across his throat. Liana checked hers and nodded. Her finger on the button of her BC, she took one last look around. Spotting what looked like white pickup sticks appearing in the now lightly disappearing sand, she shoveled them out. It was a handful of clay pipes, which she added to her bag.

"No anchor there either!" Chase called after breaking surface. He held up the gold coin. "But I found this!"

Ben cut the motor on the compressor, leaving only the soothing *clunka-clunka-clunka* of the *Wracker's* diesel. Quinn set aside binoculars he was using to keep tabs on the promontory, and slipped down to the deck. Before the divers had climbed aboard, Ben fingered his eyeglasses clean, and held the gleaming coin at arm's length. His expression wavered between a smile and a frown.

"It's a British crown! And the bloody thing is so worn we can't see the date!"

Their faces didn't fall. It was still *gold!*

"Do you think it could be a Brit ship then?" Liana asked, unzipping her wetsuit, exposing her taut bellybutton.

Barnacle Ben scratched dandruff from a bushy eyebrow. "It would be bloody unusual to find a Brit coin on a Spanish ship. A Spanish coin on an English ship is a different matter— pieces-of-eight was the international standard in them days, like the dollar is today."

Ben set the coin on the work bench and dumped out Chase's goody bag of broken pottery. ". . . It's Ching, but since thet dynasty lasted from 1614 to 1912, it's no help. And any ship out here in them days would have had broken Chinese porcelain in the hold. Young lady, how'd you make out trick 'n' treatin'?"

"The bag lady didn't do as well, I'm afraid," she said, removing potsherds from her bag.

". . . More Ching. Thet's it?"

"Well, I found these, but they're just clay pipes."

Ben took one, his craggy face cracking open into a smile. "Tremendous! We jist have to find the hallmark!" He scraped off light encrustation with a nicotine stained thumbnail. "Here's the booger . . . but what's this?"

"What's what?" Liana asked.

"This?" He held the front of the bowl out to them.

Liana gasped and gripped Chase's arm. The initials J. H. and a small anchor were embossed on it.

Quinn broke away. When he returned, he held the pipe bowl found in the cave. He took the pipe from the confused treasure hunter and held them side by side. They were identical. In a rush of words, they filled Ben in about the finds in the cave.

"If only these things could talk, eh?"

"They cin!" Ben said, creaking toward the cabin. "Thet's why I'm bloody excited!" He returned with a handful of dog-eared books. "By their shape, we cin date them within ten or twenty years of when they was made! The hallmark will tell us the manufacturer—and thus the country! *If* the manufacturer still exists, we may even be able to find out the name of the poor booger what owned them!"

The trio fidgeted while Ben fingered well-thumbed pages. He was into his third book before he found what he was looking for.

"Right around 1700 folks. We have a date finally."

"It fits with the peso! That's great!" exclaimed Liana. Then she saw Ben didn't look pleased. "Isn't it?"

"The problem is it's a bloody *English* pipe!"

". . . So it's looking like we *do* have a British ship," Chase said. "Redbeard and Blackbeard in the cave were English, not Spanish."

"I won't go thet far yet, but it's not good news," Ben said. "Did anyone notice markings on the cannons?" He frowned while Chase told him what he had seen.

"Hmmm, the broad arrow is what the Brits used to mark their guns, but determining nationality from cannons is bloody tricky. It's not uncommon to find guns from a half dozen nations on any given country's ships. Arms dealers sold to anyone thet would buy, jist like today."

Quinn cleared his throat and checked the promontory. All clear.

"If it's a Brit ship," Chase asked, "couldn't it have taken a Manila Galleon and then been blown here in a storm?"

103

Ben shook his head. "Jose did a quick survey in the Seville archives and only found four Manila Galleons thet was seized—though all *was* by the British." He dug out a ratty notebook from his nerd pack. "But the years don't match! They, uh, was 1587, 1709, 1743 and 1762."

"What about the 1709 one?" Liana asked.

Ben shook his head again. "Thet was the *Duke* what picked up Alexander Selkirk, the model fer Daniel Defoe's *Robinson Crusoe*, who was marooned in 1704. But the galleon they took was off California. Matter of fact, Selkirk was along."

"The 1743 one?" Liana again.

"Unlikely, although it was taken at the Straits of San Bernardino where the galleons entered the islands. The pesos we have was freshly minted."

The three younger members looked at each other. None were smiling.

"Chase, did you git the wood? Thet'll provide an answer. If it's Filipino, it'll be a friggin' galleon, pardon my French."

"Right!" Chase hoisted the basket up, pulled in the winch's swinging arm, and lowered it to the deck. Ben's knees cracked when he stooped.

"Good," he wheezed, patting the water filled bags. "These'll go to a dendrologist." Ben forced a nicotine stained smile. "Look, we know there's Spanish treasure around here some bloody place—we got a Spanish cross and a chest of pesos. The metal readings we got on that buried outrigger could be the motherlode—and there's only one way to find out! Are you up to movin' them anchors over?"

Chase and Liana slapped on fresh tanks and hit for the bottom. A half hour later the *Wracker* was repositioned. Surfacing, Liana shouted to Quinn to open up the mailbox, and signaled for her Nikonis. Minutes later, the couple were treated to the sight of a jumble of cannons in the emerging hole. After Liana had shot pictures, they surfaced.

"It's a load, all right," Chase called, "but not the mother we want. More cannons. And cannonballs."

They repositioned four more times . . . only to find more of the same.

"They're in three rows, four if you count those that slipped down the ballast," Chase said when they were topside again, tired and toweling, while Barnacle Ben squinted at her pictures.

"And why are they just on one side of the ballast?" Liana.

Ben puffed up a mushroom cloud on his pipe. "It's clear thet the boogers broke loose and rolled to one side of the ship, no doubt causing it to breach. When the ship went down and broke up, they all dumped out thet side." Ben suppressed a cough. "Find anything this time?"

"This brass button," Liana said, handing it to Ben.

He frowned. "It's got Britannica on it. Thet's *all* you found? Chase?"

He and Liana looked at each other. "Should we be finding more?" he asked.

Ben didn't reply, and Chase sensed he was holding something back. "We got a problem folks. We have bloody little to go on, but thet little is lookin' friggin' Brit."

He didn't pardon his French this time. Melancholy hung like a London fog over the *Wracker* that night. They should have known that discovering a treasure galleon that fast was just too easy. . . .

* * *

The next morning, despite Ben's efforts to keep up morale, it was with a fatalistic air that they repositioned over one end of Site One. Chase took his turn operating the throttle and riding shotgun while Quinn pulled on his yellow wetsuit and he and Liana headed for the basement. It took only minutes for sand to be blown away revealing the top of the ballast.

They stared at the emerging pile in confusion. Then dismay. Finally, exuberance. The rocks weren't white sedimentary like at Site Two—rather, they were distinctly gray. Granite.

This was a *different* wreck!

Then the adrenaline really punched in. The photographer spotted something shiny in the ballast and grappled for it. She inhaled so sharply she almost swallowed her reg. It was a small, brass crucifix. Quinn lunged forward. In his hand he held a brass Madonna. Thick columns of air bubbles burst upwards as they filled their bags and the basket with crucifix shaped lumps of coral.

105

Liana squealed into her mouthpiece when first one flange of an anchor, then the other, emerged from the fleeing sand. She shot a picture while Quinn measured the span.

As the end of the hull below the ballast cleared, Quinn grabbed the chainsaw and took wood samples. Then the blaster reached its limits and the prizes petered out. Their voices ran together when they popped through the ceiling.

"*Ben! The ballast is a different color!*"

"*There's Catholic stuff everywhere!*" Liana cried, hold up the cross. "Chase—*ptewn!*" She spit out water. "They're different wrecks! This one must be the galleon!"

"You're kidding!" Chase exclaimed.

"There's also an anchor, eh! Aboot four feet across!"

Ben's pipe clattered to the deck. "It's from the stern!"

"Should we start blasting around it, Ben?" Chase asked.

Ben wrestled his thoughts together. The situation had changed so fast his bloody mind couldn't keep up. "No, better to complete our survey first. We should check out the mag readings we got on the two wings. This breeze will help us drift over." He turned to the pair in the water. "If they're cannons, which they probably are, note the markings. Pass yere bags up."

The laden basket was also hoisted, and the *Wracker* was moved in record time. Chase gave Liana and Quinn several minutes to drop down before shoveling coal to the engine. Four minutes later he throttled back, revealing large cannons lying in a row in the bottom of the crater, laid bare by the mailbox, the muzzles aimed away from the ballast heap.

Liana wanted to scream with joy! Several displayed the British arrow mark—but the vast majority bore Spanish inscriptions! She was about to shoot pictures when she paused over a bronze cannon. A nail protruded from the breechlock. She studied the other big guns. The breechlocks of all the iron cannons were plugged in like manner. Puzzled, she rose and raised her camera.

She and Quinn moved the boat over to the other wing. They continued finding scores of cross shaped encrustations—and Liana also discovered a lightly encrusted bottle which she placed in her goody bag. She noted again the plugged breechlocks of the predominantly Spanish cannons.

She was about to shoot more pictures when the water around them fell silent. The diesel and compressor had shut down.

The divers shot upward, bursting out of the water beside the *Wracker*. The pounding in their hearts barely subsided when they saw Ben and Chase waving A-OK signs at them. Chase cranked over the diesel before it reluctantly caught, and with it the compressor, though Ben turned it off. It angered the divers that both men were grinning like hyenas.

Moments later, the photographer and anthropologist stood dripping on deck, torn between fatigue, fear and relief. They were so hungry that the stench of garlic sausage Ben had burned in the galley smelled almost edible.

"Geez, Chase," Liana said, mock collapsing against his chest after he had descended to the deck, "don't play that trick again! I almost wet my pants down there!"

"If that's all it takes, I just might have to do it again," he said *sotto voce* with a grin. She pinched his waist but couldn't hide another smile. She liked men with dirty minds. He began cranking up the winch.

"How'd you make out?" she asked, dropping her wetsuit into the freshwater tank, and looking over broken coral covering the sterndeck. A hammer and sledgehammer lay among the debris. Both men still looked like they had swallowed a cage of canaries. "And you've sucked enough humor from shutting the engine!"

"We *didn't* shut it down," Chase protested as he lowered the basket to the deck. "The diesel is still acting up!"

"That darned thing," Quinn complained, twirling a towel in his ear, unaware of the heightened mood. "We should look at it."

"What's so funny then?" Liana demanded.

"We thought you'd never ask!" Chase exclaimed while a beaming Ben inched toward the work bench where he had set up an acid bath. Chase flipped open a cooler and passed beer around. "Filipino champagne!"

"What for, eh?"

"To celebrate! You struck *gold!*"

"Again!" Liana exclaimed.

"Actually, it's silver, but that's what we're looking for!"

Chase led them to the work bench. Quinn whooped while Liana leaped into Chase's arms.

Laid out was a skull and crossbones Ben had made. Silver

107

crosses formed the skull, with a silver Madonna as the nose, and a chain as the smiling mouth. A silver fork and knife served as crossbones.

"Yup!" Ben rasped. "All Spanish! Unfortunately, there's no hallmarks on the cutlery so we can't establish a date—but only officers could afford these, and they lived in the stern! The ballast pile is too short for a galleon, so I'm guessing the rest is on the reef's outer side. How deep does the chart say it drops off, Doc?"

"Forever."

"Thet's what I was afraid of—but jist the same we cin celebrate because we have the back end." He winked. "Did you identify the nationalities of those cannons?"

"Spanish!" Liana replied. "Seventy percent anyway."

"Good! More confirmation!" Ben said in a voice quivering as much from excitement as age. "And the rest? The usual mix of nationalities?"

"No, just British."

Ben frowned, but didn't share any concern he had. He stood and hobbled to the basket. "As I've said before, cannons ain't definitive—but the evidence is pointin' in the right direction."

"Uh, talking about cannons." Liana described the nails in the breechlocks.

Ben's tangled brows raised. "The boogers was spiked! There's only one reason thet's done—so they wouldn't fall into enemy hands! I wish we had a bloody date. Did you bring anything else up—coins, bottles, anythin' with a hall-mark?"

Liana dug into her vest pouch. She held up the bottle.

Ben's eyes gleamed. He held it at arm's length. "Bloody fine!" he croaked as he creaked into the cabin. He was soon back, thumbing through another dog-eared reference book while his companions fidgeted and listened to their stomachs growl. A smile inched across his leathery face.

"It's English—but I wouldn't worry about thet—their glass was some of the best and found all over Europe. But—most importantly—the date is right on the bloody money! 1700! Which matches not only those pieces-of-eight—but also the other pile of ballast! This raises the specter thet the two were in a fight and got caught in a storm—" Ben began to cough so hard he spilled his beer.

Chase and Liana helped him into his lawnchair.

"G . . . go on, what was we talkin' about?" Ben pressed.

They looked at each other. That was a serious cough.

"Uh, what do you think Ben?" Dr. Quinn asked. "Could it be a Manila Galleon?"

The light brightened in Ben eyes. Suppressing a last cough, he picked up a small cannonball and meditated over it like it was Yorick's skull. Setting it down, he pulled a pen from his nerd pack and reached for Liana's Nikonos and a notebook. Like a child with a crayon, he began to draw. When finished, he leaned back.

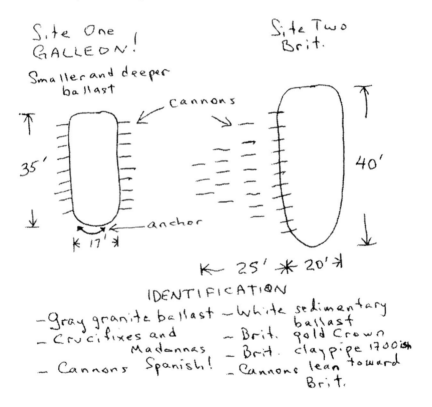

"A *Manila* Galleon I cain't say, but I'd be bloody surprised if it was anythin' other then Spanish. The pattern of cannons on Site Two looks more like a galleon, but other ships had three gundecks. There could be other reasons why there's a different

109

pattern on One—but the evidence points to it being Spanish. Until we have the wood checked, we'll act on thet assumption."

He raised a toast. There'd been serious problems hampering his enjoyment. One man was dead, Earthquake was a day overdue, and they couldn't reach him—but he was savoring this.

"But I'm sure it'll jist be a formality," he added. "I'm bloody sure we've found the ship we're lookin' fer. Once we git the diesel fixed tomorrow, let's git on it!"

* * *

"What in tarnation is thet doin' there?" Ben wheezed. He'd just laid aside an oily floorboard from beside the engine and was shining a flashlight into the bilge. Rain pitter-pattered above.

"I'm no mechanic, but it looks like a fuel pump, eh?" The anthropologist's light also illuminated a gray device spliced into the fuel line. It disappeared down into brackish water before snaking twenty feet forward to the huge, mid-deck fuel tank.

"It's a bloody electric shut-off valve!"

"A shut-off valve?"

"Yeah, and it's brand new, unlike the rest of this floating wreck. The electric wires lead forward. Doc, yere a young buck compared to me—see where they go."

Quinn wiggled into the space. His light followed color coded wires from the valve to something squarish strapped to a small, jury rigged platform in the narrow space between the tank and hull.

"There's something here!" Quinn grunted as he popped out of the hold and led Ben into the Bobbsey Twins' stateroom. Sweeping off the scatter of combs, candles and condoms, he threw aside the hatch cover and dropped to mid-calf in the brine. He sloshed to the tank's side. "*Ohmygawd*—!" It was followed by a more substantial expletive when his head whacked a beam.

"Easy there, Doc. What'd you find?"

"A *transmitter*! It's spliced into our electrical system! Wait—there's another pair of wires leading from it!" As Ben expressed surprise, Quinn followed them to the fuel tank. "Holy. . . ."

A large orange mass of plastic explosives was packed against the tank. Quinn yanked the wires out and stared at a detonator.

110

12 Intramuros

They had sailed most of the way across Manila Bay before the woman had an idea and struggled over the seats to face Jan. She pointed at his chest.

"You . . . are . . . Irish," she said in Spanish, hoping he would understand. She pronounced 'Irish' in the English manner.

Jan frowned and turned the boat into a small squall. He recognized the country but was too emotionally exhausted to try to figure out what she wanted and ignored her. She repeated her statement with greater force. Jan shook his head this time.

"No. I am a Dootchman. An American Dootchman."

Ahead at anchor lay a small galleon and a non-Spanish ship. To their port was a large flotilla—one of them with bat-wing sails spread. He had seen others from the *Raid* since they had entered Oriental waters. Hoogley had called them *junks*. Behind them rose the gray block of Intramuros, cannons bristling from great Vs slotted atop her stone ramparts. Across a river to its left lay a large residential area of bamboo huts, and beyond was jungle. The woman pointed at the sight and made the sign of the cross.

"*Spanish!*" she cried. "*Catholic!*" She crossed herself again with greater exaggeration. "*Irish!*" she repeated, desperately wanting him to understand. "*Catholic!*"

His blond brow furrowed and understanding seeped in.

"You are *Irish!*" She blunted her finger on his chest. "You are a Catholic Irishman on the *Concepcion!* Oh, Jesus Son-of-Mary please make him understand!"

Jan straightened. An Irishman—a fellow Catholic—would be within acceptance of those speaking the English tongue. The sub-

111

jugated Irish hated the English even more than the Spanish. Galleons were manned by a Babel of nationalities.

His eyes flew to the junks again. Hoogley had told him that they probably sailed from Canton—site of the English Factory! Hope cracked the rigid mask that was his face. She fell against his shoulder sobbing with relief. There was another reason she wanted to help him.

She was falling in love with him.

Jan held her with his free arm, a respite from the tension. Then another small squall rippled across the water and he gently pushed her away, needing room to navigate. Still sobbing, she crawled forward while he turned into the squall, then came about onto the starboard tack.

Soon Jan could make out the other European ship at anchor more clearly. It was a trader flying Danish colors. Denmark had remained neutral in Queen Anne's War.

Figures on both began to crowd the rails. As Jan drew closer, the woman straightened her tattered dress, then turned back and made a calming gesture, and another that Jan understood to mean that she would do the talking. It brought him his first laugh in months. She'd have to. He didn't speak a word of Spanish!

His laugh was short lived. Sailors and citizens stampeded down the jetty as Jan cut the sails and the longboat glided to the pier. He stiffened as a company of soldiers in breast plates and helmets pounded through the postern gate toward them. A cacophony of Spanish assaulted his ears but he could only look back blankly. He didn't need to speak the language to understand their common, insistent question: where was the Manila Galleon?

The soldiers clanked to a halt before them. When the master of arms boomed a question at him, Jan looked helplessly to the woman. A remarkable transformation came over her. Pulling herself up in a regal manner, she reeled off a terse litany. The crowd fell silent, and respect leapt to their eyes. Jan caught a name.

Viceroy Cruzat.

The master of arms snapped to attention and barked orders. His troops pushed back the growing throng of traders with pikes, while a corporal double-timed back through the gate. Shouts crashed down on them again as they climbed onto the jetty, but the crowd silenced when the woman raised her hand.

She made a statement. From the expressions, Jan knew she

had informed them that their long awaited treasure ship had been lost. While she parried an avalanche of questions, Jan surveyed the growing crowd. Most were men wearing waxed Van Dykes, with many smoking eight-inch-long cigars. In his rags, Jan felt conspicuous compared to how they dressed—in fine, long coats with cravats ill suited to the hot, muggy climate. An almost equal number of friars were mixed in. On the edge of the crowd stood curious natives in loincloths.

But Jan's eyes riveted on a people shuffling closer that he had never seen before. They wore blue jackets and pants, embroidered silk shoes with thick soles, and round, horse hair caps. He blanched. From the color of their skins, all were stricken with yellow fever—the same scourge that had killed his mother!

A shout turned the crowd's head. The corporal reappeared followed by four stocky natives with a sedan chair, onto which the master of arms assisted her. With a lofty gesture, she indicated to Jan to follow on foot.

He was happy to leave the diseased hordes behind, and crossed the moat's bridge into Intramuros. The carpenter in him was drawn to the Spanish architecture, most two story structures of stone block on the bottom with wood on top. By the time they reached the Plaza de Arms, word of their arrival, and the galleon's destruction, had spread and soldiers had to fight to part a channel through the mob. The chair was lowered before imposing stone steps leading to enormous bronze doors.

As the woman alighted, they swung open and a middle-aged man hurried out, flanked by guards with pikes. Among a people attired in a magnificence Jan couldn't imagine, this man was dressed with even greater splendor. He wore a long, white, powdered wig in contrast to his black Van Dyke. Cutting diagonally across his blue brocaded coat and ample wine belly was a red sash. His face betrayed suppressed emotion. Jan knew it had to be the viceroy. Cruzat.

He and the woman locked eyes and he ran half way down the steps before decorum slowed him to a more dignified pace. As the woman lifted her soiled hem and curtsied, it struck Jan with the force of a falling boom. The woman was his daughter!

The viceroy, fighting to retain his poise, offered his arm and they ascended the steps. Panic was spreading among the crowd.

A nudge prodded Jan forward and he followed into the palace and the greatest hall he had ever seen. The guards halted before French doors leading to a smaller, sparsely furnished room with stiff backed chairs, wooden sofas, and a great table. Open shutters allowed light to spill on oil paintings of starched men in starched uniforms. After the viceroy, the woman and Jan had been ushered in, the guards backed out while closing the doors.

The instant they clicked shut, decorum vanished, and she collapsed sobbing into the viceroy's arms. His voice was hoarse as he consoled her. Embarrassed, Jan turned away from the familial scene, but he couldn't turn away his ears. The viceroy was questioning her. Jan was only able to understand a few words through her sobs.

Santa Maria de la Concepcion. Baguio. Galleon. Irish.

Jan snuck a look. The viceroy swept the woman into his arms and carried her to a chair at one end of the table. Her head fell onto her crossed arms. Then the viceroy strode toward him, his hand outstretched. Ill at ease, Jan accepted his strong grip as Cruzat spoke in Spanish.

"My daughter informs me that you are Irish and were aboard the *Concepcion* when it went down in the typhoon." His grip tightened. "She also tells me that, with the Virgin's mercy, you saved her life. S . . . she says you speak little Spanish, but I must thank you from the bottom of my heart."

". . . Irish," Jan repeated.

The viceroy strode to a hanging rope with a tassle. At a bell tinkling in the next room, the doors opened, and the viceroy issued clipped orders. Once the doors closed again, His Excellency returned and, with great solicitousness, offered Jan his ornate seat at the head of the table. While Jan fought to keep his head up, the viceroy paced the teak floor, deep in thought, until a rap at the door made him look up.

Filipino servants entered carrying silver trays. The woman managed to raise her head at the smell of food. A lid was lifted revealing a roast butt of water buffalo. Steaming rice was dished onto Ching plates. Fruit was set before them. Of them, from reprovisioning stops made in the *Raid*, Jan was familiar only with coconuts. He couldn't know the others had names like papaya, pineapple, banana and orange.

They ate like ravenous beasts, Jan finishing up by reaching for one of the yellow balls. He bit through the rind, squirting juice.

Jan had never tasted anything so delicious. His malnourished body demanded another. Only after he had consumed a half dozen did he stop, and only because he had no more room. The viceroy's eyes filled with pity, then were replaced by turmoil as his thoughts were drawn to the crisis created by the galleon's demise.

Jan felt a deep, rich fatigue sink to his very marrow. The woman was already head down again, her dank, dark hair spilling over the table. Noticing this, the viceroy hurried to the hanging rope. Servants entered.

"I've ordered a bath for you," Viceroy Cruzat said in a soft voice to Jan.

Jan didn't understand what he had said but allowed himself to be led to another part of the building where a metal tub awaited. Left alone, he stripped off his worn clothes and sank into the cool depths of the water and the beautiful oblivion of sleep.

* * *

When he awoke, he was naked and in the middle of the biggest bed he had ever seen. Corner posts soared to a canopy, and cotton netting hung down all sides, muting light seeping through shuttered windows. He reached for his coconut necklace—but it was gone!

He sprang out of bed and threw back the shutters overlooking a courtyard, empty but for a native tending bougainvilleas. Jan squinted as tropical light burst into the room. His rags were nowhere in sight, although a silk shirt, britches and stockings hung from a clotheshorse, before which sat a new pair of shoes. Then he spotted his pistol and the Turk's scimitar and dagger lying on a sideboard. To his vaster relief, on it also lay his necklace.

He placed his foot beside one of the shoes. Perfect fit. Concluding they were meant for him, he dressed, and ran his fingers over the fabric, its feel as sensuous as Margaretje's skin. But the stab of heartache was sharp and he pulled himself back to reality. He was about to pull his necklace over his head, but thought better of it and stuffed it in a pocket of his britches.

He unlatched the door—and froze. A guard had been placed just outside. Jan was about to shut it when a voice hailed him. To his dismay, it was in the lilting tones of the Irish.

"Top o' the morning to ye, laddie. I've been waiting several glasses for ye to awaken. Step out here now and let me have a look at ye."

With apprehension, Jan looked onto a large sitting room, much like the one he had dined in. Slouching in a chair, with one arm resting on a table, was a man in his late twenties with rusty hair and a beard in the square, Irish style. He looked at ease in the formal surroundings despite his faded sailor's garb. Jan started as the guard marched out another door.

"Come on then, lad," the man repeated while pouring a steaming, brown liquid from a silver pot into a cup. "They've just sarved chocolate. If ye haven't had the luck to try it befare, do so. The Dons bring it from New Spain. 'Tis really a pleasant brew, though I do prefare something a mite"—he winked—"stronger meself."

Jan eased into a chair across the table and took a sip. It was delicious! Jan poured it back as fast as the hot liquid would allow, while the man studied the freckle faced boy.

"Take it easy, laddie. Savor it. The Dons will be running out soon because of the *Concepcion* sinking in that typhoon."

"*Concepcion*?" Jan repeated, his top lip lined with brown. His eyes fell on a bowl of the round, yellow fruit. A powerful craving he couldn't explain gripped him and he grabbed one.

His host looked at him in an odd manner. ". . . Aye, the *Santa Maria de la Concepcion*. The Manila Galleon. And it wouldn't hart to peel those aranges first. I'm not sarprised ye like them so much. For some reason they're the best cure to stop the ravages of the Dutch Disease—far better than purges." He named scurvy and a contemporary cure, a flush of sulfur and mercury.

Jan stiffened at the mention of his nationality. The sailor noted his reaction, but let it slide. Jan could kick himself—he had forgotten the name of the blasted galleon! He grabbed a sausage-shaped, yellow fruit with tapered ends and bit into it. As he chewed through the tough hide, the pulp oozed through breaks in the skin. The Irishman frowned, wondering why he

116

hadn't learned the proper way to eat oranges and bananas back in New Spain where they grew in abundance.

"My name is Tom O'Reilly. I'm the coxswain on the *Copenhagen* out in the bay. We just shipped a load of cinnamon from Galle, and cotton from Goa hopin' to sell it to the Dons here for their Acapulco ship. Doesn't seem like there'll be one this yare though." The Irishman spoke in good natured tones, despite the financial tragedy that had befallen his ship. "They've asked me to translate for ye. Can't say I like the arrogant prigs any better than anyone, but I can nay tarn down lendin' a hand to a fellow countryman." He chortled. "And a good Irishman ye are sportin' a black eye like that! Tell me ye's name then, laddie."

Jan hadn't known it was black. He wasn't surprised after Hoogley had slugged him. The reminder gave him a name to use. He hoped his full mouth would be taken as the reason for mangling the accent.

"John Hoogley," he replied—but he pronounced the 'J' in the Dutch fashion: Yon. And, as short as the name and as full his mouth was, he wasn't able to keep the convoluted inflections of Dutch from twisting his tongue.

The coxswain cocked his ear. "An' where ye be from in the Emarald Isle?"

Jan had only heard of one place in Ireland. "Dooblin."

Tom O'Reilly drew himself up straight in his chair. The Dutch boy shrank under the weight of his stare.

"What did ye do abard the *Concepcion* then?" Tom asked, leaning forward.

"Gooner's mate."

The Irishman's brow furrowed. He was about to ask another question when the door opened and Viceroy Cruzat strode in, followed by the young woman and the guard. Both father and daughter were tense. The woman—refreshed, groomed and beautiful in a billowing black silk mourning gown—shot Jan a cautioning glance as he stood, followed somewhat later by the Irishman. The viceroy waved them both back down with one hand while handkerchiefing sweat from his forehead with the other. He took a chair against the wall, and sat legs apart with his hands on his knees, his large stomach pressed against his silk costume. The woman sat to his

117

right, her eyes affixed to the pegged floor.

The viceroy addressed the interpreter in Spanish. The Irishman listened, nodded, then turned to the Hollander. Tom O'Reilly's eyes narrowed.

"He says to tell ye that he thanks ye on the cross of Christ"—he made the sign of the cross—"for savin' his daughter Solina's life." He paused, trying to penetrate the nervous young man's blue eyes. "He's only sarry ye couldn't a done the same far her husband who fell ill of the . . . *Dutch* . . . Disease on the crossin'."

Jan knew the Irishman was baiting him. He glanced at the young woman named Solina, who looked up, her eyes reaching out to him. Tom O'Reilly didn't miss the exchange. The Irishman—hiding his suspicions—turned to Viceroy Cruzat and spoke in Spanish. Jan heard his borrowed name used. John Hoogley. O'Reilly turned back to Jan.

"The viceroy says that he would like to help ye in anyway he can, laddie."

"I woont to go hoome."

The accent laid it broadside for O'Reilly. He pulled himself erect, his senses on full alert.

"John . . . or Yon . . . or whatever ye name is, we don't have much time. As I says, I don't care for these crap eating grape stampers any more than anyone—but ye'll have to level with me. Ye's really from the land of dikes and wooden shoes, ain't ye? Be truthful now. I'm the only man who can help ye out of this den of thieves."

Jan glanced at the viceroy and his daughter, who averted her eyes again. Fortunately, the viceroy was too wrapped up in his other concerns to have noticed Jan's distress. He had little choice. He hoped it was the right one.

"Aye, boot I live in the New Woorld. Or I shood say, did."

The coxswain nodded. Questions lined up behind his eyes. "What happened out there? Ye couldn't have been on the *Concepcion?*"

As Jan blurted out the story, Solina Cruzat began to tremble. The light of revelation filled the Irishman's eyes. O'Reilly twirled his beard, at a loss for words. Hearing the silence, Viceroy Cruzat looked up and cleared his throat. The Irishman recovered and responded at some length while Jan tried to still his

own trembling. When O'Reilly was finished, the older man nodded and said something in Spanish.

"I told him that ye'd like to return to Dublin," Tom O'Reilly
said, "but that ye have no money far passage. I presume that's the
case with ye, aye?"

Jan nodded.

"Well, don't ye worry none. He has promised to pay ye fare
with us back to Europe."

"Th . . . thank you! Thank him!"

Solina looked more at ease. Sensing Viceroy Cruzat's impa-
tience, O'Reilly turned to him. The viceroy listened, then nodded
again.

"The fat, old prig agrees," Tom O'Reilly said. "It's a good
thing. The *Sangleys* are restless. The Spanish have already locked
the gates and are holding meetings with their leaders."

The Irishman glanced at Solina Cruzat; it was apparent she
shared Jan's secret. Admiration seeped into his voice as he continued. "She's a brave wench, that one. I don't know many Don
women that would do that—particularly a viceroy's daughter."

At the sound of his title, Cruzat stood, announcing the end of
the audience. Jan jumped to his feet, followed, as usual, by the
coxswain. Viceroy Cruzat thrust his hand out to Jan and was
about to speak when they were interrupted by banging at the
door. Cruzat motioned to his guard. The door swung open and
an officer strode in and snapped to attention. A conversation in
Spanish bounded between the officer and the viceroy with increasing tension. It ended with a name that caused Cruzat to go
rigid.

"*Atagar!*" he repeated.

Tom O'Reilly and Solina Cruzat looked ill at ease. Something
was terribly wrong. The officer had no sooner left, shutting the
door behind him, before Solina burst into tears. Her hands flew
to her face a split second before the viceroy slapped her, sending
her sprawling across the floor. While she lay sobbing, the viceroy
barked an order. A guard snapped to attention and disappeared
out the door.

Viceroy Cruzat spun toward Jan and slammed his fist down
onto the table so hard that the chocolate pot jumped. His eyes
seared into Jan's, who stood shivering despite the heat wondering
what had happened.

The door swung open again. Two guards dragged a tall man wearing a matted, black robe into the room, his spindly arms draped around their necks. His head was lolling, his long, blond hair and beard as tangled as seaweed. The man named Atagar was more dead than alive but managed to raise his gaunt, sunburned face. His blurry, blue eyes registered confusion as they settled on the boy with the blond hair and freckles.

Then a malevolent smile oozed across his thin, blistered lips.

13 Guerrillas in the Mist

"Holy what?"

Ben didn't hear a reply from Quinn, just the sound of wires being yanked and another curse. Then the anthropologist popped out of the hatch like a Jack-in-the-box and slammed the transmitter on the floor. On top sat the wad of C-4 explosives.

"Oh my gawd!" the old man exclaimed.

Quinn's face was white under the grease. "The plastics could be set off by radio, and it would have made a Krakatoa out of us. I cut the power source—but there's also four pair in new electrical conduit running up the hull . . . there it is!"

He pointed at conduit emerging from a freshly drilled hole in the floor. It ran up the bulkhead and along the low ceiling before disappearing into another freshly drilled hole beside the lightbulb.

"One pair branches from the conduit into the crack between the bulkhead and ceiling," Ben said, pushing the Bobbsey Twins' meagre rack of clothes aside. He pulled a small screwdriver from his nerd pack and poked until something broke loose.

A tiny microphone tumbled out and dangled at the end of the wires.

Quinn burst onto the deck seconds later, Ben wheezing behind him. Although the sea was calm, the sky was boxed in, teasing them with drizzle but threatening to sledgehammer them with rain.

"Gawd, you look like The Monster from Greasy Lagoo—" Liana stopped short when she saw Quinn's expression. Her eyes dropped to the transmitter and plastics. "What's that?"

Chase, in the bridge, lowered binoculars with which he was trying to probe the mist. "What's what?" He looked at Quinn.

"Somebody wired us so they could cripple us or—"

"*What!*" Liana and Chase exclaimed.

"—blow us out of the water by remote. Not only that, but we found a microphone near your bed! If their shut-off valve hadn't gone on the fritz, we never would've known about it!"

Liana's and Chase's eyes locked, their uneasiness caused by more than one reason. Ben stood trying to catch his breath.

"What'll we do with the C-4?" Chase asked.

". . . We'll keep it, you never know. Let's find out where the rest of those wires go."

Ben shuffled to the cabin door and ran his claw along the conduit leading from the floor, above the lightbulb, and up and behind a ventilation screen. Using his screwdriver, he pried it off. "Here's another bloody microphone! The conduit continues through the ceiling! Chase, cin you see where it comes out up there?"

"Yeah, under our friggin' radio! I'll just lift it out of its housing . . . Oh, my gawd! There's *another* mike inside! And the last pair leads to a heating filament wrapped around a chip! Whoever did this could knock out our radio at will!"

". . . Whoever did this were letting us do the digging," Liana said. "Then, when we had the treasure, they would be able to move in and scoop it up."

The thought was sobering. That thought was also on the Beagle Boys.

"Well, they're going to have trouble doing that now!" Quinn growled. Flushed with anger, he brought the sledge-hammer down on the alien transmitter. "They must have bribed the mechanic who did the overhaul!"

Quinn stormed around the deck while Ben eased into his lawnchair, oblivious to the light rain

"But how did they find out what we're doing?" Liana asked.

The spectre of a leak was raised again. That spectre weighed 350 pounds.

"Earthquake McGoon. . . ?" Chase offered.

Quinn let out a long breath and made a face. "I can't deny the possibility this time."

* * *

Chase, on the bridge, cupped a hand to an ear and squinted over the sterndeck to the north-east. "I hear a plane! Maybe it's Earthquake!"

It was about time. He was now two days late. The crew halted dive preparations. The sound of an engine seeped through the gossamer veil.

"I dunno, it sounds too heavy to be a Cessna," Dr. Quinn cautioned, pushing his wet black hair back. "And it's sure not an F-5, certainly not in this visibility. We better cover the gear, eh?"

They yanked tarps over the equipment. As the grumble of the engine grew louder, they searched the impenetrable wall of mist.

"There it is!" Liana cried, pointing.

A floatplane dissolved out of the mist, coming in low and straight at them.

"It's a Beaver!" Quinn shouted, running to the cabin. "That's what's supplying the Beagle Boys!" Returning, he tossed the shotgun to Liana, shoved an M-16 in Ben's hands, and snapped the slide on another before dropping behind the compressor. Ben hunched to the cabin door, cursing as he was too weak to rack the bolt, wishing he had his familiar M-1 from his Carib days. Chase swept up his M-16 and jumped down to the deck where he crouched in the hatch companionway beside Liana. Her eyes flickered to the scuba tanks stacked under a tarp, and shuddered at what would happen if they were hit.

"Don't fire unless they do," Chase ordered over the growing roar of the de Havilland engine.

They ducked as the Beaver thundered over. It vanished into the mist, leaving only the receding growl of its motor, and the patter of drizzle as the weather began to close. When it was evident the plane wasn't returning, everyone drifted back onto deck.

"They were checking us oot."

"What should we do? Go on with the dive?" Liana asked, gripping the shotgun.

"I think we better wait out this weather," Chase cautioned.

"What we can't see can hurt us."

"Hey, guys, I hate to say it," Liana warned, cocking an ear to the north-east, "but I think it looped around."

Everyone scrambled back to battle stations. Chase cupped an ear—the engine was much quieter and smoother—then climbed back on deck and switched on the safety on his rifle.

"It's a Cessna," he said moments before the plane appeared out of the fog and began to lose altitude. "Earthquake McGoon, finally."

"What should we do?" Liana asked. "Confront him?"

"Better to play it cool," Chase advised and Quinn and Ben nodded.

Earthquake's pontoons plowed into the water a mere hundred yards off their stern. The dive ladder squeaked in agony as the corpulent pilot pulled himself onto deck and tied the plane's line to a mooring ring. If he noticed they were studying him, he didn't show it. They did notice that the only weapon he carried was a buck-knife.

"Sorry for bein' late, y'all," he rumbled as he pulled a crumpled envelope out of a breast pocket of his Hawaiian shirt bulging with peanuts, "but it took longer than I thought to round up everything on your grocery list." He passed the envelope to Ben Gordon. "This here telegram arrived yesterday."

Ben trembled on his glasses and studied it at arm's length. "It's from Seville," he rasped as he ripped it open. "Somethin's cockeyed though. It's from Maria, Jose's wife."

"Are you alrig—" Liana began when she saw his knees go weak.

"Oh, noooooo," he moaned as Liana and Chase grabbed him before he fell and eased him into a lawnchair. The telegram fluttered to the wet deck.

Chase scooped it up. "She says, uh, that Jose finished his research at the Archives. He was about to courier it to us but he was—oh, my gawd—*murdered!*"

"Good gawd, no!"

"It happened a few days ago! The Guardia Civil are investigating, but the only lead they have is from neighbors reporting that two men with Arab features were seen leaving the house. Maria says she was shopping."

"Arabs? That's weird. What were they after?" Liana asked.

"The only things stolen were his notes and the original ledgers from the Archives."

The eyes of the four treasure hunters burned into Earthquake.

He looked back, perplexed. "What? What did I do?"

". . . There's been other divers working the site, eh? We just learned that our boat was rigged with microphones and C-4."

The fat pilot looked stunned. "So what's that got to do with me?"

The drizzle increased, falling straight down in the dead air. The promontory disappeared behind a curtain of rain. They helped Ben, looking ten years older, to another chair in the cabin where they regrouped.

Chase couldn't shake the Drunken Bar Factor from his mind. "Earthquake, did you happen . . . accidentally . . . to mention anything to anyone anywhere about our venture?"

The Teddy suddenly became a grizzly bear. "I didn't whisper a word of it! Think of it! I'm in for a whole one percent cut if y'all find anything!"

Chase studied the big man's glare, then looked down and shook his head. "Liana, do you have those pictures?"

She zipped open her camera bag and passed them to Earthquake. "Any idea who they are?"

He flipped through them, and stopped on the group shot with the middle-aged man. He let out a whistle. "I cin tell y'all who *this* cracker is! His picture has been in the *Bulletin Today* numerous times. It's Chico Rolando!"

"Who's Chico Rolando?" Chase asked.

Quinn grabbed the picture. "I think you're *right*! I can't believe I didn't notice! He's one of the Abu Sayyef leaders, eh! Behind kidnappings and murders all over the region!"

Rain pounded on the roof.

"And he's after our treasure," Chase said. "That's why Arabs robbed Jose. Abu Sayyef is linked to al-Queda. Knowing who they are, dare we go on?"

"Mr. Detective here"—Earthquake sarcastically indicated Chase—"has a point. It's not jist the rain thet's gettin' fuggin' heavy."

Quinn turned to Earthquake. "Did you bring everything I asked for?"

"If it was an M60 you meant when you said a 'camera with the longest lens' I got thet from Jesus. I've heard easier codes to break. You cin use my flare gun."

"Flare gun? We have one. I wanted M203 *rockets* and a launch assembly for an M-16!"

Earthquake rolled his eyes. "I'll bring them next time—but I hafta warn y'all thet this is the tourist season and I'm booked up to my eyebrows. The Japanese are invading Cebu this year again."

"Try! Please!" The anthropologist turned to the crew. "Look, an M60 can spit oot 550 shells a minute and has an effective range of 1,200 yards. We ootgun them—*and* we control the wreck! We don't need the darned ledgers."

"You sure?" Chase asked. "The Philippines is your home. You're making a pretty big enemy."

"With several million bucks I can live anywhere."

". . . There's another, bigger consideration." Chase turned to the old treasure hunter, who looked like he had shrunk even more. "Ben, what was the *Atocha* worth?"

"Over 400 million."

"And the Manilas were richer. *If* there's a fortune down there and al-Queda get it," Chase said, "they'll be able to fund an international rampage that'll make 9/11 look like a grass fire. With that kind of money to throw around, what Muslim nuclear scientist can resist slipping a bomb out the back door?" The Rhodesian Ridgeback hung its ears and slouched away.

"What are you saying?" Liana asked.

". . . Maybe we should inform the military."

"Fine with me," she replied. "I've already said I'm not nuts about dealing with Islamic fanatics."

"Then we lose our once in a lifetime chance for a score like this!" Quinn objected. "Look, Abu Sayyaf don't dare bring in more people or they'll attract attention. Odds are that we only have the Beagle Boys to deal with. And deal with them we *can*."

"And if we can't?" Liana pressed. "We're putting the West's security at serious risk."

"If we're in trouble, we can act. Can you imagine the stampede if we broadcast on the open channel that a treasure galleon is here? And we have Earthquake to blow the whistle if we disappear. The world's safe!"

Chase turned to Liana. "He's got a point."

She considered, then nodded. "I hate giving up too."

"Ben?"

"I'll go with whatever you decide," he said, pulling the piece-of-eight from his pocket and fingering it. "I jist don't want to go back to thet bloody armchair in The Trophy Room."

"It's decided then—we stay." The Ridgeback trotted back wagging its tail. "I just hope we're not making the biggest mistake of our lives. It'll be calamitous if we're wrong."

"Y'all are nuts, but thet's jist my opinion." Earthquake glanced at the weather. "We better get the plane unloaded so I can get above this crap before it gits worse."

"I have a couple of things to fly out," Ben rasped. Despite his depression, he pulled himself from the chair and inched to a desk on which rested a small box containing one of the clay pipes. He passed it to the pilot, along with a handful of dollars and a paper with addresses. "This goes to a colleague in London." He pointed an arthritic finger at a sack. "Thet holds wood to be tested in the States. If you courier them, we should have results in two weeks."

Earthquake grabbed the sack. Within fifteen minutes, the machine-gun was offloaded and the plane dissolved into the rain, leaving the uneasy treasure hunters behind.

* * *

"Okay," Quinn called from the bridge's roof, "Fort *Wracker* is open for business!"

The machine-gun's tripod had been bolted atop the wheelhouse and could be covered by an Explorers Club flag lying ready. Quinn swung the big gun around in a circle, then aimed it skyward.

The rain had sputtered out, leaving a thick mist that was steaming off as the sun sneaked between an elephant stampede of dark clouds. The promontory's top floated above a fogbank obliterating the point and the view to the south. Chase was thankful the sea was so still that the sound of a motor would skip through the fog to them.

He bit into a canned tuna sandwich Liana had prepared. Barnacle Ben ignored lunch and sat facing out to sea, fingering the piece-of-eight. He was lost in thoughts of Jose, convinced he was responsible for his old comrade's death. His last treasure

127

hunt had turned into a nightmare.

"Before we hit the water," Quinn said, joining them on deck, "I'll pick up those reinforcements Batuta promised. Lolo's funeral has to be over." He wolfed down a sandwich, grabbed his Tilley hat and M-16, and climbed into the Zodiac.

Chase watched the craft skim toward the river mouth. When it was about to disappear into mist 800 yards away and Chase was turning to grab another sandwich, the motor screamed. The writer turned back to see the boat wallow and the engine run down. It sounded like Quinn had accidentally slipped it into neutral with the throttle wide open.

"What the. . . . ?" Chase muttered.

The relaxed cough of the Merc's idle was replaced by another scream as Quinn cranked the handle open, but the Zodiac didn't move. The engine fell silent. Chase flew up to the bridge and grabbed binoculars. He squinted through the mist as Quinn's silhouette tilted the motor and leaned over to inspect the transom. Then the anthropologist looked over his shoulder and appeared to start.

"What going on!" Chase said as Quinn scrambled for his M-16. Lowering his binoculars, all Chase could see where Quinn's attention had been focused was the low fogbank.

Something above it caught the writer's eye—a mirror winked through fingers of mist above the main body! It came from the brown crest of the promontory. Then an elephant stepped into the path of the sun and the signal disappeared.

A single-stroke engine banged to life in the fog.

"Ben! Liana!" Chase shouted, stringing the binoculars around his neck. "Raise the mailbox! Cut the anchor lines! Quinn's in trouble! Then, Liana, get up here as fast as you can!"

He snapped the key over and punched the start button while Liana hooked the crane to the mailbox. An instant after the diesel caught, a loud *cruuuunch* ground from the stern, all but drowning out Ben's curses and Liana's shrieks to put the engine in neutral. Chase did—but too late. The flimsy mailbox had been torn to shreds by the propeller.

"Quinn left it in gear!" Chase said as he jammed the throttle forward again. The *Wracker* picked up speed, dragging the last anchor thirty feet before Liana managed to sever the line.

"Take the helm!" Chase shouted as Liana leaped up to the bridge and he to the roof. Quinn was hunkered down, his M-16 peeking over the Zodiac. A fuming Ben wheezed forward with his M-16. The hammer of the gasoline engine somewhere in the fog grew louder and closer.

"There!" Liana screamed. "The other side of Quinn and just to starboard! Coming out of the mist! They've spotted him!"

Like a ghostly Viking ship with outriggers, the port bow corner of the huge *banca* dissolved out of the fog, bearing down on the Zodiac at full speed. Chase fingered off a warning burst back of the *banca*, zipping a row of geysers.

It was enough—the boat came about, hoping to race back into the fog. When its side was presented, Chase stitched a long burst of tracer and shells across the apparition. Just before the M60 spit out the last shell in the bandoleer, one of the human silhouettes aboard was knocked over. Then the *banca* dissolved into the mist.

"Head straight for it, Liana!" Chase fed another ammo belt into the gun.

"I am!"

Ben cursed while he wrestled with the M-16 bolt.

"I don't dare shoot!" Chase shouted. The *banca* had popped out of the fog again—but now was beyond the Zodiac and bearing down on it fast. The *Wracker* still had at least 300 yards to go.

Chase raised binoculars and watched helplessly as Quinn threw his hands into the air and was manhandled aboard the *banca*. Then the faster outrigger shot back into the fog—but not before unleashing a hailstorm of lead at the *Wracker*, sending the remaining three crew members diving for cover.

* * *

"The amazing thing is thet bloody eggbeater stayed on thet long," Ben wheezed as Liana lowered the Mercury by crane to Chase in the Zodiac.

The sheer pin holding the propeller had been hit during the firefight when Lolo had been killed. It had finally worked out and the prop had spun off. The *Wracker* was back anchored over Site One—as far from the promontory as possible. It was less than two hours since Quinn's kidnapping. They were still traumatized.

"Good thing that fogbank ended where it did or their ambush might have worked," Liana said.

"They must want the *Wracker*, so they can do their own hunt," Chase said.

"How did they get that close without being heard?" Liana asked.

"An electric motor," Ben replied, unable to suppress a cough.

Chase eased the Merc onto its housing, tightened the clamps, and snapped in the fuel line before climbing back aboard the *Wracker*. "Sorry about your mailbox, Ben," he said, anxiety tracing his voice.

What was left of it hung by a metal thread.

"Weren't your fault. May as well drop it to the bottom fer now." He nodded to their airlift. "We still have this. It'll jist take longer. There's more important things to worry about."

Chase's eyes wandered to the promontory, now visible. The weather system had blown away leaving a sky as blue as a Sung bowl. The freshly scrubbed colors along shore were vivid. It was difficult to imagine that this peaceful scene had witnessed violence.

"All we can do is wait and see what they want for ransom," Chase worried. "And I can guess what it'll be: Quinn for the treasure, after we've brought it up—"

"Hold your horses!" Ben shouted, pointing in the direction of the river.

A dugout *banca* angled in their direction.

"I'll run out and meet them," Liana said, reaching for the Zodiac's line.

"Wait, it could be a trick," Chase warned, checking the clip in his M-16.

Liana paused. They watched as the *banca* paddled closer.

"I . . . don't . . . believe it," rasped Ben, following their progress through binoculars.

"Believe what?" Liana asked. Her palms were sticky on the shotgun.

"Here, my eyes ain't so good no more." He handed the binocs to Chase. "Who's thet in the middle?"

Chase raised the glasses. "What the. . . ! It's *Quinn*! With Batuta and a young native!" It was the one with the sharp eyes who had held the leader's RPG.

Liana grabbed the binoculars. "My gawd!"

"Sorry for taking so long bringing reinforcements, eh?" the anthropologist mumbled through cracked lips several minutes later as the *banca* glided alongside. He'd been badly beaten and one eye was swollen almost shut. "But I had to take a detour."

"How'd you get away?" Chase demanded as he helped the anthropologist onto deck.

Quinn's hand drifted to a bruise on his side as he eased into a lawnchair, not in any condition to speak just then. Liana grabbed the First Aid Kit and dabbed Quinn's face with peroxide, while pots and pans clattered in the galley as Barnacle Ben heated water.

"Agila and I will stay with you," Batuta said, his attitude unchanged. He turned and spoke in the softer Batak dialect, and Agila began transferring supplies from the *banca* to the *Wracker*. They had brought AKs, ponchos, bananas and rice wrapped in banana leaf.

Liana looked from Quinn to the Batak leader for an explanation.

"Dr. Quinn was very fortunate. My man on the promontory spotted their *banca* through the fog and tried to signal you. When Dr. Quinn was captured, our man notified the vil-lage. We knew the ter-rorists had moved to a new camp on Palawan ten kilometers down where there's fresh water." Batuta's tight lips parted in something approximating a smile. "They did not know that scouts were watching, and that we were just waiting for Lolo's funeral to end before attacking. If we could have gotten closer, we could have cleaned them out but they spotted us, and we managed to kill only one before they got away in their *banca*."

"I escaped in the confusion." Quinn guzzled from a canteen, then looked at Batuta with gratitude. "He saved my life. U...unfortunatcly, Chico Rolando wasn't the one they whacked, but at least the Beagle Boys are down to seven. They tried to take advantage of the fog to commandeer the *Wracker*, but had to settle for me. He was furious another one of his men got blasted when they grabbed me. That was you, Chase? Good shot. Bag Lady, will you please stop that!"

She gave up trying to be Florence Nightingale.

The Batak leader stood with crossed arms listening with an air of disdain. Agila finished transferring supplies, picked up his Kalashnikov, and took up position on the bow where he watched the promontory like a hawk.

"Batuta, any idea where they went?" Chase asked.

"Further down the coast, probably to establish a new camp."

Ben arrived with hot water but Quinn waved him off. Looking lost and useless again, the old treasure hunter set it aside and crouched to his lawnchair.

"What did you learn about them?" Liana pressed.

The anthropologist's bruised face grew dark. "I found oot where the leak came from. Rolando bragged when I asked how he learned we were treasure hunting . . . from one of their spies who hangs oot in Cebu bars picking up information."

Chase dropped his head and massaged the back of his neck.

"Earthquake regularly flies there," Liana muttered.

Quinn nodded. "Rolando said it was Earthquake who let them in on it."

"You make it sound like he's with them," Liana said.

Quinn shook his head. "That's the way Rolando put it—but I don't believe for a minute he knew what he was doing. Everything in his past is as anti-terrorist as you can find! Cripes sake, he worked for the CIA! He thinks Attila the Hun was a panty hose wearing faggot! He was probably conned by some Filipino drinking 'buddy' like you guessed Chase. What does he stand to gain, eh?"

"Maybe one percent wasn't a big enough cut?" Liana offered. "He wouldn't be the first spook to have gone bad for money."

"One percent of the *Atocha* is four friggin' million bucks, pardon my Spanish."

"But even two percent is eight mil," Chase said. ". . . But why hook up with terrorists, who everyone knows can't be trusted? When he must know more reliable people? There's something here we don't understand."

The anthropologist made a weak gesture. "Whatever, we have a lot of work ahead and we're under pressure to get it done and ootta here as fast as possible, eh? I think we should get onto Site One asap." He noticed what was left of the mailbox.

"Somebody left the *Wracker* in gear," Liana said.

Quinn rolled his eyes. "Oh crap! Sorry!"

"We'll manage. How bad are them ribs, Doc? Cin you dive?"

"Gimme a day or two." He hoisted himself to his feet, limped to the compressor, and began hooking up a tank. "Well? Let's get at it, eh!"

"'He will persevere and will curse the day he heard of it. . . .'"

Quinn looked at the speaker but said nothing. The man had saved his life.

"Yes, yes Batuta, we know—Joseph Conrad," Chase said. But the Curse was beginning to haunt him.

Liana, too, worried that Batuta—and Conrad—were right, that they were caught in the golden cobweb of Conrad's Curse.

Her worries were suddenly magnified by Ben. He doubled over in his chair gasping. She rushed to his side but there was nothing she could do. They stood by helpless while Ben hawked his throat and spit out a large gob onto the deck. He tried to hide it with his shoe but he wasn't fast enough.

It was red.

14 Fort Santiago

The first thing Jan saw when he regained consciousness was the block and tackle above his head. He lay on the stone floor in only his silk britches, every cell in his body screaming in pain. Pain from being hoisted by his wrists tied behind his back. Pain from being beaten by cane poles. Pain from having strips of linen and water forced down his throat.

A volcanic surge of water and swollen cloth spewed out of his mouth. The only other sound was the dank, hollow drip of water. Both were blotted out by a roll of thunder, climaxing in an enormous *craaack*. The stench of vomit, blood and death in the stone chamber was overwhelming.

Jan managed to raise his head. Light oozed through rusting bars of the single small window. A teak rack in the middle of the room cast dim shadows. Jan closed his eyes to block out the sight. He hoped for a fast end, but it was a mercy he couldn't expect.

Hearing a throat clear, he forced his eyes open and made out two figures in the shadows. One, standing, a sailor, looked familiar. The other, dressed in black, was seated. It had been the Jesuit who, with exacting skill, had supervised the torture. Jan's teeth chattered. The next round must be upon him. He waited for that malice laden voice, weakened though it was, to speak. Instead, the voice he heard was filled with emotion.

"J . . . John . . . it's Tom O'Reilly."

Jan moved his lips but all that issued forth was a gurgle.

"John . . . or whatever ye's name is . . . this sadistic son-of-a-dog is Father Ignacio del Atagar. He 'asked' me here to translate. Cin ye understand me laddie?"

Jan again tried to speak. It was enough. O'Reilly saw it.

"He claims to be a Jesuit—though he's the strangest Black Robe I've ever seen, I'll tell ye." Fear had replaced insolence in his voice.

Jan managed to find his. It was a broken thing. "He's w . . . with the . . . the Inquisition?"

"The Inquisition has nay operated in some years. But he's got power over the viceroy." He dropped his head before continuing in quiet, clear tones. "He got the entire stary from Solina Cruzat—"

The gaunt man in black cut the coxswain short with a spiel in Spanish. Two men Jan remembered well stepped from shadows, yanked him to his feet, and slammed him into a rough chair. His chin fell and he caught a glimpse of his distended belly before he gasped as one of them grabbed a fistful of his long, blond hair and jerked his head back. O'Reilly cleared his throat again.

"The gentleman wants me to get to the point. Solina Cruzat told him about an iron chest ye had. He wants to know what happened to it. It's vary impartant to him."

Jan saw with clarity honed by pain that giving up the statue wouldn't save his life. In any case, he no longer feared death. It was a deliverer. So hell with him. Hell with the crap eating Don!

"I th . . . threw it ooverboard." Jan felt a flicker of satisfaction.

The reply to the Irishman's translation was instantly forthcoming. The lanky clergyman shouted and tried to stand but fell back in his chair. O'Reilly asked something in Spanish. The answer was short and harsh. The translator turned back to Jan.

"He won't tell me what was in it. I presume it's gold cobs though. He won't accept that ye threw it overbard. Why would ye do that?"

"It was . . . wasn't coobs," Jan managed, his resolve strengthening. "It was platinum. Worthless."

O'Reilly translated. Father Ignacio del Atagar fidgeted. His words spat like cobra's venom.

"Where John? Quickly now—he's impatient."

". . . Oo . . . oot in the middle of the ocean. *Deep*," Jon replied, relishing revenge. What use the strange cargo was to the Don he couldn't care less.

Atagar slammed his fist on his armrest. Such a torrent of abuse flowed forth that the coxswain stepped aside like he'd been struck.

"John . . . I have to tell ye bad news . . . though I don't think ye expect anything less. The situation is deteriorating. The city's in an uproar for ye blood. Not only is Queen Anne's War on—and may she prevail—but ye took their annual galleon. The *Sangleys* have shut their shops. Manila is a powder keg. We're finishing re-rigging and provisioning the *Copenhagen* as fast as we can. We hope to raise anchor with the moon's peak tide in a couple of days. . . ." His voice trailed off when he came to the most difficult part.

Jan managed to fix his blue eyes on the Irishman. "How?"

". . . Tamorrow at daybreak they's going to tie ye to the . . . to the mouth of a cannon overlooking the Pasig River so the *Sangleys* can witness . . . the execution. The Spanish are passing the ward amongst them now, to try to defuse the situation."

Jan swooned—but from relief. His deliverance would be soon. Seawater from a bucket slammed into his face, washing him back to his muddied senses. He blinked to see the Irishman leaning over him, his face full of concern.

"Cin I have a priest come to take confession? Are ye Catholic?"

Never had his disgust for all things Christian plumbed deeper, and a quart of watery vomit disgorged onto his lap, causing O'Reilly to jump back. When Jan was able to catch his breath, he waved the Irishman away. A voice screamed orders. Rough hands seized him. Terror gripped him. The rack. It had to be the rack now.

Instead, they drew him up before Father Ignacio del Atagar who, with new found strength, stood. Shaking with fury, the Spaniard jerked his thumb toward the heavy door.

"It's the dungeon far ye, John. I do much wish there was *somethin'* I could do—"

A knife-edged glance from Atagar cut the coxswain short. Jan tried to thank the Irishman, but his lips felt like rubber. Then he was dragged through the door and down a narrow, dank passageway.

* * *

136

Jan remembered the cell from the previous night. The entrance was a hole in the floor covered by a rusty grate. He was dropped the few feet to the sloped bottom and tumbled down a short incline into a cramped pit, splashing face first into brackish water seeping from a floor grate. His survival instincts flickering, he found strength to stagger to his feet, only to strike his head on the low ceiling, causing him to fall back into the water.

Light filtered through a barred window and muted against white sedimentary river rocks mortared to form the cell. Rain dimpled the Pasig River flowing outside the window. He hoped the rising tide wouldn't push the river back as high as it had the previous night—muddy water rising through the lower grill had left him with only the top six inches of the cell to breath. It was a space he shared with swimming rats.

His hand trembled into his pocket. For what it was worth, the coconut shell was still there. If Solina Cruzat had guessed what it was, she hadn't betrayed him.

Someone grunted from the top grate. A wooden bowl had been placed on a ledge just below the opening. Jan crawled to the entrance and slurped mush until he bit down on something long and rubbery. It was a rat's tail. With disgust, he flicked it into the calf deep water.

He raked his fingers through the gruel until he felt something furry. Gagging, Jan lifted out the stewed carcass, the flesh slipping with a plop back into his bowl, leaving the sopping fur in his hand. He threw it aside as an enormous surge of water spewed from his mouth and nose. He wheezed, water having rushed down his windpipe. Then another and another horrid flood of clear vomit gushed out. Somehow, he managed to hang onto the bowl.

Gasping, he lay back against the rocky incline until his breathing calmed. He felt his stomach. It was flat again and the terrible cramps gone. His ravaged body crying out for nourishment, Jan fought back revulsion as he trembled his fingers back into the bowl. As he raised the dripping corpse to his lips, Jan tried to think of his favorite meal back in New York, rabbit stew. He nibbled a tiny shoulder. The taste was strong but acceptable. Then his hunger rose, and soon all that was left of the rat was ribs and guts stringing through his fingers. Tossing them aside, he gulped the contents of the bowl.

The bowl clattered down the incline to bob in the rising water. He fell onto his back and stared up at the grate, his chest heaving. The last thought staggering through his mind before he plunged into the escape of sleep was that it was his last supper.

* * *

Jan was dreaming of a beautiful, tropical waterfall when he began to drift up from the depths of that sweet oblivion. He was lying under its warm flow, the cleansing water washing his face. The lilt of laughter filled the crystalline air. A smile formed and he opened his mouth to drink in the pure, clean liquid.

The laughter turned harsher, throatier, louder—then dissolved into rough voices in a tongue he didn't understand. The waterfall slowed, then stopped, except for a few last spurts that splattered onto his face. Jan's eyes popped open.

Standing above him, looking down through the iron bars of the grate, were two Spanish soldiers. They were laughing and hitching up their pants.

Jan sprang to his feet spitting. He banged his head on the ceiling again and fell forward into the water. To his alarm, it had risen to his chest. Still reeling, he swirled water over his face. Then he ploughed back below the smirking men.

Shaking his fist, he unleashed every curse he had learned in eight months of sailing. The soldiers traded a joke and roared again. One of them placed his hands on his stomach, then threw them outward.

"*Boom!*" he boomed.

He was about to repeat the joke when another—louder—boom from across the river resounded though the dungeon. At the same instant a great *crash* shook the building, followed by Spanish shouts. The guards blanched and disappeared in a rattle of scabbards.

Jan scrambled to the small window overlooking the river. Water reached almost up to the bottom sill. Through the drizzle and dusk across the narrow Pasig he made out figures in blue running for cover. Beyond the mouth of the river, the junks had withdrawn beyond range of Fort Santiago's cannons. It was probably one of the junks' cannons that had been smuggled into the Parian.

A great flash of fire roared out from across the river. Jan flinched as a cannonball slammed into the fortifications, shaking the water in his cell. Spanish cannons overhead began to belch flame and fury. Smoke curled down the sides of the ramparts as buildings across the river disintegrated and fires broke out.

A full blooded insurrection had broken out among the *Sangleys.*

Jan's more immediate concern was the rising water. Through the bars, he could see whitecaps where the flood tide fought its own battle with the monsoon filled river. Murky water swirled up through the lower grate. If it kept rising at its present rate, the Spaniards would have a limp body to tie to the mouth of the cannon in the morning.

Jan plowed through the water to the upper grate again. He shouted until he was hoarse, but his calls were drowned out by the louder voices of the guns. In growing desperation, he returned to the window and tried to shake the bars. Although he was surprised at the strength the sleep and swill had given him, they didn't budge.

The water had crept up another three inchs in the time he had been awake. He remembered something Tom O'Reilly had said. The tides were rising.

Jan gasped and flailed backward. A yellow face had burst out of the water inches from his own, on the other side of the bars, the head shaved but for a wet topknot. The face was that of a boy hardly older than Jan. His slanted eyes gleamed with fear. There was something in his hand that made Jan's heart beat faster. The visitor looked both ways, then began sawing at the bars.

"Thunder and lightning!" Jan exclaimed. Forget the yellow fever! He pushed forward through the water and gripped the other end of the blade so they could work in unison. By the time they had sawed through only one bar, the water had risen. Waves slopped over the window sill into his cell.

They were starting on their second when the *Sangley's* head kicked forward, the violence of the movement tearing the saw from Jan's grip. He stared at a red hole in the back of his would be savior's head just before he slipped into the water. A stray shot from across the river. One of his own people.

139

Jan lunged for the submerged arm that had held the saw—
and cried out. His hand was empty. Jan let the *Sangley's* body bob
downstream. Clearance was now reduced to less than a foot.

Somewhere beyond the ceiling grate a candle flickered. In a
last bid for survival, Jan clenched the grill and shook it with all his
might. He called and cursed and spat like a caged lynx, but in the
end was left with no more than ragged vocal chords and inches
of clearance as the tide inexorably rose. Defeated, he drifted
down into the water, wanting just to drown and end his agony.

His cell suddenly exploded into a boiling maelstrom. Jan spun
head over heels, limbs flailing. He knew he was dying and he
happily surrendered to it, his spirit rising until he looked down
with dispassion on his body being flung around like a rag doll's.
Nature's beautiful music reverberated through his being again,
and all was peace in the pandemonium. Recognizing the Light,
with eagerness he moved toward it—but was stopped a second
time by the Figures in White. One in the background wore something elaborate on his head.

Haven't I completed my destiny, Jan asked? I took the
woman home.

No, that was only part of your purpose, they replied, turning
him back.

But how can I survive this?

The Figures smiled.

Who are you?

The light, the music, the Figures in White, to his disappointment, withdrew and he descended again.

He found himself back in his body with two inches of clearance choking and gasping and wondering why, again, he had been
returned to this veil of tears. He had no idea what had happened
until his wide eyes settled on the window.

It no longer existed. The bars had been blown into a tangle
by a *Sangley* cannonball.

A dazed Jan squeezed through the hole and into the agitated
stream. Above on the ramparts, arquebuses *cracked* and cannons
breathed death and destruction on the Parian. He was relieved
that the swirling smoke helped hide him because the rain had
paused. Floating fifty yards ahead was the *Sangley's* body.

Jan knew he must look just as dead in order to live. Scrap-
ing mud from the side of the ramparts, he rubbed it over his

face and into his hair, then eased out into the stream. Concussions from the Spanish cannons were deafening, and shots from the Chinese whizzed overhead and splashed around him. Water slapped his face as he bounced into the No Man's Land where sea clashed with river. Jan kicked with all his might to stay afloat as he bounced through the whitecaps. Then he reached the calmer current beyond which carried him far out into the darkened bay.

Before him rose the magenta glow of the Manila Bay sunset. Behind, the flash and roar of battle receded. The entire Parian was aflame, its reflection dancing against the walls of Fort Santiago.

A new terror swept into his mind. He still had to flank the river's riptide-like current and the battle, then swim back to shore, and he was weakening fast. It was all he could do to tread water.

Jan drew in a sharp breath.

Silhouetted against the crimson sky only a hundred feet away lay a Chinese junk. He wouldn't have spotted it except that it was spreading its bat-wing sails. Worse, it had spotted him. The mud had washed off his face! The *Sangleys* would mistake him for a Spaniard who had fallen from the ramparts! The junk bore down on him, sing-songy shouts filling the air. Then the sails folded and the junk stilled feet away. Menacing figures holding torches leaned over the gunwale.

Jan wasn't about to give up without a fight—not after all he'd been through. One thrust a spear in his direction. He brushed it aside and was raising his last burst of energy to curse them and their mothers when a female voice called out.

"John? John Hoogley?"

Jan was thunderstruck. Solina Cruzat leaned over the gunwale, holding her hair aside.

This time Jan gripped the extended gaff hook and allowed himself to be drawn to the vessel's side. With his remaining strength, he pulled himself up a rope ladder before hands dragged him onto deck. He lay panting while the woman knelt beside him. Her face was a slate of fear and concern.

"Pardon, but I happy to see you velly well. We much wolly."

141

Jan looked up at the speaker. A wizened old man placed his hands together and bowed. Long, gray whiskers sprouted from a mole on his cheek.

"Wh . . . who are yoo?"

Solina Cruzat clasped Jan's hands and looked up at the old man with gratitude.

"I *Sangrey* but no can tell you name. Solly—best you no know. I fliend of Missy Cluzat long time, since before she go back to New Spain to meet future husband two galleon before. I tlade in Manila rong time. I lea'n rittle bit Spanish in Manila, rittle bit English in Canton. I see many ploblem like this. Many *Sangrey* clazy. Tlade bad one time, they get angly. Be patient and tlade always get good again." He turned to a more immediate concern. "Where boy?"

"Boy. . . ?" Jan asked while Solina dabbed his forehead with a handkerchief. Then he shook his head. The old man nodded but there was no change in his expression.

"No ploblem. We take you away. Missy Cluzat must go velly soon to Catholic temple. There she be safe from papa who beat her."

Jan brushed her hair aside. Her lip was split. Written on her face was dishonor and disgrace—but also determination. She forced a smile, then looked to the Chinaman.

"We must go quick quick. Solly."

Two young *Sangleys* clambered down into a sampan. Jan staggered to his feet, clutched a rigging line, and turned to the old *Sangley*.

"Can . . . can yoo take me to Canton?"

"Yes, that what Missy Cluzat want—but no can do light away. I wait until after tlouble. When Spanish leady, I tlade my silk. They have to build new Manila Galleon or Manila bloke." His grin squeezed his already narrow eyes. "Plices be velly good."

"What do I doo in the meantime?"

"I take you up coast and leave you where nobody rive, but much water and fluit. We leave you lice. Missy Cluzat bling you weapons so you shoot wild animal. You stay for one, maybe two month before I pick you up. Then we go Canton."

Jan was torn between relief and anxiety. Back to the jungle. But the old man had said that there were no cannibals or head-hunters.

Solina turned to the old man and spoke with a heavy voice. Her eyes were wet as they turned back to Jan.

"She ask if anything else she can do for you."

". . . Can she take a letter for me? And give it to the Irish-man—Tom O'Reilly—aboard the *Coopenhagen*?"

The *Sangley* translated it into sing-songy Spanish.

"*Sí*"

The Chinaman placed his hands together and bowed again. "Be velly fast. I send for wliting box."

A minion disappeared below, returning seconds later with a black lacquer container. He set it on the deck before Jan, who dropped to his knees and stared at the beautiful box in confusion. The ancient mariner prepared it for him. Jan dipped the brush into the ink jar. Drops dripped onto rice paper while he collected his thoughts—then he began to write in Dutch.

Solina glided to the gunwale where she stared at the raging battle. Sparks danced high above the conflagration in the Parian. The *Sangley* cannon had been silenced, but the Spanish guns continued to pound the quarter, their distant sound indistinguishable from thunder still rolling across the sky.

"I'm doon," Jan said.

The Chinaman blotted it, then folded the letter in thicker paper, tied it with string, and secured it with chopped sealing wax. Then he passed the envelope to Jan. His hand trembled as he wrote:

Guert Van Larmancaller
New York

Knowing how fragile the chance was the communiqué would arrive, he passed it to the old *Sangley* like it was a butterfly. He bowed, then shuffled to Solina Cruzat. She slipped it into a pocket, then reached down into the shadows. There was the clatter of metal as she picked up something. The Dutchman staggered to his feet as she glided toward him with a sword, dagger, a pistol with a powder horn and a bag of shot.

"This is my father's best sword," she said in Spanish.

It was an ornate ceremonial weapon with the most beautiful worked belt he had ever seen. He slipped the glistening blade a few inches out of the filigreed scabbard. The qualities of Toledo steel were legendary. The viceroy would be furious to discover it missing. Jan didn't know what to say.

A tear trickled down her cheek. Jan felt a rising tide of emotion as she reached for his hand and guided it to her round belly. Her lips trembled.

"T . . . thank you. You're the bravest, finest, most beautiful man I have ever met, and I wish to God that you were Spanish because I would love and care for you forever. If . . . if God grants me a son"—she pointed from her belly to Jan—"I will name him Juan, after you, John. It is really you who gave him life—more than my husband who was an arrogant simp my father forced upon me." Her lips tightened. "No one will force me to do anything against my will ever again. . . ."

She trailed off, knowing Jan couldn't understand, and that the *Sangley* translator had retreated beyond earshot out of respect. A tear rolled down her other cheek as she pulled away.

Jan's own eyes brimmed. He did understand that she planned to name the baby after him and was deeply moved. "Thank you."

Her face knotted as she turned and hurried away. She stepped down into the sampan and signaled to move off. They were sculling away when Jan remembered that she didn't know his real name! He was about to call but checked himself. It wouldn't matter. John. Jan. Juan. They were all the same anyway.

Their eyes held until the sampan dissolved into the darkness and the sad song of her sobs was swallowed by the night. Then he turned away, his eyes flooding, toward the last, faint glow of the sunset over Manila Bay.

He whispered a prayer to the Figures in White asking that she be well taken care of. He whispered another prayer asking that the letter arrive.

15 The Mailbox

Liana squeezed water out of her hair. She was wrung dry herself, ready to hang up her fins and return to her first passion, photography. It was one, she noted, that had evaporated as she had dived deeper into the watery world of treasure hunting.

Chase flopped down on deck, too tired to unscrew his regulator. He was thinking it was time he called the magazine and told them he was ready to go back on assignment.

The deck was covered with broken coral. Ben, in his familiar lawnchair fingering the piece-of-eight, stifled a cough and stared off at a Batak fishing *banca* far beyond the reef. His dream of discovering a last treasure seemed as distant. Batuta looked pleased. Agila, atop the bridge, looked as sharp-eyed as ever.

"Darn," was all Dr. Quinn could say. The anthropologist had taken only two days off to recover from his beating before gearing up and taking his shift down in the watery mines.

It had been two weeks of anxiety, knowing seven armed terrorists lurked beyond the promontory. It was an anxiety not eased knowing that vigilant and vengeful Batak were positioned atop it. Two weeks of not knowing if Earthquake had betrayed them. Two weeks of working the airlift and underwater jackhammer and chainsaw. Two weeks of nerve-shredding noise from the compressor and engine. Two weeks of lugging anchors, eating Ben's cooking, and twenty-four hour watches. Two weeks of drilling holes all over Site One until the cannons and ballast lay exposed. Two weeks of Batuta's escalating smugness. Two weeks of exhausting work and, in Ben's words, salty friggin' all. If they had the mailbox, they could have done the same amount of work in two days.

"Why aren't we finding anything?" Chase muttered.

Ben Gordon let out a long wheeze. It was time to acknowledge his mistakes. He knew they hadn't done enough research—hell's bells, they hadn't done *any* research to determine if the wreck was even listed with the House of Trade! Every booger in the business knows that the first step is to wait until word is in from Seville!

But he knew thet his young partners had ants in their pants, and he didn't want to step on 'em. Worse, he knew that the old pro himself had been grasping for golden straws—hoping he could finger treasure one last time before his turn came to cross the bar. His breathing was becoming more difficult. He knew what it was. He didn't need any bloody Dr. Mengele to tell him. But if thet last feel came from a Manila Galleon, he would die with a smile.

He hadn't been a proper mentor to his partners—but in the time left, he resolved to do his best by them. He sucked on his unlit pipe and concentrated. Most disturbing was the evidence—or rather the lack thereof. Incidental finds were few—too few—and right from the beginning on Site Two. Ben knew why, but he had been in denial. But that wasn't the only problem.

What little evidence they had indicated that the wreck on Site One was *not* Spanish after all! Pewter and more cutlery had been found—this time with English hallmarks. There were also too many English bottles to be coincidental.

But why—*why*—the overwhelming Catholic evidence to the contrary?

Although seventy percent of the guns were Spanish, why did the rest bear *only* the British broad arrow mark? The Spaniards didn't win many battles with the canny English. It would be unusual for the Iberians to carry so many seized, or even purchased, British guns. Not so the English carrying Spanish.

But most telling was the pattern of ballast and cannons he had drawn. The site below clearly indicated it had a single gun deck like many fast British warships—unlike Site Two which left a pattern of a tri-level galleon. It even had half its cannons on the ballast—something common in the Carib. Why it contained British artifacts, he couldn't explain, but it was time to face reality. To announce that they had failed, that the wreck below them was Limey. To announce why the wrecks gave up so few artifacts . . .

why Site One, if it was the Spanish ship, had cannons in that *banca* outrigger pattern. . . .

Ben pocketed the piece-of-eight and cleared his throat. The action turned into a wracking cough, one of his worst. His partners pretended they didn't hear, a polite conspiracy. When it had died down, he made another gasping attempt to speak—but Batuta raised a finger. His ear was to the sky. A hum wavered in with the breeze, turning into a drone. Ben's barnacled eardrums were the last to hear the approaching plane. It was not without relief that he had been granted a reprieve.

"Somewhere in the clouds over Palawan," Batuta said.

Chase cocked his ear. "I think it's Earthquake. But why would he be coming from that direction?"

Batuta and Agila gripped their Kalashnikovs while the crew stood poised to draw tarps. The Cessna burst out of the river mouth and banked toward them. Seconds later, everyone ducked as it roared overhead. An empty beer can clattered into the bottom of the *banca*.

"That answers your question," Liana said sarcastically.

The float plane circled and landed. The crew tried to affect a casual attitude as the prop fluttered to a stop, and Earthquake eased his hulk onto the pontoon and threw a line to Quinn. The dive ladder screeched as the monstrous pilot hoisted himself aboard and grinned. His smile dissolved when he saw their grim expressions.

"Y'all don't appreciate a li'l humor, huh?" Spotting Batuta, his face lit up, but his outstretched mitt was met with a cold look. "Anyway, I brought grub, thet case of rockets and the launch assembly, and a case of beer. I also have mail." He waggled a fat thumb over his shoulder in the direction of the plane. "How's your fuel holdin' out?"

"Still have a drum of diesel, thanks," Quinn replied, trying to downplay his partners' wariness. "But we're low on gas for the compressor and the Zodiac . . . however I don't think we'll need more."

". . . Don't look so good, huh?" Earthquake cast an appraising eye over the deck. "Anyway, if you need anything, gimme a call. Now, how about offloadin' thet trash. I gotta fug off after a Mig. Hafta haul some Frenchies down to Boracay to burn their warts off on the beach."

Quinn climbed into the cockpit and passed a twenty-four-pack of San Miguel beer down to Chase on the pontoon, who set it on the deck. It had already been opened and two cans were missing. Earthquake pulled out a third, popped the tab, and tossed it into the drink.

"Loose Shoes!" Earthquake boomed the Air America toast, raising his beer to Agila who studied the enormous pilot in awe.

Liana turned away in disgust. McGoon took a long pull, then squeezed himself into a lawnchair, and began littering the deck with peanut shells while Quinn and Chase ferried supplies aboard the *Wracker*. The anthropologist carried the correspondence as he and Chase climbed back aboard the boat. Quinn dropped the papers on the work bench, and threw back the lid to the metal box containing the M203s. He looked up at Earthquake. "One's missing."

"Really? Thet's all there was." Then Earthquake grinned. "You don't need 'em all anyhow. Whadya think Abu Sayyef are anyway? A fuggin' army?"

"Very funny," Dr. Quinn said as he lugged the rocket case into the cabin. He returned and attached the launch assembly to his M-16.

Earthquake sighed and lifted his elephantine frame onto his flip-flops, crushed the empty aluminum can against his head, and tossed it into the sea. The Bobbsey's Twins' lips tightened but they said nothing. The pilot bent over, half mooning them as he scooped out another two cans. "I was hopin' to enjoy a Mig with y'all," he said as he jiggled toward the dive ladder, "but I've been to happier funerals."

The crew relaxed only when the Cessna finally rose into the air. The lawnchair Earthquake had been sitting in looked like a work by Picasso.

"Your friend seemed in a hur-ry to leave," Batuta said while Liana used a gaff hook to retrieve the floating beer can.

"We didn't exactly lay oot a welcome mat," Quinn said as he picked up the mail. "What do we have here? Three couri-ered envelopes for Barnacle Ben, and a letter for you, Chase. Sorry, Bag Lady—nothing. But don't be hurt, no one loves me either."

Ben trembled on his glasses and leaned back, checking the return address on one. "This is from London about the pipes," he said without enthusiasm. Announcing the end could wait until after mail.

"Not that it'll help," Chase mumbled. His letter had been sent to him in care of the *LA Times* and forwarded to his address in New York, where his old girl friend had sent it on to Quinn's. He checked the return.

C. Larman. He recognized neither the name nor the Palm Springs address. No doubt another one of the letters he received whenever an article was published. It could wait. He set it aside.

Ben stretched his arm out to read the return on a second envelope. "It's from Jose's widow, Maria!" He clawed it open. A typewritten note was stapled to a Xerox of an old chart, and that to another Xerox of typing. "She found copies of some of Jose's notes. Here's a chart showin' both wrecks."

"*What*! May I see them, please?" Dr. Quinn asked.

Chase and Liana sandwiched the Canuck as their eyes roamed across the chart. The date '1704' was quilled in a flowery hand.

"Oh, my gawd," Liana whispered as she gripped Chase's arm.

It clearly marked the ship they had been diving on as *British*.

It just as clearly marked the other at Site Two as *Spanish*!

Quinn's face lit up as he speed read the final page, then he handed them to the writer and broke away. Liana's shoulder touched Chase's as they read.

"It's part of Jose's summary," Quinn cheered, "of a Board of Inquiry called to investigate the sinking! *And it was a Manila Galleon*! It was called the *Santa Maria de la Immaculate Concepcion*! They should have called it the *Misconcepcion* for all the trouble we've had! What else, Chase!"

"Jose says it went down June 24, 1704 in a typhoon following a battle with a British privateer! There were two survivors. One was an Ignacio del Atagar, and the other a Solina Cruzat, the daughter of the viceroy, interestingly enough."

"My gawd—her father headed the inquiry!"

"Right! And the privateer also went down in the storm. They testified that they—listen to this—forced the Spanish to *exchange* ships because the British vessel took such a beating!"

"And *both* were blown *here*!" Liana shrieked. "*That* explains why the cannons were spiked! And it explains the religious items

149

here too! On the galleon, it explains the gold Crown and the English pipes!"

"And there was only one survivor from the privateer—a young unidentified Dutchman."

Ben ripped his third envelope open. "It's the wood analysis with corroboration. Site One is English elm and oak, and Two is teak."

"This is *fabulous*! We know *conclusively* that the other ship is the Manila Galleon!"

Ben finally ripped open his first envelope, and his jaw dropped. "Them clay pipes tell us the name of one of the privateers! They was custom manufactured in 1703 at, uh"—he stretched the letter out to arm's length—"Stanley Perkins and Sons in Liverpool fer a John Hogley . . . no . . . *Hoogley*. He listed his address as a ship named the . . . the *Raid*."

"My gawd—we have the names of *both* ships!"

"The latest Perkins takes a keen interest in his family's company's history and tracked the *Raid* down in Lloyd's of London's archives! A Dennis Seagrave and this Hoogley fellow purchased it in Liverpool in January 1703. They, uh, refitted the booger, obtained a privateering license, and sailed in June. It was reported callin' in at New York fer an endorsement of their Letter of Marque, then sailed 'apparently' fer the Caribbean." He looked up and pushed his glasses up onto his bald pate. "The booger was never heard from again!"

The crew looked stunned. Batuta stared tight lipped out to sea.

"Does it say how the woman survived, Chase?" Liana asked.

While he and Liana huddled reading, Ben stared at the chart dangling from the writer's hand and sobered. It confirmed to him why further search would be in vain. They would have to be told . . . but not right now. They had ants in their pants again. Hell's bells—he might even let them dive a few more days! Let them hang onto their dream a while longer. Let him hang on to his.

". . . No, there's no mention," Chase said, his finger running down the page. It stopped. "Wait! Listen to this! Jose says it was a Manila bound galleon 'laden with pesos.' Ben, how many did you say that Manila Galleon in 1597 carried?"

150

"12,000,000," he replied with a forced smile.

Liana shrieked and flew into Chase's arms. He pirouetted with her before returning to the letter. "The rest is missing," he said, flipping over the page and seeing only air.

"Who cares!" Dr. Quinn cheered. "We know where the galleon is!"

". . . Ben," Chase said, becoming aware of the treasure hunter's lack of enthusiasm. "What's the matter?"

"Oh, I . . . I jist wish thet there was more paperwork. Jose always did separate reports on each set of documents—and a Master Report summarizing everything." He forced another smile and took the papers from Chase. "This is the best bloody chart I've seen in years of diving! I'd suggest we start airliftin' the livin' crap out of the *Concepcion* as soon as possible, pardon my French!" Knowing his display of enthusiasm wasn't convincing, he added, "All this reminds me of Jose. . . ."

Chase nodded with sympathy.

"I'll radio Earthquake to fly in more fuel eh?" Quinn said, hurrying toward the companionway. "We'll start on it tomorrow morning!"

Liana snapped open beers and passed them around. Agila reached down to accept the strange coconut container and took a sip. He made a face and set it aside. Batuta, with an irritated wave, was the only one to refuse.

"Chase, aren't you going to read your letter?"

"Huh? Oh, yeah. Thanks Liana."

He sat on a box and ripped it open. There were four sheets, one a newspaper clipping. He guessed right. It was from a reader.

"Hey, Bag Lady!" She paused from combing her flaming tresses out. "It's from someone who read our Hansel and Gretel yarn!" He held up the tearsheet. It fluttered in the breeze, the picture of the two heads figuring prominently.

"Great!" She sidled next to him, bent her head between her knees, and continued brushing while he sorted through the papers. One was a Xeroxed letter. From the archaic handwriting, the original was centuries old, and a brush had been used instead of a quill. Ink drops stained the paper. The language belonged to one of the Germanic tongues. On a page beneath was a translation. Puzzled, he set them aside, pushed his sun

streaked hair away from his eyes, and skimmed the monogrammed cover letter. His tanned face drained.

"What's the matter?" Liana asked, setting the hairbrush aside.

Chase shoved the letter into her hands. She looked at him,
then at the page. Her green eyes broadened as they rolled down
the lines.

Dear Mr. Ballantyne,

I was extremely intrigued by your article. I have
reason to suspect—however vaguely—that the
young man in the picture was an early relation. My
suspicions have partly to do with the enclosed letter
(actually a Xerox; the original I have passed down to
my eldest son) which has been in my family for generations.

It was mailed by the brother of my ancestor
Guert Van Larmancaller (by the mid-1700s, the
name was anglicized to its present form). Guert was
a prosperous developer in New York in the early
1700s and married to a Margaretje de Peyster from
another family of prominent builders. They had only
one child, a son named Jan. I'm ten generations
down. He was named after his uncle Jan who left
New York to go to sea as a boy.

I'm particularly intrigued because the features of
the "boy in the bottle" bear a startling resemblance
to early portraits of family members, especially
Guert's and Margaretje's son. I'll bet if his eyes were
open, they would be blue.

Chase and Liana looked at each other, experiencing déjà vu.
Then they dove back into the letter.

Most arresting is the tattoo on his forehead. Your
article speculated that it looks like a 'pirate treasure
map.' I have reason to believe that this is the case—
though the treasure is of dubious value. Like you, I'm
hypothesizing that he applied the tattoo as a communication—knowing his head would be preserved.

It may be mere coincidence, but this fits with the enclosed, enigmatic letter Jan mailed to Guert from the Philippines. It's written in old Dutch which I had translated, and which is enclosed.

That the heads in the jars are from the Philippines also raises my suspicions (and, I might say, excitement).

If you have information connecting the two, I'd very much appreciate your informing me. My private phone number is on the masthead. This has been <u>the</u> family mystery for three centuries.

Most sincerely yours,
Conrad Larman

Chase's head jerked back like he'd been hit by Mike Tyson.

"What's the matter?" Liana asked.

"Do you know who Conrad Larman *is*?" Chase hadn't considered that the 'C' stood for Conrad.

". . . It sounds familiar."

The radio spat static as Quinn brought Earthquake up.

"Conrad Larman is—*was*, he's retired—one of the biggest property developers in the States! You're heard of The Larman Museum, certainly?"

"Of course!" Situated off Rodeo Drive and dedicated to Mesoamerican culture, it was becoming one of the most controversial museums in the world. Part of it was due to its vast acquisition budget.

"He's *the* Larman! He now devotes his life to his first love—archaeology!"

"Really!" They plunged into the translated letter from the young man named Jan Van Larmancaller.

Spanish Philippines
June 1704

My Dear Brother Guert,

I have little time and my adventures are too many to tell. The *Raid* took a Manila Galleon. We trans-

153

ferred to the Spanish ship because ours was sinking but struck a reef. I was the only survivor from the crew.

I hid something many leagues distance from Manila that is worthless but which the Dons consider to be of value. I don't dare reveal what or where it is because this letter might be opened. But remember my favorite stew? It's in a cave in the left foot. Somehow I will send the rest of the map.

I am very homesick. Especially give my love to Margaretje and the child.

Your loving brother,
Jan

"This is *incredible*! Look at the date! *He* was on the *Raid*! And we know a young Dutchman survived the shipwreck!"

The déjà vu built.

"Earthquake says he has a break in bookings the day after tomorrow," Quinn said, descending to the deck. He raised his beer but stopped it half way to his lips. "What's with you two?"

"Ben! You remember!" Chase exclaimed, already on his feet, Liana at his side. They blurted out the story of the heads in the Trophy Room. "It's possible *that* boy was on the *Raid*!" Chase shoved the papers into the old treasure hunter's gnarled hands.

Ben's eyes lit up. While he shuffled through the sheets, Quinn set his beer aside and looked over the old man's shoulder. Batuta stared out to sea with even tighter lips. Agila never stopped eying the point.

"We should look into this, worthless or not!" the old man said.

"Absolutely!" Chase exclaimed.

"We need a break anyway," Liana agreed, "and a change is as good as a rest. Quinn?"

"Say no more, eh!" Quinn grinned. "'Remember my favorite stew?' 'It's in a cave in the left foot.' And Earthquake thinks *I* have stupid codes! What the heck could it mean?"

Liana snapped her fingers and ran down into the hold. There was the sound of rummaging, then her red locks flared up through the hatch. She held a hand mirror. Taking the newspaper article from Ben, she spread it out on the work bench and placed the mirror above the pickled head's forehead.

The tattooed image reversed.

"This could be a map of this very coast!" she exclaimed.

Seconds later Quinn spread out their British Admiralty Chart with the newspaper clipping and mirror on top while the crew crowded around.

". . . There's superficial similarities," Ben coughed as he traced his bent finger along the map's coastline, "like this deep lagoon, but thet's jist about it." He raised his head. The lagoon cut inland a quarter of a mile away.

"Just a minute!" Chase said. "Ben, hand me that 1704 chart."

The writer laid the newspaper picture above it and applied the mirror. They sucked in their breaths as one.

"My gawd! It's a perfect match! The coast has *changed* in 300 years!"

"That's right," Chase grinned. "Just like in the jar cave! An earthquake, and I don't mean McGoon. Jan Van Larmancaller started drawing his map at this lagoon and continued as he traveled up island!"

"But where does this arrow point to?" Liana asked. "The one with the '6 zeemijlen?'"

They turned to Batuta, still looking stonily out to sea. Chase fought down excitement as he sidled up to him and pointed.

"Uh, Batuta, that lagoon. What's up there?"

"A river, Mr. Ballentyne," he spat. "An underground river."

* * *

"Chase, I'm having second thoughts about leaving the *Wracker*," Liana called from the *banca's* bow as it skimmed over the surface of the lagoon. "What if the Beagle Boys return?"

The Batak *banca* glided toward a limestone cliff at the head of the lagoon. The mouth of the underground river was hidden behind foliage, but a gentle current told them it was there. Batuta had no idea how far back it extended as it, too, was hallowed.

"My dear Bag Lady, relax. They haven't been seen in two

weeks. And even if their Muslim brains are addled from beating them on the ground five times a day, they're not stupid enough to try anything on a clear morning—especially since they know we have the M60. If anything goes down, they can take care of it."

"Sorry, you're right." He certainly was last night when she had smoked one of Quinn's joints, which always acted as an aphrodesiac on her, and he had done just that on her. He was so good she was having second thoughts about her *We'll Sing in the Sunshine* philosophy. She pushed her wet thoughts aside as the *banca* glided under branches and they beheld the entrance.

It was thirty feet across with stalectites hanging almost to the water in places. Liana shipped her paddle and hung onto a bough while Chase reached into his safari shirt for a lighter. Gas burped into a Coleman lamp. He switched on the GPS as the *banca* slipped inside. Stark light from the lamp burst against gray, limestone walls. After paddling a hundred feet, Chase checked the GPS. "We're looking at three hours!"

"We better get going then."

The cave initially meandered, opening into some huge galleries, before straightening, often with long cracks running the length of the ceiling.

"Looks like a fault line," Liana said. Her voice sounded eerie and hollow.

The heightened hiss of lamp and drip and dip of paddle was joined by the occasional plink of water from stalactites. Time became timeless in the magnificent monotony.

". . . Liana, that destiny thing we talked about. You experienced déjà vu too when we read Larman's letter, didn't you?"

"Yes! What a coincidence."

"Yeah, that's all it could be. Interesting though."

Their emotions were transported by the moody mystery of the underground river, and they fell back on their own thoughts. Chase's turned to the difficulty he was going to have parting, when it came time. But part they must. It couldn't work out.

When he next checked the GPS, he did a double take. They had paddled for three hours without thought of rest, and it had seemed like twenty minutes. The realization was unsettling. thought that he hadn't noticed unsettled him.

"The GPS says we're there," he whispered, aware of the awe in his voice.

"I suppose we should be watching for some kind of 'foot.' And why are we whispering?"

They laughed, and paddled on, senses sharpened.

"Hey, we're coming up to something, Chase!"

The light at the edge of their lamp's reach flickered against an obstacle in their path. It was another few paddle strokes before they recognized it as a great, natural column dividing the flow, and that the cave had widened into a massive cavern. Chase guided the dugout to the port side of the column.

"Look!" Liana gasped. She pointed to the left. Above a low, dry shelf that drew back several yards from the water's edge were black markings on the wall. Chase held the *banca* stationary in the stream while Liana grappled for her flashlight.

Three, foot high black initials in old fashioned script with a date punched them in the eyes: J.V.L. 1704

"Oh, my gawd! *Jan . . . Van . . . Larmancaller!*"

Chase dug his paddle into the water and the outrigger crunched against the ledge. Grabbing her camera, Liana scrambled out and held the boat while Chase jumped out and secured the line to a fallen stalactite. As he untied the Coleman lamp, Liana sprayed the beam of her flashlight against the limestone.

"He used torch smoke to write!"

Chase held up the hissing lamp. "What are these marks beside his initials?"

". . . Who knows?" Liana said, sweeping her light around the small ledge. "Let's find whatever he hid."

But like Mother Hubbard's cupboard, the ledge was bare.

"It must have been washed off," Chase said. "The ledge was high and dry all year when Jan was here, but not during today's monsoons."

The high water mark formed a line just below the initials.

"Maybe we're not the first to be here since Jan." Liana shone her flashlight into the steely flow but the beam only penetrated inches. "We could bring tanks, underwater lights and ropes, but I wonder if we should bother. He said it was worthless anyway."

"Just a minute!" Chase said, moving back to the wall and raising the lamp again. "Remember the part in Jan's letter about his 'favorite stew?' This looks like a *rabbit's footprint in snow!* They would have been common in Manhattan's forests in Jan's day! That might explain the left foot!"

They stared at each other, then back at the smoked markings.

"Ridiculous as it sounds, I think you're right. But how does that help us?"

A heavy drip of water somewhere in the tunnel echoed.

"The map on his forehead only provides the first clue to where the thing is! This is a cave alright—but it's *not* the cave he hid whatever he had. We just have to figure out where that one is! There has to be . . . hills . . . or something nearby shaped like a rabbit's foot! There's caves everywhere here!"

"Makes sense. I'll shoot pictures, then we better get back. I still don't like being away this long."

Flashes beat against the walls of the cavern, then they clambered back into the *banca*. They took one last look at the initials and the rabbit's foot smudged on the wall, wondering when next it would see the light of lamp. Then they dug their paddles into the stream, hoping they would find the *Wracker* and its caretakers in good health.

* * *

They did, though they worried about their own health when Ben greeted them with cold liver and onions fried in rancid butter. The look on Batuta's face was no more appetizing.

"So you say we have another mystery, do we?" Ben coughed as he used coral to weigh down the corners of a topographic map of Palawan. "If there's a rabbit's foot pattern to the hills, we should be able to find it! It would have to be close to the coast."

In a short time their faces lengthened.

"Nothing here I can see," Chase said.

Gloom descended. Batuta strode over and glanced at the map.

"Did I hear right?" he asked with acid in his voice. "You are looking for a rabbit's foot pattern?"

They looked at him. It wasn't often he offered anything.

"There," he said, waving his hand out to sea. It had chopped up and heavy swells rolled over the outer reef. "Just off the underground river."

They stared in confusion. There was nothing but the tiny island with the sprig of coconut trees. Then Chase's face opened and he removed the topographic map revealing the Admiralty Chart.

He slammed his finger down on a group of shoals beside the island.

"Batuta's right! They fit the pattern! That little island is the *rabbit's left foot.*"

While Batuta slouched back to the shade, Chase ranged through the charts until he came to the one from 1704. No sooner had he spread it out than all four treasure hunters sucked in their breaths again.

The shoals were marked as *islands.*

"It's those earthquakes again!" Chase said. "The islands did an Atlantis!"

They squinted at the sprig of coconuts rising from the azure sea.

". . . Treasure Island," Liana whispered.

16 Marooned

Jan cursed.

A full month he had been beached on Luzon's forehead and what were the first sails he sees? Not the bat-wings of the junk that was supposed to carry him to Canton—but rather the squared canvas of a small galleon! Worse, a longboat was being lowered!

He looked behind him. Scruffily jungled coastal flats stretched back a dozen miles before sweeping up the mile high Cordillera Mountains. Cutting into them was a prominent canyon, which was why the old *Sangley* had chosen this spot to maroon him. A landmark. Had he been betrayed?

Jan scrambled back from the scrub bordering the broad beach and sprinted to his palm frond bivouac. Sweeping together the Toledo sword, dagger and flintlock Solina Cruzat had given him, along with a bag of dried fish and rice, he ran inland, his destination an inactive volcanic vent cone 200 yards away. By the time he had slipped and slid up the rear of the cindered slope, the longboat was butting onto the beach.

Jan cursed again.

It was exactly where the *Sangleys* had dropped him off! He could see his camp, just inside the fringe of scrubby jungle. Two groups spilled onto the beach. One consisted of a dozen Filipino coolies. A beam of sunlight breaking through clouds glinted off chest plates and helmets of a half dozen soldiers. Something leaped out of the boat, and Jan felt a shiver down his spine.

Bloodhounds. Two.

A second, colder shudder followed. One figure—clearly in command—gripped his attention. He had a long, yellow beard and hair and was robed in black.

The Jesuit—Father Ignacio del Atagar!

The Chinaman *had* to have betrayed him! His hand drifted to his coconut shell necklace as coolies hoisted a chest out of the boat that looked like the strongbox he had hidden! Had the Spaniards discovered the letter destined for Guert? Had Solina Cruzat been feigning unconsciousness when he had buried the chest? Had she been forced to betray him?

Distant yelping announced the discovery of his camp. Jan cursed yet again—in his haste, he had forgotten his silk britches! Jan skidded, tripped and rolled his way to the cone's base, tearing the more practical floppy blue garments the *Sangley* had given him. He started this way, then that, as he tried to decide which way to go. Then he looked up at the cloud encircled Cordillera. The head of the canyon, like the inner bow of a ship, offered a natural route up to the plateau. Jan struck off, fighting panic, planning strategy. The first thing he had to do was lose the dogs.

He tacked to his left and charged through thin jungle toward the brook watering his camp. Scrambling upstream, slipping, sliding and falling again and again, he managed a hundred yards before the yelps grew louder. Then he crossed over to the other bank and ran inland along an animal path.

Five minutes later the bloodhounds ran up to the edge of the stream where Jan had entered and sniffed around. It was another minute before the Spanish expedition caught up and halted. A sergeant pointed at Jan's footprints disappearing into the water.

The man in black, lost in thought, fingered Jan's britches. Then he tossed them aside and waved his men forward. The soldiers continued their march inland, ignoring Jan's route.

* * *

It was noon the next day before an exhausted Jan dragged himself onto the plateau. He lay gasping until the cold of the altitude made him shiver. The sky had cleared but for a few cumulus clouds. He looked back along his steep route. He knew the Spaniards were still on his trail. From his camp half way up the night before, he had spotted their campfires between the valley's bulwarks. So worried was he that he hadn't been able to sleep until deep into the night—and when he had woken, the sun had been up at least two hours. To his horror, their thin line wasn't far behind.

Jan staggered to his feet to take his bearings and was startled by a familiar sound from Manhattan's forests—the whisper of wind through pines. He stood at the edge of an evergreen forest. He took a step forward—then stopped. Before him was a small, hard packed clearing. Three footpaths led from it—two in either direction along the plateau's lip, really a cliff except for this spot, and the third inland. The site was a lookout! Cannibals might have witnessed his ascent!

After melting into the forest, he loaded his pistol, then paralleled the trail leading inland. Jan stalked it for a mile as it wound over rough terrain until he came to a large clearing. Taking a chance, he scurried across it. When he had proceded into the forest beyond a hundred feet, he heard a muffled cry and a bumblebee whizzing past his head. Jan dove behind a pine tree, fanning his pistol. The cry was repeated—issuing from a bush on a low rise. A huge, reptilian tail flicked out from behind it, then disappeared. An instant later, snake and prey tumbled into view.

To Jan's horror, a native was in the grip of an enormous python.

Rushing forward, Jan aimed at the serpent's wavering head. The loud shot was wasted—he missed! Throwing the pistol aside, Jan whipped out his sword. Four feet of curling tail sought a grip on a brown leg. The Toledo steel sliced through it with ease.

The reptile reacted by uncoiling and striking at Jan. He slashed blindly—and the snake's head flew over his shoulder, leaving its body writhing. The terrified native crabbed backward and slapped his scabbard, but his machete had fallen out. The native was certain he had been spared from the constrictor only so his head could be taken. He stared at Jan's long, glistening machete in awe.

While Jan retrieved his flintlock, he kept a wary eye on the man. Naked but for swirling tattoos and a red, striped loincloth that reached his knees, he was a few years older than Jan, well built and handsome, despite a haircut that looked like the

162

barber had used a bowl as a template. Jan didn't know what to do with him. He only knew that he needed a friend desperately—even a cannibal.

Seeing the native's weapons behind the bush, Jan picked them up and passed them to him. So dumbfounded was the young man that Jan had to urge them onto him. With wonder, the native stood and gripped the proffered spear and machete. As Jan stooped to pick up his longbow, he realized that hadn't been a bee flying by—it had been an arrow. Just the same, Jan passed the bewildered man the weapon.

Scooping up the man's ornate headdress—made with a plume of feathers and a monkey skull—Jan held it out. The native's eyes registered continuing confusion as he fitted it over his head.

"I . . . am . . . Jan," the Dutchman said in Dutch, pointing to himself.

". . . I . . . am . . . Jan."

"No." Jan shook his hand and tapped his chest. "*Jan.*" He pointed at the native and raised his eyebrows, hoping the expression was universal. It was.

"Mansu?" Curiosity seeped into his dark eyes as fear drained away.

A noise on the path hushed them. The native swept up his shield and faded deeper into the underbrush, urging Jan with downward sweeps of his hand to follow. They stole a short distance before crouching and looking back. Thirteen warriors pounded past in the direction of the clearing. Jan noted that the red and blue pattern of their loincloths was different than Mansu's. He also noted that the leading warrior wore a feathered headdress similar to his new friend's, but that the men following sported woven straw skull caps. It dawned on Jan that Mansu was also a leader, and he wondered where his men were.

"Kalinga," Mansu whispered as he nubbed his chin forward. He patted his tattooed chest with pride. "Ifugao!"

Mansu slipped deeper into the forest, Jan on his bare heels. The muscular native padded up the back of a steep hill to the scrubby crest where five rattan backpacks lay. From this height Jan was able to glimpse into the interior, a panorama of rugged mountains and deep, verdant valleys. A league distant, man-made terraces stacked up the side of a valley like a giant's staircase, and still water in the pools shimmered in the sunlight. Jan guessed they were fish ponds.

They elbowed forward to shrubs at the edge of a limestone cliff overlooking the clearing Jan had crossed. There, the Kalinga milled in a state of agitation. Jan realized that his flint-lock had alerted them—they had no doubt been monitoring the Spaniards' progress. He gulped when it occurred to him that they had also probably been following his own.

Jan reloaded while Mansu studied the unfamiliar weapon with derision. If its smoke and thunder couldn't scare a huge snake, how could it frighten Igorots? Never.

Hearing bushes rustle behind them, Jan started if Mansu didn't. A lean, young warrior wearing a simple rattan cap and the same red striped loincloth as Mansu appeared carrying a little girl's head, the stump dripping blood. Jan looked up into a face as shocked as his own. The native let out a small cry and grabbed the headhunting axe in his loincloth—but a harsh whisper and explanation from Mansu stayed his hand. He eyed the pre-pubescent head and his companion with disdain. The newcomer, caught between embarrassment and pride, stowed it in a backpack.

"Dar," Mansu said, indicating the newcomer.

Two more headhunters appeared amidst rustles of bush, followed by the fifth. All were around eighteen, muscular and sported the same haircut—and all were as startled to see Jan as the first. Unlike the first—to the New Yorker's relief—they were empty handed. As Mansu whispered an explanation, their suspicions morphed into incredulity, then a warmth and acceptance that took Jan by surprise. One squatted before him and stared unblinking into Jan's blue eyes. Another wiped his finger across his cheek and looked at it, wondering why the freckles didn't rub off.

Mansu hissed and the men keened to distant barking. The Kalinga grew more restless and fell back to the interior side of the clearing just as the bloodhounds galloped out of the trail opposite. One was felled by an arrow and rolled before lying still. Its companion yelped as another arrow caught it in the flank. A third finished it off.

The Spaniards poured into the clearing moments later. Spotting the Kalinga, the soldiers formed a scrimmage line while the Filipino bearers dropped their packs and huddled behind them. Only a hundred feet separated arquebuses from bows and spears.

The tall, thin figure of Father Ignacio del Atagar strode to the vanguard of his company. So great was Jan's fear and loathing of the man that it was several seconds before it registered that he had changed costumes—and in a most peculiar manner.

Gone was the black robe. In its place, his blond beard cascaded down a shimmering white, silk robe. A crucifix was nowhere to be seen, but in his hand was a staff. But most striking was his headgear. He wore an extravagantly feathered headdress—similar to the one in the strongbox. Towering above the other players, Atagar dominated the field.

17 Treasure Island

In Guinness Book record time, the anchors were raised and the *Wracker* was coughing louder than Ben toward the break in the reef, then north-east. Behind bobbed red floats fastened to airlines to the jackhammer, chainsaw and airlift.

"There's got to be a submerged cave," Chase said.

"Exactly," Quinn said as they closed the distance and the anthropologist eased back on the throttle. "I don't want to get any closer, eh?"

A hundred feet ahead sat the lone island, an equal distance across. Beyond, the sea's watery fingers ran through grassy hair atop three submerged islands, now coral heads. Despite their being on the lee side, the island offered so little protection that the boat rocked. The sea had risen, although the wind was still no more than a breeze, and the sun continued to blast from an untarnished sky. The waves were a hangover from a storm somewhere over the north-east horizon.

"The tide chart says we're within days of the month's low tide," Chase said. "Right now we're a half hour from slack tide."

Taking up binoculars he accidentally drew in Liana's magnificent backside as she leaned over the bow. Sighing, he raised them and refocused on the island. The beach rose at a gentle angle twenty-five feet before meeting vegetation. The foliage at the base of the coconut trees, though sparse, was just thick enough to prevent seeing through.

"Best circle around the island, Quinn," Chase said. He didn't have to say that Abu Sayyef were on his mind.

"There won't be anyone there, eh?"

"Humor me."

"Why would any Beagle Boys be th—"

"Just do it, okay?"

Quinn sighed and eased the throttle forward. The old boat waddled around to the windward side, and Chase tried to scope through the vegetation, to no avail. He moved his magnified circle of vision lower until it was filled with sand. He swept it back and forth—and blinked. He shoved the glasses at Quinn and pointed.

"There on the beach, just up from those boulders. Footprints—and they're sure not Friday's!"

Quinn shifted into neutral and grabbed the binoculars. "You're right."

"Liana! Batuta!" Chase shouted as he climbed up to the machine-gun. "Battle stations! There's someone there!"

While Quinn fought to keep the bow to the island, and waves slopped over the stern, Liana ran back to the sterndeck. Grabbing an M-16, she knelt behind the compressor. Batuta dropped beside her with his Kalashnikov and shouted in Batak. Agila ran just forward of the bridge, his automatic at the ready. Ben picked up an M-16 and fell back in his lawnchair, cursing as he again tried to rack the bolt on the bloody modern contraption.

"Hey, they were probably left by a Batak fisherman having shore lunch," Quinn called up to Chase. He was losing the battle with the waves and the bow was bobbing around, exposing their port side to the island.

"I don't remember seeing any in this area. Let's not take chances."

The *Wracker* shuddered as Chase swept the machine-gun across the tree tops. Fronds exploded and coconuts clumped to the sand. Then all was silent again but for the wash of waves.

". . . Okay, since that didn't wake anyone up—" Chase began—but was cut off by a long, loud burst from an automatic on the island slamming slugs into the bridge and cobwebbing the bridge's side window. Quinn ducked while the crew reacted—delivering a broadside that ripped the foliage to pieces, chewed bark off trees, and kicked up sand geysers. By the time their guns fell silent, magazines spent, their ears were ringing and only the crash of palm fronds issued from the island. The trees looked like they were from the Ypres Salient.

167

"That should have sent Friday well into next week," Chase called as he raised his binocs. ". . . But what's left of the vegetation's still thick enough that I can't see a body, or bodies." He fed a fresh ammo belt into the M60 as he looked around for Liana, only relaxing when their eyes locked. Ben was having a coughing fit, having given up on the M-16. Chase was about to ask after Batuta and Agila when Quinn bellowed.

"The gas drum! Get it off the boat!"

The fifty-five gallon barrel was spouting diesel from several bullet holes. Batuta and Liana threw aside their weapons and rushed to it. They pushed it onto its side, then rolled it over the edge. It hit the water with a great splash and disappeared, leaving widening rainbow patterns. Batuta sloshed pails of water across the deck while Liana mopped.

"Great, now we're a floating Presto log," Chase muttered. The only environment that concerned them right then was the one they stood on. "What's our fuel gauge say, Quinn?"

"Low!" Quinn grabbed the mike. "I'll try to pull up Earthquake . . . . Oh no! A bullet whacked our radio!" He slammed the mike back into its cradle.

A cry from the bow grabbed their attention. It came from Batuta who had gone in search of his colleague. Liana reached Agila a moment after him.

"Oh gawd no. . . ."

Batuta knelt over the sprawled body of the young Batak. He lay face up, a pool of blood widening from his lower back. A round, red hole formed a second belly button beside the original. Agila was still conscious, his bright eyes registering the calm curiosity of shock.

"Get the First Aid Kit!" Liana cried as Ben, having recovered, arrived.

After leaning over the roof's edge to look down on the scene, Chase scrambled down to the deck, while Ben called up to Quinn what had happened. By the time the writer arrived with the kit, Liana and Batuta had just finished gently rolling the young warrior onto his side.

"Oh, my gawd." Torn intestines oozed out of a gaping exit wound. No one had to say that his condition was hopeless.

"I curse the day *I* heard of this treas-ure!" Batuta spat as they bound the wound as best they could.

Conrad's Curse swept through their minds.

"We should take him back to the village," Chase said in a quiet voice.

Batuta nodded, relayed the suggestion to Agila, and was about to rise when the wounded young man gripped his arm. Batuta didn't like what he heard, but nodded again.

"He wants to take the body on the island with us."

Chase nodded, understanding the importance to the young Batak.

"Batuta, I'll go with you to pick him up," Dr. Quinn called. "Chase, take the helm."

"No, stay there," Chase said as he slapped a fresh clip into an M-16 and turned toward the Zodiac. "I'm closer, and you're more experienced with the bridge."

Quinn saw argument was useless. "I better pull over to the lee side first," he said, announcing defeat trying to keep the boat stationary.

"No, Dr. Quinn! Those boulders give us our only cover once we land."

Quinn didn't like it—the sea was getting heavier—but he held their position. "Who's going to ride shotgun in case someone survived that barrage?"

"I will."

Liana climbed to the top of the wheelhouse. Chase jumped into the Zodiac, while Batuta snapped a fresh banana clip into his AK-47 and joined him. Being exposed, Chase approached the boulders as fast as the heavy surf would allow. Reaching the beach, they leaped out and dragged the boat up onto the narrow strip of sand between the boulders and the sea. Chase glanced back at the *Wracker*. Liana wouldn't be any help with the M60 if they ran into trouble—the risk of hitting them would be too great.

"Take that side," Chase said, nodding to the left, then flicked his M-16 onto rock 'n' roll.

Like a panther, the native angled up the sandy incline. Chase cut to the right, slowed by the talcum powder sand. It flashed to him that this is what the marines at Iwo Jima faced. As at Jima, the attack came from the left.

BLAM! BLAM! BLAM!

Chase hit the sand while Batuta dropped to a crouch. Only twenty feet beyond him, a Filipino in camouflage charged from behind the scrub in a bansai attack. His left arm was blown away—but he was wildly firing a Beretta 92F pistol with his remaining hand. Batuta snapped off a three shot burst and the attacker rolled, coming to rest a dozen feet from him.

"Thank gaw—" Chase began—but cut himself off when the terrorist staggered to his knees, pistol still in hand.

Batuta squeezed his trigger—but his rifle didn't respond.

"*Crap!*" Chase shouted. He couldn't shoot—Batuta was between them! Liana didn't dare fire. Leaping to his feet, Chase ran toward them.

The terrorist shakily raised his pistol as Batuta threw his rifle aside and whipped out his machete. Chase knew there was no time for either of them to stop the man.

Two shots rang out.

At the sound of the first—from the handgun—Batuta spun like a dust devil. The next killed the Muslim. Chase glanced back at the *Wracker*. Quinn lowered an M-16.

Batuta was writhing as Chase dropped to his knees beside him.

"Good shot, Mr. Ballentyne!" For once, his eyes were filled with something approaching warmth.

"It was Quinn. Where are you hit?" Chase's eyes swept over the native's muscular body. There was no sign of blood.

"I'm not wound-ed. I, uh . . . tripped."

Behind them, a small outcropping of coral protruded from the sand. Batuta had a sprained sense of pride in addition to a sprained ankle.

Leaving him, Chase crouched up the beach, M-16 at the ready. He peeked through what was left of the foliage, and was relieved that his view was unimpeded across the island. Confetti-like vegetation littered the interior. His grip on the M-16 tightened when he saw the terrorist's blood trail leading to two foxholes. He approached with caution. Supplies filled one. Blood was splattered on the sandy lip of the other, and an AK and an arm lay in it.

Chase shifted his attention to the cache. A walkie-talkie and a spotting scope lay atop a pile of scuba gear and banana clips. Beside it lay a cooler. Chase flicked the top open with his barrel tip.

It was filled with bottled water and rice wrapped in banana leaves, most of the ice having melted. Satisfied, he clicked the safety on his weapon and hurried back to Batuta.

"I didn't have it snapped all the way in," Batuta said sheepishly, holding up his banana clip.

"I'll take you back to the *Wracker* first," he said as he pulled Batuta's arm around his shoulders and hoisted him to his feet. "Then I'll return for the one armed bandit." Remembering the mess Lolo had left, Chase wanted a poncho. The writer limped him to the Zodiac and they bounced out to the mother ship.

"My gawd! How bad is Batuta hit?"

"He's fine. Get the First Aid Kit." Chase helped him aboard and looked up at Quinn. The anthropologist was chalk white as he stared at the island and the man he had killed. "Good shot. Thanks from Batuta."

"D . . . darned lucky shot, but Liana didn't dare try."

Chase called up what he had found while Liana began taping Batuta's ankle. "It looks like after the Beagle Boys failed to ambush us, they went back to their first plan—wait for us to bring up the treasure, then somehow scoop it."

"I think you're right. I *have* to get this darned boat around to the lee side."

"Wait, I have to go back for Friday. Batuta, lend me your poncho."

"I don't think the young feller needs his anymore, Chase," Ben rasped, appearing from the bow.

Batuta looked like he was going to faint. He pushed Liana aside and hopped forward where he lowered himself beside the motionless body of the young Batak. Agila's eyes stared at the sky. He was surrounded by a huge pool of blood.

"Get away from us!" Batuta barked.

Liana and Chase, who had followed, retreated to the sterndeck where Chase leaned against the compressor, his head hanging. Lolo. Now Agila. Bad things come in threes. Who's next? At the sound of Ben hacking, he turned away.

"I . . . I don't want Friday's body aboard," Quinn called as he maneuvered the boat to the lee side. "If Batuta wants it, he can send a *banca* later."

Liana understood Quinn's feelings. "Two dead men over something worthless. Forget it. Let's go back to the Manila Galleon."

"Heck with *that*!" Quinn countered. "I want to find out what I had to kill a man for! What got Agila killed over! *I'll* do the dive."

Chase and Liana stared in surprise at the latest outburst from the normally polite anthropologist.

"What's the point?" Liana argued.

"We should check the booger out." Despite the bloodshed Ben, wiping his mouth after his latest fit, wasn't in a hurry to return to the old site. He knew what they would find. What they wouldn't find. "I'll take the helm, Doc."

Liana rolled her eyes. "Chase—talk sense into them!"

". . . Liana, if we don't find out what it is, it'll nag us for the rest of our lives." Déjà vu was enveloping him again.

She shook her head. ". . . Well, let me gear up with Quinn then. We're losing our slack tide and your ears will slow us down."

"Fair enough."

Ben climbed sloth-like to the bridge while Liana grabbed her red wetsuit off its hook.

"Ben, it's pretty rough, even on the lee side," Quinn said. "The sea's continuing to rise. Best pull off the island a bit."

Ben put it in reverse while Quinn slipped down to the deck and pulled on his yellow wetsuit.

"I suggest we take different levels ten feet apart," Liana said as they cinched weight belts, "with the top diver ten feet down, and circle the island. If we don't find a cave, we'll drop deeper. I'll take the lower position. Should we take the metal detector?"

"Definitely, and don't forget your flashlight," Quinn replied as he flicked on his underwater light and the detector to check them. "Ready?"

With their hands to their masks, they plunged in. Eight feet below the surface swells, the sea was calm. The island dropped steeply and was dressed in a lace slip of coral, embroidered with multi-hued fish. With Liana's bubbles percolating to the right of Quinn, they began to swim counter-clockwise around the island. They had finned a quarter of the way around when Liana rolled onto her back and, with urgent gesticulations, signaled Quinn to join her. He floated down under a parachute of bubbles holding the detector and flashlight in one hand.

Before them yawned a cave eight feet across, the entrance hung with a bead curtain of tiny, silver fish. Quinn fingered the detector's switch, drifting up a little as he did. He looked back at Liana just in time to see her reach out to grasp coral to anchor herself in the rising current. Quinn's reaction was instantaneous. He grabbed her by the hair and yanked her upward. Her hands flew to his and her eyes sprung open. Quinn pointed.

She corkscrewed to see a small Crown of Thorns, effectively invisible among the colorful garble of coral. Picking the starfish up by a toe, Quinn frisbeed it over the edge, where it spun in slow motion into the depths. Then he poked the metal detector into the cave and kicked forward, his flashlight in his other hand.

Thousands of dwarf herring, as if joined by a single nervous system, spread around him like a halo until he passed through, the fish closing behind. Liana was about to follow when Quinn suddenly kicked backward, sending the herring scurrying. Sensing panic, she backpedaled, air bubbles exploding from their regulators blinding them.

A pair of large sharks who had been sleeping in the cave rocketed out, their tails fanning the divers aside, and disappeared into the mist.

A terrified Liana jabbed her thumbs upward, but Quinn made a calming gesture. With his thumb on his BC's charge button, he motioned for her to stay near the relative protection of the coral. As she grappled for the knife on her calf, he blasted air into his vest and rose.

"Bring the boat over!" Quinn shouted after he popped through the surface. Quinn swam out until Barnacle Ben skillfully moved the Wracker alongside him. "We found a cave but it had tenants! Pass the sharksticks. Don't look so worried, Chase. They gave us a bit of a scare but . . . ptwwee . . . they were just harmless reef sharks. But a shark is a shark to Liana. I want to make her feel safe."

Chase quickly loaded two rods and passed them down. Minutes later, a grateful Liana slipped her knife back into its sheath and gripped one of the sharksticks.

Quinn glided inside, stopped, and probed the now empty cave with his flashlight. Liana joined him, her beam peeking this way and that. The cave was round, as if a giant toredo worm had created it, and the tawny sides smooth except for small fan corals. The bottom was flat but for a few juvenile stalagmites. Their beams found the end only thirty feet back and there was nothing in it, worthless or not. Setting his sharkstick aside, Quinn waved the detector's head over the surface. Nothing. He kicked forward and repeated the procedure, being careful not to kick up the fine sediments. Nothing again.

He was almost to the end when he froze. The needle twitched. He waved it over the surface again. Nothing. He finned forward a yard, and his eyes widened as the needle rose. He kicked ahead, sending up a small cloud of silt as a fin flicked the floor. He waved the wand again.

The needle hammered the pin.

Quinn pulled up short, his head banging against the ceiling. Oblivious to the pain, he sank and slowed his sweep until the needle pressed against the pin, refusing to budge.

Liana set her sharkstick aside and pulled up beside him, her light searching out the detector's dial. He heard her squeal in delight.

Setting the detector aside, Quinn slipped his knife out and plunged it into the sand. They were greeted by the unmistakable ding of metal. Trying to temper excitement, they palmed the sand, sending up clouds of sediments. Three inches down, Quinn's hand brushed against something hard. Their flashlights shone onto blackened iron, the surface mottled by corrosion.

Throwing caution to the currents, they dug like badgers, their tanks clanging against the walls. Within seconds, they were blinded by a thick cloud bank. By the time they had finished, the only way they knew that they had excavated an iron chest was by feel.

Quinn's hand sought out a handle but it broke away. He tried to lift the box but was only able to raise one end. Whatever it was, it was too heavy without the handle, even underwater, to pull out by hand.

The anthropologist groped for Liana's arm and signaled to leave. After fumbling blindly for their sharkstick, flashlights and the detector, they banged and scraped their way to the entrance. A thick, dirty cloud drifted like smoke from a window of a house fire, which then was flagged away by the current. Quinn motioned to Liana to stay again, set his flashlight aside, and was about to fire his BC when she grabbed his arm.

A shark, like an apparition, glided out of the mist seventy-five feet away, then disappeared. Quinn showed her his palm again, grabbed his sharkstick, and ascended. He broke through the surface, waving frantically. Worried he was in trouble, Ben gunned the boat over to him.

"*Jackpot!*" Dr. Quinn shouted, taking a mouthful of water when a wave hit him in the face. He hacked out a good chunk of the South China Sea before he was able to continue. "We found a strongbox! It's. . . ." His joy faded when Batuta glared. Subdued, Quinn passed the detector to Chase. "Darned sharks are oot and aboot—*ptwweee*—scaring Liana."

"We better git the lead out, Doc. This bloody chop is as rough as a Havana streetwalker."

"It's way back in the cave and too heavy to drag to the entrance," Quinn said. "Chase, you better gear up—"

"Better idea," the writer said, unhooking the winch line from the basket and passing it to Quinn. His excitement was tempered by Agila's death.

Quinn fought the rising underwater breeze as the tide picked up speed to reach the cave and a relieved Liana. Setting their sharksticks inside the entrance, they inched in, the beams from their flashlights punching ahead. Silt hovered like cigarette smoke, but enough had settled that they could see. Using the rope, they trussed the box like a parcel for the post. When they had finished sweeping an incline, the cave was again as black as Ben's lungs, forcing them to grope to the entrance.

After emerging, they had to hang onto the winch line to keep from being blown away. Seventy-five feet off the island bobbed the *Wracker's* barnacled bottom, and the surface was choppier and visibility closing. Quinn signaled to Liana to surface and tell them to start the winch. Gripping her sharkstick and flashlight, she pulled herself up the rope, while warily looking around. Once topside, she bobbed in the waves, then Quinn heard the diesel revving up to provide power to the winch.

As slack was taken out of the line, he set his flashlight by his sharkstick. The line snapped taut and vibrated like a violin string. Quinn kicked inside the cave, blindly following the rope until his hand struck the chest. With him guiding it around stalagmites, the strongbox was dragged like a toy, and in minutes was at the entrance.

The winch line snaked at a forty-five degree angle toward the now invisible *Wracker*. Quinn hung onto the rope as the chest was dragged to the edge of the mouth. Then off.

Quinn flagged out like ship's colors in a *baguio* as the heavy box arched into watery space, terrifying a green turtle which flapped away panic-stricken. The box swung back and forth like a pendulum before settling vertically. At a signal from Liana, still in the water supervising, Ben chugged toward the safety of deeper water, trolling the chest like a giant lure, Quinn the live bait. After the boat stopped and the box settled vertically again, Chase began to hoist it.

As it ascended, Quinn checked the chest's condition. It was eaten through in several places, but was reasonably intact. He looked up through the murk. Liana's red form came into view, her masked eyes looking down at him. The winch groaned to a stop when the load was just below the surface. Quinn surfaced, bobbing in the now three foot swells, and gripped the line beside Liana.

"How's it look, Quinn?" Chase called. "Will it hold together if we haul her up?"

The anthropologist yanked out his reg, careful this time to keep waves on his back. "Should be okay. Just take it slow."

The winch groaned as the box broke through the surface and inched out of the water.

"You wasn't foolin' thet sucker is heavy!"

With effort, Chase swung the crane's arm over the rocking deck and lowered the chest. Liana and Quinn passed up their tanks and climbed aboard, their wetsuits torn in several places. Liana was more than happy to be out of the shark infested water.

"You're one gutsy bag lady," Chase said, tossing her a towel.

"Hey, a woman has to do what a woman has to do."

Satisfied they were drifting away from the shoals and parallel to the outer reef, Ben made his way down the companionway. "Let's have a look at what's so heavy and worthless as boobs on a buffalo, pardon my French."

The divers were too eager to see what they had found to remove their wetsuits first.

"My gawd, look at the lock eye! It's bent! And the lock is missing!"

Their collective minds pictured the broken lock in the bridge. Chase tried the lid but it was rusted shut. Water leaked out of rust holes.

"One of you young fellers roll over thet acetylene carriage."

Quinn jumped to it.

"Wait!" Chase said as Ben pulled on goggles. "Before you fire that up, we better wash the deck down again. It stinks up here. The fuel seeped into the wood. Somebody give me a hand."

A few minutes later they stood back with fire extinguishers ready as Chase nodded to Ben, but the extra precautions weren't needed. Ten minutes later shrapnel sizzled on the wet deck as Ben pushed the goggles back on his forehead. With a tap from a hammer, the rusty top fell inward with a crash. Chase pulled on leather gloves and reached down the two inches to the lid's edge with pliers and lifted it out. Their eyes widened as the steaming slab clunked onto the deck.

In the bottom lay a gleaming statue of a naked man with slightly bent knees. The same thought flashed through their minds.

Silver!

"My gawd! How could Jan think *this* was worthless!"

Chase and Liana exchanged glances. They were experiencing it again—and the strongest ever. Déjà vu.

"What the hay is it?" Ben asked.

"Except for the beard," Liana said, "it looks like an Ifugao *bolul*! Don't you think so, Quinn?"

"The resemblance is uncanny!"

"I saw several in Banaue," Liana said. "Many are squating also, but none are as remarkable as this!"

"Ifu what? What're you talkin' about?" Ben rasped.

Liana turned to Quinn. "You're the expert."

"Uh, the Igorots are several related headhunting tribes with names like Benguit, Bontok and Kalinga, the most warlike. The Ifugao are the most famous because of their rice terraces. They're the world's largest, dating back 2,000 years, and if stretched end-to-end would reach half way around the planet. The *bolul* is their rice god. It's only the Ifugao who use them."

"What fer?" Ben asked, running his hand over the statue.

"They're animists. After harvest, they hold feasts called *canaos*, and drink vast quantities of rice wine they brew in these three gallon Ming and Ching trade jars. They also sacrifice animals and check the internal organs for signs—gall bladderology being an art of divination among them. Then they pour blood over the rice gods to propitiate them in hopes that succeeding crops will be bountiful. They held *canaos* after successful headhunting expedition too, of course, but these lasted ten days."

"Headhunters? No kiddin'?" Ben said.

"They stopped the practice in the early 1900s," Quinn replied, unable to take his eyes off the unusual *bolul*, "though they took several Japanese heads during WWII. General Yamashita retreated into their territory. And there's reports of the odd body turning up headless until the 1970s. Headhunting brought honor, eh? Retribution was swift too—the family of the person who had lost his head had to exact revenge or face ostracizing, and anyone in the offending village was fair game. Thus, heads rolled back and forth for centuries. Filipinos, you may have noticed"—he indicated Batuta—"have a thing about revenge. It's said that young women greatly favored men who took many heads."

Chase recognized the details and jokes coming verbatim from his book. The writer had been waiting for a break in the conversation. "You know, it could also be a statue of—"

"Jist a cotton pickin' minute. I'm not so friggin' sure thet it is silver. . . ." Barnacle Ben wiggled on his glasses.

"Why not?" Chase asked. He could pass on his observation later.

"The booger should be oxidized black as the inside of a shark's stomach! Cin you lads git it out of there?"

They looked at each other, then fell to it.

". . . Geeeeeez," Quinn said in a constricted voice as they lifted it, "this thing must weigh over 300 pounds!"

They thumped it onto the deck upright and Ben knelt beside it. Cocking an ear, he tapped the piece-of-eight against the statue's head. He repeated against the beard. Then his face opened up and he ran his hands over the statue like a blind man might do.

". . . In . . . incredible," he muttered.

"What?" Quinn asked.

"It's pla . . . platinum."

"*Platinum!*" the crew exclaimed.

Batuta left Agila and inched to the edge of the group where he regarded the statue with disdain. Ben creaked to his feet and wiped away a tear. The statue was the answer to his Dream.

"Yippers, this beautiful . . . *wonderfull* . . . little booger is worth a fortune."

"My gawd! How could Jan think it was *worthless*?"

"Because in his day, it was," Ben grinned. "Platinum was an unimportant by-product of silver mining."

"Why was it on the *Santa Maria de la Immaculate Concepcion*?" Chase asked.

18 The Moment of Truth

Atagar's dazzling costume was bizarre to Jan, but not so to Mansu. The Ifugao leader whispered to his comrades while pointing from his own headdress to the Spaniard's. They nodded. The white man led a headhunting party.

The Kalinga thought so too. Taunts rose from their ranks, and they stuck their tongues out aggressively at the outnumbered Spaniards.

Atagar turned back and gesticulated airily. Two terrified coolies hurried the strongbox forward. Jan's eyes seared into it. It wasn't the chest he had buried in the cave after all! This one was wood!

From it the porters lifted a white statue and set it on the ground before Atagar facing the Kalinga. Jan's brow furrowed. It was identical to the one he had hidden, but by the ease with which this one was handled, it was whitewashed wood. He *hadn't* been the object of their expedition after all! The Spanish woman and the *Sangley* hadn't betrayed him!

One of the coolies retreated to his companions while the other stood quaking beside Atagar's imperious figure.

The appearance of the bearded statue gave the Kalinga pause. Many pointed from it to the towering white man with a similar beard. If Atagar was trying to convert the natives to Christianity, he was going about it in too strange a manner for the young Dutchman to comprehend. His new found friends were even more perplexed.

Emboldened by the Kalinga reaction, the Spaniard raised his free hand to the sun, then swept it down to the statue before slapping palm to chest. So grand were his words that they drifted up to Jan.

"Vera . . . ?'" Jan repeated, recognizing a woman's name thundered with prominence.

The coolie loudly translated the Spaniard's proclamation into Igorot. The Kalinga looked bewildered. Then their leader pointed from the tall man to his statue and made a comment, causing laughter to wash over Jan's hilltop balcony. Hearing giggling, he turned to see Mansu and his friends having trouble containing themselves.

It was Atagar's turn to look bewildered. He admonished his translator, then faced the warriors again, his mouth and hands moving. Whatever he said, it caused the Kalinga's laughter to leap to new heights. Tears ran down the faces of Mansu and his fellows.

Agitated movements betrayed Atagar's frustration. He raised his staff, shook it, and shouted something. He shouldn't have. The Kalinga took it as an aggressive gesture. Their laughter stopped and with a blood-curdling cry, they attacked, unleashing a typhoon of spears and arrows. Clouds of smoke burst from arquebuses, their great reports rolling down the valleys. The Kalinga stopped dead in their tracks and stared in astonishment at six natives lying motionless or writhing. One of them was their leader.

Jan's companions were no less astounded, and Mansu glanced with new found respect at his pistol.

Two solders, the translator and another coolie lay dead or wounded, while the remaining porters ran screaming back down the trail. Atagar stumbled back while his soldiers frantically reloaded.

The bewildered Kalinga fell back and regrouped. By the time they had decided on another charge, the Spaniards were raising their muskets. Both sides fired simultaneous broadsides. The second Spanish volley blew down another three warriors—but two more soldiers fell. While the surviving four Kalinga charged with axes raised, the remaining two soldiers unsheathed swords.

Jan wasn't able to witness the outcome. Mansu, face bursting with joy, grabbed his pack and signaled him to follow. By the time their group reached the battlefield, only two figures remained. One was a soldier with a bloody sword. He was cut down by Ifugao arrows.

The other was the tall figure in white who stood in shock surveying his bloody field of dreams. The staff slipped from his hand as the Ifugao surrounded him shouting and laughing. He stared flabbergasted at Mansu when the native knocked his headdress off. So stunned was he that he made no effort to ward off their teasing spear thrusts.

Jan stepped into the clearing and glared at the man he loathed even more than de Peyster. Such was Atagar's dismay upon recognizing him that the Ifugao paused in their cat-and-mouse game. Jan unsheathed his Toledo blade and wove through the bloody bodies, oblivious to the moans of the dying. Atagar dropped to his knees. Jan kicked him in the face, knocking him onto his back, blood bursting from a broken nose.

A death rattle caught in the Spaniard's throat as the tip of Jan's blade nicked his throat, drawing blood. The Jesuit looked up along the icy blade to the glacial eyes of the Dutch boy. Jan bared his teeth and was about to plunge the blade when Mansu grasped his arm. Sternfaced, he pointed at the Spaniard, then tapped himself on the chest. Frustration knotted Jan's guts, but he willed himself to step back.

He waited for Mansu to take the pleasure he so craved, but he had other plans. While his ecstatic companions beheaded the dead and wounded, Mansu stripped a loincloth off a Kalinga corpse and tossed it to the Spaniard. Atagar stood and stared at it blankly. Only when Mansu thrust the statue into his arms did he understand that he was being taken prisoner, and hope glimmered in his blue eyes. After quickly changing, he clung to the statue like it was a life raft.

Jan seethed, but tried to satisfy himself with the thought that the Jesuit's fate at the hands of headhunting cannibals had to be the most gruesome imaginable.

Mansu turned to decapitating and said something that communicated haste, for his men quickened their gruesome work. Feeling his gorge rising, Jan waved at Mansu and started back down the path toward the cliff. He didn't want to miss the *Sangley* junk. Whatever de Peyster had in store for him, he was prepared to accept it, for *nothing* could be worse than what he'd been through. Mansu, although surprised at his new friend's abrupt departure, raised a bloody axe in salute.

Jan jogged halfway to the lookout site before skidding to a stop. Excited voices ahead around a bend had caught his attention. Slinking into the brush, he crouched forward. The hair on his nape stood as he witnessed a large party of Kalinga butchering the coolies.

Jan retreated—then ran as fast as he could back to the clearing. Only Mansu's quick reactions spared him from joining the other bodies strewn across the field. Jan pointed down the trail and made a slashing gesture across his neck—galvanizing the Ifugao. While Mansu stripped off another Kalinga loincloth and threw it to him, the others sped their work. In seconds they had fitted tumplines supporting dripping packs, scooped the dead dogs under their arms, and had dissolved into the forest.

Behind them lay the headless bodies of over thirty people, including the little girl's head which had been hidden, with embarrassment, in bushes. With them staggered the pale Spaniard grasping the strange, wooden idol.

19 Feeding Time at the Aquarium

"This slop's getting worse," Chase said, grabbing an M-16 and heading for the bridge. Waves slapped against the *Wracker's* hull. "Before it gets dark, we better get back to the site."

Quinn unzipped his wetsuit, then caught himself. "Darn it, I left my dive light and sharkstick down there!" He reached for his BC. "Chase, take the *Wracker* closer please so I don't have so far to swim. Liana, don't bother gearing up, it's just a quick bounce."

No one could dispute the light's value, and Liana was relieved she didn't have to jump into the shark soup again. Chase bounced the bow around in the waves, then chugged closer to the cave site. He stopped a hundred feet short of the island.

"If I'm not back by Canada Day," Quinn joked, "please send oot a Labrador Retriever, eh?"

He plunged in, his bubbles disappearing in the chop.

* * *

"What's keeping him?" Liana worried, checking her watch. She had long since removed her wetsuit. "Twenty minutes have gone by!"

"I know!" Chase was also alarmed. The bounce should have taken five.

"I can't see ten feet into this pea soup. It's too choppy to see his bubbles."

"Is the cave hard to find or what?"

"Not at all." She looked up. Hints of sunset pink traced feathery clouds. "Let's give him a few more minutes."

They waited with increasing apprehension. Even Ben pulled his eyes off the statue to look over the water.

"Oh gawd, I never should have let him dive alone. It's against all the rules. Maybe he's run into sharks."

"Ben, take the wheel," Chase ordered. "I'm going to gear up—"

"Didyouhearthat?" Liana exclaimed.

"What?"

"A muffled sound—like a *whump*."

"Thet's his sharkstick!"

"Oh gawd! What can we do?"

Chase flicked his M-16 onto rock 'n' roll.

"*Look!*" shouted Batuta, pointing.

Midway between them and the island the water churned. Dr. Garnet Quinn's body was jerked halfway out of the sea, his waist hammerlocked in a shark's jaws. It shook its head, tearing a chunk out. Then another shark hit, collapsing his inflated BC. Before Chase could shoot, the anthropologist disappeared in a crimson maelstrom. Heavy waves washed away the horrible scene, leaving fragments of his yellow wetsuit and an expanding amoeba of blood.

Even Batuta was stunned. Then Liana broke into tears as she recalled how he had saved her life less than an hour before.

* * *

"We have no choice," Chase said. "We have to abandon the hunt this time." Lolo. Agila. Now Quinn. He was right, bad things came in threes.

He had just returned from tossing the anchor beside one of the red floats marking the excavation site. The sky was staining inky blue, blotting out the sunset, as the early tropical night descended. The wind was little more than a whisper and the water relatively quiet in the inner reef. Chase flicked a switch, bathing the sterndeck with light, before continuing.

"There's not enough diesel to make Ulugon Bay, and not even enough gas to make it in the Zodiac. We're going to have to wait for Earthquake. And hope he arrives tomorrow as scheduled."

And hope he's on our side.

"We're gonna have to keep a careful watch tonight," Ben said, looking down at the decked dive ladder. His joy had been shortlived. "The Beagle Boys have to know thet their puppy is fish food, and they're gonna be mad as bulls booted in the butt, pardon my French."

Chase nodded. "Batuta, we'll have to ask you to enjoy our hospitality for another night. I can't risk running you and Agila in with night falling."

"Anything to help see your back at the earliest opportunity, Mr. Ballentyne. I'll even take the first watch."

Chase turned away. The abrasive native was right—the writer was cursing the day he heard of the treasure. He turned to Liana, her eyes red. He couldn't figure her out, such a paragon of boldness and blunder, of strength and weakness.

"I'll take the midnight watch, if someone cin cock this stupid rifle." Ben shuffled his lawnchair beside the statue, and sat with his hand resting on a platinum shoulder. "I cain't sleep anyhow."

Chase racked the bolt, flicked on the safety, and passed it back to him. "Wake me at 4:00 a.m. then," the writer said, putting his arm around Liana. "Come on Bag Lady, we're long due for some rest."

She hugged his arm as he led her to their quarters.

* * *

Chase sat up, instantly awake. Their quarters were black as the inside of python.

"Hmmmmmgff . . ?" Liana mumbled beside him on the futon.

"Hush!"

Then she heard it above the slapping of waves against the hull. The dive ladder was squeaking. Someone was climbing aboard the *Wracker.*

20 Banaue

The trek lasted five days, long enough for Jan to lose his appetite. It wasn't due just to the putrefying heads. He had wondered why they had brought the dead dogs. He learned at lunch time.

With each step away from the coast, his desperation grew. By the time they had lost their Kalinga trackers, he was so deep into headhunting territory that he had no choice but to stay with Mansu and his colleagues.

It was five days of tension and danger, of traveling through pine forests on the heights and jungle in the valleys, skirting enemy villages and terraces and avoiding detection at all costs. Five days of shivering at night with only the Kalinga loincloth for warmth, which he knew was necessary to blend in better. But it was five days of a solicitous Mansu protecting him, doing his best to make him comfortable.

It was also five days of controlling his urge to slash the Spaniard's throat. But for him, he would be aboard the *Copenhagan* sailing home to New York, Guert and Margaretje! It was five days of watching Atagar recover and renew his bizarre sense of purpose, whatever it was. For all five days, he carried the statue like a new born, which rankled Jan even more because it reminded him of his own child.

It was the early afternoon of the fifth when Mansu hailed guards wearing similar loinclothes atop a high ridge. While the band was greeted with whoops and backslapping, Jan found himself standing at the head of the most enormous terraced valley he had seen.

187

"Banaue!" Mansu beamed. "The naval of the world!"

Thousands of fish ponds filled the huge bowl, though now that he was standing beside one, he was puzzled why neat rows of grass grew out of it. Huts with coconut trees were clumped among the terraces. On the valley floor sat a neat village of thatched, wooden huts on stilts. As exhausted as he was, Jan didn't fail to recognize the stunning beauty and grandeur of the scene.

He looked back to see Atagar dipping a hand into an irrigation channel, a smile touching his lips, just before Mansu kicked him forward.

As they wove down snake-and-ladder steps to the village, the entire population of the valley, perhaps 2,000, abandoned fishing and other chores to rush to meet them. As the expedition neared the bottom, the carpenter in Jan emerged and he studied the architecture. Ladders led up to entrances of sturdy lodges constructed of wide planks, each hut about ten feet on a side, most with smoke sifting through thick, thatched roofs. The homes were placed with no regard to plan, but Jan felt a comfortable, airy feeling to the tidy town. Even the ground was paved with flagstones.

With Mansu strutting like Caesar, their triumphant procession entered imperial Banaue, sending pigs squealing and chickens squawking before them. Villagers ran up cheering—only to stop short when they beheld the two white men. Naked children ran screaming to mothers. Men eyed Jan's sword with as much suspicion and envy as they eyed the white men's enemy loincloths with disdain.

All regarded the statue with curiosity.

Jan blinked. Beautiful, young—bare-breasted—women were everywhere! All kinds of breasts! Big breasts, little breasts, all firm, upraised breasts! He was equally astonished to see that their jewelry was made of gold and silver! They wore skirts with the same red pattern as the men's loincloths. He flushed when he realized that many, once they overcame their initial surprise, regarded him with mutual admiration. It was something he hadn't experienced since Margaretje and her girl friends.

Their arrival acted as a tonic to the Jesuit also. He strode, purple nose askew, as if he were the true head of the cavalcade.

Like a Pied Piper, Mansu led the growing crowd past a central clearing, bare but for a teak tree, into the sparse suburbs where he halted before a hut, the mob flowing around them in a horseshoe. Jan's eyes had been fixed on the feast of breasts, but this hut grabbed his attention. It was like any other—but for rows of human skulls along the sides. Mansu called up to the open door.

Tree trunk legs crossed as a thick man crouched out of the shadows and sat on the threshold as if it were a throne. He was about seventy and still powerfully built, with a huge belly overhanging his loincloth, and a bowl of platinum hair. His eyes gleamed with intelligence as they flickered over the assembly, taking in the strangers.

"Tonapa," Mansu said in an aside to Jan.

Recognizing that he was in the presence of the chief, Atagar pulled himself up to his full height.

At a signal from Mansu, his comrades proudly dumped their baskets. While Jan fought down his rising gorge, the valley dwellers pressed forward with cries of admiration. Chief Tonapa studied the heads, beamed and made an announcement that elicited a cheer. One word stood out.

Canao.

The chief's smile disappeared as he turned his attention to the captives. A grinning Mansu gripped Jan around the shoulders like a brother and drew him forward. As his words spilled out, contempt in the crowd's eyes was replaced by an intense warmth which took Jan by surprise.

Also taking him by surprise were the hideous smiles on the older citizens—their mouths the crimson of blood, their teeth blackened stumps. Some horrible disease was surely sweeping the village—especially when many spat red saliva onto the ground. Jan couldn't know it was betel nut.

But his concern was swept aside by the bright smiles from the young women. Tonapa beamed down on him too, his red-and-black smile faltering only when his eyes drifted to Jan's beautiful machete.

Mansu turned to the Spaniard and pointed to the ground. With great nobility, the Spaniard set the statue down facing the chief. By Atagar's expansive gestures it was apparent he was building himself up to something.

189

As Mansu spoke in snide tones, the chief studied the statue, then whispered over his shoulder. Two smooth female arms extended from the darkness and passed him a statue covered with a rough, black coating. Atagar brightened and struggled to keep his equanimity as the chief passed it down to Mansu.

"*Bolul!*" Mansu beamed to Jan as he set it beside the white statue.

The Hollander blinked again. If the '*bolul*' had a beard, it would be virtually identical to the Spaniard's, excepting size and color. The crowd whispered among themselves.

Seizing the moment, Ignacio del Atagar strode forward. While Mansu and his troops giggled, with great significance Atagar raised his hands to the sun, then swept them down to behold the rice god.

"*Bolul!*" he announced in a voice filled with thunder and lightning. He raised his hands to the sun again, then lowered them to his chest. "*BOLUL!*" The Spaniard opened his arms as if to embrace the crowd and smiled beatifically. "Vera—"

Someone at the back of the class snickered. It grew into a titter, then general laughter, and finally a thunderous roar, drowning out the Spaniard's words. The chief's big belly jiggled and Mansu and his friends laughed loudest of all. Even Jan had to laugh, even if he didn't know what he was laughing at. With his broken nose, Atagar looked even more ridiculous.

His thin shoulders slumped. As the laughter subsided, Mansu kicked the white statue onto its side. Such was the look of dismay on the Spaniard's face that a fresh round of mirth broke out. It rose to laughter again when Mansu struck him in the solar plexus with the butt of his spear, dropping the Spaniard to his knees, gasping.

A movement in the chief's doorway caused Jan to glance up. And his laughter died on his lips.

A girl, perhaps sixteen, peered around the doorsill to see what was so funny. Glistening, black hair fell like a waterfall down one side of a gorgeous face. Gold earrings and a silver necklace graced mahogany skin, and swirling tattoos adorned each shoulder. Her breasts were full and voluptuous. Movement beside Jan jolted him out of his reverie.

Mansu stepped forward, chest swelling. Smirking up at her, he swept his hand over the grizzly trophies. She looked away indifferently. While Mansu deflated, her doe eyes caught sight of Jan and her lips parted. His hair and skin were the color of gold, and that of his eyes had to have been stolen from the sky. Then she smiled the most beautiful smile Jan had ever seen.

Because of an agitated movement beside him, Jan pried his eyes off her. Mansu shot him a sharp look before offering the broken Spaniard to the chief. His face showed pleasure and he issued an order. Dar and the boys seized Atagar, threw him onto his back, and wrestled a foot onto a stone mortar while Mansu lifted the white statue above his head. The sound of the Spaniard's tibia *snapping* was followed by a horrible scream. To laughter, Mansu threw Atagar's statue into a pig wallow. Oblivious to the Spaniard's howls, he and Dar dragged him to a nearby hut and pushed him up through the door. They didn't stand a guard. One wasn't necessary.

Jan was unnerved by the brutality and the crowd's light-hearted reaction to it, but upon glancing up, his concerns dissolved. The girl's glistening smile and jeweled eyes beamed down on him. The chief's sharp eyes noted the mutual attraction, and his lips curled into a bemused smile. He spoke to her in a soft voice and she disappeared again. When she reappeared, it was to pass Jan an Ifugao loincloth.

"T . . . thank you," he croaked in Dutch.

She understood the courtesy by his manner and smiled. Mansu returned, his own sharp eyes flickering from the girl to Jan while the chief called for someone in the crowd.

"Saging?"

A wizened woman befitting her name pushed forward. After the chief said something to her, she made a downward sweeping motion to Jan and hobbled away on the tender feet of the old. Jan cast a last glance at the girl before following, but her expression had turned neutral since Mansu had returned.

The old woman led him to a hut near the Spaniard's and, with surprising agility, climbed the short ladder to the closed doors, two slabs of wood. A puzzled Jan watched as she broke a single knotted straw looped through leather eyes serving as the lock, then slid the panels apart. After climbing down, she smiled cavernously and fluttered a bony hand toward the hut.

191

"And t . . . thank you too."

Jan climbed to inspect his new surroundings. It was bare but for a raised firepit in one corner, a dusty quating *bolul* in another, a dustier *Sangley* trade jar in a third, and handwoven baskets in the fourth. Stacked on rafters were bundled sheaves; the hut was normally a granary. Seeds littered the slab floor. He recognized them as rice—their staple aboard the *Raid* once they reached the Orient. He looked at the sheaves again—and could have slapped himself! The ponds weren't used to raise fish! They grew rice!

The old woman's smiling face appeared at the top of the ladder, and she handed him a red blanket, and a wooden bowl heaped with steaming rice and a wooden spoon. Jan studied the attractive scalloped design on the bowl, and the spoon, its handle fashioned like a *bolul*, with admiration. After wolfing down the food, laying aside weapons and switching loincloths, he lay on his back with his feet toward the door.

With hunger satiated, his body cried out for sleep, but his mind raced. He couldn't take it off all the lovely girls! And how they looked at him! Most vivid was the angel behind the chief! She was even more beautiful than Margaretje! More beautiful than any girl he had ever seen! He shook his head. And she was a . . . headhunter and a cannibal!

The thought was sobering. He wasn't a prisoner, but he was captive nonetheless. Finding his way back to the coast through unfamiliar and hostile country would be impossible without a guide. Chances of meeting the *Sangley* junk diminished with each day. He felt the same sinking feeling as when he had boarded the *Raid* in New York.

But if he had learned anything in the past ten months, it was to survive—and here in Banaue he was being welcomed. With hard won maturity, he knew he had to put aside his feelings for Margaretje. That part of his life was over.

A gecko above him chirped. He wished it was louder, that it would blot out the muttered Papist prayers and moans drifting from the Spaniard's hut.

A giggle startled him. Pulling himself up onto his elbows, Jan looked at a pretty face framed by his feet. The girl put her hand to her mouth, then scampered down the ladder. Jan looked to see what she found so amusing—and blushed. His white dangler had flopped out of his poorly tied loincloth. Embarrassed, he rolled onto his side and tucked it back in. Through the doorway, he saw her—about thirteen he guessed from her budding breasts—scurry to a giggle of girls with baskets on their hips. She spoke with animation as she held her hands several inches apart.

His ears burning, Jan was about to slink back into the shadows when his heart skipped. The tallest of the girls was the gorgeous one, and her breasts swelled when their eyes met. Her gaze, full of invitation and curiosity, melted his embarrassment, and a smile burst onto his face.

Without taking eyes off him, she spoke to her younger friend in a voice that carried the trill of brightly colored birds. The smaller girl nodded, scampered to Jan's hut, and climbed the rungs until her face was level with the threshold again. Eyes twinkling, she pointed back at her taller friend.

"Maganda!" She then pointed at him.

"Jan?"

The girl skipped back to her friends. Maganda's eyes glistened when she heard his name.

Their faces clouded when the old woman's crackling voice interrupted their recess. It came from where festive preparations appeared to be underway. Sobering, they readjusted their baskets and strolled away to their chores. Maganda dawdled, then turned, an upraised breast in silhouette. She dazzled him with a smile, then her lips moved in pantomime.

"Jan," they said.

". . . Maganda," he whispered.

She skipped to catch up with her friends. The last he saw of her was her tight bottom swaying around the corner of a hut. Jan let out a great breath and dropped his head. To his embarrassment, his saker was primed and ready for action.

* * *

A moan seeped into Jan's dream of swimming nude with Maganda in a warm pool. Then a *tap-tap-tapping* roughened the water's surface and it grew colder and she faded away.

He awakened shivering from a nap with the sound of the Spaniard's moans drifting over. Jan rubbed his eyes and pulled himself onto an elbow. Dar stood on Jan's ladder, urging him with a broad smile to follow. Seeing that he carried weapons, Jan strapped on his blades and followed. The valley's population filled the clearing. As he was led before the chief standing at the head, Jan wondered why each family held a *bolul*. Behind the chief stood Saging, who the Dutch boy guessed was his wife. To the chief's left stood the tribal council; to his right, the headhunting party with Mansu in full feathered regalia.

The chief greeted him warmly, though his eyes cheated to Jan's sword. The young Dutchman smiled a greeting to Mansu but was startled when the headhunter regarded him coolly. Before he could wonder why, he saw that they were surrounded by a semi-circle of Spanish and Kalinga heads atop high stakes. Buzzing flies formed halos around each of them. The stench was awful to Jan. To the Ifugao, it was attractive, like blue cheese is to some.

At a word from Chief Tonapa, the head table sat on mats laid on the flagstones. The gathering followed in kind, leaving a large space between the two parties. Mansu and his men sat to the chief's immediate right. Smiling, the chief patted the mat to his left. Jan accepted, the honor not lost on him. Neither was it lost on him the chief's growing interest in his sword.

From a trade jar, girls filled decoratively carved wooden drinking bowls and passed them to the chief and his entourage. Rice kernels floated in a milky liquid. Other young women moved through the crowd with ladles. When everyone was served, the chief rose and made a flamboyant speech punctuated with sweeps of his arm toward Mansu and his brave band. They were the pride of Banaue.

At a cue Jan missed, everyone threw back their heads and drained their bowls. Jan followed. It had a mild, sour flavor, but there was the cut of alcohol below the surface.

As Mansu rose and launched into a proud recalling of events, Jan's eyes searched the crowd. Many were already refilling bowls at stations. It took some time to find the gorgeous face he was looking for, with many girls betraying disappointment when he passed them over. Maganda sat with her friends to one side, her face a study in impassivity. Then her young friend elbowed her and giggled. An embarrassed smile broke onto Maganda's face. Jan turned away to save her discomfort, and when he couldn't help looking back, she was scolding her friends.

Mansu finished his speech and sat to deafening cheers, but Jan's smile disappeared when the headhunter cast a sharp look at him. Chastised, Jan avoided further eye contact with him by accepting another bowl of rice wine.

Two dazzling eyes he couldn't avoid belonged to Maganda. Those large orbs flickered to meet his each time he glanced in her direction. Few things escaped Mansu's pin-prick irises, and from his new friend's reaction it was dawning on Jan that he was intruding on territory already staked out.

As each headhunter strutted in turn, and the celebrants drank like sailors, the *canao* grew more festive. Speeches gave way to ritual dancing to drums, flutes, cymbals and stringed bamboo instruments, which escalated into festive dancing as the wine fueled even the old to hobble onto gnarled feet. Jan was swept up in the earthy, good spirits. As the villagers lost themselves in revelry, Jan and Maganda grew more emboldened, their eyes meeting and lingering.

No sooner was his bowl emptied than it was refilled. No sooner had it been refilled than the chief raised his in another toast to the headhunters' stupendous success. Jan was throwing back his thirtieth bowl, and the crowd was wobbly, when Mansu and his men rose and staggered away on some mission.

With Mansu gone, Maganda's and Jan's eyes seized each other, only separating when Mansu led a water buffalo forward. The drunken headhunters gathered around it with machetes. At a signal from Mansu, they converged, blades flashing and hacking. The buffalo made a long, pitiful bellow before dropping to its knees, then rolling like a large ball onto its side. Jan's mouth fell open at the barbarity and fury with which they butchered the animal—one warrior staggering from the killfest bleeding from serious wounds himself. Within fifteen minutes, nothing was left of the beast but bones, blood and the bag of guts.

Mansu swaggered forward and slit it open, spilling out steaming offal. The chief and entourage rose and, with Jan in tow, staggered before the writhing intestines, villagers drunkenly jockeying for position. Gripping a large, slippery lobe of liver, Mansu paused with great drama. A hush fell. With considerable flair, Mansu threw the organ back, revealing a large, green gall bladder.

"Aaaaah!" rose from the assembly. Faces beamed, heads nodded.

Jan frowned. They seemed to have found a positive 'sign' in the guts, like Manhattan Indians with their sticks and bones. Villagers pressed forward with their *boluls*. With the heart, Mansu anointed as many as possible before the tap ran dry. Then he ladled blood from the abdominal cavity over the rest.

After the rice gods' appetites had been satiated, Mansu stumbled to the pig wallow and dragged out Atagar's statue. Returning with it to a huge bonfire his comrades were building, he threw it onto the flames, an action eliciting renewed laughter.

Villagers stuck chunks of meat onto spits and spears and began roasting, actually burning, their feast. The *canao* was reaching altitude.

* * *

It was well after dark and the first day of the *canao* was winding down before Saging helped the sodden chief home. To Jan's disappointment, Maganda followed—but not before casting him a last, longing look.

Although tired and wobbly himself, on his way back to his hut Jan prided himself that despite everyone making sure he drank far more than his share, he had held his own. He had the *Raid's* daily beer ration to thank for that. Then his smile disappeared when he remembered Mansu's change of heart. Jan felt awful, but he couldn't help himself. This girl. . . .

He was half way up his ladder, and had just pushed his scabbard through the door when a pebble struck the wall beside him. Turning, it took him a blurry moment to recognize the outline of a familiar figure a hut away. A smile burst onto his face. Maganda made a flirtatious downward sweep.

His fatigue vanished, but by the time Jan slipped down the ladder, she had too. He rushed to the corner where he had last seen her and squinted into the darkness. Something moved in a grove on the edge of the village. Maganda stepped out of the shadows just long enough for him to recognize her in the moonlight, then dissolved back into the gloom.

His heart beating like a hummingbird's, Jan hurried to join her. Slipping her hand into his, she led him several yards into the darkened woods where, to his surprise, she drew him to the ground. Jan felt a reed mat as they lay down. Soft streaks of silvery moonlight broke through the brush and spottled her body and face in lace. Her eyes sparkled as her lips parted.

She placed his trembling hand on her breast. Her features relaxing into passion, her hand drifted to his loincloth. His rapidly priming saker sprang free and he sucked in his breath at her touch. She explored its smooth, hard surface with wonder, verifying that, indeed, this beautiful golden boy was built like their men. Throwing her shawl aside, she lay spread, desiring final confirmation. Jan wasted no time.

Normally, he would have blown his wad after the first few strokes, it having been so long since his embraces with the passionate Margaretje, but tonight his gunpowder was dampened by wine. They wrestled and rolled and her sighs grew longer and louder until bursting into wet, loud gasps. With a long, low wail, he fired a broadside into her.

Immediately, she pushed him off, adjusted her shawl, and stood. Dumbfounded, he fumbled on his loincloth and followed her to the edge of the jungle. There, he looked down into her eyes, unsure what he would see. It all had been so sudden. What he saw melted his heart.

It was love at first sight.

She gave him a lingering hug, then urged him to return in haste to his hut. With reluctance, he left her while she remained in the shadows. It was only when he was in his lodge that she faded into the darkness.

Jan's soaring emotions were checked by a movement in the shadows two huts away. A figure topped with feathers stepped out, then disappeared again.

Jan's heart sank. Mansu had been spying on them.

* * *

Jan was delighted when a smiling Maganda tapped at his door, awakening him, the next morning. He slid the panels apart to find her holding two wooden bowls heaped with rice and greens. She set one on his threshold and, after checking that no one was watching, stuck her forearm out and made a fist.

"Jan!" she laughed.

He sputtered thanks. After warming him with another smile, she glided toward the Spaniard's hut with the other bowl. Jan's eyes followed every sensuous move. She stirred passions he didn't know existed—passions that even Margaretje hadn't aroused.

And then he thought of Mansu having caught them in the act, and his boiling blood stilled.

* * *

The *canao* continued for days—as did their nightly trysts. Jan noticed they weren't the only young couples sneaking into the jungle. It seemed to be the accepted manner of courting.

He avoided the now surly headhunter as best he could. Likewise, Dar and the other single men now avoided Jan. They didn't like the sensation he caused among the girls. If they would have known, they would have brought only his head home.

Atagar's moans reached a climax on the fifth day. It was on that morning that Maganda returned to Jan after delivering breakfast to the Jesuit, her eyes wet with worry, and made a now familiar downwave. He followed the brisk pace she set to the Spaniard's hut. After slipping up the ladder and inside, she urged him to follow. Reluctantly, he did.

The stench of rotting flesh hit Jan. The ashen Spaniard sat slumped with his back against a wall. A storm cloud of flies swirled around his putrid leg. His eyes had the look of a man staring into his own coffin. Atagar mumbled incoherently. Jan gagged and turned to the door, but Maganda gripped his arm. With imploring eyes, she pointed to Atagar's lips, then opened her palm.

Jan could only shrug, shake his head, and look perplexed—hoping one of the gesticulations translated across the cultures. One did. She turned back with worried eyes to her semi-delirious charge. After days of listening to groaning from the Spaniard's hut, Jan could no longer stave off growing pity—try as he might.

Ignacio del Atagar managed to raise his head. "*Aguaa*," he moaned. Maganda held a spoonful of rice to his lips.

"*Aguaaaa*," Atagar repeated. His hand trembled toward the porcelain jar.

Cursing his compulsion for compassion, Jan scooped out a

bowl of water and held it to his lips. Atagar slurped, then accepted a spoonful of rice. As they fed him, the dim candlelight behind Atagar's eyes flickered brighter. Finally he nodded before his bearded chin lolled back onto his thin chest.

After cutting off the lower foot of the Spaniard's loincloth, Jan washed his wound, gagging as squirming maggots fell to the floor. Unable to stand it any longer, Jan turned to the door, but a bony hand stopped him. Jan shuddered and shook it off.

"*Gracias,*" Atagar rasped.

Jan studied his pasty face. The care was having an effect, Atagar was on the edge of lucidity. Curiosity ate at Jan's mind. He pointed at a cobwebbed *bolul* in a corner, shrugged, then swept his palm toward the village.

The question stirred something deep within Atagar, for the darkest of depressions filled his sunken eyes and he began to ramble. Then the ramble grew into a rage as he tapped into some hidden well of strength. It took Jan and Maganda aback.

Sputtering, he pointed at their apparel . . . then to her jewelry . . . to a tumpline hanging from the rafters. He gesticulated like he was using a blowgun . . . stabbed a finger at a woman working a backstrap loom nearby . . . swept it in the direction of the rice terraces . . . then flung it in a gesture of contempt at the sun.

But he saved his greatest fury for the *bolul.* Spittle foamed on his lips as he cursed and kicked at it with his good leg. Then, spent, he collapsed while a horrified Maganda swept the rice god up and held it to her bosom.

None of it made any sense at all. Jan had understood only one word—it was the woman's name Atagar had thundered at the Kalinga. The one he claimed his statue was called. The one he—quixotically—claimed to be.

"Vera?" Jan repeated. He was unsure if Atagar could even hear him.

The Don could, and a bitter laugh welled out of the dark recesses of his soul. But it was a private joke—one filled with the most bitter of disappointment, and scorn for all.

Then the candle behind his eyes burned down and he was reduced to muttering.

* * *

"What's this?" Jan asked using sign language.

Maganda had taken him on a tour of the valley. They had followed the creek running along its bottom into the country-side, where he paused at the base of a hill. A hole had been dug wide enough for a man to crawl into. Scattered around the entrance was rubble. Jan crouched and peered inside, but it was too dark to see.

Her reply was to finger her earrings.

"Gold?" he asked. He poked amongst the quartz rubble until he seized a rock. He stared at a golden seam the thickness of his palm!

"Goooold?" she repeated, the word strange on her tongue.

"*Ja! Gold!*" He leapt to his feet. It was everywhere! For the *taking!*

She gave him a peculiar look, wondering why he was so ex-cited about a common stone they used merely to make jewelry. Anyone could use the mine, and there were several. She knew of places much more interesting—such as a bamboo grove nearby where they could make love. As she giggled and pulled him toward it, he dropped the rock and looked back with wonder.

* * *

Jan sat up, suddenly wide awake. He had been having a night-mare. In it a screaming Atagar had been chasing him—to drag him back to Fort Santiago's torture chamber.

Another scream—from outside—rended the air. Jan slid his door panels open to darkness. There was a nightmare in progress alright—but it belonged to Ignacio del Atagar. Mansu and Dar, holding torches, were dragging him by his scrawny shoulders. He howled as his twisted foot bumped along flag-stones.

Jan scuttled down the ladder and followed to the central clearing. Most of the villagers were already there, waiting with grim, drunken anticipation. Torch light lit the scene. Jan stopped cold.

A new stake had been raised.

Atagar's eyes fixed on it and he screamed like a wounded rabbit. They threw the Don at the chief's feet. Tonapa was in an expansive, if drunken mood, joking with his entourage as he tested the blade of his headhunting axe.

Jan caught the eye of a naked, little girl in the corral of bodies fencing the Spaniard in. She clutched at her mother's shawl. The Dutch boy was shocked that she should be there, for surely they would butcher his corpse like they did the buffalo and eat it too. Jan forced a smile for her. She buried her face in her mother's skirt.

Chief Tonapa barked an order and set his feet apart. A grinning Batuta and Dar yanked Atagar to his knees, twisted him so his side was to the chief, and stepped aside.

"*Bolul! Vera—*" Father Ignacio del Atagar's head tumbled and a four foot geyser of blood spurted from the stump as his body collapsed.

The little girl looked puzzled. A grinning Chief Tonapa picked up the Spaniard's head by its long yellow hair and held it aloft, admiring the trophy, then nodded his gratitude to Mansu. He responded deferentially, then dipped his headhunting axe in the now weak pulsations of blood. While he fingered a lick from the blade, he fixed his eyes on Jan.

Jan swallowed. The message was clear.

21 Pirates of the South China Sea

As the dive ladder squeaked again, Chase fumbled in the darkness for Quinn's 9mm and flicked the safety. His watch read 3:06 a.m. The ladder squeaked again as it took a second weight. Chase groped for the companionway, inched upward, and peeked through the hatch. The new moon cast silver light and shadows across the deck and onto agitated waves beyond, the wind having risen. His view of the dive ladder blocked by the compressor, Chase slipped behind it.

The ladder squeaked a third time.

Chase peered around the compressor. Two stocky men in black wetsuits and scuba tanks with masks pulled up onto their foreheads strained as they passed the statue to a man in the Zodiac. Another stood guard with a speargun.

Where's Ben? Chase thought. *It's his watch!*

Chase aimed at the guard.

Something cold, wet and sharp pricked the side of Chase's neck.

"Don't move," a voice with a Filipino accent whispered.

He froze. The pistol was lifted from his hand.

A throat—female—cleared behind them. Startled, the man turned, the knife shifting from Chase's neck. A flash exploded in the diver's face. At the same instance, Chase swept the arm aside and launched him overboard where he landed with a loud splash. Something heavy clattered to the darkened deck. The pistol.

Liana's head protruded from the hatch, camera in hand. The two startled thieves lost their grip on the statue. It fell,

202

banging against the gunwale, then plunged into the water. The figure in the Zodiac rolled backwards into the sea and disappeared.

The half blinded guard swung his speargun toward Chase, who dived back behind the compressor as the spear thudded into the side of the cabin. No time to search for the 9mm, Chase sprung to his feet and charged the man, now fumbling for a knife. The writer lashed out with a side kick, catching him in the solar plexus. The intruder flew backwards into the water, sending up a great splash before disappearing.

While one of the last two fumbled for another speargun, his mate lunged with a knife. Chase seized his wrist and they grappled until they crashed to the deck, the Filipino on top, his knife hand breaking free. While the diver with the speargun hurried to assist, Chase threw up his arms to protect himself from the knife—when something snapped into the side of the man's head, jerking it to the one side. Then he fell off Chase, his knife clattering to the deck. One of Lolo's arrows protruded from the man's ear.

The diver with the speargun stopped dead, turned, and ran for the edge. He made it—but not alive. The report of a pistol was lost in the ear-splitting explosion of his scuba tank. It rocketed him overboard, breaking his back, jagged, aluminum shards curling into his sides. As the boom echoed off trees, Liana lowered the Beretta. Batuta, Lolo's bow reloaded and half drawn, stood favoring his bad leg and smiling. Revenge was his.

Chase raced up the companionway to the bridge and racked the bolt on an M-16. Starlight dancing on the chop gave them reasonable visibility but not enough. Grabbing their flare gun, he fired it. It popped open high above them and drifted down, casting a harsh, artificial light over the scene, before sizzling out in the sea. Nobody. Switching on their searchlight, Chase swept it in a circle, across the wall of coconut trees and far out to sea. Nothing. He slipped back down the companionway, grabbed a dive light, and ran around the cabin.

"Where's Ben! I can't find him. Check over the side!"

A groan issued from Liana as she leaned over the stern. Ben's body floated face down. Chase was too overcome to speak. He gaffed Ben's work shirt and drew him to the dive ladder where he lifted the old treasure hunter's limp, sopping body onto deck. Liana hauled up the ladder while Batuta stood guard.

"What was he doing on deck?" Liana cried. "He should have been on the bridge?"

"Here's why," Chase managed, his flashlight illuminating pliers and wire at the stern. A rhythmic rattle betrayed that the exhaust had shaken loose. "He must have been leaning over rewiring it when he was grabbed and pulled overboard."

". . . The Beagle Boys were going to steal our Zodiac," Liana said, "and their *banca* isn't around. Where did they come from? And how did they know we had the statue?"

"My men only guard the promon-tory during the day. The terrorists must have slipped in at night, stockpiled scuba gear, and hid men on the beach."

"Exactly," Chase muttered, "Friday wasn't the only one watching us. That's where they must be swimming to right now." He turned to Liana, his eyes burning into hers. "By the way, thanks."

"A woman has to do. . . ," she tried to joke.

Chase turned to thank Batuta, but the Batak leader looked away. "Let's have a look at these guys," he said instead.

He shone his flashlight into the face of the diver with the arrow protruding from his ear. The man had heavy features with a nose like a double-barrel shotgun, but now those features lay in the sloven relaxation of death. Chase recognized him from Liana's pictures.

"We should have shots of them, just in case," Liana said, looking at her Nikonis. "I'll get another camera."

While she slipped below, Chase beamed his light into the Zodiac. The oars had been lined and an alien pair of fins lay in the bottom.

"Be interesting to see how far they would have gotten with so little fuel," he said to Batuta.

When he didn't reply, Chase snapped off the light. Liana popped up from the hatch with her camera bag, which she set by the gunwale. She snapped pictures of the corpse's face.

The body of the other Filipino floated face down, his head thumping against the hull in the heavy waves. His twisted scuba tank was as recognizable as his back. Chase used the gaff to roll him over into the beam of the flashlight he had passed to Liana. His face was pockmarked, and water sloshed into his open mouth. Liana set the light aside and raised her

Nikon, but it didn't flash.

"I need a fresh memory card. Chase, hold the flashlight for me." With the writer providing light, Liana dug into her camera bag and fished out a new card. After slipping the full one into a plastic sleeve, and installing the new one, they returned to the body.

"This Beagle is even uglier than the other one," Chase muttered as her flash lit up the grizzly sight.

The wind continued to rise and water slapped harder against the hull.

"What do we do now?" she asked as she slipped her camera back into her bag. "That's five of the litter down, but still leaves four."

"We have the M60. We can wait for Earthquake in safety." He didn't want to speculate on McGoon's loyalty. He was their only hope.

"What about the statue?"

"We'll hoist it up at daybreak. I'll drop down. It shouldn't take more than a few minutes."

". . . That's what Quinn said."

Ignoring the implications, Chase turned to Batuta. "Can you climb up to the bridge with that ankle? We'll need your help operating the diesel and winch."

"Anything to hurry you along, Mr. Ballentyne."

"You don't quit, do y—"

Chase was cut off by Liana screaming. A gaping jaw full of teeth raged up out of the brine. A shark seized one of the dead Filipino's arms and shook it like a pit bull until it tore loose. Liana jumped into Chase's arms as another hit the corpse from the other side. As they retreated to mid-deck, the sea boiled.

". . . Can't say that Filipino food isn't popular," Chase muttered.

"It was also Quinn who said maneaters aren't a prob . . . wait! Where's my camera bag!" Freeing herself from Chase, she grabbed his flashlight and hurried back to the gunwale. The bag was nowhere to be seen. Overcoming her fear, she peeked over the side. A rubber squeeze bulb bobbed in the swirling water. "Oh no! It got kicked overboard!"

Chase had seen her nude, but never so naked. "Once we flog that statue, you can buy thousands of—"

A loud splash behind them spun them around. Batuta had just rolled the other body overboard.

"What are you doing!" Liana demanded.

"What does it look like, Miss Eastlake? I'm clearing the deck."

"But that'll attract more hungry sharks!" Liana shrieked.

". . . If anything, it might fill them up."

They tore into breakfast like lumberjacks.

"Thanks," Liana said. "That's all we need. We have to dive tomorrow."

Batuta wasn't about to admit he had made a mistake. Chase fought back his own fury. He didn't know how much longer he could put up with the grating Batak before he fed *him* to the sharks. Then he caught himself—but for their quest, Batuta's grandfather and friend would still be alive.

"Batuta, help me carry Ben and Agila into the cabin where they'll be out of the sun. Then I'll show you how to operate the bridge, and we better move the machine-gun down to the deck so it's handy if the Boys try anything from shore."

Liana could see that he didn't like the fact that they were only 400 yards away, well within firing range. "Maybe we should move and come back at dawn?"

"We'll take our chances. AKs are notoriously inaccurate at this range, but the M60 isn't and they know that."

Chase took another look at the water and worked his jaw. The sharks had already cleaned up their plates and disappeared, but he doubted if they had gone very far to rest and digest.

22 Rites of Manhood

"Hey!" Jan laughed as Maganda "accidentally" bumped him with her backside, almost knocking him from a dike into a rice paddy. He splashed a handful of water at her, but before she could retaliate by pulling off his loincloth, he grabbed her wrists and they fell to the ground wrestling. She was a strong, quick girl and it took some time before he could pin her. After he did, and they lay in a tangle of arms and legs, he realized their panting wasn't all from exertion.

Two months was long enough for Jan to have learned a smattering of Ifugao. Long enough to have fallen hopelessly in love with Maganda, and to have become thoroughly enchanted with her people, despite their awesome contradictions. A greater juxtaposition of horror and hospitality, of sensitivity and slaughter, of artistic beauty and barbarism he could not imagine. Neither could he envision a more honest people— citizens left possessions lying everywhere and anywhere. Theft was unheard of. They could even have as many wives as they wished!

Adding to his joy was the relief of learning that they weren't cannibals after all. The Jesuit's headless body had been dragged to the forest, dumped into a freshly dug hole, and covered over. His skull, the flesh boiled away, now smiled down from an honored place on Chief Tonapa's hut. Jan made a point of avoiding it.

As he understood more of the language, he learned why Maganda was so much younger than the chief and his wife. They were her grandparents. Jan had been shocked as she described how her parents had lost their heads to Kalinga head-hunters while gathering wild mushrooms. That his own father had been slaughtered by savages too only strengthened their bond.

With the exception of Mansu, Dar and the other unmarried men, Jan had been welcomed with open arms. His carpentry skills found him respect, and life was simple and good. He felt so at home that his feelings of being trapped dissolved. He knew it was ridiculous, but he felt like he was fated to be here—to be with Maganda. Indeed, thoughts of Margaretje had retreated to the distant horizon of his mind.

He'd been mulling something for weeks—and this seemed like the perfect time to bring it up. He held up his finger. She looked at him with expectation, as it was his signal that he had a new word he wished to learn. Jan placed his index fingers together and raised his eyebrows.

"Make love?" she giggled and flicked his loincloth. She glanced to one side. A banana grove lay not far away.

Although tempted, Jan shook his head, and signaled that his meaning was close.

". . . Marriage?" she frowned.

"Marriage," he repeated in Ifugao with a wide smile.

Maganda's face clouded. Standing, she turned her back and waded into the paddy field and began plucking snails off rice blades and dropping them into a small basket attached to her waist. Confused and hurt, Jan joined her.

* * *

"Spirits happy today!" Maganda exclaimed.

She spoke in baby talk so he could understand, but she was pleased at how fast he soaked up the language. She had been keeping him company high in the forest while he adzed a plank.

"Spirits?"

"Yes, of course," she replied, looking at him funny. "Everything has a spirit, even us. We just spirits in bodies. Sometime spirits speak in little voices inside you. You know that, no?"

His mind leaped back to the moment the longboat had shot through the foam. It was an experience which had awakened such thoughts, one reinforced when the *Sangley* cannonball had struck his cell. But both had left him still with much to learn—certainly whatever his mysterious "destiny" was.

"Tell me," Jan said, pushing back his hair which Maganda had cut in Ifugao fashion.

"Look at Sun God. He most important god and very happy today. Look how He shines! Sometimes, He no happy and burns crops. Plant spirits also happy—look at flowers everywhere. Listen to laughter of water spirit in stream there, and soothing song of gentle pine tree spirit, and happy sound of birds!"

Jan felt like lightning had struck him! They were the very sounds he had heard when he saw the White Light! He looked around . . . listening . . . looking . . . smelling. Yes, *yes*! He recognized the spirits! He only couldn't believe he hadn't before! All of Nature was alive—*ALIVE*! So unlike the sterility and irrelevance of church where doors kept it out! That the sun was the most important god in the pantheon was perfectly logical!

". . . Are you alright?" Maganda asked.

Jan's head was spinning. "Y . . . yes! Sure!"

The epiphany flooded in to fill his spiritual vacuum.

* * *

"What happen?" Jan asked.

The entire valley was gathering before the tribal council. Before it stood a middle-aged wretch, his head hanging in shame. Jan recognized him, a farmer who lived by the creek, too poor to afford even one wife. His plots were subject to such frequent floods that in a good year he might manage to grow only one crop, whereas his higher neighbors harvested two and sometimes three. His retaining walls had collapsed in the same *baguio* that had struck the *Concepcion* and *Raid*.

Maganda made a contemptuous face. "He break straw lock on someone's granary and steal rice. God of Locks very angry when Ifugao steal, and make flood or no rain, so we punish so God can see."

Unlike spirits in mountains and trees which he could hear and smell, Jan couldn't relate to this strange god, and relegated it, as he did prophesizing from gall bladders, to superstition. Not so the Ifugao. He had never seen Chief Tonapa so indignant, nor the crowd's mood so ugly. After a harangue, the chief ripped off the thief's loincloth leaving him naked, stripped of his tribe. Fighting tears, the man picked up the machete and bow and spear the chief threw at his feet, and trudged through the glowering assembly. Several spat in his face, some struck him.

"Where he go to?" Jan asked.

Maganda waved her hand. Who cares?

Jan followed the course of the dejected man as he wound his way up the terraces. Then he disappeared over the ridge.

Jan never saw him again, and he was certain it couldn't have been long before a *canao* was being celebrated in a neighboring Kalinga, Bontoc or Benguit village.

* * *

"What that?"

"Betel nut," she answered.

By now he knew *that*—he just didn't know why people took it, because of what it did over time, turning mouths red and teeth black. He wasn't pleased that Maganda had taken up the habit, but thus far her mouth remained fresh as a flower.

She shaved slivers from an areca nut into a bamboo container and added a pinch of lime. After mashing both, she shook the coarse powder onto a heart shaped betel leaf. This she folded like the *Sangley* letter and passed to him. Jan didn't notice her hidden smile.

He pressed it into his cheek like he had seen others do and bit into it. Immediately, a flashflood of saliva surged into his mouth. The taste was so vile and bitter he gagged and spit it out, but still his mouth gushed like a waterfall, and the horrible taste remained.

Maganda laughed so hard tears burst to her eyes. "Very good, yes?" she teased as she prepared a chew for herself.

He still didn't know why people took it.

* * *

It was his fourth month in Banaue before Jan broached the subject of marriage again. Despite the murderous look in Mansu's eyes, Jan was determined to make her his wife. If the Igorots could have two or more, he felt entitled to one.

210

He felt a fresh urgency. In recent weeks, he sensed a growing coolness from Maganda. He knew she loved him, yet he sensed she harbored growing shame being with him for some reason. Chief Tonopa's attitude too was increasingly one of a superior toward one insufficient and inadequate. The other young men, once apprehensive about him, now began cracking jokes behind his back. Even Maganda's girl friends had begun to giggle when he passed. She chose to hide behind their inability to communicate well as an excuse not to talk about it. Worse, he had spotted her flirting with Mansu.

He had been de-barking a lodge pole in the forest when his love for this enigmatic, gorgeous, high spirited creature overcame him. He had practiced what he was going to say for days. Dropping his adz, he gripped her by the shoulders.

"I love you. You marry me?" he urged in his best broken Ifugao.

Tears burst to Maganda's eyes and she pulled back and tried to turn away. He seized her arm, and was about to demand of her why not—when he threw her aside.

Two Kalinga crashed toward them with axes raised. Jan grappled for his sword, knowing he didn't have time, but the leader pulled up short in surprise when he spotted Jan's golden features. His friend ran into his back, tripped and tumbled. The leader recovered and resumed his attack—but Jan had had time to unsheath his sword. His broad slash severed not only the Kalinga's head, but also the upraised hand holding the axe. Forward momentum caused his spurting body to slam against Jan before collapsing.

A bloody Jan just had time to recover before meeting the second headhunter. They circled, the headhunter's eyes flickering to the awe-inspiring Toledo blade. Then he lunged, but the quick Dutch boy plunged the blade all the way through his tattooed chest.

After stepping on his stomach and yanking the sword out, he ran to Maganda, reaching for her hand. "*We go! Maybe more!*"

"NO!" To his astonishment, she was ecstatic. Her next words tumbled out so fast he wasn't able to catch any of them. She tugged at his free arm and pointed at the heads.

He looked at them. Then at her. Then understood. "You want me bring *them*? You *crazy*!"

"*Bring!*"

Seeing that she wouldn't leave without the grizzly trophies, he raised his sword and decapitated the second Kalinga. Grabbing their heads by the hair with his free hand, they ran through the pines to the valley where her exhilarated cries spread the alarm. Women threw down hoes and rushed for the safety of the village, while men seized weapons and galloped to the ridge.

Jan had never seen Maganda in such rapture as they entered Banaue, panting. While villagers encircled them, she explained what had happened in an intoxicated voice, her eyes flashing toward Jan with adoration. Citizens who had begun to ignore Jan now beamed at him as he, with revulsion, threw the heads onto the flagstones.

The crowd parted as Chief Tonapa and Grandmother Saging rushed toward them, their expressions wrapped in worry. Maganda threw her arms around their necks. Their demeanor changed as her words tumbled out, and both shot looks of pride at Jan. The confused Dutch boy almost dropped his bloodied sword when the chief grabbed him in a bearhug, oblivious to the blood covering him. Then Tonapa pulled away and shouted something to the assembly Jan didn't catch. Cheers rose. Maganda ran up to Jan, gripped his hand, and jumped up and down, her breasts dancing with her. Because everyone was speaking in a blur of words, he had no idea what was going on.

"What is happen?"

Maganda's eyes sparkled as, with great deliberation, she pointed at him, then to herself. Then she pressed her index fingers together.

While a thunderstruck Jan realized that the roadblock to their marriage had been because he hadn't taken a head, she squealed and threw her arms around him.

* * *

"Grandson, a married man must own land," Chief Tonapa said, waving a thick arm over a paddy field three-quarters of the way up the valley wall.

It was the next day and Jan's regular routine had been uprooted. He hadn't seen Maganda since she had skipped away with her grandmother the day before. She was with her girl friends in a happy frenzy making wedding arrangements.

Jan nodded. He wasn't sure if Chief Tonapa was giving it to him or what.

"But a man must *buy* land. Understand—*buy?*"

Jan didn't, but when the chief pointed from the field to his sword he caught on. The offer was fair, even if Jan was reluctant to part with his most prized possession. He still had the flintlock. More important—he finally had Maganda.

Jan unstrapped his belt, caressed the Toledo scabbard's metallic embroidery a last, loving time. Then he handed it to the Chief. A broad smile spread across his strong features as he strapped it on.

Jan was now a man of means.

* * *

The next day he stood before the tribal council. His summons had been unexpected, which was disturbing—a feeling exacerbated by Chief Tonapa's troubled expression. It was obvious the council had discussed his place in Ifugao society. That Mansu stood to one side gloating didn't bode well.

With a heavy heart Chief Tonapa, the Toledo blade strapped to his middle, put a hand on Jan's shoulder. "Because your yellow head would be a great prize to other villages, knowledge of your presence in Banaue would bring us great danger. . . . I must forbid you from climbing higher than your land. Understand?"

Jan felt that sinking feeling again. He suspected it was a decision that had been brewing for some time.

Chief Tonapa handed Jan a hoe. Jan flushed. Working paddy was the exclusive domain of women.

"I'm sorry," Tonapa said while Mansu smirked. "We'll miss your skills as a carpenter, but you must contribute in other ways if you can't go into the forest for wood."

Jan trudged away, feelings of being a prisoner returning. And, although the chief hadn't meant it to be taken that way, humiliation was unavoidable.

* * *

213

The marriage ceremony was simple. The next day, they stood before the villagers and announced that they were man and wife.

The reception was more traditional. Chief Tonapa, as the bride's guardian, staged a huge feast and ensured that rice wine flowed like monsoon floods. He not only had two water buffaloes butchered—and the condition of the gall bladders brought cheers, for they signaled good fortune for the young couple—but he presented the newlyweds with another plot of paddy. Grandmother Saging gifted them with the hut Jan had been borrowing, along with the granary that had served as Atagar's prison. Their new holdings were more than enough to sustain them in comfort until they inherited Chief Tonapa's and Grandmother Saging's substantial holdings. Jan had married into wealth and status. Their future was bright and secure.

Many girls were saddened that the Golden Boy didn't want additional wives—but that very attitude caused the young men to do another about face. Dar and the boys crowded around him laughing and slapping him on the back like the good old days.

One cloud marred their perfect day. Mansu drank too much and in the middle of the reception, broke his spear over his thigh and stalked away.

* * *

"What this?"

They had retired home for their honeymoon, freshly tidied by Maganda. Jan's pistol, shot bag and powder horn had been moved from a ledge to pegs and a shrine set up in their place. It held an ancient, wooden statuette of a smiling, nude, pregnant woman with her arms open. Before it lay rice, banana and flower offerings.

"Chantico! Grandmother must have placed it there! It's been in her family generations!"

"Chantico?"

"Goddess of Love and Fertility! She will make sure we have many beautiful children!"

"*You* will ensure we have beautiful children," he laughed. The thought sparked a yearning to replace his lost child.

She embraced him, placing her head against his chest. "Not only that, but Chantico will ensure we're together forever—even after we die."

Jan didn't believe in idols. He'd seen enough bloody Jesus Christs nailed to crosses, and 'virgins' living with men and yet managed to give birth, back in New York. He couldn't believe how people could believe that stuff. *Boluls* he took with a grain of salt, but he wasn't beyond humoring her. "True?"

"Oh, yes! And there it's always summer, and lots to eat!"

"I no have to hoe fields?"

She laughed. "No, there everything is perfect. Just like you."

Jan picked up one of Maganda's betel nuts. "Chantico like this?"

"She *loves* it! Like me!"

"Then it hers," he said, placing it before the idol.

The love in Maganda's eyes took on another gleam as her hand drifted down his flat belly. He slid the door shut, but a beam of light still caught Chantico smiling on them.

They were sure they would live happily ever after.

23 Jack-in-the-Box

"By the time I gear up there'll be enough light," Chase said.

The sun was bursting over the Palawanian mountains. The wind continued rising, adding to the height of waves breaking over the reef, causing the red floats attached to the air lines to bob like Halloween apples. Chase studied the still shadowed shoreline and small point with binoculars, but all was barren except for the balloon basket.

He traded binocs for Polaroids and leaned over the lee of the bow and frowned. He couldn't see ten feet because of stirred up sediment. Standing, he signaled and Batuta cranked the diesel over, and Liana fired up the compressor. The racket banged back off the trees. "That should take care of the sharks," Chase shouted as he slipped into his BC. "I'll drop down and get the statue . . . what are you doing?"

The woman who was terrified of sharks was pulling her vest on.

"I want my camera equipment! If I can get it into freshwater, maybe it can be salvaged."

"I can get it. Remember what happened to Quinn."

"I do—that's why we're going *together*. Besides, you don't know what was in my bag, and you might miss something."

He had learned it was no use arguing once she made up her mind about something. Chase turned to Batuta who had descended to the stern deck. "If they follow their usual pattern, it'll be most dangerous once we have the statue up." The machine-gun was set up behind a barricade facing shore. "You know how to use it?"

"I'll manage," came the contemptuous reply.

Chase dropped the basket to the basement, then gaffed the two floats connected to the chainsaw and jackhammer and attached their lines to the compressor.

"What'd you do that for?" she asked as he hurried to catch up with Liana who was buckling her weight belt.

"I have to blow water out of the lines, otherwise we'll never get them aboard."

They did a last scan along shore, and for sharks, then grabbed sharksticks, and jumped overboard. As Chase followed the basket rope down, he corkscrewed, watching for maneaters. He wished Liana wasn't in such a panic to retrieve her stupid equipment—abandoning her own safety procedures, she had all but disappeared into the mist below. Alarmed, Chase pinched his nose and blew as hard as he could. His right ear popped open, but a sharp pain in the left stopped him at fifteen feet. He yanked down on the rope, gliding up a fathom until the pain subsided. His face contorted as he pinched his nose and blew again. This time, the stubborn ear popped like a champagne cork.

He looked down between his fins. Liana was nowhere to be seen! Above him, the *Wracker's* hull was only just visible through the murk. Chase pulled himself head first down the rope. He was a dozen feet off the bottom before a row of cannons leached out of the mist. Settled between two culverins was the exploded scuba tank with a few shreds of rubber suiting. It was all that remained of the diver.

Chase's anxiety retreated somewhat as Liana's form appeared. She was on the bottom stuffing cameras into her bag. The photographer kicked off, evidently having spotted one beyond the range of Chase's vision. He was about to look for the statue when he sucked in his breath.

A dark form glided out of the mist behind Liana. It wasn't a shark. It was a diver in a black wetsuit and rebreathing equipment with a knife. He kicked to catch up to her, unaware of Chase hovering above. The writer propelled himself down the basket rope, his sharkstick extended. To his horror a second figure in black, also with bubble-less equipment, appeared behind the first, wielding a harpoon.

The forward diver grabbed one of Liana's fins. She turned, expecting to see Chase. Her eyes registered surprise—then terror as the man gripped her ankle and yanked her toward him. Before she could react, he ripped the sharkstick from her hands and clawed for her regulator. Just as he yanked it out, Chase jammed his sharkstick into the diver's lower side. The shotgun shell exploded with a *WHOMPH*, and a cloud of red burst from his back. He twisted away in agony.

The second diver pulled up in surprise. Leaving Liana flailing for her regulator, Chase dropped his sharkstick, yanked out his knife, and kicked toward him. The writer raised his arm defensively as the man fired his harpoon. Chase felt little pain as the arrow punched through his forearm, the barb sticking out four inches—but his hand sprang open, the knife dropping.

While Chase pulled up to draw the harpoon through to the long cord attached to the gun, the driver fumbled for his knife. Chase turned just in time to grab the diver's wrist with both hands. Though his right was now weak, he twisted the attacker's wrist back, but they were underwater and tumbled over and over. The cord, harpoon and gun trailing from Chase's bleeding arm tangled them like a spider's cocoon.

Chase didn't dare let go—even as the diver's free hand shot toward his reg. The writer took a breath a moment before it was yanked out. With all his strength, Chase twisted the Muslim's arm behind his back and forced him face down on the sand. He wrestled for the terrorist's regulator with his weakened hand, fighting against time, but he had clamped his free hand over his mouthpiece. Chase tore the man's mask off.

His lungs begging for air, Chase groped for his own air line. He yanked on it—but his reg jammed between his tank and vest. The Filipino only had to wait until Chase had to release his grip and kick for the surface. Then he merely had to grab Chase's ankle, and it would be all over.

Chase was about to—had to—break free when he spotted a large Crown of Thorns a foot ahead of the man's head.

With strength born of desperation, Chase gripped the man's hair, heaved him forward—and jammed his head onto the spikes. The poisonous barbs stabbed into the back of the Beagle Boy's paw and he reacted with such violence that he yanked his regulator out. The starfish tumbled back onto the sand. While the diver flailed for his regulator, Chase caught a glimpse of his face.

It was Chico Rolando. Rage fueled Chase and he wrestled the Abu Sayyef leader back over the deadly starfish. Rolando managed to grip his reg but his hand was paralyzing, and it fell free. Chase hoped the terrorist's eyes were wide open when he jammed his face onto the Crown of Thorns and pushed down with all his might.

The effects were immediate as the black spikes pierced his eyes and brain. Rolando screamed—Chase could actually hear him—and expelled his air in a huge mushroom cloud, then convulsed, before going limp.

Chase—his own lungs screaming—grabbed Rolando's regulator and stuffed it into his mouth, and panted like he'd just completed the 800 meter at the Olympics.

Rolando's motionless body lay on its back, his arms spread like Christ's. The less Christian arms of the starfish wiggled as it tried to free itself from the Abu Sayyef leader's face.

The writer switched the terrorist's reg for his own. While cutting through the harpoon cord he looked for Liana, wondering why she hadn't come to his assistance. He didn't have to look long or far to learn why. She was under a third diver with a rebreather, his back to Chase. Her regulator had been yanked out again, her mask was off, and her eyes were wide as she fought the much stronger man. Her sharkstick was nowhere to be seen. The knives were too far away.

The chainsaw lay on the sand. Flickers of a horror movie Chase had seen flashed through his mind as he fumbled for the button with his stiffening finger. Liana's attacker pinned her wrists on the sand on either side of her head and waited for her to give up her last breath.

It was his last.

The high pitched whine of the chainsaw startled him into turning his head. He released Liana and kicked off to escape but it was too late—Chase drove the spinning teeth into his stomach. The diver gripped the whirling blade but his fingers flew away as Chase eviscerated him. Intestines mix-mastered in a cloud, and small, multi-colored fish shot in to nip at undigested *adobos*.

Chase corkscrewed, the bloody buzzsaw still flying, searching for other attackers, but in the limited visibility, he could see no one. The chainsaw fell silent as Chase dropped it to the sand and finned to Liana, she holding her regulator to her mouth with both hands and hyperventilating. When she caught her breath and bearings, she kicked in panic away from the cloud of innards surrounding her.

They had no time to waste. Noise or no noise, carnage like this was going to attract sharks. Chase grabbed her mask and handed it to her. While she cleared it, he unsnapped her weight belt and jabbed his thumb skyward. She hesitated, looking around for her camera bag and the rest of her gear. Chase shook his fist at her, and she responded by shooting him a bird. She shoveled the last of her equipment into her bag before firing her vest.

Chase looked back and forth, searching for the statue. It was only feet away. Grabbing the chainsaw again, he kicked to the basket and severed the line. Gripping the end, Chase booted toward the statue, chainsaw in tow. Cursing his numbing hand, Chase looped the rope under the figure's armpits, tied a bowline, then searched in vain for Liana's sharkstick.

A reef shark cruised out of the mist and honed in on the filleted diver like a missile. Smaller fish shot away as the shark tore out a jawful of human rope. Another shark streaked in behind. It seized a drumstick and shook the body like it was a rag doll, causing more stuffing to come loose.

In a blur, Chase dropped his weight belt, grabbed the chainsaw, fired his BC, and kicked toward the surface while more gray shapes flew to the scent. As he neared the surface, he yanked off his fins and unzipped his vest so he could exit the blood bath as fast as possible. Just then another shark, and the largest of all, glided in. It flicked its head, then picked up the blood trail leading from Chase's arm.

The killing machine struck toward him. Chase locked the chainsaw's trigger to 'on' and prayed that his stiffening hand wouldn't be the end of him. The unexpected noise startled the shark, because at the last moment it veered away. Chase glanced up. Liana was nowhere to be seen, and the choppy surface was coming down on him fast. He would be helpless there, but he didn't dare free a hand to empty his vest.

The shark circled, whipping its tail. Chase twisted to keep the flailing chainsaw pointed at the brute, hoping its high-pitched scream would keep it at bay. It didn't. So sudden was the attack that Chase had little time to react. The predator rolled onto its side, its eyes hooded and its lips drew back over jagged white teeth in a deadly grin.

It streaked right into the chainsaw. The long blade slipped down its throat like a tongue depressor, the saw's teeth tearing at the shark's insides. With unimaginable strength and speed, it twisted away, ripping the chainsaw from Chase's weakened grip. Then the shark rolled belly up, the still roaring chainsaw slipping from its mouth and falling toward the sea floor. Another shark attacked the bucking saw, but wrenched away as the blade ripped the bottom half of its mouth away. Others closed on the injured sharks.

Chase was helpless as one streaked toward him. He struggled out of his vest, hoping to face the tank toward the onrushing shark. He didn't have time. Chase was even with the bottom of the hull. The surface was mere feet above. The shark was closer.

Three white streaks cut through the water from above with muffled rifle reports, the shots punching into the predator. Its mouth slammed shut and it was already dead when its blunt nose rammed Chase, knocking the wind out of him.

He burst through the rough surface, the roar of the compressor exploding in his ears. M-16s and AK-47s cracked as Liana and Batuta drilled holes in the water around him. Chase abandoned his vest, his arms a blur as he crawled toward the *Wracker*. He grabbed the ladder, but his right hand was useless and he fell back. On his second try, Liana grabbed his arm, and he bellied over onto the deck just ahead of a white shape that shot from the depths, clamping down on air inches behind his heels. Batuta punched the killer back down with a burst that left powder burns on Chase's leg.

"Reel it in!" he gasped.

He lay panting while Batuta hopped to the winch. It whined as the statue began its ascent. Chase tried to sit up but he was too spent. Liana pressed his head to her bikinied breasts and swept matted hair from his eyes. He felt her love penetrating his terror, dissolving it, and he realized only then just how strong their bond had become, one forged in the crucible of combat.

His breathing subsiding, Chase pulled away. A delta of blood poured down his forearm.

"You're bleeding!"

"Yeah, it's that time of the month," he muttered.

"Very funny."

She was half way to the cabin for the First Aid Kit when the winch strained, and she paused. The line whipped sideways through the water as if they had hooked an enormous trout.

"An enormous shark has it!" Batuta shouted as the *Wracker* tilted towards the line. "I've stopped the winch but the rope is going to break!"

"Hit the release!" Chase shouted.

Batuta looked for it, then threw his hands in the air. "Where is it!"

Liana looked at Chase's bleeding arm.

"Forget the Kit, Liana! Hit the lever on the other side!"

Before she could react, the line danced slack and the boat rocked back to an even keel. They stared at the limp line—then breathed again as it tautened and the statue settled. The trout had spit the fly.

"Thank gawd we got out of there before he arrived!" Chase pulled himself to his feet, compressing the wound with his hand. "I'm okay Bag Lady. Let's get the statue up first!"

She was torn, but swept up Batuta's AK-47 as he pulled the winch's throttle and it began groaning again.

"It's about to surface!" the native shoulted. "And that shark is after it again!"

A silver surge shot upward, its mouth open. Inches before the statue broke surface, the shark's teeth clamped on a platinum leg. Liana's rifle cracked. The shark released its awful grip, and drifted away trailing blood. Its mates converged on it while Batuta hoisted the statue out of the water. Early morning sun glistened off its wet sides.

"Stop Batuta!" she cried. "The shark bit the rope!"

Strands snapped and twisted free above the knot. Batuta leaned out and grabbed the winch's arm and began pulling it in. Chase positioned himself to grab the prize.

"Hurry!" she screamed "It's unraveling fast!"

The statue was almost over the gunwale. Below, crimson water churned.

"*Ohmygawd!*"

The rope snapped.

The statue slammed down onto the gunwale's edge just as

Chase grabbed its right arm with both hands, but his right slipped away, smearing the statue with blood. It tilted toward the water, but he hung on and cried out for help. Batuta crashed down beside him, his strong hands grappling the statue's other arm. Its motion stopped—but only for a moment before it continued arm wrestling them to the mat.

"It's too heavy!" Batuta exclaimed.

Its base slipped toward the water, stopping with only an inch gripping the gunwale.

"Liana! My arm's useless!"

Her hand shot between them and gripped the metallic beard. As the three cursed and grunted, the statue angled back. Then it tumbled with them onto deck with a heavy *crash*. They lay breathing heavily and staring at the dripping statue.

"I th . . . think we should stick to fishing for walleye from now on," Chase managed.

Liana didn't appreciate the humor. It was too close for her. Too close for Chase. Much, much too close for Lolo . . . and Agila . . . and Ben . . . and Quinn. She picked herself up and hurried to the cabin for the First Aid Kit. Returning, she crouched beside Chase and opened it.

"We appreciate your help Batuta," the writer said. "Best cut the diesel and the compressor. We need to save fuel."

Liana turned Chase's arm. "Oh, my gawd. This is an ugly gash!"

The motors throbbed down to a resounding silence that left their ears ringing.

"Did you find all your camera gear?" he asked while she cleaned and dressed the wound. He was acutely aware that if he would have gone down alone, he wouldn't have stood a chance.

"It's in the freshwater tank. Fortunately, the memory chips were in a waterproof pack. I'm carrying them here from now on." She patted an outline in her bikini top.

He pulled himself to his feet when she was done. "Now all we have to do is wait for Earthquake to fly in with that fuel." *And hope he's on our side.*

Chase ignored his throbbing arm as he scanned the water around them. They would have to leave their equipment littering the basement. Shading his eyes with his good hand, Chase squinted toward the small point. The balloon basket sat on the margin of the waving coconut trees.

"Batuta, I have two last favors to ask . . . don't look like that, please . . . then we'll be out of your hair. Oh, we'll be back to excavate the galleon with another crew, but we won't need you anymore—and that's a promise."

"Last favors are best favors, Mr. Ballentyne." He offered one of his rare smiles.

"Stay with us until Earthquake arrives."

Batuta smirked. "And if he doesn't?"

Chase turned away. He didn't have an answer.

"And your other request?"

"Give me a hand getting that balloon aboard. Two cripples are better than one."

"Chase—leave it!"

"It belongs to a friend of Ben's and mine Liana," Chase replied, climbing into the Zodiac. "Don't worry, there's only one Beagle Boy left—and he's with their *banca* wherever it is."

A less than mollified Liana stationed herself behind the M60 and watched the Zodiac streak toward shore. Chase cut the outboard as the boat ran up onto the beach. Leaving their weapons behind, Chase helped Batuta hobble toward the basket.

"I thought we left the balloon and blaster inside," Chase frowned. "How did it get behind—"

They froze. A man had popped out of the basket like a Jack-in-the-box, an AK-47 in his hands.

"Don't move."

Chase and Batuta looked like they had seen a ghost.

24 The Great Escape

"I not welcome in Banaue anymore," Jan muttered in near perfect Ifugao. "I . . . I think I must leave. Somehow return to my old village."

He and Maganda sat on a dike, she taking a betel break. Jan fingered his coconut shell necklace and looked at the verdant rice terraces across the valley. After nine months, the once beautiful sight now looked as appealing as a quarry. The dreary diet of rice, yam, taro and beans made hardtack sound inviting. It was no wonder headhunters attacked sacrificial animals with such frenzy—it was virtually the only time they ate meat.

He certainly didn't like women's work. It was too hard. It was no wonder the older women, like Grandmother Saging, looked so much older than their husbands. Jan's back was so sore sometimes he had to walk bent like her. Worse, he was now openly laughed at behind his aching back.

But most unsettling, his renewed state of grace had worn off. A state of siege was a constant among Igorots—and none wanted pressure increased. It wasn't unknown for enemy headhunters to take advantage of a *baguio* to skulk deep into the valley. Word could leak that Jan lived there. He was not only being treated as a pariah again, but there were expressions of violence in some quarters. Jan put his callused hand over hers. He didn't want to leave her, but he saw no choice.

Maganda spat a red stream into the water and squeezed his fingers. "I'll go with you."

"W . . . what?"

Maganda's eyes were wet. "I have thought about it too. I don't know how long Grandfather will live. Then Mansu will be made chief. . . ."

Chief Tonapa had begun complaining about abdominal pain and was losing weight. She had seen it happen before. A bad spirit had possessed him and in a few months he would shrivel and die. Only the number of skulls decorating Mansu's lodge approached those of Chief Tonapa's. Jan's days were as numbered as the chief's. He would be banished—he was simply too great a risk to the community.

"But this is your home, your people. . . ?"

"Jan, I have never met anyone like you, so gentle and kind. You make my life so much easier, not just in the fields. Without you . . . I can't imagine. . . ."

And there were other reasons. Jan had told her fantastic stories about his village—with huts soaring four stories to scrape the very sky. It raised questions that perhaps Banaue wasn't the center of the universe after all! Perhaps they could go there in one of the big bowls that he described, that floated on a puddle so large one couldn't see the other side. The bowls that moved by the wind spirit blowing enormous shawls tied to trees.

There perhaps she might become pregnant and bear the child he so desperately wanted. She couldn't understand why Chantico hadn't blessed them, unless she had other plans for them. It certainly wasn't from lack of trying!

Jan clutched her hand. With her knowledge of Igorot ways, they just might survive the trek to the coast! They could make their way to Manila where, surely, he could secretly contact Solina Cruzat, and she could arrange passage to Canton on a junk! With Ifugao gold, they could book with a trader to London—and from there to New York!

"B . . . but what about Margaretje?" His inherent honesty compelled him tell Maganda about her and the child. She had taken it without so much as a blink.

"You can take her as a second wife," she replied, her tone insinuating that she would remain Number One.

It suddenly seemed so possible! With gold, you could do anything in America! He could rescue Margaretje from her shameful existence, and whisk the two women he loved south to the Carolinas and buy one of the fledging plantations!

Yes, as the honeymoon gave way to drudgery, thoughts of Margaretje had returned.

"But how? If we go, your grandfather will send warriors after us, thinking I kidnapped you! I watched all the time! Mansu never takes his eyes off me!"

That's what worried her most. It wasn't beyond Mansu to arrange an accident—ambushing her husband and burying his head to make it look like an enemy raiding party had been responsible. The social climate was prime for just such an incident. For that reason she rarely let Jan out of her sight. That Mansu hadn't taken action sooner was only because the young Dutchman had saved his life—but this carried less and less currency with each day.

"We need a distraction," she said as she stood, announcing an end to the betel break.

Jan picked up a handful of rice shoots and waded into the paddy field. A distraction. How do you create a distraction in a valley constantly on the highest level of alertness?

It found him.

* * *

"Jan! Look! They're back!"

Across the valley, a band of warriors skipped down the steps. It was the most recent headhunting expedition—Young Turks out to break Mansu and his team's legendary record. They had been away almost three weeks, and tensions had been high, fearing they had lost their own heads. But from their ebullient manner and heavy backpacks, it was clear they had done well.

Maganda swept aside long hair blowing across her eyes. One carried a large, square, green object. "What's that?"

Jan squinted but it was too far away. Farmers were dropping tools and rushing toward the village.

"Go, I'll finish," Maganda said, pinching his bottom. Men always wanted to see the trophies.

Normally, the thought repulsed Jan, but he'd do anything to get out of planting. After kissing her cheek, he joined the exodus.

Mansu and Dar were already there, trying to look nonchalant

as a mountain of heads were dumped before an ailing Chief Tonapa. He sat in his doorway with the Spanish sword across his lap, and congratulated the exuberant party in a raspy voice. Jan gave Mansu a wide berth, but the warrior spotted him and scowled. He rolled heads over with his foot to check ages and sexes, and smiled. True, there were more than his team took— but many were women and children. There was one Spaniard's—a significant trophy—but even with that they didn't represent a true challenge to his record.

Villagers pressed around the large, square object. They considered it a great prize.

"We attacked a lowland hut where one of the white people lived," the headhunter with the plumed headdress announced, smirking at Mansu. No one had ventured that far afield before, the odor rising from the heads confirming the distance. "We took his head! And *this*! The metal will make jewelry and tools!"

Jan couldn't believe it.

"Jan, what is it?" the headhunting leader demanded.

It was the distraction he and Maganda were looking for! It was something found in virtually every home in New York!

It was a copper still, oxidized by the tropical humidity.

"I . . . it's a magic, uh, bowl for make rice wine into firewater." Jan recalled the name American savages gave whiskey. Lying didn't come easy to him, but he was learning it was sometimes necessary.

"Fire water?" Chief Tonapa repeated.

"Yes! Magic water that burn like fire! To my people it is a spirit—the Great Spirit!"

Villagers looked dubious as Jan lifted one end, checking its condition. It was intact—but something rattled inside. He unfastened catches securing the lid and his heart leapt. Coiled inside was copper tubing, and two large bundles wrapped in thick, cloth layers. He lifted one out and unwrapped it while the natives pushed closer.

It was a handblown, glass jar with a large lid. He held it up so sunlight glinted through its green sides. The Ifugao murmured among themselves. You could see right through it! The jar itself was truly magic!

"Firewater is poured into the magic jars. One must handle

them with great care. They break very easily, like *Sangley* water jars, and the God of Jars would be furious—even more than the God of Locks." Jan repacked and replaced it inside the still.

"What's it for, this firewater?" The cynic was Mansu.

Jan's mind raced. "In my people's *canao*—for a boy or girl to become an adult, they must prove they can drink much of it! But it is very hot and not easy!"

There wasn't a headhunter there who didn't take the bait.

"Do you know how to make this magic firewater?" the chief asked in a voice not as robust as usual. "This . . . this Great Spirit that makes boys men and girls women?"

"Yes."

A renewed respect germinated in villagers' eyes.

"But it won't be ready until the *canao's* last day," he tempered. "And I need help."

The chief was intrigued. "How? I'll tell them."

"I need all houses to make rice wine—as much as possible! And I'll need many *Sangley* jars to put the firewater in!"

* * *

Jan could tell by the way Maganda stoked their fire that she was nervous about the plan, though it hadn't stopped her from joining in wholeheartedly.

"I know a hole dug in the forest where there's no more gold or silver," she whispered. "I'll take food at different times and hide it." She set the green stick aside and flew into his arms. "Close the door! Make love to me!"

As Jan turned to slide the panels, blood drained from his freckled face. Mansu's back receded behind the next hut.

Jan groped in the dark for her. They made love desperately . . . deliberately . . . then, finally, deliciously.

* * *

"Show us this 'firewater,'" Mansu sneered.

Pine logs crackled and snapped beneath the still, its copper tubing coiling from the top through an irrigation waterfall. Curious men squatted around it in silence. It was the sixth day, the wine was ready, and Jan had just finished running the first batch through the still and into one of the green jars.

He was prepared to meet just such a challenge. That it came from Mansu delighted him. Jan poured a bowl full of the clear liquid and lit a taper. Summoning all the drama he could, he raised the bowl and chanted the Dutch Reformed Church's liturgy. Then, he lowered it so all could see, and touched the taper to the surface.

Jaws fell as a blue flame danced above the liquid. One man dared to steal his finger forward, but snatched it back with a cry. Mansu tried not to appear impressed.

But Jan wasn't through yet. Borrowing theatrics from Father Ignacio del Atagar, he raised the flaming bowl to the sun, switched to Dutch, and boomed: "Scare the crap out of this stupid son-of-a-gun and his friends!"

He flung the contents into the fire.

WHOOOOOOOOOOOOOOMPH!

The headhunters shrieked and crabbed backwards. Dogs barked, chicken squawked, pigs squealed and all ran for their lives and—best of all—Mansu tripped over his feet and fell. While the Ifugao looked at each other, Mansu jumped up and stalked away. Jan hid a grin as he attached the glass lid to the jar with beeswax.

Then he sobered. By causing Mansu to lose face, the last few coins he held for saving the headhunter's life had just been spent.

* * *

It was near the end of the day and Maganda was helping. Jan had three long days of distilling ahead when Chief Tonapa approached with the council. The old man walked slowly, but no one dared offer assistance. Jan noticed that he had cinched Toledo sword's belt in another notch. The chief regarded the glass and ceramic jars already filled, then began wiggling a lid loose.

"No, no, no!" Jan protested, wanting to husband it.

"Why? It's ready, isn't it?"

"The Fire God, uh, has to taste each batch first or he'll be angry!" Maganda looked away. Jan especially hated to lie to his father-in-law, who had always been good to them.

The chief nodded, understanding the priorities of the gods. "But Mansu tells me that the Fire God got angry when he tasted it."

"No, it's the opposite! The better the magic water, the bigger the Fire God's expression of *joy*!"

Chief Tonapa let the explanation ferment, then nodded.

"I will show you how powerful the firewater spirit is. Maganda, could you bring me a small bowl with a lid, and a chicken gall bladder from the *canao*?"

While she hurried away, the chief held his side, his breathing hinting at suppressed pain. In a few minutes she returned with a Ming jar. As the chief and his retinue edged closer, Jan filled it with moonshine and dropped in the gall bladder. Then he replaced the lid and sealed it with bee's wax.

"No matter if the meat is left five days or forever, it will remain the same! But it must be closed tight with beeswax, or the Great Spirit will sneak out over time."

Jan's words made a deep impression. Chief Tonapa accepted the jar, turned, and limped back in the direction of the *canao*.

* * *

"Our supplies ready?" Jan whispered. He was exhausted from long days of distilling—but their home and granary were filled with brimming trade jars, all safely secured by straw locks. They had just enough room to sleep.

"In the cave," Maganda said as she lay down. Light from a tallow lamp flickered across worry lines. "Is that backpack ready for me to take?"

"Yes." Jan closed the lid. He hoped the fifty pounds of gold wouldn't slow them. Lifting his powder horn from its peg, he opened it. Unable to see in the dim light, he dipped his finger inside—and a cold wave swept over him. He beat the horn against his palm, trying to shake gunpowder into his hand.

"What's the matter?" She had pulled herself up onto an elbow.

"The powder for my weapon is gone! It no work without it!"

". . . Y . . . you didn't tell me what it was. I thought it was your drinking bowl! It was filled with dirt so I washed it!"

Jan groaned.

"I . . . I can find a bow and arrow!"

"I don't know how to shoot one good. Can you?"

". . . No."

"Don't bother then," he said, suppressing anger.

He lay beside her. While he brooded what to do about the loss, she wept. He didn't have much time to think. The next day they would make their escape.

* * *

A rooster crowing woke Jan from a shallow sleep. Raising himself onto an elbow, he slid the door open. A tentative smile touched his lips. It was cloudy and—better—misty. He turned to Maganda. It was evident from her eyes that she hadn't slept well either.

"You're sure?" he whispered. "You don't have to come."

"I do."

* * *

A constricted yelp attracted Jan's attention. Looking up from rows of firewater jars he was assembling within the semi-circle of heads, he saw a man and his dog. The headhunter had tied a noose around the pet's neck, flipped the other end of the line over a branch of the tree growing in the clearing, and two accomplices were hoisting Fido. The grinning owner stepped forward with a club. The first blow caved in the dog's ribcage and it hung fibrillating, its eyes wide. The second blow broke its back.

Already sickened by the stench of green, maggot-crawling heads, Jan looked away. Another thing he wouldn't miss was dog meat, nor how the Ifugao prepared it. The women—Maganda included—who had been helping him carry jars hurried to inspect the gall bladder. A groan rose from the assembly. Fright filled Maganda's eyes as she ran up to him.

"The gall bladder was *white* instead of dark!" Her voice dropped. "We must not go today!"

Jan felt that familiar sinking feeling again. It was time to break away from their superstitions. Back on Manhattan, spirits in sycamore trees and brooks would still exist—but not so rooting around in animal guts predicting the future. The dog was old and sick.

"The firewater is ready!" he hissed. "We can no wait!"

"But Jan!" Her lips quivered. "The gods are sending a sign that—"

"No 'buts.' We *must* go today or we lose our chance!" He hated himself for manipulating her. "You heard how joyous the Fire God was when I gave him firewater! And the Fire God is the son of the Sun God, the most powerful of all. Which gods send messages through gall bladders?"

"I . . . I don't know."

"You see? Minor gods. And the Sun God has even sent us mist today because we have pleased his son. What better sign is there than *that*?"

". . . Y . . . yes, you're right. But—"

"Don't worry, even if the signs in the gall bladder are right and we're brought back, they won't punish *you*. You can go anywhere you want—not like me."

"But I care what happens to y—!"

"Hush! Someone is come!"

Reluctantly, Maganda helped Jan finish arranging the jars.

* * *

Chief Tonapa, sitting with the headhunting party and council on either side, nodded toward the jars assembled before him. Just beyond sat the entire population of the valley, except for sentries, with Mansu and Dar standing at the crowd's edge. Everyone bore a drinking bowl and anticipation was high. Jan glanced at Maganda. She turned away, unable to bear seeing her grandfather deceived—especially since it was obvious that his pains were worse today. So bad that he wasn't wearing his pride—the Toledo blade.

Imitating the dramatic gestures of Dutch Reformed priests, Jan dipped a drinking bowl into a jar and touched a taper to it. As blue flames danced, awe rippled through the crowd. Jan raised it in the direction of the Sun God somewhere high in the cloudy sky.

"May they have hangovers they'll never forget!" he intoned in Dutch.

Lowering the bowl, he blew out the flames, then took a sip, knowing they would follow his example. That little boiled all the way down to the orlop deck. Touching the taper to the bowl again, he offered it to Chief Tonapa. He stood with difficulty and accepted.

"Drink very little, Grandfather," Jan cautioned as the old man faced the villagers. "The firewater is very, very strong."

The chief toasted the sun, then Jan's face drained as Tonapa didn't blow it out, but rather threw back the entire contents! His eyes and cheeks bulged like a keg of gunpowder had exploded in his head, then he doubled over gasping. The crowd surged to its feet. Maganda and her grandmother flew to his side. Jan tensed as Mansu and Dar's hands slipped to their axes.

A wheezing Chief Tonapa waved everyone back. When he managed to straighten, his eyes were watery and his face betel nut red. Then a broad smile lit up his face. No one was more relieved than Jan as the mood swung back to joy. Hands drifted from weapons, but Maganda was almost as white as Jan.

The headhunting squad was next to partake. In emulation of their chief—and in response to Jan's earlier challenge—they tossed it back flames and all. Villagers pressed forward as Jan and Maganda ladled out firewater, touching each with burning tapers. A primitive band struck up a beat. Hooting and hollering men soon began pulling women forward to dance. As the band fueled up, their tempo increased to a frenzy—and so did the revelry.

Jan smiled—he had never seen the Ifugao celebrate with such wild abandon.

* * *

By late afternoon, the most prominent sound was that of snoring, the second of wretching, the third of groaning from burned lips and mouths. Villagers lay everywhere, oblivious to a cold rain that had begun. Maganda tucked a shawl over her grandparents, who lay snoring on their mats. The last member of the band, unaware that he had been playing alone and out of tune, nodded off.

Jan set the wooden dipper aside, relieved that his resistance to alcohol had built up on the *Raid*. Between that and faking toasts, the firewater had done little more than fire his courage. He was also relieved that he had distilled as much as he had: the hard drinking Ifugao had left only a few gallons.

He drew a tense Maganda aside. He had been worrying all day how to replace his priceless flintlock. "I need Spanish sword."

She stared at him in horror. "*No!* The God of Locks would be furious!"

"Keep your voice down. It's not stealing! It's a fair trade! Your grandparents get all their property back! I get my sword! We not survive without it! And the God of Locks doesn't live where we are going!"

She wavered. Against her better judgment, she hiked her shawl and hurried to their own hut. There, she wrapped a hoe in a blanket, then inched up the ladder to her grandparents' home and, with trembling hands, broke the straw knot. She quickly wrapped the sword in the blanket with only the hoe blade showing.

After returning and exchanging a rigid nod with Jan, who was helping the drooling headhunting leader, his plumed hat askew, take another drink, she struck out ahead. He waited until she had disappeared into the mist a quarter of the way up the terrace steps before picking up a hoe. The few villagers not comatose paid scant attention as he strode in the direction of his fields.

As he climbed, Jan sent a prayer to the Sun God thanking Him for the poor visibility. By the time he was half way up, the village was hidden not only from his view, but from that of the sentries who stood with backs to the valley, squinting into the mist. Jan waited with bated breath until the nearest guard looked away, then slipped into the clouded forest. He didn't take a real breath until he had padded a hundred yards.

Dropping the hoe, he pulled out his dagger and looked for Maganda. Anxiety gripped him until he caught sight of her waving in the distance. Quickly joining her, he strapped on the Toledo sword, both acutely aware of the awful finality of their decision. She crouched before a limestone ridge piled with debris, threw pine boughs aside, and crawled into the long abandoned mine. Jan stood guard, wanting to put as much distance between them and the village as possible during the night.

Maganda scurried out, eyes wide. "Our backpacks!"

"What is happened?"

"Gone!"

"Wha—"

An arrow slammed into a pine tree next to them, its feathers vibrating. Grabbing Maganda, they dived into the debris. His eyes swept the forest. He didn't have to look long or far.

Mansu stepped out from behind a bush with his bow relined. Dar and other armed Ifugao drifted toward them from hiding places. Jan's nemesis stuck out his tongue, then a smile spread across his features as he eyed Maganda. Reaching behind the bush where he had been hidden, he dragged out two backpacks and dropped them.

Rice and gold spilled onto the pine needle covered forest floor.

25 The Betrayed

"Qu . . . Quinn!" Chase exclaimed.

Batuta stood on the sand beside him, frozen in mid-limp. Their eyes swept from the familiar face to the Kalashnikov in his grasp.

"Yes, the Eskimo himself. Now, step back while I get out of this damned thing. And, Batuta—your machete—on the sand. *Do it!*"

They reeled back as if from a blow, Batuta flopping his weapon to the sand. Speechless, they watched the anthropologist crawl out of the balloon basket. A bloody bandage was wrapped around a thigh, and a wad of papers protruded from the back pocket of cutoffs.

"What's going on?" Chase demanded.

"The three divers. What happened to them?"

"You knew?"

"Of course. They were to ambush you, but I saw you haul up the statue. Well?"

"Shark food, Dr. Quinn."

A smile touched his lips, and he nodded toward the basket. "Get this thing into the boat and let's get back to the *Wracker*. I'll be taking the Zodiac, and this'll be your only chance to get it. Get moving!"

Dr. Jekyll had Hyded again. As they walked the basket down the beach and Quinn leaned into the jungle for a gas can, they noted a radio, supplies and scope there. With the basket in the bow, they lumbered back to the mother ship. Long before they reached it, they could see Liana following them with binoculars.

"Best put down the gun, Liana," Chase advised as the Zodiac glided alongside, and Chase looked over his shoulder to eye Quinn's AK-47 aimed at their backs.

Mystified, she set the Beretta on the work bench. Chase and Batuta ascended the dive ladder, and stepped back while Quinn joined them aboard.

"Now, exchange the balloon for the statue," he said, checking that the pistol's clip was full before laying his AK aside.

"What is going—"

"He's ripping us off, Liana!" Chase exploded. "Quinn— there's tons and tons of silver down there! What's gotten into you?"

"That can be your share," he said wryly. His eyes skimmed the horizon. There were no other vessels, no planes. "Now do as I damned well say! Move it!"

Fifteen minutes later the trade had been made. Quinn threw a coiled rope to Liana.

"Now, Bag Lady, tie their hands behind their backs and to the compressor, starting with your boy friend. Earthquake can free you when he arrives. Down on your butts you two. Move it!"

Batuta eased his injured ankle out as he sat facing shore, and Chase lowered himself to his right. Diesel odor seeped from the decking. Once they were tied, Quinn bound Liana next to Chase, then checked the mens' bonds. Satisfied, he stood and shoved the 9mm in the front of his cutoffs.

"Why Quinn?" Liana pleaded.

"For one thing, the name's not Quinn. The real Quinn's a croaker."

"*What!*" Chase and Liana exclaimed. Even Batuta was taken aback.

"Smuggling dope and artifacts from around Southeast Asia is my game. I've been working out of the Philippines for years. I heard about the real Quinn, of course, having gone bamboo in Banaue, eking out a living, drinking too much rice wine. He tried to get away from that by moving to Puerto Princesa, but it didn't pan out. I ran into him when he moved to Manila and was staying at a cheap pensione. It's amazing how easy it is to become bosom buddies with a drunk by standing a few drinks. He was lonely and broke—and said he had a few items he had collected over the years he wanted to sell, but was so out of the loop he had no idea how. I offered to help. He took me to a storehouse. The sucker had a small *fortune* in trade jars and ethnology! I arranged with Jesus to break in and clean it out. . . . Unfortunately, Quinn showed up. . . ." He drew his finger across his throat.

"Jesus! I can't believe what I'm hearing!"

"Yes—Jesus—Bag Lady. He's obviously more than just my houseboy and driver. I wasn't pleased to learn JC had crucified Quinn—like most sots, he had his charm. Jesus fed him to the sharks." He grinned. "Those were his collections you sold, Chase. I don't dare go back to the States."

"Oh, no, you even made me your accomplice. . . ."

Quinn checked his watch, and began shaking and separating gas cans.

"Over my Migs Quinn'd told me about this planned cave expedition—including the probability of finding ceramics and gold jewelry. He'd also told me that *National Geographic* had to bow out at the last minute." He shrugged. "It would be a shame to see that Writ go to waste."

Chase swore while Quinn grinned again.

"To make sure Dr. Quinn wasn't reported missing, I went to his pensione—they were happy to have someone pay his arrears and take his stuff. Unfortunately, waiting for him was a fax from *National Geographic*. It said you would be coming after all! I thought the caper was over—but then I figured, hey, Quinn and I are about the same age and size and I even have his clothes! There was no author's photo on the dustcover of his book. I just had to bone up on it, and Fox's on the Tabon caves, and throw in a few 'ehs,' eh? After making sure the warehouse rent was paid up to date, I rented an apartment under his name. I could use your expedition to case the joint." He grinned widest of all. "There was enough time under the terms of the Writ to return for the valuables later."

"You bast-ard!"

"But then we discovered the silver! But I hadn't figured on that son-of-a-pig Jesus! You see, I also dabble in guns. He's my contact with Abu Sayyef. What better cover for a Filipino Muslim named Mohammed than a name like Jesus? While snooping in my apartment he found the silver block, although I had it under lock. Although the little jerk was happy to pocket the 5,000 dollars I cut him for the collection heist, he saw the potential of this find for his fellow Islamic fanatics—and the havoc it would reap internationally. While you were in New York and the bag lady was playing touristo, I was dragged into a car, blindfolded, and taken to Rolando. I had no choice but to own up and strike a deal."

"A deal?" Liana asked.

"Yeah, we would salvage the wreck and warehouse it. Afterwards, the treasure would be 'stolen.' Having used the Writ under false pretenses, we couldn't very well go to the authorities." He paused. "I was then to market it anonymously and receive half."

"Why was Chico Rolando diving then, Dr. Queenn?"

"He didn't trust me."

"The man was a good judge of character."

Quinn ignored Chase's comment as he lowered gas cans into the Zodiac. "He wanted to keep an eye on us and, being impatient, do some preliminary work before we arrived. His radio had gone on the fritz—I figured that out when his *banca* first appeared. Otherwise Jesus could have contacted him to let them know we had left Manila early, they would have covered their test holes, and we never would have known they were here." He rolled his eyes. "Then you dummies had to chase them like drugstore cowboys, getting Lolo killed!"

"So you obviously recognized Rolando from my photos!"

"But I didn't want to say so—it might have frightened you off. To boost your confidence, I ordered in artillery. I banked on Jesus not being able to radio Rolando for clearance, so he had to accept my explanation about pirates."

"So Earthquake wasn't in with them," Chase said.

"No, but it didn't hurt to make the fat slob look like he was."

He strode into the cabin. Pots and pans clattered before he emerged carrying food and supplies, including his clothes and beloved stash. After dropping them into the Zodiac, he returned to the cabin. This time he reappeared with Ben's alarm clock. Setting it on the work bench, he fished into the tool box for a screwdriver. Quinn began unscrewing the clock's back.

"If they were just going to keep an eye on us," Chase asked, "why did they try to attack us in the fog?"

"Besides bringing a new radio, the Beaver that buzzed us an hour before flew in Jose's stolen reports. Know what Rolando read in them?" He paused for effect. "That both ships had been salvaged."

"*What!*" Liana exclaimed. Even Batuta looked flabbergasted.

"The Spanish in old Manila had pearl divers strip the wrecks clean. Before the drop in land level, the ships were more accessible 300 years ago. They would have gotten the cannons but another *baguio* covered them up."

"That explains why Ben lost his enthusiasm," Chase said. "He figured that out."

Quinn set the clock's back cover aside. "Rolando was so choked he tried to blow us up by remote—and was *really* choked when nothing happened! *That's* why they tried to bushwhack us—but they ran out of fog and into your M60, Chase. They settled for me when the Zodiac's prop flew off." Quinn paled. "They beat the crap out of me."

"It must have taken some beating to get it all out." Chase muttered.

"Rolando threw Jose's papers in my face—including the Master Report. He told me to read it because it was my 'death warrant.'" He pulled the papers out of his shorts and held them up. "Jose wrote that the only thing that *hadn't* been salvaged was one chest of silver—which spearchucker here found—and a 150 kilo 'silver' statue. After centuries in the water, there'd be no detail left, hence little antiquity value. Its metal worth would only be about 25,000 dollars. No wonder Rolando was choked, considering what he had expected! I flipped through to a document Jose had translated into English."

He sifted a sheet from the others.

"It concerned this 'silver' statue. The translation was stapled to the original and a Xerox copy. Jose had circled a word on the latter, and in the margin was handwriting. I read Spanish." He paused for effect again. "That circled word was *platino*—which means *platinum*. It's very close to their word for silver—*plata*! Jose had memoed *himself to change the Master Report to reflect that the statue was made of platinum and not silver*! But his notes were stolen, and he was murdered before he could do it!"

Quinn beamed at the gleaming statue.

"The metal is worth almost 4,000,000 dollars—but its antiquity value? The sky's the limit! I pointed the mistake out to Rolando. The sleazebag apologized profusely for my beating. He came up with a plan, part of which was for me to 'escape.'"

241

Tossing the papers on the work bench, he flicked open a jackknife and began fiddling in the back of the clock. Chase and Liana looked at each other.

"And the rest of it?" Chase tried to hide his uneasiness as he watched Quinn work.

"I knew the statue could have been aboard *either* ship. I needed a ploy to get us over to the other wreck if the one we were on proved fruitless. When this was the case, I radioed Rolando during one of my watches. He, in the meantime, had had the papers flown to Manila. He radioed Jesus to send a couriered envelope faked to look like it came from Jose's wife in Seville."

"I don't believe this," Liana muttered.

"But while the note was fake," Quinn grinned as he stripped plastic coating from wires, "the chart and first page from Jose's summary of the Board of Inquiry Report were authentic."

"And Conrad Larman's letter arrived at the same time," Chase muttered.

"Saving us useless diving! It told me why the Spanish hadn't found the statue—this pirate Jan had ripped it off! His clues led to Treasure Island!"

"Did you know Friday was there?" Chase asked, his uneasiness growing as Quinn rummaged for electrical tape. "And another by the balloon?"

"Certainly. I hoped we could do the dive without incident—but you spotted his footprint! Both lookouts were undoubtedly screaming into their radios. Once the pheasant was flushed, I couldn't let him be taken alive, and have him squawking to me in front of you to save his butt. But whacking him created a dilemma—Rolando would conclude I was throwing my lot in with you. We were low on fuel—sitting ducks. Before he either used RPGs at night, or sent divers with timed charges, I had—"

"Sounds like the security provided by the M60 was an illusion," Chase interrupted.

"Most of humanity lives with one or another," Quinn shrugged. "Look at what religion has brought us to internationally? I merely provided one for you."

"Oh, gawd, does he have to philosophize!"

"I had to get Rolando on the radio to convince him I wasn't betraying him—but it was shot up! So I had to get off the *Wracker* to Friday's walkie-talkie."

242

"And so you faked your death," Chase said. "That was Friday in your wetsuit."

He dug wire from the toolkit, and began stripping ends. Liana and Batuta looked at Chase uneasily.

"I jabbed the sharkstick into his stomach. The blood and guts was all it took to call the sharks in for nummies while I ducked into the cave. Before you were anchored back over the wreck sites, I was screaming into that walkie-talkie. I had less trouble than I expected convincing Rolando that Friday's death couldn't be helped. Fortunately, he had no problems sacrificing another man who, in his grand illusion, would be in Paradise being ravaged by virgins anyway."

Quinn glanced skyward again as he twisted wire ends together and wrapped them in tape.

"What are you doing?" Liana demanded.

"That night they snuck in with the *banca* and met me by the balloon basket, then a Beagle Boy took their boat back. We waited until we saw Barnacle Ben's pipe, then Rolando sent us out in scuba gear."

"You waited for him *specifically*!" Chase sputtered.

"I knew how to lure him down from the bridge. Come on—the old geezer was ready to croak anyway."

"And you unwrapped the wir-ors around the exhaust pipe."

Quinn shrugged as he ripped off a piece of tape with his teeth.

"And you pulled him under," Chase spat. "You rotten scumbag!"

"No, one of Rolando's men did." Quinn's eyes flickered to the horizon again as he hurried to wrap the last join in the wires. "We would have made a clean escape if you lovebirds wouldn't have woken. My job was to operate the Zodiac—but I hit the water as soon as fur flew. Rolando was choked when only three of us returned—and with no statue. So he went out with rebreathing equipment and waited."

He grinned and set the clock on the work bench.

"Rolando liked my idea of musical wetsuits on Treasure Island. The plan was to ambush whoever came down, slip into their wetsuit, and then climb aboard the *Wracker* taking you by surprise." He grinned broader. "But I still had my eye on that statue for myself."

"Naturally," Chase mumbled. He couldn't believe all this was going on behind their backs.

"As we swam to shore after the abortive night raid, I had purposely cut my leg, and told Rolando it happened when I rolled off the Zodiac. With sharks around, I couldn't be expected to dive anymore. If Rolando succeeded in commandeering the *Wracker*, fine, I'd market the statue, keep the money and disappear. If not, I'd wait by the basket for you. It was a win win situation."

Quinn stood back admiring his handiwork. Two long wires dangled from the back of Ben's clock.

"What *are* you doing?" Liana demanded again.

Quinn disappeared into the cabin. When he returned, Chase knew their worst nightmare was coming true. In Quinn's hand was the lump of C-4.

26 Chantico

Jan lay breathing heavily in their darkened hut, any movement causing waves of pain to wash up from his broken leg. Crumpled beside him was Maganda, one leg twisted. She had fainted when the rock had been brought down. He tried to understand why they had done this to her? Before he found an answer, an undertow of pain sucked him into its dark depths.

When he regained consciousness, a soft hand caressed his brow. A great sadness filled her eyes. Jan lifted himself onto his elbows and stared at his leg. A flurry of flies flew around white bone protruded through purple skin. The pain had reduced to a dull throb. He glanced at Maganda's limb and looked away.

"I'm sorry," he pleaded, guilt racking him. "If it wasn't for me, you wouldn't be in this mess."

She replied by stroking his tousled hair.

The grumble of distant thunder drew his attention outside. Sharp light cut through a wound in the clouds and stabbed through the door. From the sun's position, Jan was startled to see that he had been unconscious almost a day.

A heavy silence lay over Banaue. The village seemed deserted, and even dogs stepped warily. The *canao* had been brought to a premature end.

Jan turned back to his wife. There was no acrimony in her gaze, only affection. His own well of love rushed up to meet hers. He was about to tell her so when there was movement outside their door. Maganda's wide irises contracted when she saw one of the gathering was her grandfather. Jan shuddered. It had been the chief, in a drunken rage, who had ordered their crippling.

On his right stood Mansu, looking distressed. On Tonapo's left huddled three nervous elders, two cradling the green jars. The third held the vessel containing the chicken's gall bladder. The lid had been removed and the organ lay unblemished. Behind gathered the tense, sickly remainder of the tribal council.

Chief Tonapa stepped forward, his large frame shrunk more than the disease gnawing his body should have caused. His face was haggard, his eyes filled with anxiety and pain. As they flickered to Maganda, she looked down in shame. His face hardened as he turned to Jan.

"You have put at risk our very existence! If we would have been attacked, we would have been slaughtered to a man! It is the greatest crime ever committed! Your punishment will be appropriate!"

The chief turned back to his granddaughter, and his voice lost its animosity. "Y . . . you normally would have been spared, and a lesser punishment applied . . . but you were seen yesterday st . . . stealing my sword." He held up the scabbard. "T . . . this is the most serious theft in memory, and the God of Lock's anger has been swift."

The assembly shrank with fear as his statement was punctuated by a closer roll of thunder.

"W . . . while there is opposition to the punishment which must be meted out"—the chief glanced at the distraught Mansu—"the consensus i . . . is that the Ifugao people would be subject to the most awful retribution if it wasn't."

He turned back to the tribal council, his eyes imploring. One of them nodded toward the Ming jar. Chief Tonapa picked out the intact organ. His voice was so quiet Jan had to strain to hear. He spoke to Maganda, but his words were meant for both.

"It is my terrible duty to inform you that you will be . . . killed and . . . and . . . your h . . . heads displayed for all time . . . so the God of Locks can witness the depths of our regret for welcoming the white man and his terrible firewater god into our midst. . . . The gall bladders tell us tomorrow morning is the best time . . . before the rising Sun God."

The words struck like bolts of lightning.

Fighting back tears, the chief hurried away. Just before he disappeared around a corner, his entourage in tow, Mansu halted and looked back. With eyes mirroring a broken heart, he viewed the shock on Maganda's face. The headhunter turned to Jan, his eyes flinted, and he slapped his machete. Then he was gone.

Maganda crumpled into Jan's arms. His mind raced, seeking an avenue of escape, but every way he turned, he stumbled . . . onto his shattered leg. His short life flashed before him. During all of it he had been moved to sow good—but the only harvest he had reaped was pain. Maybe the accursed Calvanists were right about being born to suffer! He had sown it for Margaretje. For Guert. Even for Solina Cruzat, facing the wrath of her father and community. Now he had sown it for Maganda, her grandparents, and the village. The Figures in White had forced him back to fulfill some "destiny"—but he had done nothing but bring ruin! *That* was his *destiny?*

Maganda sobbed. He held her, his eyes welling as he tried to absorb her pain, her fear, her shame, his shame.

* * *

"Jan."

". . . Huh?"

Her gentle voice nudged him from thoughts absorbing him during the day. She had lain in his arms through most of it, lost in her own.

She raised herself onto her backside and nodded toward Chantico's shrine. A beam of late afternoon light had broken through the clouds and slanted through the door, illuminating the figurine. Maganda had come to some resolution. Her eyes were moist.

"This way is best. Even if we reached your village"—she eyed him with a jealous squint—"I'm not sure you would have let Margaretje just be Number Two wife. She was able to bear your child." Her eyes found the shrine again. "Chantico has decided we aren't to be so blessed. Her reasons are wise, so we don't leave orphans." She smiled. "But She assures us of being together . . . after . . . ever after."

His eyes shifted to the statuette, and his distrust of idols flickered.

"Lovers become beautiful spirits, like butterflies." She dabbed lime onto a leaf and wrapped in a slice of areca nut. "The sound of birds and babbling brooks—that's the laughter of

247

lovers in Chantico's world. That will be us."

Her faith was so matter-of-fact—so persuasive. He looked harder at Chantico—and suddenly saw her in a new light. In an epiphany, he realized that the world of everlasting life and bliss offered by the Figures in White was the same as that offered by Chantico! In an epiphany, he realized they *would* be together! As he knew *all* he loved eventually would be. Guert. Margaretje. His child. Or what is a heaven for? In an epiphany, he realized that all idols—the *boluls*, Jesus Christs, the Buddhas Hoogley had told him about, Chantico—were merely representations to help people communicate with the mysterious spirit world.

A great weight lifted and tranquility descended. He felt the same profound peace he had experienced when the longboat shot through the surf. When the *Sangley* cannonball had struck his dungeon.

Jan thought of Guert and Margaretje and his child and his heart filled with love. He prayed to Chantico that Guert would marry and prosper, and felt a connection. He prayed that Margaretje would overcome the stigma of bearing an illegitimate child and find happiness. He prayed his child would grow up happy, prosper, and have children of its own, and they would have children of their own, and all would prosper and be happy.

He felt a powerful urge to bequeath something material. Jan's thoughts drifted to the strongbox he had buried, its contents his only chattel. He had written Guert cryptically about its existence—if he had even received the letter. But was the statue not worthless? Then an idea struck him. Was it not an idol as well? A representation? Perhaps its material value lay in its spiritual worth to someone, somewhere . . . sometime?

With growing obsession, he looked around the hut. He had no quill. No paper. No manner in which to deliver another letter. But as if guided, he turned to gaze out the door toward the central clearing with its spiked heads. While fingering his coconut shell necklace, his thoughts drifted to the two jars of moonshine. He was detached from the image of their heads floating inside . . . even warmed by the idea that they would be together. In a trance, Jan's eyes shifted to the tattoos on Maganda's shoulders. The idea didn't seem ludicrous. Indeed, it seemed somehow . . . certain.

While Maganda sat absorbed in her betel nut and the happy, perfect world they would share, he picked up her sewing thorn.

He searched for something he could use as ink. Maganda spitting out a stream of betel drew his attention. She had missed the doorway and the crimson gob splattered against the sill. Maganda looked at him askance as Jan fingered it and smiled.

"Spit in here," he said, holding a wooden bowl.

She frowned, but did as he bid. Dragging the *Sangley* jar over, he let the water settle, then looked inside. A mirror.

He snapped his necklace from his neck and his heart sank. The markings scratched onto it months earlier were all but worn away! Reaching for a blackened stick in the firepit, he crushed charcoal between his fingers, rubbed them across the shell, then wiped the piece clean on his loincloth. He sighed with relief.

The map of the coastline, with the underground river marked by an arrow, was again clear.

While Maganda looked on curiously, Jan dipped the thorn into the betel juice, leaned over the jar, and made the first prick in his forehead. . . .

* * *

By the time he had finished, his face was tight from pain. He wiped blood and betel off his face with the end of his loincloth, leaned over the jar, and smiled. The message was clear.

Maganda smiled too, and touched her own tattoos. She understood. He was arming himself for their spiritual journey so that he could run the gauntlet of demons and reach their safe haven in the afterlife. Both protected—and with Chantico's blessing—they would make it together.

Neither thought they would be able to sleep that night, but they slipped into each other's arms and drifted into a slumber as deep and sweet as death itself.

27 *Tick-tick-tick*

A jolt like electricity surged through the three captives. They struggled against their bonds as Quinn attached the detonator to the wires and buried it in the plastic explosives, but it was no use.

"You said you were going to leave us, you sleazebag!" Liana shrieked.

"I *am* going to leave you!" He pointed to different points out to sea. "There, over there—and waaay over there."

"Your sense of humor leaves something to be desired," Chase said.

"Why did you bring the balloon aboard then?" Liana demanded while Batuta's eyes cut into Quinn like poisoned darts.

"An old German trick," Quinn smiled. "The garden path leading to the showers."

Batuta returned to fighting his bonds.

"But why kill us, Quinn?" Liana screamed.

"Those old reliables—so there'll be no partners or witnesses, of course!" He shrugged. "And so it'll appear that I was killed too, naturally. When that last Beagle Boy in the *banca* hears the explosion, he's going to investigate and will conclude we all went up in smoke. I don't want to be looking over my shoulder for Abu Sayyef and al-Queda the rest of my life."

Quinn checked his watch again and hurried back into the cabin. He returned lugging the case of rockets. After setting the alarm clock and C-4 on top, he disappeared down the hatch. A minute later he scrambled back up on deck. Sweeping up the AK and shotgun, he strode to the Zodiac.

250

"A near empty fuel tank creates an even bigger blast than a full one," he smiled as he untied the line.

"When Earthquake arrives and sees wreckage," Chase shouted, "he's going to radio in the military! You won't get far!"

The dive ladder squeaked for the final time as Quinn stepped down into the Zodiac. "Please don't grasp at straws, eh?" he said like the Quinn of old as he shook the Mercury's gas tank. Full enough. "I told Earthquake on Rolando's radio that we picked up diesel in Ulugon Bay with the Zodiac. He won't be around for two weeks. By that time I'll be sipping caipirinhas on Copacabana, but everytime I punch 1703 into an ATM machine, I'll think of you. Yeah, I cleaned off some of those pieces-of-eight to learn the date too." He scratched his chin. "A question. Are any of you having out of body experiences?"

"What are you talking about?" Chase demanded.

"Just curious. I understand you're supposed to have them just before you croak, and you only have ten minutes."

"This is *murder*!" Liana shrieked. "Where's your conscience?"

"Conscience? I've honestly never understood the concept." His voice hardened as the Mercury revved to life. "Sorry, have to run. Rolando radioed in the Beaver to pick up the statue—and it's due in a half hour. Have a nice friggin' day. Pardon *my* French."

He tinkled his fingers at them as the Zodiac pulled away. They flailed against their bonds.

"It's no use!" Liana cried. She couldn't believe it. She was worried about her lousy cameras!

"Keep trying!" Chase's bleeding arm pulsated.

Quinn described a large circle around the *Wracker*, looking for the best seat to enjoy the fireworks.

"Just a minute . . . do you hear that?" Batuta tipped his ear to the sky.

"What?" Chase retorted. "Harps?"

"No! A plane!"

A faint drone rose and fell over the slap of waves against the hull.

"You're right," Liana said as the sound grew louder. "But it's coming from the direction of the promontory."

". . . Sounds like the Beaver arriving early," Chase said. "It checked in with the *banca* first." He craned to catch sight of the plane, but the changing wind bobbed the boat around, facing them up island.

Quinn cruised in another circle around the *Wracker*, oblivious to the approaching aircraft.

"I don't know why that scumbag can't hear it!" Liana cried, leaning forward to look past the men's chests.

"He just did!" Batuta said.

The Zodiac stopped three hundred yards off the seaward side of the *Wracker*. Quinn searched the sky, then cranked the throttle wide open, almost falling overboard as the Zodiac wheeled around.

"He lost his AK!" Batuta said. "He's heading for the underground river! Look, one side of the Zodiac is leaning into the water! The statue has shifted!"

Quinn stopped, grabbed the shotgun, and scrambled forward to center the load. The growl of plane's engine grew louder. Batuta twisted his neck until he could see the dry hump of the promontory. A floatplane banked around the point, 200 feet above the water.

"It's the Beaver alright!" the native continued. "And it's coming right at us!"

The whine of the outboard drew their attention as Quinn raced toward the lagoon. Like a dog after a rabbit, the Beaver banked after it, slipping down to fifty feet. As it roared overhead, Quinn's shotgun blasted three times. The surprised Beaver leapt up and banked out to sea, its port mooring line freed by the blast.

"Quinn's heading straight for shore!" Liana shouted.

Goose bumps rippled across their bodies as the seconds ticked off. Mesmerized, they followed the Zodiac as it sped toward the beach. The Beaver drifted at a safe distance over the South China Sea, wings wobbling as the pilot checked for damage.

"Here it comes again!" Liana cried.

The Beaver plummeting like a hawk after prey. Quinn triggered off two more blasts, one splattering the windshield.

Something large and rectangular tumbled out the pilot's door. It plunged into the sea inches ahead of the small boat, sending up an umbrella of water that cascaded into the Zodiac.

"What was that!" Chase asked.

The floatplane clawed for height, barely clearing the coconut trees and upcroppings beyond, then curled in a tight cul-de-sac turn for a second run—this time head on. The plane's nose lowered like a bull's and a roar rose as the pilot punched the throttle. The Zodiac whizzed toward shore.

"Quinn is go-ing to make it this time!"

The Zodiac skimmed into the quieter water of the shallows. The Beaver dropped so low over the coconut trees edging the beach that fronds shook. The pilot's door pressed open. The charging beasts met head on. Quinn half stood in the Zodiac, his arm pointed toward the plane, the *BLAM-BLAM-BLAM-BLAM* of his Beretta carrying to the *Wracker.*

Another rectangular object tumbled from the Beaver at 150 knots. This time it hit the Zodiac's bow causing the rear to buck like a horse, throwing Quinn clear over the nose and into the water. The rubber boat flopped back down and all but disappeared beneath waves as it floundered and stopped. Quinn was nowhere to be seen.

The plane's pontoons skipped over the water like stones, and the wings wobbled before regaining balance and climbing at a steep angle. The Beaver stalked around the sky, searching for its enemy.

"*My gawd, Quinn's still alive!*"

He stood and plowed toward shore, the hand with the pistol flailing as he towed the drowned Zodiac by its line. Suddenly, Quinn stopped cold.

"What in. . . ?" Chase questioned as the Beaver roared again.

Quinn looked from the plane to shore, his pistol wavering with uncertainty. Then he turned toward the trees and began to raise the gun. A streak blurred out from shore before he could fire.

"*An arrow!*" Batuta shouted as it *thunked* into Quinn's chest.

His 9mm slipped from his grip, and he toppled backwards into the sea. A Batak warrior stepped out from the treeline, relining his bow. Around his neck hung binoculars. Batuta cheered, then caught himself. They weren't out of hot water yet. The Beaver circled, checked them out, then banked for a touchdown.

"The Beaver has landed," Liana mumbled, her photographic life flashing before her eyes.

There couldn't be more than a minute left on the clock. Chase pressed his shoulder to Liana's. "You said this relationship couldn't last forever anyway."

"Oh, it's forever all right. It's just that forever isn't very long."

"You know what I mean."

"I . . . I do. And, just so you know, I'd been wondering if a dog would mind me in and out of its life."

The Abu Sayyef plane gunned toward the *Wracker*.

"And just so you know, I hoped—"

"With any luck, he'll go up with us," Batuta interrupted.

Glare from the sun against the pellet-peppered windshield obliterated a view of the cockpit. The prop fanned down to an idle as the floatplane glided up to the *Wracker* and the muzzle of an M-16 poked through the pilot's window. A large head poked out behind it. The fat face was florid with fury.

"*Oh, my gawddddddd!*"

"Thet sucker made me waste two fuggin' cases of beer!" Earthquake McGoon boomed, his eyes darting from the cabin door to the hatch. "Any more of them suckers around?"

It flashed to Chase that McGoon had said he was looking for a bigger plane! "A bomb is timed to explode! Get us offa here!"

McGoon's eyes bulged. He charged onto the *Wracker*, peanuts flying, and sliced through their bonds with his buckknife. "Don't waste time gettin' inside!" he thundered as he wobbled back to the plane. "Jump on the pontoons!"

Liana grabbed the M-16 with the launch assembly, leaped down to the port float, and grabbed Batuta's arm when he hopped down and his ankle buckled. Chase ran after them—then skidded to a stop.

"*What are you doing?*" Liana shrieked. She hadn't given her cameras a second thought for a change—what could be so important to Chase? Earthquake was driving the throttle home when the writer ran to the work bench, scooped up Jose's papers and, crammed them into his trunks. At a full run, he dived off the *Wracker*. Batuta grabbed his hand.

"*No!*" Liana screamed as their poor grip slipped apart.

The plane picked up speed, leaving Chase behind in water fanned into a mist. Something burned along his body. The line! He grappled for it with his good hand and was yanked forward.

As the Beaver gained speed, he rolled onto his back, wings of water shooting up either side of him.

They were hardly clear before the *Wracker* disappeared in an enormous explosion. Liana and Batuta ducked under the wing as shrapnel splashed around them, burning pieces of wood making the sea look like a huge, watery birthday cake. Only when the last pieces had drifted down did Earthquake pull back on the throttle, and the plane sank with sluggish grace into the water. It was just in time. Chase couldn't have held on a second longer.

"*You almost got yourself killed!*" Liana screamed as she and Batuta helped the writer onto the pontoon. She hugged his head to her breasts.

"We have to git the fug outta here, y'all!" Earthquake bellowed out the door. "The starboard pontoon's hit and takin' on water! Walk across the struts to the other pontoon and git your butts in here!"

"We have to drop Batuta off first!" Liana shouted.

"Let the spearchucker swim! It ain't far!"

"There's sharks everywhere!"

Chase stood. "And we have to get the statue in the Zodiac!"

"What's so fuggin' important about a statue?" Earthquake rumbled as he leaned out to eyeball the struts. They seemed intact. Patches of wing looked like toredo worms had attended the birthday party.

"It's platinum!" Liana shouted.

Earthquake's eyebrows bobbed. After slamming the door, the plane plowed toward the Zodiac, only the tube tops showing. Midway between it and the beach, Quinn's body floated face up in a patch of pink water. The arrow protruded like a mast from his chest.

"Look!" Batuta cried.

A trilogy of fins streaked toward Quinn's body while the warrior on the beach stepped back. The sharks struck like a pack of wolves, tearing apart the man falsely known as Dr. Garnet Quinn with terrible efficiency.

"I told you good things came in threes," Liana said, cocking the rifle when nothing was left of him. She snapped off two shots. The boiling water calmed as two sharks rolled onto their bellies, and the third streaked back into the deep.

Chase looked at his arm. Blood trickled from the bandage. He had been little more than trolled live bait.

Earthquake nudged the port pontoon against the water-logged Zodiac. Splintered floorboards forward were testament to the awesome power of the Filipino saint, San Miguel. The statue gleamed beneath a blanket of foam and water. Chase jumped into the boat, but there was no way he could lift it, certainly not with his useless hand. Batuta's leg was gibbled, and Liana wasn't strong enough.

"Here ya puny little tar!" Earthquake threw down one end of a rope. "And hurry the fug up! Thet pontoon is taking on water fast, and there's more sharks comin'!"

Two fins wiggled along the blood trail toward the Zodiac. Liana shouldered the M-16 and pulled the trigger—but nothing happened.

"Chase! It's jammed! And the Zodiac's so low they can slip right into it!"

He snaked the rope around the statue's chest and tied a bowline. As he scrambled back onto the pontoon just ahead of the sharks McGoon, with a loud grunt, hoisted the statue up and onto the float. While Batuta steadied it and Earthquake glared down, Chase jumped back onto the pontoon and lashed it to the forward strut. *Cracks* from Liana's cleared M-16 hurried him.

"I don't know why I'm still hel-ping," Batuta muttered.

"Because you know the sooner it's aboard," Chase said through barred teeth as he cinched a reef knot, "the sooner you'll never see us again!"

Despite the weight on the port pontoon, the right wing dipped at a dangerous angle.

"Batuta!" Liana cried. "Now's your chance! It's not far to shore."

He dived in and swam with all speed. The warrior waded out to meet him, bow half drawn. Other Batak, attracted by the explosion, ran along the beach toward them.

"Y'all git yore fuggin' butts in here! We're sinkin' like the Titanic!"

As Chase and Liana clambered in, Earthquake grabbed the M-16 and set it on a burlap sack between the seats. The last thing they saw of Batuta before Earthquake eased the throttle forward was him being helped up the beach.

McGoon's face pinched as the Beaver pushed through the water, the starboard pontoon causing the nose to dip and yaw.

"We're in deep doo-doo," McGoon rumbled as Chase strapped into the passenger seat. "Everytime I feed 'er juice, she wants to do a Red October. We may have to dump the statue!"

Chase looked over his shoulder. The storage hold reached back to the tail. "Bag Lady! Back there!"

They wedged into the narrow tip. If the Red October dived, they didn't stand a chance.

"Come on baby . . . coooome onnnnn. . . !" The Beaver rocked like a hobby horse in the heavy seas but gained speed. "Thazzit baby . . . thazzit it . . . up, up . . . uuuup we goooo! *Yeeee-hawwwww!*"

The plane stepped up onto the waves—and burst ahead. Earthquake rammed the throttle home and rotated, the de Havilland giving his ample beer gut ample room. Joint-jolting pounding was replaced by smooth vibrations as it rose. Sea water rained from the riddled pontoon. The writer looked down at the scattered wreckage and sent out a short prayer for Ben and Agila. At least they had had a proper Viking funeral.

"The Beaver didn't get the reputation as the greatest bush plane in the world for nothing," Earthquake grumbled as Chase climbed back into the passenger seat and squinted. They were flying up island straight into the rising sun. "Well, thet's thet fer thet fake fuggin' cracker Quinn!"

"You know?" Liana and Chase chimed.

"Indeed!" Earthquake boomed, yanking his ballcap down. "I'm happy to see the hairy sucker deader then Uncle Albert's left butt. I managed to throw a couple Migs under your seat, Chase. Grab me one."

"How did you find out?" Chase asked, passing him a beer. Blood oozed through his soaked bandage. Catching Liana's eye, he pointed at the First Aid Kit in the back.

While McGoon jockeyed for altitude, he poured half the can down and belched. He grabbed the rag and angrily wiped the windshield. "I knew something was fishy as boobs on a buffalo when he radioed me with all thet code bull about wantin' a machine-gun and rockets! Jeeez, what was he doing with weapons like thet? And I mean Jesus Cabez. I got them from him! He was obviously more than jist a fuggin' houseboy! Thet's why I was late. I was checking things out!"

"And we thought you were the leak," Chase said. "Sorry."

"Fergit it. Y'all were being bullcapped to by a pro. Whadya know about him?"

Chase filled Earthquake in on what Quinn had told them, while Liana peeled off Chase's old dressing and grimaced. It was infected. She rummaged through the kit while Earthquake nodded.

"Thet's what we figured—a small time gun runner!" Earthquake said as he reached up to the trim control.

"What do you mean, 'we?'" Chase asked.

"I took everything to my friends in the CIA. They traced the M60 to a theft from a Taiwanese base, but the M203s took longer, which is why I didn't bring them all out right away. Know where the suckers came from?" He took another swig.

"Well?" Chase said as Liana applied peroxide and a new dressing.

"A corrupt Thai general. A dud turned up at an aborted Abu Sayyef bank robbery in Zamboanga. Thet *really* got The Company's attention! They lifted his fingerprints from the ammo box. He turned out to be a guy named Robert Baudru—a con man with a record Stateside as long as my leg, before he shifted operations here. The DEA in Thailand also have a file on 'im."

He fished into his breast pocket for peanuts. He looked even more peeved when he came up with only one.

"The spooks contacted the Filipinos who put a tail on our little Jesus—or Mohammed, as you say. They followed him to a house next to the American embassy! They kicked in the door, there was a short firefight, and Jesus was crucified. Every room was crammed with nitrate fertilizer and diesel! The Filipinos then kicked in Baudru's door, and found a room stacked with ordnance, including cases of Beretta 92Fs. Thet's the standard US military sidearm, and it came from thet Thai sucker too! The Filipinos naturally wanted to know where Baudru was. I said I didn't know—thet he had radioed me to get the stuff from Jesus, and he would radio later where to deliver it. The Filipinos grudgingly bought it, but the Caspers just winked at me. They understood!"

"Why didn't you tell the spooks?" Liana asked as she finished Chase's bandage.

"Because I wanted the sucker, which was fine with the CIA! They just wanted him off'd. The spooks were callin' me Earthquake McBaboon for gettin' involved with him in the first place! I was gonna rip his leg off and use it to bat his head clear across the islands!"

Liana made a face.

"I was gonna grab him when I flew in the diesel fuel—but the jerk radioed me this morning to cancel! I didn't believe fer one fuggin' minute thet y'all was gonna risk leaving the *Wracker* to spin into Ulugon Bay! And to transport several hundred pounds of diesel thet far in a *Zodiac?* Come on! I may be fat, but I'm not stupid."

He poured back another quarter can of beer before continuing.

"I knew yere butts had to be in a sling. I fired up the Beaver I jist bought, thinkin' thet would be the best chance to git close to the cracker—and their *banca.*" Earthquake grinned. "There was only one jerk aboard when I taxied up to it, and he thought it was his Boys."

"What did you do?" Liana asked.

Earthquake lifted a corner of the burlap, revealing a .357. "I thought it was a false alarm when I saw y'all sunbathin' on deck—but then Quinn-slash-Baudru took a poke at me with his shotgun and thet's all I fuggin' needed!" He chortled. "Did you see him fly butt-over-rice-bowl?"

Chase heard a *tick-tick-tick* somewhere on the aircraft. He wouldn't have thought anything of it, but Earthquake whipped his head around.

"*Hear that!*" he roared, throwing the beer over his shoulder, missing Liana's head by inches. He rammed the throttle to the dash and laid the Beaver onto its right paw. "*We're under fire!*"

28 Through a Glass Darkly

Roosters crowing roused Jan from a dream sailing in a magnificent ship across a calm, windless ocean. Light was everywhere, and ethereal music blasted from an unsullied sky.

It drifted away as he pulled himself onto his backside, and became aware of throbbing in his leg. A red dawn bled across the sky, and the air was heavy, cold, wet. Jan shivered, then Maganda's hand overlaid his and he looked into her calm, assured eyes. They turned to watch the villagers, faces filled with fear and foreboding, gather for their sacrifice.

Maganda threw her arms around his neck as a dozen men led by Mansu strode toward their lodge. His eyes filled with fire when they fell on Jan, but as they flickered to Maganda, his bottom lip quivered. The couple looked back to Chantico. She smiled encouragement.

"It's ti—" Mansu began, but a sharp look from Maganda cut him short.

Jan helped her to the entrance, her face tightening in pain, and down to two Ifugao who had made a chair with their arms. As they carried her through a parting in the Red Sea of spectators toward the clearing, she twisted back to look at Jan, panic flying to her eyes.

He all but dropped down the ladder in his haste to catch up. The Dutchman bit back pain as rough hands dragged him to the center of the clearing. Maganda was already on her knees. Fear on her face dissolved into happiness as they lowered Jan on her right. They gripped hands.

A snatch of music—the low of pines, the babble of brooks,

birds—drifted on the breeze.

Before them a monument to their folly had been constructed. Atop a foundation of stone sat the still. A large opening, like double doors, had been cut and the metal curled back. Inside rested the two homebrew filled jars. It looked so ludicrous Jan almost laughed. Even the condenser coil curled out of the top.

To one side sat the tribal council, studying the angry sky with apprehension. The couple surveyed the silent, sullen, sickly wall of bodies staring at them. Many eyed Jan's odd tattoo, their expressions conveying they hoped it failed to protect him. But Maganda had been popular, and sobs revealed islands of compassion. Her young girl friend put her hand to her face and ran away.

Jan caught the eye of a naked little girl huddled against her mother's shawl. He recognized her—the same child as at Atagar's execution. Jan smiled and winked. She shyly smiled back, her tiny fist flying to her mouth.

Jan and Maganda had never felt so close. Murmurs passed through the crowd as it saw the tranquility with which they faced their end.

The music mounted.

A squeeze of Maganda's hand drew Jan's attention forward. Chief Tonapa weakly stepped forward, unable to mask his emotions. Wailing rose from his hut. Saging.

"We all know what must be done," he said. He, too, glanced at the reddening sky. And nodded.

Executioners materialized and positioned themselves on either side of the couple. The Dutchman was thankful Dar had been lent the Toledo blade. It was an act of kindness by Chief Tonapa for his granddaughter.

Jan glanced up at the man by his side. To no surprise, it was Mansu, but his hands were trembling. His eyes were fixed on Maganda, blissfully unaware of his presence. Those shaking hands worried Jan. As the headhunter's eyes flickered down to him, Jan stuck out his tongue. Mansu's face set, and he gripped his headhunting axe with both hands. Jan faced forward with a tiny smile.

The music grew so loud, Jan couldn't understand how no one but he seemed to hear it.

There was only the word to give. A hush fell.

29 Vera

The Beaver banked so hard, it threatened to rip the wings off. The *tick-tick* sound disappeared.

"Can y'all see the sucker?" Earthquake hollered.

"It's the Abu Sayyef Beaver!" Chase shouted.

Earthquake flipped the plane level and punched the yoke forward, rocketing them upward against their seat belts. "Hang on. I'll show them suckers how to fly!"

"*Earthquaaaaaake!*"

"Quit yere belly achin' back there—I reinforced this sucker."

The choppy South China Sea rushed to meet them.

"It's fallen behind," Chase shouted, "but it's diving too!"

"Good! See thet river! We're goin' fer a cruise!"

"*River?*" Liana squeaked. "*That's a creek!*"

"Even fuggin' better!"

A moment before they kamikazied a school of dolphins, Earthquake pulled up. The Beaver almost slapped its tail as it leveled out feet above the deck. The water was a turquoise streak as they rushed toward the narrow river mouth. Karst formations on either side staircased inland towards the mountains. The Bobbsey Twins were rigid as Earthquake whipped around a curve and shot down a straightaway, the jungle on each shore a green blur. Then the contents of their stomachs sloshed to the other side as he banked around another bend. Ahead, two enormous limestone sentinels straddled the river—the gap narrower than the Beaver's wings. Beyond, jungle swept up the mountainside.

"Pray thet there's a valley wide enough on the other side to level out."

Chase and Liana did as they were told as McGoon lay the Beaver on its side and threaded the needle. He popped the wing back up and scratched upward through the mist, chasing clouds that sat atop the mountains like gray fedoras. Earthquake dropped his side window, stuck his head into the slipstream, and looked back. Peanut shells kicked up into a storm.

"I see 'em!" He slammed the window just before they shot into the clouds, and banked to port, eyeing his instruments. "They chickened out and are circlin' fer height over the sea, and their butts are to us! They won't know which way we turned—or if we even made it."

They burst into sunlight on top of the hat brim. Liana's eyes opened to wide angle as the blunt tip of a mountain flashed by only a hundred feet off their starboard.

Earthquake reached between the seats and threw off the burlap, revealing the missing M203 rocket. "Yeah, I thought I'd keep one. Ya never know when it might come in handy." He let the plane fly itself, skipping over the surface of the clouds eastward into the sun while he loaded the rocket launcher. "Hang onto it, Chase. We're gonna trap us a beaver!"

Slowing, he circled back and eased the plane to the edge of the hat brim and peeked over. Sunlight glinted off a windshield a mile away and a thousand feet below.

"They cain't see us, sun's burnin' into their eyes. See? The dumb sucks are circlin' again, still lookin' fer us, or our wreckage."

He eased the throttle forward and slipped into a shallow dive, the plane picking up momentum. A smile spread across his leathery features as the terrorist Beaver completed its maneuver, and began flying parallel to the coast towards the south-west. McGoon plunged toward it, easing back on the throttle only when they were so close that they were buffeted in its wake. Earthquake dropped his side window open. Peanut shells swirled again.

"Now, pass me thet toy."

He jammed the M-16's muzzle out the window. In a move as graceful as a ballerina's, he dipsy-doodled the plane over and forward so that they lay a hundred feet off the starboard wing. Two Filipinos in white barong shirts were aboard, the muzzle of an AK-47 sticking up between the passenger's legs. Both men craned landward.

"Maybe I should toot my horn," Earthquake cackled.

The passenger glanced to the right and did a double take. His mouth flapped as he raised the alarm. The pilot leaned forward and terror filled his face as they stared at Earthquake's broad smile, and the rocket launcher leading them like a duck. The Abu Sayyef pilot desperately tried to bank away while the passenger fumbled with his window.

"Git ready to find out all them virgins waitin' fer ya are barn-yard pigs," Earthquake said as he squeezed the trigger.

The last thing the wide-eyed passenger saw was the rocket streaking toward him. Then the terrorist beaver exploded in a huge, fiery cloud of reds, yellows and glinting metal that rocked Earthquake's plane.

"Not much pelt left," Earthquake chortled as he snapped his window and circled the site. Torn aluminum slapped down into the sea. "Chase, thet other Mig!"

Chase fumbled for the beer while Earthquake leveled out. He took a satisfying pull, let out a triumphant belch, and reached for his rag.

"Now, what's the story on this fuggin' statue?"

If Earthquake wasn't so fat and ugly himself, Chase might have kissed him. He tumbled out an explanation then, remembering Jose's papers, worked the soppy bundle out of his trunks.

"Oh, thank heavens! They're not torn, just stuck together! Pass them back here. I still have a couple of long fingernails."

Liana separated the matted sheets, papering the floor and seat with them. Original documents, translations, Xeroxes and a chart dripped water.

"Here's the Master Report! . . . Jose writes that the *Santa Maria de la Concepcion* ledger wasn't with the other Manila-Acapulco trade files. He happened on it in an area devoted to Top Secret documents! He writes that's why the sinking isn't in-cluded in published accounts of Manila Galleons taken by raiders. I wonder why it was there?"

"Good question. Go on."

"Quinn, er, Baudru wasn't lying. Everything was salvaged except one chest of pesos, and another holding a 150 kilogram *silver* statue." She traded the document for another. "Here's the rest of Jose's summary of the Board of Inquiry Report! My gawd! They salvaged over *13,500,000 pieces-of-eight!*"

265

Chase twisted back in his seat while Earthquake let out a whistle.

"The viceroy complains that the superstitious Filipino divers refused to touch the bodies, so they couldn't recover the crucifixes in the *Raid's* hold!" She picked up another dripping sheet. "Here's the xerox with *platino* circled with Jose's notes in the margin! This is the one that saved Quinn's butt when Rolando nabbed him!" She picked up the translation. "Wow! It's from Viceroy Cruzat to the King of Spain, Philip V! It's marked *Top Secret*!" She read in a breathless voice.

"Castle of San Diego
Acapulco, New Spain
May 5, 1705

Your Majesty:

Regarding the activities of Marquis Ignacio del Atagar who was empowered on the special mission by Your Highness, it is my grave duty to report the following:

Although the Marquis, disguised as a Jesuit, survived the naval engagement with the English pirates and subsequent typhoon, we were unable to recover a chest containing items central to his mission. These included a feathered headdress, costume, and a 150 kilogram silver (*no, platinum*) statue of Vira-ko-cha.'"

"Vera? Thet's a dame's name. I thought I saw a beard on the sucker?"

"*Viracocha*—one word!" Chase exclaimed. "I thought it was Viracocha myself when I first laid eyes on it! He was the top god of Mesoamerica! Viracocha was the name the Incas gave him! The one you're probably more familiar with is his Aztec reincarnation—Quetzalcoatl!"

"The Plumed Serpent!" Liana exclaimed.

"Huh?"

"You know the story, Earthquake! He was a tall, blue eyed white man with yellow hair and beard wearing a luminous, white robe, sandals, and carrying a staff. Legend states that he sailed

266

into the Pacific promising to return. The Aztecs mistook Cortez for him!"

"What was this Atagar looney-toon doin' with a statue of him?"

The Bobbsey Twins looked blank. She returned to the translation.

> "Despite the loss, Atagar was intransigent. After recuperating, he commanded me to assign a ship and soldiers, such was his determination to expand the Dominion of the Spanish Crown, first by the conquest of the terrible Igorot headhunters for their heathen souls and long coveted gold and silver mines, followed by the conquest and Christianization of China—"

"What?" Chase gasped. "*China?* Atagar fancied himself a *conquistador?*"

Liana hurried on.

> "To this end, he further commanded me to have constructed a replica of said statue, headdress and costume for the Igorot campaign. Should it succeed, he felt the second mission on the continent could be achieved if he secured platinum from the liberated mines to recreate the statue of Viracocha.
>
> His arguments, on this and his previous visit to study pagan ways, that the conquests could be executed in the manner of Hernan Cortez and Francisco Pizarro with a handful of men, were made with great conviction—"

"Was he thinking that Quetzalcoatl was *here* too?" Chase interrupted. "Left? And promised to return, like he did in Mesoamerica?"

> "He argued with passion that the many similarities of Igorot to Aztec, Mayan and Inca culture pointed to a connection. He emphasized the strikingly similar apparel, gold jewelry, terraced fields and

irrigation systems, the use of tumplines, backstrap looms and blowguns, and even, like the Incas, their preference for residing among mountains. That both Cusco and Banaue were considered the 'navel of the world' bore great import.

He argued most vociferously that the Igorot feathered headdresses were representations of the Plumed Serpent. That both their beliefs in spirits and a sun god weren't hapstance.

Most dogmatically, he argued the astonishing similarity between the Igorot's chief idol, bolul, and the statues of Viracocha was more than could be co-incidental—"

"'Chief idol!'" Chase scoffed. "The *bolul* was just the Ifugao rice god!"

"Central to his plan was to display the most impressive representation of Viracocha in existence. He was convinced the savages could not fail to see the connection between their standing boluls, the bearded statue of Viracocha, and his bearded self.

Concerning his Cathay aspirations, he was convinced that the idol Buddha was the latest manifestation of Viracocha, and that the Emperor was his descendent."

The sunburnt serpent of Palawan swam off the starboard wing.

"Atagar claimed the reason the Emperor was secluded behind the walls of the Forbidden City, and that one looked upon his face only upon pain of death was because of his fair skin and blue eyes. Atagar was convinced that Viracocha, after siring the first in a long line of God-Emperors, left as was his habit. That the Emperor claimed to be a god was of utmost significance to Atagar.

He was supremely confident that he would be welcomed into the Forbidden City. Once there, in the manner of Cortez and Pizarro before him, he intended to seize the Emperor."

"And thus seize control of China!"

"When last seen, the Marquis sailed on their mission. It is my terrible belief that these brave souls working to expand Your Highness' most holy Christian Dominion have failed."

"What was this sucker thinkin' of? Conquerin' fuggin' *China* with a handful of men!"

"Think about it!" Chase exclaimed. "Cortez was outnumbered 500-1! Pizarro did the same number on the Incas! Remember that during one of the *Sangley* uprisings, 700 soldiers wiped out 23,000 Chinese! With a track record like that—wouldn't *you* think it could be done!"

Earthquake and Liana nodded. He banked away from Palawan in the direction of Manila.

"How could this guy take this Quetzalwhatever legend seriously though?" Earthquake asked.

"Hey, I don't doubt that he lived!" Chase replied. "Troy was a legend too until Heinrich Schliemann dug it up."

"Sure," Liana countered. "Like El Dorado, the Fountain of Youth, and the Seven Cities of Gold."

"No—more like Jesus Christ, Buddha and Mohammed. I had time on the New York flights to think about our earlier conversation on the jumbo. Look, the Quetzalcoatl legend says he came from the east. Probably he and his band of fishermen or traders were blown onto the Canary Current off North Africa. No one argues that the mid Atlantic is a difficult crossing anymore—people have *windsurfed* it! Fortunately, he was a good man, unlike the Spaniards who followed. He taught the primitive people he met in Mexico to live in organized communities with governments and laws, hieroglyphic writing, pyramid building, astronomy, sun worship, megalithic carving—the works! It's the only way to account for the complex Mesoamerican civilization that sprang up overnight!"

Liana acceded the point as Chase raised a finger.

"And he also tried to teach them to live in peace, to be loving, to be charitable. Quetzalcoatl was a *prophet*—the 'messiah' of Mesoamerica! In fact, his teachings were so strikingly similar to those of the Ten Commandments that Spanish friars initially mistook Quetzalcoatl for St. Thomas. In Peru, they confused Viracocha with St. Bartholomew! He was against blood sacrifices."

"What happened then? The Aztecs ripped prisoners' beating hearts out?"

"The same thing as in Christianity—priests perverted the original message in their personal quest for power. Which is worse, a fast Aztec death—or a lingering Catholic one being stretched on a rack, with red hot pincers, on in an iron maiden?"

Earthquake searched his pocket for a peanut. Finding none, he pulled out a cigar.

"We'd have his entire story, except that Spaniard missionaries destroyed virtually all the native books, records *and* statues of him. *They succeeded in doing to Mesoamerican religion what they failed to do with Judaism during the Inquisition—destroy it.* It was one of the worst cases of cultural—and religious—genocide in history! Except for a few statues of Quetzalcoatl and a handful of codices, there isn't much left. It's as if all that remained of Christianity were a few crucifixes and the Dead Sea Scrolls." The writer paused. "This platinum statue must be one of the rare ones that survived. It found its way into Atagar's hands."

Liana waved away smoke. "But how did he ever think that Quetzalcoatl-slash-Viracocha ended up here?"

"Viracocha had another name—Kon-Tiki."

"Thor Heyerdahl!"

"Right. Atagar recognized the same thing that Thor did—that the Humboldt current swept every Manila Galleon to the Philippines since Cortez sent Ferdinand Magellan into the Pacific. There's statues like Quetzalcoatl-slash-Viracocha-slash-Kon-Tiki and *boluls* all across Polynesia! Don't forget that Captain Cook was killed on Hawaii after being mistaken for their white god hero Lono." Chase's voice swelled. "Atagar had talent as an anthropologist! Like Thor, he was one of the first Diffusionists!"

"And Atagar figured that Quetzalcoatl met the Igorots?"

"Yes. The cultural similarities exist! To Atagar, they were proof that Quetzalcoatl brought them!" Chase wobbled his hand. "Here, an Isolationist would argue, with justification, that things like blowguns, bows and arrows, tumplines and terraces developed independently, or were carried over the Bering Strait."

Earthquake tapped his fat fingertips on the yoke in boredom, preferring bars to history. Chase continued.

"Even if he knew that 'Buddha' means the 'enlightened one' and not 'plumed serpent,' it's not surprising that he concluded that they were one and the same because Viracocha certainly *was* an enlightened one too—and both their teachings of good thinking and living were strikingly similar!"

They flew without speaking over the whitecapped sea for several minutes, the bray of the motor broken by the rumble of Earthquake's stomach.

"He was one gutsy son-of-a-gun," Liana said as the incredible—flawed—ambitions of the Spaniard sank in. "Still, think if Atagar would have been correct and succeeded! The entire Far East would have been Spanish! Spain would have been rich and powerful beyond imagination!" Her pause wasn't meant to be dramatic but it was. "Marquis Ignacio del Atagar would have become the greatest conquistador of all! World history would have been radically rewritten! Spanish would be the de facto universal language, not English! His name would be as famous as Columbus'."

Ahead, the dry mountains of Luzon rose from the sea.

". . . Instead . . . nothing," Chase replied. "Not even a footnote."

Liana smoothed a document. "I didn't read the addendum:

> It is my equally grave duty to report that a revolt against Your Highness's authority invested in my person broke out after we quashed the most recent Sangley rebellion. In the passions of the day, it was widely perceived that Your Agent was responsible for the loss of the Manila Galleon.
>
> Unable to carry out my duties, and fearing for the safety of myself, my daughter and grandson, I boarded the next Acapulco galleon. The Viceroy of New Spain has sent the governor of Acapulco to Manila to take command.
>
> In his place, I am discharging duties in Acapulco, and implore Your Highness to assign me to a

more congenial posting. The conditions are most in-
tolerable due to the scorching heat, boredom, gnats,
mosquitoes and command of but a troop."

Liana looked for another sheet. "That's it!"

". . . Poor booger, as ol' Barnacle Ben would say," Chase
chuckled. "Sounds like he was the scapegoat."

The Beaver bounced through potholes in the sky before hitting the straight and level again. Liana began gathering the sheets
up.

"What's this?" She found an ATM card stuck behind one of
them.

Chase took it, flipped it over—and his face lit up. "It's
Baudru's! From his off shore account!"

They looked at each other, stunned.

"Hey guys, this is our day! For the statue, I guess the choice is
between Sotheby's or Christie's! The sky's going to be the limit
for what sounds like the rarest pre-Columbian artifact ever!"

". . . Uh, I think I may have a third choice for ol' Vera here,"
Chase said with an impish smile.

30 The Figures in White

Jan floated above the scene, looking down on the assembly. To his left hovered Maganda, enjoying the sensation. They held hands. The music rose.

They watched with detachment as Chief Tonapa closed his eyes and nodded.

The images of the people Jan loved passed before his unearthly vision as the blades swept down in slow motion.

Maganda. Chief Tonapa. Grandmother Saging. Guert. Solina. Margaretje. And his . . . son.

The light was never brighter as they approached. Maganda looked at Jan with wonder, then ahead at the Figures in White.

Have I completed my destiny? It'll be pretty hard to send me back this time if I haven't.

The Figures in White laughed and stepped aside.

Yes, yes you have.

The tallest stepped forward from the background to welcome them. On his head was an ornate feather headdress.

31 The Explorers Club

"So this is the famous Trophy Room," Conrad Larman exclaimed, striding into the open beamed hall. "I've put off joining too long!"

With healthy good looks and athletically built despite being in his sixties, Larman neither looked nor acted like one of America's richest men. He was entirely without pretension, and had a kindly nature. In rumpled khakis, he could have been mistaken for a white haired anthropologist on his way to the field—which is precisely where he was heading when Chase's phone call reached him. Without hesitation, Larman had changed his Lear's flight plan from Lima to La Guardia.

"It's quite a sight alright," Chase replied as he tagged behind he and Liana, his eyes cheating to her backside. Nope, not bad at all.

"Those are the heads?" Larman asked, his voice quickening. He pointed with the rolled Spanish chart.

"That's correct, Mr. Larman," Liana replied.

"I've told you, the name's Con—as in Kon-Tiki, but with a C. And my wife's name is Marg."

"Sorry . . . Con."

Con strode to the cabinet and slipped out eyeglasses. It was the moment of truth. The Board of Inquiry summary and Liana's photos in the underground river had brought Con to his feet. In the previous two days, his pre-Columbian experts had been authenticating and appraising the statue.

The Bobbsey Twins retreated to the *bolul*. She reached into her new camera bag and recorded for posterity the moment Conrad Larman leaned forward, his eyes soaking in the tranquil features of what he believed was his ancestor's brother. After an eternity, he turned to the other head, his lips parting in admiration. Looking back at Jan, he raised the chart with trembling hands. His eyes rose and fell as he compared the coastline with the tattoo wavering across Jan's forehead.

When he straightened, the retired construction magnate was moved to his very foundations. "T . . . there is no doubt. The loooong family mystery is solved."

He accepted Liana's proffered hanky and dabbed his cheek.

"Excuse me . . . my friends, but it . . . it's uncanny—the familial resemblance is even more noticeable up close. If I had pictures of me when I was a youngster, you'd be struck as much as I am by the similarity. My hair was a shade darker but just as much of a tousle, and I had freckles once, if you can imagine, scattered across a nose just like that." He blew that nose. "It . . . it makes me wish that my Great-Whichever-Grandfather Guert was in the jar so I could see what *he* looked like."

Chase and Liana remained silent, their arms touching. This was Conrad Larman's day.

"Not only is Uncle Jan back home after all these centuries, but his mysterious inheritance has finally reached the family— even if I have to purchase it, and purchase it I gladly will do."

Con wiped away his last tear and lay the chart on a table. Reaching into a breast pocket, he pulled out a checkbook and a Parker Doufold fountain pen.

"There's just the matter of price. The appraisers had considerable difficulty. A significant figure was 20,000,000 dollars."

He leaned over the table and wrote. Liana and Chase shared glances. They were being made a flat offer—but 20,000,000 had been the lowest appraisal!

"But twenty was *preposterous!*" Con thrust them the check.

They looked at it—and blinked. It was the highest appraisal. 58,000,000 dollars.

It was written on a Bahamanian bank. A twinkle danced in Con's blue eyes. "I dare say if I had to buy it at auction, I would have paid considerably more."

"T . . . thank you," they managed. Earthquake would be pleased with his cut. Barnacle's Ben's share would fund an exploration grant in oceanography at the club in his name, while Baudru's account would fill a seat in anthropology in the real Dr.

Quinn's honor.

"The most astounding thing is that I have been searching for just such a statue for decades—long before I built the museum! I don't know if you're aware, but the most important wing of The Larman is dedicated to Quetzalcoatl in all His reincarnations. It's a stunning coincidence that the finest example that *exists* comes from Uncle Jan! It's almost as if there was a . . . grander purpose behind all this! My lifetime passion has been to restore Quetzalcoatl to His place of prominence among the pantheon of great religious teachers."

Chase and Liana looked at each other again as a tsunami of déjà vu washed over them, then dissipated, never to return.

"Did the Spanish ever get their hands on that Igorot gold?" Con asked.

"No," Chase replied as Liana slipped the check into her camera bag. "It wasn't until we Yanks arrived in the late nineteenth century that they were conquered—and it was because of the Remington repeating rifle. After that, the silver and gold was mined. It still is today. The Philippines is the world's eighth largest gold supplier."

". . . I only wish I could acquire the heads themselves," Con said, turning back to the case. "Out of the question, of course. . . ."

"Uh, perhaps I could introduce you to the club president?" Chase offered.

"Wonderful idea! I think under the circumstances . . . and a suitable donation—"

"Jade! Jade! Wait!" Chase turned back to Con. "That was her poking her head in the door."

Conrad Larman beamed as the writer made introductions. He winked at them before following the president to her office.

With Con gone, the check suddenly seemed to weigh down Liana's bag as though the entire treasure of the *Santa Maria de la Concepcion* was buried in it.

"Well, lady with the bag of money—let's have another look at it! I was afraid Con's last name was Man there for a moment."

Staring at the check, Chase felt a rush he hadn't experienced since he won a trip to Disneyland as a kid.

"'There is something about a treasure," Liana echoed, "that fastens itself upon a man's mind. . . .'"

"So much for Conrad's curse. We didn't know it, but we had the wrong Conrad in mind all along!"

"You're going to be able to buy some Rhodesian Ridgeback. Do I get to help pick a name? . . . Even if we're not sure if this is going to work out?"

"How about Destiny?"

"Not bad." She slipped the check back into her bag. A smile traced her lips. "I have another theory about fate we can test."

"Yeah?"

"You know the one that says good things come in threes?" she said with bedrooms in her eyes.

"Uh huh," he uh huhed, tucking himself into those eyes.

"Why don't we buy a bottle of Cristal, head back to the Plaza, and prove that hypothesis again?"

Epilogue

After they strolled out of the room, its usual deep serenity returned.

Then, from somewhere, the soft low of wind through pines could be heard, faintly at first. It was followed by the babble of a brook, then the chirp of a tropical bird. From behind the jars fluttered two butterflies. They danced into the middle of the room.

Upon hearing approaching voices, the butterflies flitted back behind the jars, and the music faded to silence.

Post-Expedition Notes

The genesis for this novel came about in a most unusual manner. In 1982, I was on assignment for the Smithsonian Institution and Vancouver's Museum of Anthropology to collect masks and ceremonial paraphernalia among the exorcist Devil Dancers of Sri Lanka. After a day of rummaging in the jungle, I'd dine on shark steak and Lion Lager while enjoying the magnificent sunsets over the Indian Ocean at the beautiful beach village of Hikkaduwa.

There I met a Manhattan couple. When he learned I was an ethnologist, he offered that he had an unusual tribal collection . . . human heads. When we met the next evening, he brought shots of his eccentric—to say the least—collection, and they are much as described in the opening scene in the Trophy Room of The Explorers Club.

Most startling among his remarkable photos were the heads of a beautiful young couple floating in separate jars—and in a stunning state of preservation! Equally intriguing were their quixotic, tranquil expressions.

His information was that they had lived in nineteenth century Hawaii, that the tousle haired lad had worked on a whaler and had jumped ship when the couple had become romantically involved. They had apparently broken a tribal taboo which had led to them losing their, well, bodies. The heads weren't lost. They were in these jars.

The images of the attractive young couple in the jars percolated in my mind for years. This novel is the result, and I hope it does honor to the real couple, whoever they were, and whatever their real story was. I'm sure it was one full of adventure, love and butterflies.

About the Author

Jason Schoonover has been a writer and an anthropologist since the 1970s. As a field collector of primitive art and antiquities, his collections are found in museums around the world and in private collections. South and Southeast Asia are his main areas of interest. Besides novel writing, he's been widely published in newspapers and magazines, including as a columnist, and has a background as a writer/director/producer in radio, film, television and on stage. His adventure-thriller *Thai Gold* was an international bestseller, and he was profiled in Jerry Hopkins' *Bangkok Babylon: The Real-Life Exploits of Bangkok's Legendary Expatriates Are Often Stranger Than Fiction.* Jason is a Fellow of The Explorers Club of New York and a member of the Foreign Correspondents Club of Thailand. He divides his time between Bangkok, Thailand; Saskatoon, Saskatchewan, Canada; and the rest of the world. Canoeing old Canadian fur trade and exploration routes is a favorite passion. The Imperial Dragon Lady, Su Hattori, has kindly been enduring the unendurable since 1988.

CPSIA information can be obtained at www.ICGtesting.com
Printed in the USA
LVOW11s1121040915

452859LV00001B/75/P